The Autobiography Of Fezziwig

DANNY KUHN

DEDICATION

To S.K., who said I should write books.

CONTENTS

WORDS FOR *THE AUTOBIOGRAPHY
OF FEZZIWIG:*

"A true look at a remarkable time, so full of historical facts and characters as to be totally believable as autobiography. It reminds us of the astounding array of scientific, literary, and philosophical geniuses rubbing elbows in the eighteenth century London coffeehouses, and of the social and political unrest of the day. As Fezziwig says, 'The only thing that outlives us, as our legacy, is the good we do for others.' Mr. Dickens would be pleased!"

PART THE FIRST: *BEGINNINGS*

My Dear Daughters,

Desiring to be remembered for something other than once being naked and lost in the forest with Dr. Benjamin Franklin, I will endeavor to set down for you some account of the other anecdotes which, strung together, have made up my journey on this earth. Many of them you have heard while allowing your doting father his vice of storytelling; some may be new to you only because the misty veil between the real and the imagined is growing more translucent every day.

In the words of my old departed American friend, "Hereby, too, I shall indulge the inclination so natural in old men, to be talking of themselves and their own past actions."

It seems a poor investment indeed to allow the inventory of knowledge accumulated over a lifetime to be lost with a final breath. In business, even the fury of storm or fire should not cause such a total loss; consider this missal to be my Lloyd's of Lombard Street insurance contract against it. As you are the beneficiaries, I pray it is worth your time.

Your Loving Father,

William Lucian Fezziwig

* * * * * * *

In the conversations often heard in the coffeehouses among men of business, boasting of one's relations and acquaintances is a type of sport. Almost no statement is complete without adding a name of note, such as "Why, I remember discussing this very thing with my grandfather when I was a lad...he was intimate with Newton, you will remember, and some say many of the latter's ideas originated with my progenitor." The connexion with noble birth or association is a condiment, as necessary for the enjoyment of coffee as mustard is to the enjoyment of beef.

I have scant stores in the realm of family history, simply because I did not think to ask when I had the opportunity. I know not who my grandfather was, and all memories of my own father were made in my first seventeen years, as I never saw him again past that age. I also never again met another Fezziwig, nor heard of others with my name, despite a life with more travel than many men. I did, once, see a bill of sale from Normandy signed by a man named Fessevig. I have thought that, perhaps, my ancestors were descended from the ancient Norse invaders of those environs, and their way to Britannia was paved by an earlier William.

My entrance to the world came in 1721, on land associated with what was known as Nene Manor, Lincolnshire. My mother, who I believe to have been known previous to marriage as Sarah Billingsley, sacrificed her life to allow mine; that is, she died in childbirth. It is my understanding she was young and delicate, of about sixteen years, and with no other children. I recently returned to find more about her and her family, with limited success.

My father, Lemuel Fezziwig, was older and engaged in agriculture. I have no knowledge of how I was nursed, or who helped my father raise an infant. There is only a vague memory of warmth and tenderness shown to me, a voice, and a fragment of melody:

Jockey was a piper's son,

And fell in love when he was young;

But all the tunes that he could play,

Was o'er the hills, and far away.

You may well remember me singing that to you.

When I say my father was engaged in agriculture, I mean he was a farmer. He planted a small plot close by our single timber and thatch house, and tended the sheep held in common with the others on the manor. He had a cow during most of my childhood, and, as early as I can remember, I helped with these animals and the turnips, cabbages, leeks, spinach, and peas grown in the close, and with hay from the wolds. The house had a hearth and stone floor, a table, bed, and chest. The cobblestones extended past the walls for some little distance, leading me to think the floor had been part of a larger, more ancient structure, and the hut built upon it at a later time.

My father was not tall, but was of a substantial girth. His face was in a perpetual state of sadness, with features that seemed to want to drip down it and create a puddle at his feet. (The wrinkles of smiles and laughter deeply crease my face today, and I would have it no other way. I always felt my happier predisposition must have come from my mother.) He was not prone to drink, except at Christmastime, and then in a moderate fashion.

3

While he did not nurture me in the physical way in which I doted on you, he was kind and patient, especially when compared to many of the other fathers of that time and place. He was a man of numbers rather than letters, or, for that matter, spoken words.

The only book in our house was a leather bound ledger, which he kept assiduously. While little more than utilitarian conversation passed between us, I knew his love for me, and remember often sensing him looking upon me when he thought I took no notice. At those times, I knew he was thinking of my mother, some of whose features he said I shared.

Most of my playmates were the children of other common holders on the manor, and, when not more productively employed, we made great sport of exploring the fields, forests, and streams. There were still swaths of great trees back then, having been preserved for the pleasure of the manor. The area was replete with ancient ruins, walls and tumble-downs and trenches and stones perfect for boyish battles between Cavaliers and Roundheads. Fishing, berry picking, and building water wheels for the small stream were favorite pastimes of mine, but many of my creations met unfortunate ends when the flock became unruly while being taken to drink.

My own education (or, at least that not gleaned by nature and her minions) was supplied by my father for figures and ciphers, and by my great friend Pricilla for letters. Her father, Reverend Meade, was the local vicar. My experience with vicars, to this day, tells me they are of two types: those who exude heaven on earth, and those who project a warmer disposition presumably from a much hotter place. Reverend Meade was of the latter type. He wore a scowl as gratefully as most men wear a greatcoat in winter.

Many clergymen warn that their flock is on the precipice of damnation, but few seem so satisfied at the prospect as Meade. It was rumored that, while his disdain for everyone was clear, he particularly disliked my father and me, because he believed my mother, taken in her youth, was from a family of Papists. I know not if that was true, but have confidence she is at peace, regardless of small differences in the beliefs.

While Pricilla and the other Meade children suffered mightily from their father's foulness and fists, they, of both sexes, did learn to read and write. Pricilla, in turn, taught me, from *The Pilgrim's Progress* and pieces of Holy Scripture, often under the sun while seated on an ancient wall, making sure not to stain the pages with the wild blackberry juice that dappled on our fingers. My delight in her, my curiosity and my constant thought of her, all increased as I approached manhood.

If these days seem idyllic to someone, such as yourselves, who were reared in the great city, I will not try to convince you otherwise. While we worked to exhaustion and had not but bare sustenance to show for it, we knew little else and were quite satisfied with our lot. I do not remember giving much concern about the future, and knew nothing of the wider world. All that began to change in my sixteenth year.

We seldom had others visit our small house. Most smallholders saw one another in the fields or with the flock every day, so visited little. That winter, other men began to crowd around our small table over a candle at night and talk with my father in hushed tones. He would often find a reason to send me out into the dark during those times, to check on the animals or fetch water or wood. If I ever inquired after the point of those nighttime gatherings, my father would just say "Naught" in a way that made it clear to me I should pursue it no further.

5

The other young fellows also noticed anxiety among their fathers and had a wide range of ideas about the origin. Some thought we would soon be defending ourselves against the Pretender, or the Spanish, or the French, and we assured one another that we could dispatch whole brigades of the enemy by leading them into the bogs at night. Others thought it had to do with Walpole, or a great beast in the forest, or plans to take passage to America.

I was sure the change came about because of a word I frequently heard while my ear was pressed upon the door without Father's knowledge, a word spat out with disgust like a worm accidently consumed with a slice of apple. Though I knew not the meaning of the word, I was certain nothing good could come of *containment*.

The meetings became more frequent and animated during the time when the winter Manor Court approached. On the appointed day, my father's countenance was even more grim than ever. I felt I was old enough to join the men of the manor, but my father would have none of it. He trudged off through the frost and left me with instructions for chores already a part of my daily routine.

He was gone far longer than usual for Court days; I was worried that something foul had happened but dared not leave the house after dark. At length, the oaken door swung open and he went straight to the hearth, sat down, and stared into the smoky, unwilling flame. He spoke not the rest of the night, but would, in turn, stare at the hearth, and then at me for uncomfortable minutes. I eventually fell into an unproductive sleep, but, on the dawn, he looked like he had not moved since the evening before, speaking not a word of whatever distracted him so.

The rest of the winter passed uneventfully, at least to my knowing. The dark meetings continued, but with less frequency, and my father seemed to produce the unmistakable haze of someone with something to hide, but possessed of a great desire to appear the contrary. My contemporaries still had ideas that some great catastrophe was possible, but the overall feeling was that it was not immediate, and was soon supplanted by the busy work of spring.

For those who make their living from the earth, spring is a time like no other, at once exhausting and hopeful. Father was, for his time, a scientific man. He experimented with different techniques in the close, while often frustrated that the other smallholders did not share his willingness for innovation in the commons. At the time, I was not so impressed by his modernity and curiosity, as it often made work for me that my mates did not share. The vegetable plots of the other holders were planted and harvested; little more. The Fezziwig plot, in comparison, was continually manured with droppings from the sheep, after a long mellowing in a pile that I regularly turned. I was fascinated by how much heat the pile generated, even in winter, and many a time warmed my stiff hands over its comfort.

A thick cover of leaves and needles covered the plot after the plants sprouted, meaning many a backbreaking trip into the forest with a large rush basket. It was not sufficient for Father's plan for mellow manure to be spread upon these leaves; nay, the leaves had to be raked away, the manure applied, and the leaves returned. Woe was upon me if, in this process, I injured the tender stem of a new plant.

In that particular spring, Father came upon an idea to increase the size of turnips and parsnips. He called it "digging it double," the logic being that looser soil would present fewer obstructions for growth. He directed me to dig that section of the plot twice as deep as usual, and deposit a layer of mellow manure at the bottom, removing all stones and clods from the till. The first stage of this endeavor produced numerous blisters on my hands, despite their being already heavily calloused. It also produced the most amazing event in my life up until that time.

I had been hard at my task all day, and silently bemoaning my fate, as is common for boys of that age. The lower soil was very hard, as if it had been purposely compacted at some ancient time, and full of stones. Just at dusk, my hoe struck a stone of large size and peculiarly regular shape. Unable to lift it out, I continued to dig around it, only to find another identical stone beside it. Determined to not have these two stones haunting my dreams for the night, I dug wide around them and finally found an edge to grip and heave with great effort.

In the centre of the flat, hard earth under the further stone, I saw a tiny glint of yellow in the failing light. First thinking it another stone but intrigued by its colour, I plucked an object out of the muck and wiped off the soil, aided by my spittle. It was clearly not a natural object, about half as large as my hand.

The thing was made of yellow metal, roughly oblong in shape, and possessing a socket on one end. The other end was fashioned into the head of a lion, with one eye being a bright blue stone with many facets; the other eye was missing. All around was filigree decoration, though one side was compressed to make the fine work indiscernible. The other side had the words (if, indeed, words they be…I have not met one who could interpret them, though I assume they are of the old language) HEHT GEWYRCAN worked into the design. It was, overall, the most beautiful object I had ever seen.

Father had not yet returned from the commons. The jewel

shone even more brightly when I washed it with water, and held it up to the light of a candle. The one lion's eye burned from within, and the gold (for, what else could the yellow metal be?) was like liquid fire dancing around its regal master.

When Father came in, he looked weary and was taken aback at my excited babbling; that is, until he saw the glint of the jewel in the candlelight. I had never before seen such a look of wonderment in his eyes, the sparkle of which almost matched the one remaining in the lion's face. He gasped, laughed, cried, all seemingly at once. I well remember how he closed his eyes tightly and rubbed his face roughly, then slowly opened them to view the sight, repeating this action many times. He bade me to recount the smallest detail of finding the jewel, over and over.

When our jubilation caused us to reach emotional fatigue and the muscles of our mouths ached from the effort, a cloud came over Father's face.

"Will, you must do the hardest and gravest thing you have yet done, but it is also the most important. You must not speak a word of this jewel to anyone. Anyone. You must not allow any word or action tomorrow to be different from those today. This is life or death, Will."

"But Father, surely this find is of value! We can improve our lot. God has sent us a gift that has been awaiting us in the earth for only He knows how long!" I cried.

Father's complexion was always very pale, especially for one who made his living out of doors. In the light of the candle, I could see that what little blood was usually present had drained, and he shone white. He raised a finger to his lips.

"We have not done ourselves a service by being so loud, Will, but no man could be otherwise, I'm sure. It can't happen again. It's not God that is of concern, Will. It's man. These are dangerous days – dangerous days! Many times I have seen blessings become curses when times are evil. I have said naught about it to you, but I was in war once. I know that everything can be taken from a man without reason, other than that someone stronger desires it."

"No one can take it, Father! It is ours! I found it in our own close plot! There can be no other claim but that!" I cried, loud enough to bring a scowl to Father's pale face.

"I'm afraid you know little of life," he sighed. "But, we must be thankful for what God has sent us, and keep our wits. Have you thought that there could be even more?" I hadn't, in my excitement. "It could bring attention if someone saw a candle in the close at night. Besides, I think it has begun to rain. We must both continue our routine tomorrow, as if nothing is different from any other day. I will go to the common, and you will dig the close plot. But, carefully, for God's sake, carefully! Sort through every clod. I will mention that we are increasing our planting, so it will look natural for you to do it. And remember, not a word! Not a nod or wink or haughty look. Our lives may depend upon it, Will."

By then, the candle was almost spent. Father took up a stone in the corner that I had never seen before removed, and, to my surprise, there were two copper coins hidden under it. He made a depression for the jewel, wrapped it in a small scrap of skin, and placed the stone over it, sweeping grit into the crack so that it appeared undisturbed. He hugged me, a first for some years, and laid to rest.

Rest came not for me. My thoughts ran faster than one of my water wheels in the rain-swollen stream. They showed me feasts of great joints and fine clothing with silver buttons and carriages drawn by four. Then, as could be expected for a lad of that age, I thought of Pricilla, and her sharing with me those riches, and a bed covered in silk.

Upon sunrise, Father repeated his warnings and instructions of the night before, and left for the commons. The rain had ended, but left the ground wet and sticky. Still, I went to my task with enthusiasm, digging deep into the plot and carefully mashing through the clods turned up. I found more stones that had at least one worked face, but no more whole and still in place.

By evening, I had tilled the entire plot to a point past which suspicion would be raised, with no richer result than worms, grubs, roots, and stones. My hands and back pained me greatly, but not as much as having no additional good news for my father that evening. He hid his disappointment, but I could tell he was continuing to consider what to do next with the great treasure in hand, lying patiently under the stone in the corner.

The soil in the plot had been worked so thoroughly that planting was an easy task, and I still held hope (ultimately unrealised) of turning up something of value. After a few days, Father was again ready to discuss our situation.

"Will, you are a smart boy. There has been no hiding from you that there are troubles. All smallholders hang by a thread. You know we could not live off just the produce of our close plot."

At this point, my father did something I had seen him do but seldom. He smiled broadly and made a jest of sorts. "Unless, you could continue to coax from it the type of fruit it yielded of late." His usual countenance quickly returned. "Things are changing. Great mills are hungry, and the commons have always been used to provide for smallholders, with a little to spare for payments. Somehow - you know I am not a scholar - Lords are taking what has been used in common and pushing the smallholders off it. They say the land belongs to the manors, and now that there can be some profit from it, the manors are exercising their rights."

"But, how?" I sputtered. Father held up his hand.

"I don't know. I have heard it is like Eden. Adam and Eve used the Garden in common until it pleased the Lord to reclaim it. That is the talk when the other holders come by night. Parliament and the King know of this unjust practice. It has happened all over England, and it is allowed."

He sighed deeply and stared for a moment. "We hear that, in some places, the holders try to resist, and meet bad ends. Other holders will come again tonight, though I am loath for them to be here. We must be careful. Men's desperation match the times." His eyes briefly shifted to the stone in the corner. "But, perhaps God has sent us a way. There are places where a small amount of gold can give a man enough land to live unmolested and thrive by his sweat without fear. "

"You mean, leave this place?" I asked, unbelieving. Though possessed of a curiosity of the world common to a young man, I had, on that day, never been more than two miles from the hut in which I was born.

"I see no other way," he replied. "I hear that, when this happens, many go to the cities to work in the mills and live as close as mice in a box and their days are few. Your, ah, *produce* may be God's way to help us avoid that end. But how to use it? To whom can we turn with trust?"

"What does it matter, Father?" I asked. "The treasure is ours. We must go to a city and sell it, and buy a new plot." I envisioned us in well-appointed house, with a separate chamber, where Pricilla and I quietly laughed and shushed one another lest Father hear our passion.

"No, no," he shook his head. "If a country man such as me is found hawking such a gem, an inquiry would be raised. What do we know of commerce in the city?"

It was at that moment I resolved that I would, someday, know something of commerce in the city.

He continued. "Just like the charters that allow the commons to be taken, there could be devilish, ancient ones that would make the treasure the property of the manor. It is the way of the world. The rich are uninterested in the things possessed by those who toil, be it their children or their land or their labour or their souls, until some value in those things is seen. Then, we are suddenly poor stewards, and the mighty do us the great service of taking those things from us to manage them more efficiently." These last words were bitterroot and vinegar.

Father pushed himself back partially from the table. "Who is the most learned man here who is not of the manor family?" he asked.

"The only man of letters not of the manor family is the vicar," I said, giving him the obvious answer.

"And what do you think of him? Not his *daughter*. Of him." When he said daughter, I saw an expression of both amusement and consternation, if the two can coexist.

"God forgive me, but he is a terrible man. Learned, yes, but you know how he condemns everyone and everything. He is of violent temper with his family. Other than judgment, Father, I see nothing of Christ in the man."

"Nor do I," he agreed, "But I see little choice. He is the only neutral party with learning in history and law. As vile as he may be, he is a man of God. He is bound to do His work when called upon, is he not? Clearly, God has brought this treasure to us, Will. There is no other explanation. The ancients did not take up a stone and lay down a jewel knowing that William Fezziwig would some day be in need whilst planting turnips."

He paused for a moment. "He took something from us when you were born, Will. He has now decided to give something back. Despite all my prayers for guidance, He has shown no other path than to turn to His servant. I know of none other who can advise us. We must show the jewel to the vicar and ask for his help in turning it into a future for you. Can you see another way?"

I could not. "But, pray, take heed, Father. More than once, what looked like the best things plucked from our plot turned out to be rotten in the core."

"I know, and am proud that you are so observant," he said. "But somehow I know that God is making it up to us, and shan't allow us to go wrong, as long as we trust Him."

With this, our course was set.

We continued to appear most ordinary to the world for another few days, until Father came early from the commons just ahead of the vicar. Before I could speak my desire to attend the discussion, he pointed me toward the close with a single "Naught," and I knew it would do no good to argue.

I tried to listen at the door, but the voices from within were so low that they yielded nothing to slake my curiosity and fear. I barely pulled away from the door in time to avoid being discovered as it was pushed open and the vicar strode out, his face like stone. He spoke not, but aimed himself at the lane and disappeared. I entered to find Father still seated.

"He is a hard man, Will, but he will help us. The Church will have to share in our proceeds, and so will he for his trouble. He said he couldn't help but to question God's will to send such a treasure to people like us, but that what is done is done. He will make inquiry on our behalf, and we will sell the jewel and start afresh as freeholders."

"Where will we go? What will we buy? Will we be far?" The first real change in my young life was upon me.

"There will be time for all of that. We will finish out the season. But, we must see land in the flush of summer, to know its worth to us. We have much to do. When we are settled, I want to look for you an apprenticeship in a trade, Will. A foul change is going to make it hard to live as a freeholder in days to come."

I lay down that night with visions of what the future may be like, visions I look back upon now and smile. I knew so little of the world at that time, because all I had for comparison was within sight of that stone hut.

In the middle of the night, I thought I heard an owl in my fitful slumber. Then, with a great rush, six men in black cloaks were instantly in the hut, holding my father and me with short swords at our throats. A seventh man came in with a lantern, and I recognized his as a man of the manor. He held the lantern up to Father's face.

"So this is the digger who thinks the world is his," he sneered. He went to the corner and bent to the stones. "Cobbles in good order. At least this sty will be easily mucked. Ah, here we are. This one will do."

If possible, my fear and anger rose even more sharply, for I knew the wretch had found what he sought. I heard a sharp intake of breath, and the figure rose, looking at the jewel by lantern light. He held the jewel up higher and spoke to the brigands holding us. "God has smiled on the just. You will share the benefit. We have other visits tonight as well, and some diggers have daughters instead of this s---e," he said, cocking his head toward me with a sneer. The other men gave one another lascivious glances.

"Take it and leave us!" cried Father. "We will be gone on the morrow."

The man smirked. "Two truths and a falsehood, digger. I will take it, and you will be gone tomorrow. But I will not leave you. I have full authority of the manor and the sheriff. What would be your penalty for poaching a stag? Or stealing from the manor stores? And yet, you've done greater evil. Do you think we know not what you conspire, with the other digger vermin? You think you will resist a rightful order of containment. You know better than God on how to order the world? It's not just your body you will lose, digger, but your soul! Take him!"

With that, three of the men drug father out. His words, "Will! No! Will!" I can still hear, and they have awakened me from my sleep many times. That was the last time I heard my father's voice. I never saw him again, or, despite later inquiries, know certain of his fate. In my heart, I know my father did not see the next dawn, and sleeps in a field, abandoned and unknown. Scarce a day for many years passed without my pondering what I could have done to save him. Even now, I know naught. I had kept the secret of the jewel in my heart, and I am certain Father had done the same.

To all but the vicar.

The man came so close to my face I could smell his stench.

"What else is here, boy? What else is here?" I was too alarmed to think of any response that could help my situation, so I resorted to the truth." "Naught!" I cried. One of the men holding me struck me several times on the face, and then in the middle. "Naught! Naught!" I cried again.

"We shall see. Get rid of him!" the man spat, and the brigands bound my hands and feet, and tied a filthy rag around my mouth. They drug me out, and I saw that, during our tribulation, a cart filled with hay had come to the hut. The driver made a hole in the hay, and the men holding me pulled a putrid pouch of wool over my head so that I could not see. I felt myself being heaved into the cart and covered with hay.

Between the tight cloth in my mouth, the hood, and the hay, I could not breathe. I struggled to rise, but, as soon as I did, I was struck several times with something heavy and rough. I lay still for a moment, gagging, then panic overcame me and I struggled again, with the same result. "Lay still, d--- you!" I heard. "You will get the cudgel each time I see you move, until your brains colour the hay if need be!" I tried to comply, but the sensation was the same as I imagine that of a drowning man, and I struggled once more. I suddenly felt a searing pain on the side of my head, and my shuttered eyes were illuminated with points of light.

I know not how much time passed. My head throbbed, and I heard roaring in my ears, and each bone and muscle ached. I awoke being roughly handled out of the cart and thrown onto cobblestones. I heard a heavy door slam shut and being locked. With difficulty due to the pain from the blow, I shook off the hood. There was sunlight streaming through small cracks; I must have been dead to the world throughout the rest of the night.

DANNY KUHN

I was in a round timber structure, low ceilinged, and filled with barrels. By the look and smell, I surmised I was in a granary. A strange one it was, though, for I heard the heavy creak of moving timber and stone above me and the whole structure seemed built to turn on its axis. Through my haze, it came to me that my prison must be the roundhouse of a post mill, of which I had heard described, but not before seen.

Oh, daughters! Even after these many years, I cannot describe the sorrow I felt laying there! I felt sad, so sad, that I was alive and that my torment had not ended quickly. I was sure it was about to do so, but, instead of dying as a man, I was to die bound as a sheep for slaughter. A day before, I had visions of hope and a new life; now, none of God's children were so low. I sobbed, thankful that the tears running down my face and into my mouth helped me expel, around the bloody cloth still secured there, the hay chaff caked inside.

Soon, the door swung open and I was blinded by the bright sunlight. A large, slovenly man came in and clamped a shackle to my ankle; the other end he secured to a post. He cut the tethers on my feet and the cloth from my mouth. He said "I'm going to free your hands, boy, but if you raise 'em, I will beat the life out of you. I'm not sure I want you alive anyhow." He brandished a club, and I believed his words. He cut the rope around my wrists. I could feel no sensation in my hands at all.

The man leaned back on the wall, as if pondering what to do next. He ducked back out of the low doorway, and reentered with a clay pot of water and half a loaf. Hungry though I was, I first drank to clear the debris caked in my throat and then ate the bread, avoiding the eyes of my captor.

"How old are you, boy?" he asked offhandedly.

"Seventeen."

"Pfft. I would think they have been hard ones, by your look. But who could tell, under all that." My clothes had, from my being bound, become unnaturally soiled with waste as well as covered with blood, and I had no shoes or stockings, owing to my abrupt apprehension. "We'll clean you up and you will start earning your bread." He left again.

A short while later, a younger man brought in a wooden tub, two buckets of hot water, a sliver of soap, and a rag. All my questions to him were met by only a blank stare, and I assumed he was deaf. He freed me enough to wash, and brought in a set of clothes, which he left on a barrel top.

The clothes were tight fitting, for I was not particularly tall, yet of solid build. They were, though, of finer weave, manufacture, and cut than any I had ever worn. The shirt was frilled at the cuff and around the neck. The waistcoat was plain, and the breeches buttoned below the knee. The coat was long, and embroidered on the edges and pockets. The shoes had heels and silver buckles. These, particularly, caused me discomfort, as I had never worn more than farmer's shoes.

Having supped, bathed, and shed my fouled clothing, I was again able to think clearly and access my situation. I assumed I was in the post-mill closest to the Nene manor, which I knew to be the Waltham Mill. I could see no means of escape, the shackle already cutting into my ankle. I tried to tell myself I would soon be reunited with my father and the legitimacy of our situation, and at least our little house, if not the jewel, would be restored. Only two other times in my life did I have such a plea to God that time be turned back, just a day. You will likely surmise which those other times might be.

My despair had little time to fester before the large man returned, this time with a tall, thin companion. One look revealed the newcomer to be a gentleman of means, with rich clothing and a golden head on his walking stick.

"'Ere he is, m'Lord." the large man said, nodding toward me. The tall man scowled, at me, and took snuff from a gold box in this pocket.

"Have you ever worked in a household, boy, or only in the dirt?" He sniffed.

"My father and I are freeholders, sir, and we have been kidnapped from our home by brigands. Pray, I need your assistance in returning to Nene Manor."

The two men exchanged a look of derision. "There are no longer freeholders on Nene, and you are indentured to me, such as you are. You will be working in the household. If you are diligent, your life will be tolerable, and you will one day be free. If not, I will sell you to the Indies plantations, where I have interests. It's a short life there. I won't have insolence, even for a day."

With that, the two men left and continued conversation, little of which I could hear. In a short while, the young deaf man came in and tied my hands, which I did not resist, feeling it futile. He unlocked the shackle from the post but secured it to my other ankle, and led me to a waggon. He tied my shackles to a ring in the back, and mounted the seat to begin our journey.

That was the first time I had opportunity to view my prison from the outside. Under less dire circumstances, I would have been interested in the sight of the great wheel turning slowly in the light wind. (I later learned the mill was already quite ancient at the time of my captivity, but blew down in a storm some few years thence, and I was not sorry for it. I know it has since been rebuilt and stands today.)

By this time dusk approached, but being again in the fresh air rejuvenated me. The surrounding fields were much like those I knew at Nene, though perhaps a bit lower. We arrived at a formidable manor house after a short journey, and two liveried servants, one appearing younger than myself, met the waggon. Neither spoke, but they took me to a downstairs chamber. I had never seen so fine a house.

The chamber was windowless, and was apparently a cupboard, though no stores were present at the time. A straw tick lay in the corner, with a porcelain chamber pot opposite. There was nothing more, save a welcomed water jar and a plate with bread and cheese. When the door closed, it was exceedingly dark. I lay on the tick, overwhelmed by fatigue and sadness, but the chamber was warm and comfortable, so I entered a fitful sleep.

At some time in the dead of the night, I heard the lock click, and the door swung open. The young servant appeared, his pale face ghostlike by the flicker of a thin candle. He put a finger to his lips, produced a key, and my shackles were soon on the floor. As I rubbed blood back into my ankles, his lips came close to my ear.

"It is clear to me you are not here of your own will." His voice was strangely hoarse and dry for one so young. "You know not what awaits. By God, if it means my life - and it very well may - I won't see it happen to someone else. My life is forfeit. When he comes for you and you are missing, I will likely be discovered. At least it may deliver me from my torment. He is the devil." He choked on the next words. "He does things to me you cannot imagine." He composed himself and continued. "Follow the lane past the stables. You must be quiet, for the stable boys will be questioned. You will come to a proper road, the Brigsley Road. I know not from where you came, but the near settlement is the port at Great Grimsby. Walk right, and you will reach it mid morning. Keep to the side and be able to hide yourself quickly. You will be pursued."

He tiptoed me down the hall and out a door with such rapidity that I was able to say naught a word to him, and often wondered of his fate since. I was suddenly alone in the cool night, and stealthily followed my liberator's instructions. The moon was new, and I stumbled more than once, trying to make as much haste as possible. I encountered no one else on the road until just after dawn; I easily avoided a slow waggon by hiding behind a nearby stile. Eventually, I passed houses coming alive with the work of mid-morning, and was seen by a few inhabitants, but my presence was only acknowledged with a nod, if at all.

After climbing the final rise, I saw the village, with its docks and the Humber estuary. Now that I have been a resident of the City of London for many years and traveled to others nearly as great, I know Great Grimsby is, compared, but a spot on the map, though its port is of great merit in the fishing industry. On that day, though, my eyes had never seen such a busy place, or as many buildings, or so much water.

I nervously made my way toward the quay, knowing nothing else to do. My ignorance of the ways of such a village was great; I decided that looking like I had purpose would make me less conspicuous. I once considered finding a magistrate to tell of my kidnapping, but, for all I knew, I was thought a criminal, a runaway indenture, or a manor thief. For a moment, my inclination was to find a clergyman with whom to share my saga, but, in my glowing anger towards Vicar Meade's treachery (for, what else could have happened?), that thought quickly evaporated.

Hunger and thirst had returned. I found a barrel of rainwater at the side of a tiled building and drank, straining out the small wiggly things through my hands. While my thirst was slaked, it did little for my hunger. The smell of meat and bread and porridge being prepared was carried on the smoke from many buildings, making my emptiness even worse.

Evening began to fall, and the business of the docks dissipated. The proprietors of hawking carts trundled them away and I found myself more or less alone, able to duck into the shadows if someone should pass. Behind the market, I found several cheese skins and a burnt half-loaf and limp carrots in the heap; they were wrapped in cabbage leaves and barely soiled. Many a finer meal since has been far less appreciated.

The centre cobbled street was mainly silent, but I heard music and raucous language from the unimproved side lane, and I was able to view the source from a concealed corner. It was my first sight of a gin-house, and I understood it little, but I knew there were food and drink and light and a warm hearth and human companionship. Lost in my loneliness, I was shocked back into the present by a feminine voice.

"What 'ave we 'ere? Ready for a bit o' bachelor's fare, my love? You look the age, you do!" I had not noticed the young woman as she approached. To my great surprise, she lowered her bodice and showed me underneath, the like of which I had not before seen. I turned and ran, as she called after me, "Don't run, love! They shan't bite, you know!" I ran into a side lane and found a three-sided shed that became my lodging for the night.

How my life had changed in only two risings of the sun! The loss and fear and loneliness overcame me, and I sobbed so loudly that I held my face with both hands to avoid being discovered. I could only think of the verse I had learned to read under Pricilla's tutelage, "My God, My God, why hath thou abandoned me?"

When the next dawn came, I knew naught but to repeat the previous day. I found water to drink and made my way to the quay. A cadre of men, young and old, was unloading a great ship, carrying bales and casks and loading them onto waiting waggons. I did not realise it at the time, but Providence planted the idea that, since I had no other plan, I should fall in and help in the effort. No one seemed to notice that I did not belong to the gang, and even that small measure of human contact felt satisfying. On the deck of the ship, I saw, for my first time, a man with skin as dark as night, an African.

At mid day, my heart leapt when loaves and cheese were distributed from a large rush basket. I tried to hide my greediness as I ate mine, and went back to the work of unloading for the rest of the day. The chore was finished near dusk, and I began to wonder what I was going to do next, having no other prospect but another night in the cold shed alone with my despair.

I was walking away when a tall, old man blocked my path, and I almost trembled with fear when he accosted me. "Hold, lad!" he called. I considered running as I had from the strumpet the night before, but thought better of it, since there was no edge of accusation in his voice. "Hilli-ho, what have we here?" he asked, as he looked me toe to head. "A pretty fine suit, but this is not the first day the boy has seen toil, I'll wager. What is your name?"

"Will, um, Gainsborough." I lied, still not knowing that I may not be the subject of a sheriff's search.

"Humph," the man huffed, showing his doubt. "A

formidable name to match the suit, but I'm still not sure of the boy." He folded his arms, with his battered walking stick held by its middle. He wore his own hair and a tri-corn. His suit gave the impression that it was of fine manufacture, but aging and having been worn somewhat carelessly. "Have you worked for me before?" he asked.

"No, Sir," I said, trying to appear nonchalant. "I am newly arrived from Quick, and in search of situation. My family is desirous of the clergy for me as a vocation, but I feel I am not suited for it." A lie begins like a spark on tender, but soon is capable of fanning itself.

"No lust for the life of a country vicar, hm? Ho, I can't say that I blame you!" He smiled, and I saw the first glint of kindness in eyes that I had seen in days, since seeing my father the evening before our capture. "So, since you are from a family with ambitions for their son, am I to assume you can read and write?"

"Aye, Sir, and cipher."

"Capital! Where are your lodgings?"

I had to decide with haste whether to continue my subterfuge, or tell the truth, or at least a version of it.

"At present, Sir, I am between lodgings. It will be my activity for the evening, to find what Great Grimsby has available."

"I thought as much," he said. "Well, Will *Gainsborough*, I conduct myself in a way in which I later regret almost daily. This day, I will offer you a position, if you can keep it. That," he pointed at the largest building on the quay with his stick, "is my warehouse. You are strong, not afraid to put your back into it, and, at least you tell me, can write and cipher. Business is brisk, and I am in need. There is room in the garret for you, if your possessions are scant. Which, I conjecture, they just may be. As fact, do you have *anything* you will need to retrieve?"

"No, Sir." I replied, embarrassed. Only three days previous, Father and I were preparing to benefit from an ancient treasure of great value. But, standing there, I had only the clothes on my body, which were not actually mine.

I pondered the man's offer. The events of the prior days had, quite understandably, made me very suspicious of the human race, but something in the man's manner made me believe I could trust him. And, what other prospect did I have?

"Much obliged for your offer of employment, Sir. I promise you will not regret our meeting."

"Ho, it wouldn't be the first time I have heard that and been proved wrong!" he snorted. "Be warned. If I find you, and so much as a needle, gone on the morrow, you will rue our meeting. You *Will* be found, Will *Gainsborough*." He frowned. "Do you use tobacco?"

"No, Sir. Neither snuff nor a pipe."

"Good. Don't begin. Unhealthy habit." At this, he fumbled with a silver snuffbox and took a pinch up his ample nostril. His face loosened. "Chirrup! Come along, then!"

I followed the man, who along the way identified himself as Mr. John Spills, ("A warehouseman named Spills. No need to say it; there will be naught I haven't heard.") into the warehouse, where several men were finishing for the evening. It was the biggest building I had ever entered, filled with orderly rows of bales and hogsheads and chests, and relatively clean and neat. I was led up a ladder to find a small straw-tick bed with blanket, a desk with quill, inkwell and candle, and the necessary basin, jug, and bucket.

Mr. Spills indicated he would soon return, and did so shortly with a thick slice of bread and cold mutton. He also tossed down a worn nightshirt. "This is almost ready for the ragman, but could still be of service," he said. "I have some other matters. I will see you down in the warehouse at dawn, Will *Gainsborough*," he concluded, and climbed back down the ladder.

The room was dusty and close, but warmth arose from the space below, bringing with it domestic smells of cotton and grain. No longer being observed, I wolfed the food and donned the nightshirt. For the first time in days, I allowed a small stream of peace to trickle into my soul, and I slept.

I was awake before dawn, and it took me a few moments to remember where I was, and how I had gotten there. Thinking back over the events of the previous day, a realisation came to me that has been reconfirmed over the years. If I had not been wearing the suit of a gentleman, no matter how I came about it, or how tough and calloused the hide within, Mr. Spills would never have picked me out of the crowd, and I would have awakened again in a three-sided shed with an empty stomach. The suit made him assume I could read and write, which I could do only through my coincidental friendship with Pricilla Meade. My ambition and hard work on the quay was not enough, in itself. The other men also had those. Persons provided with a good suit, no matter if they worked for it themselves, have an advantage in the eyes of the world. Perception trumps fact, and station reigns over all.

After attending necessities and dressing, I descended into

the warehouse at almost the same moment Mr. Spills arrived. He had a jug with porridge, and poured some into a bowl on a small, rough table. He looked over figures in a leather-bound ledger while I ate, and, when I finished, he said. "Read, write, and cipher, he can, this vicar-not-to-be from Quick. Let's see how you can earn your keep. Add these columns, and then subtract these expenses. And write an entry saying I have taken you in." I took up a quill and did the calculations, then asked, "Is this day 25 April, Sir?"

"26. Tempis fugit," he replied.

I wrote:

Apr 26, This day took into my employ one William Gainsborough, late of Quick.

I pushed the ledger toward him, feeling somewhat nervous. He evidently had already done the calculations and knew the sum, for he gave it but a glance, then read the entry.

"Yo ho, yes. Very good. I hope you are as honest in all things as you were in at least *part* of our conversation yesterday, William. You shall work with me, and with Barkers, my clerk. If you are needed quayside, like yesterday, you will work with Gibbon, but I suspect there will be enough to occupy you with the inventory and books."

Mr. Spills pulled a great watch from his coat and peered at it. It was gold and gleaming, and, to me, seemed the size of a turnip. He noticed my stare.

"Ah, it is a thing to see, is it not? I am not vain, as you can see from my dress, but watches have always intrigued me. You know exactly what they require, and if you provide that requirement, they go about their job without complaint." He handed me the watch to examine. It was the first time I had ever held one. It was the second most beautiful thing I had ever seen. I read its inscription: "Time SPILLS, to be Caught."

"Chirrup, here is Barkers now," he said, breaking the spell of the timepiece.

A plump young man, of about twenty years, pale complexion, and red hair, came in and nodded to Mr. Spills. His suit was fine, but his eyes bloodshot. He looked as if his sleep was little, and his breath gave clue as to how he spent late hours. Mr. Spills gave introduction and instructions for the day, and left me with Barkers as other men began to come in and out of the warehouse on sundry missions.

Despite my initial negative impression, Barkers turned out to be a fair companion. He talked softly, giving the impression that loud noises caused him pain even if emanating from his own throat. He showed me the order of the warehouse, and we sat with ledgers while he explained the business and its record-keeping methods.

"It's good to have some help again," he said. "I had another helper, but he went to London with his family. I don't talk much with the others - coarse sort, no letters - so we will get on and perhaps I will burn fewer candles. At least, fewer at work rather than play!" The last words came with a wink and crooked smile.

Mr. Spills was in the business of commodities, importing mainly cotton and tobacco from America, and molasses from the West Indies. The molasses went to distillers and was exported back to America, along with finished cloth. Tobacco was distributed in the Midlands, and he also arranged for the transportation of grain to London. "At least, we used to send grain to London," explained Barkers. "Of late, the demand for gin in the city has become such that the grain we send is now liquid. Not that we don't withhold enough sufficient for ourselves, of course," he laughed.

Over the next few weeks, I was a student most eager, and worked diligently to prove to Mr. Spills that he had made a good decision. Barkers and I got along well, as he seemed relieved to share his work in order to comfort his aching head from nights spent in the gin-house. I learned that Mr. Spills had both suppliers and customers in the north, and had been of service to the Crown with certain information concerning the Jacobites some years before, and thus had favored status as a man of business. He and his wife, who was as round as Spills was tall, were childless, and were generally fair taskmasters, as long as those in their employ were diligent and honest.

"He's always been level with me," confided Barkers. "In fact, he has indulged me a time or two when the cards went against me. But, I know I wouldn't cross 'im. I heard he once beat a 'prentice half to death with his stick, after finding the bloke had nicked half a crown. Deserved it, though, I guess. And he doesn't suffer laggards. He is tolerant of many things, but not idleness. You will note I am diligent in my work, even when I am, ah, suffering from flux." He rolled his eyes.

As summer drew nigh, my life began to take on a comfortable routine, and I dwelt less on the past. I grieved for my losses, but my needs were met, and I had some promise for the future. The nightmares, replaying the scene of my capture and Father being drug away by brigands, still came, but less often. I could not completely dispel the gnawing fear that the sheriff would take me away to the fine house on Brigsley Road in the middle of the night to face unspeakable defilement, but that shrank with time as well.

Barkers was, indeed, a diligent worker, even when quite

clearly suffering the effects of too much drink the night before. He spoke little of his past or family. His habit, while not otherwise occupied, was to draw on small scraps of paper. His sketches of other workers bore such good likeness, that I thought he could have made a fair living doing them as a vocation. What I enjoyed most was his drawings of animals; birds, fishes, horses, dogs.

"I wish I could make drawings, but I have no talent," I said one day.

"Tut. 'Tisn't talent. It's like learning your letters. It just takes practice. Here, draw over this dog several times, and see if you are not able to draw it yourself." I was pleased to practice under his watch and, as you know, I retain joy in doing little drawings even today.

As our friendship deepened, Barkers gave me another gift I retain to this day. He taught me to play whist. While my drawings would never rival his, I did seem to have natural talent at the game, and he soon enthusiastically embraced me as his partner whenever we could find another pair among the workers, especially just after pay had been distributed.

One day, Barkers convinced me to sup with him in the evening, instead of buying meat at the market and eating in the warehouse, as was my habit. He led me to the gin-house I had seen on my first night in Great Grimsby. The great room was loud and hot and smelled of sweat, with a fiddler screeching away and regular bursts of laughter at bawdy jokes. I spent more than I wanted on oysters and mutton and beer. Barkers drank copious amounts of gin, and insisted that I drink a dram of it as well. I choked; it was like swallowing a burning pine bough. Barkers thought my cough most amusing.

Barkers' gait was unsteady as we rose to leave, and I

understood clearly why he looked and felt so badly upon the dawn. A young lady met us just outside the door, and the blood rose in my face as I recognized her as the same I had run away from months before.

"Ah, Barkers, now there's the lad I have been looking for. It shouldn't be so hard to find you, though, now should it, love?" she twittered. "Oose your friend here? Oh, we're going to all make right good sport of it tonight, now, are we?" She laughed and put her hand on my chest.

"This is Will," he said, unsteadily. "Will is all work and no play, until tonight. C'm on, Will." He attempted to pull my arm around the young woman, but I resisted.

"Wot's a matter, love?" insisted the woman. "Not much cost, split between you, now, if that's the worry." I pushed past them and hurried back to the warehouse. That night, I thought about Pricilla and wondered if she missed me, and whether I would ever see her again.

Barkers was both bleary and sheepish the next morning. I decide to take advantage of his misery to ask him a question I had pondered for some time, but weighed carefully before asking.

"The books don't show it all." I said. "You know they do not. I work on the whole inventory, but more comes and goes than is on the pages." He was quite shaken. "No, you're wrong. You are still just learning our methods."

"That's not true!" I protested. "What about the casks of…"

"You're WRONG, Will!" he shouted with ferocity that surprised me. "Now shut up and do your work!"

The rest of the day passed in stony silence, except for a few exchanges out of necessity. Mr. Spills came that night, when everyone else was gone.

"So, Will *Gainsborough*," he began. "Let's begin with your telling me your real name."

"It's..." I was about to persist in my lie, but saw a fire in his eyes that made me reconsider. "It's William Lucian Fezziwig, Sir, and I am most grateful for the kindness you have shown me. My father was a freeholder at Nene, but was taken away by men from the manor after treachery from a vicar." My words began as a trickle, but began to rush like a stream. "I fear the worst for him, and I have no other family. I was bound and kidnapped and shackled in a post-mill and sold to indenture for a man in a great house, but a servant boy of his helped me escape in order to save me from a fate of unnatural violence." It all spilled out, like water from a jug, except for the treasure. I still considered myself under my father's admonishment to speak of it not. I also realised I was in the presence of a smuggler who, if caught, could hang.

Mr. Spills leaned back and frowned. "I see. I believe you. I know of containment, and its consequences. Now you listen, and believe *me*," he said, fiercely pointing his finger. "I knew you were smart enough that you would soon figure out our business. The *rest* of the business. I have been of great service to the Crown, at risk to myself. You well know that I pay considerable taxes. Every bushel of grain and bale of cotton is counted and paid upon, every shilling. Those things feed and clothe our people, what grain doesn't go to gin. Even that makes tolerable the wretched lives of the country folk who have, like you, been forced from their homes into the city. Absent taxes, I would be a richer man, but I am a most loyal subject and don't complain." He took a deep breath, and paused long enough to take snuff from the well-worn silver box.

"The playthings of the rich, like brandy, tea, silk, lace, those things are not necessities and add little production to the economy, yet are taxed to a point of no profit, thanks to Walpole. The rich will have their pleasures, regardless. If I fail to provide them, my other business will suffer. Everyone avoids duty on those goods, Will. *Everyone.*"

The last statement, and perhaps the effect of the snuff, seemed to calm him. He continued. "I have another warehouse, hidden to the north, into which ships are unloaded by night. The goods are brought here and re-shipped, secreted in barrels and bales. A few people enjoy generous gifts from me to assure their silence in the matter." He sighed. "You are hard working, smart, and honest, William *Fezziwig*. You are not taken with gin and night women, like poor Barkers. I knew we would have this conversation eventually, but I dreaded it. Because now, you know that you too are a smuggler, and, should we all be found out, shall hang as high as me and the rest, though my feet will dangle closer to the ground."

He looked sad as he continued. "Barkers has gone down a ruinous path, and it troubles me. His mother was employed by Mrs. Spills as a house-servant, and she bore him after hiding the fact she was with child until almost the hour of his birth. We know not the father; his mother was Mary Barkers, and she gave the babe not another name. While I considered what to do, his mother left in the night. We never heard of her again. Barkers was only a few days old, so, at my own expense, I sent him to be raised by a small merchant family whose baby had just died. I was counseled to send the baby to an orphanage instead, but I could not do it. I had him educated and brought back to work here when he became of age. Yes, there were wags and rumormongers who tormented Mrs. Spills by conjecturing that I was the father, but, as the child grew with characteristics so different from mine, those tales dissipated. So, his thirst for gin and whores is not from a life of want. He serves me well, but I have seen many young men travel the path he has set upon, and the destination is almost always the same."

"And you, Mr. *Fezziwig*, conspirator and smuggler, have great promise. I believe you will avoid the path Barkers has chosen. You have talent, and I need you. The kindness I have shown you will be rewarded, I trust, by your continued association. If you choose otherwise, that I understand. But take care. Those to whom you might think to expose the *rest* of our business may just be enjoying my generosity as well."

My head spun. Mr. Spills had, indeed, been my benefactor, and my station had improved immeasurably.

"I am deeply indebted to you, Mr. Spills. In a way, I owe you my life, and I am happy, if I may, to continue to repay you with my deepest loyalty and affection."

The old man smiled and held out his hand. "I am most obliged, Mr. William Fezziwig." He seemed to revel in pronouncing my name, now that he had discovered it. He pulled out his snuffbox again. "And now, it is high time for you to disregard my advice on taking up the habit of snuff."

Over the next months, my life became both busier and more productive. I felt my discovery had caused Mr. Spills to take me fully into his confidence, and involve me in more important workings of the business. Barkers seemed sullen toward me for a short time, but his usual humour soon returned, as I began helping him with the *rest* of the business, as we referred to it.

I was, on occasion, invited to dine with Mr. and Mrs. Spills, and he assigned a worker to teach me to ride, an opportunity I did not have in my prior years of ox carts. I began to assist with inventory, as it was unloaded from ships at night, at a shallow cove north of the village. I also found, to my surprise, that the commerce was so great as to render the warehouse insufficient, and other buildings in the vicinity were used as for temporary storage. One of these happened to be the greatest building in the town, the Minster of St. James. The vicar, it seemed, was quite fond of brandy in need of a temporary home.

In November, news came that a great storm had killed thousands - perhaps hundreds of thousands - in India. Mr. Spills was grim over the matter, and mentioned thoughtfully that raging water knows naught Christian nor Hindoo nor Jew nor Mohammedan. He did, though, teach me a valuable lesson in commerce.

"Will, it is human to revel in comfort. When things go well, men tend to keep doing what they are doing to preserve it. The problem, though, is that even nature, even the weather such as we see today, never stands still. We must be ready to change with it, and think about what will be needed tomorrow. If we are poised to provide it first, we swim while others sink."

He was silent for a moment, and then continued. "The tragedy has sent the East India Company into disarray. Their trade in silk and cotton and tea will become dear for some time. By chance, I have on hand stores of silk and tea that will become more profitable. I have little cotton at present, but my supply is the American colonies, and will continue unabated, though I'm sure the price will rise. We are well situated, but must increase our trade in London in order to take complete advantage. Every year, there are fewer people of means, in actual fact, fewer people at all, in the countryside, while London is filling like a barrel during a rainstorm. *Containment...*" he seemed to regret the word, then went on as if he had not uttered it. "Hm. We need our own agent there. I have already made provision to buy a building on the Lea, and we will need to hire four or five strong men. Barkers will go, though, I admit, I fear what the temptations of the city will do to him."

Winter approached, and the weather turned quite grey, chill and damp. We did not know at first that it was the beginning of a series of the worst winters, those of 1738 through 1740, in memory. Mr. Spills had me move into a small chamber in a dependency of the warehouse, to benefit from its fireplace. As I moved my belongings, which now included several suits of clothing, I remembered my first night in the garret, and the feeling of peace it had brought me after days of being handled so roughly.

Business was very brisk, as my master's prediction of the effect of the India tragedy on trade turned out to be correct, and the demand for brandy, offloaded under darkness, naturally increased as Christmastime neared.

As the quality of the weather waned, so did Barkers and his health. That he was Frenchified was not unexpected, given his propensities, and he became more consumptive as the winter dampness encroached from the sea. In mid-December, Mr. Spills came to me in the evening.

"Will, it's clear Barkers will not be able to travel to London. It may be a decision made by Providence. If Great Grimsby brings him to such a state, what would the great city do to him?" I was not prepared for what came next.

"You must go in his stead."

"But Sir, I have been naught but in this county in my life!" I protested. Under his glare, I remembered my loyalty. "Surely not alone, Sir. To accompany you?"

"No, Will, I am also not prepared for the rigors of travel this winter. I have given you good instruction, both in business and in judgment. You are not yet well traveled, but the remedy for that is, well, travel. We have an advantage in that a distant relative of mine is well-situated midway, and you will be received there to refresh yourself and continue on. I know I can trust you in this, Will."

That night, my thoughts raced, as they had not in some time. I had heard tales of the great city since childhood, and reveled in their repetition. But I lacked confidence that I could carry out my obligation. Only months before, I had been tilling soil in the close in order to plant turnips, and I have revealed how that turned out.

I was surprised to find Barkers neither glad nor disappointed at the news that he would remain in Great Grimsby. He full well knew his health would not allow him to complete the trip. He joined Mr. Spills in preparing me for my journey, and wished me Godspeed when the day of my departure arrived.

"You have all you need, and the directions are simple," assured Mr. Spills. "You will waylay with my relation, Regis Bracebridge. He will be expecting you, and, I have to say, I have a bit of envy of visiting him at Christmastime. His manor is ancient and worn, but his manner is opposite." Mr. Spills grinned and winked, as he often did when he was proud of his playful words. "His hospitality is considerable. Like many old families, his is abundant in land but not in liquidity. He has loyal servants, though, and plenty on the table, and keeps the season well, from my memory of long ago. Safe travels, Will. I know your trip will be *profitable*. Chirrup!"

With that, I was off, alone, into the winter.

I followed the shore south, and soon snow was swirling around me. Nervous about reaching my destination for the night before becoming lost or prey for highwaymen in the dark, I coaxed the most out of the compliant, steady bay serving as my mount. I was relieved when Skegness came into view before the light failed, and the inn was sufficient. The new experience and freedom were both scary and exhilarating. I continued my journey early the next morning, eventually turning away from the coast and toward Stamford, to leave Lincolnshire for the first time in my life.

The cold was ferocious, seeping into every joint. A shiver accompanied each breath, and the frost accumulated thickly on my face. The inns became less inviting as I progressed, being those used primarily by drovers, but they were nonetheless welcome sights to my smarting, frozen eyes each night. My travel was considerably slowed by the weather, and I did not arrive at Bracebridge Manor until more than two hours after darkness had fallen, so my fatigue was great.

The manor was large and ancient, but, by an almost full moon, I could see parts of it were in need of repair. It was covered in ivy almost in its entirety, with snow and ice hanging in the vines, but even that was not sufficient to cover all the voids in the walls. On one wing, part of the roof and collapsed, but the main part of the manor, which I took to be the original hall, was brightly lit, and I could hear voices from within.

A servant, whose livery seemed as ancient as the manor, impeccably clean and neatly fit but threadbare, met me at the door. He took my greatcoat and led me into the bright, warm hall, where about a dozen members of the family were assembled. They were accompanied by four small, brown and white spaniels, which announced my arrival with howls that would wake the dead.

A middle-aged man of distinguished look met me with

enthusiasm "Ah, my great-cousin John's man! Capital! " He cried. "I was beginning to think the winter had taken you! I am Regis Bracebridge, and you are a welcome visitor, indeed! Warm yourself. You look a sight! The Wassail bowl is hot. Warm yourself inward and outward!"

I had seldom heard words more welcome. I stood in front of the fire and drank the hot liquid, feeling life flow back into my frozen limbs. After giving me a moment to thaw, Mr. Bracebridge introduced me to the assembly, mostly his own extended family, including five children, an old mother, and assorted Bracebridges of various lines explained to me, but then promptly forgotten in the rush of senses. The remains of a roasted joint were on the server, and I ate and drank liberally, at the insistence of my host.

The hall had a soaring ceiling and wood paneled walls. Artifacts of times past hung on the walls, paintings, armor pieces and sundry weapons having no edge. Most noticeable, though, was the great quantity of pine, holly, and other greenery decorating everything in sight. I had never had a better host, and I was included in the conversation as much as I would allow myself. The liveried servant returned, this time with a fiddle, and the whole band, young and old, began to dance with such enthusiasm that I feared the ancient armaments might leap from the walls and decapitate the revelers below. I was surprised to find that the servants, after making sure all was in order, joined the foray as apparent equals.

"Will! Will! Surely your legs have thawed by now. Join the dance!" my host admonished.

I was quite embarrassed, but thought honesty was owed to such a fine host. "I regret, kind sir, that I know not how."

He seemed surprised by this, but determined to find a

remedy. "Tut! We're born with dance, my son; it's only the cares of commerce that cause us to forget! It is a perfect job for my Caddy to help you recover your memories. There is no finer dancer in the county. Caddy! To your work!"

Caddy was the elder Bracebridge daughter. She wore a pale yellow bell-sleeved gown, and her hair was of a similar hue. Her complexion was fine and smooth, though some of the day would consider her features to be somewhat broad. The first thing I noticed, though, was her smile, which was warm, gay, and sincere. I could feel my face flush, but no longer from the cold. She took me by the hand without hesitation.

"Oh, you poor dear, I think you're still cold!" she said, clasping my hand in hers. "Just watch and listen to the music, and do what I do. It's all for the fun of it!" she laughed, and I had never heard a sweeter, purer sound. "Ah, see James!" she pointed toward one of her brothers. "See how he cuts! Now you try." Though fatigued by days of cold travel, I was at an energetic and nimble season of life, and very soon was able to join with only an occasional trip or flattened toe.

The youngest and oldest of the gathering began to drift away, and, by midnight, a good evening had to come to an end. Goodnights were bade, and the servant led me to a small chamber with a comfortable bed and lively fire at the hearth. My traveling roll was already there, with my nightshirt spread out awaiting my tired body. As is my habit, I spent a moment thinking of my situation before allowing sleep to overtake me. My world had changed greatly in a few months. I held in my hand a great treasure, but it was taken from me. Opportunity and, perhaps, Providence, had led me to a life very different from that I left. That night, my only regret was that my father could not share in my fortune.

I slept later than my usual time of arising, and found the fire had been stoked, indicating my sleep must have been sound indeed. I dressed and descended to the hall, where the males of the family were assembled.

"Ho, Will! Capital! In time to accompany us to cut the log!" my host exclaimed. The servant brought my greatcoat, now dry and brushed. I accompanied them outside, where the snow had stopped, but left a thick, clean layer of white covering the landscape. Not far, Mr. Bracebridge pointed out a great oak along the edge of the forest. "That's the one!" He pointed. "I girdled it two years ago, so it would be standing dry and seasoned to provide the Yule log. A fine one it will be!"

We all took turns with the ax, and soon had the great, heavy log hoisted on our shoulders, making our way back to the manor house. Leaving the log outside, we entered to find the fair sex of the family assembled at the table, awaiting our return to break their fast. I was seated beside Caddy, who made conversation while we ate cold meat from the night before, bread, porridge with butter, small beer and tea.

The rest of Christmas Eve day was spent with more pleasantries, especially games. I was familiar with most of them from childhood, including Hot Cockles and Shoe-the-Wild-Horse. Some of the card games they played were new to me, though, and I happily allowed Caddy to guide me through the intricacies of Gleek and Quadrille. When someone suggested whist instead, I became much more confident, and was, with time, proclaimed a master of the game.

Toward evening, we were called to assemble in the chapel, and warned that greatcoats were in order.

Coats, indeed! After following the family and servants down a disused corridor and entering the chapel, I looked up and saw twinkling stars through a substantial hole in the roof. Tiles still littered the floor, and a thin layer of snow covered the pews. Mr. Bracebridge read the prayers, and his elder son the scriptures. I knew most of the carols from childhood, and soon felt the warmth of Christmastime, despite the chill.

The prayers and silence thereafter gave me pause to think. My recent experiences with clergy had been frigid, indeed. Reverend Meade's treachery had cost me everything, including my father, and sent me on a road to a short and defiled life. The masters of the Minster in Great Grimsby were little better, being more *profit* than *prophet*, to be sure. Yet, along the way, things happened. A young man risked his life, wretched though it was, to save me from suffering his fate. I was wearing a fine suit of clothes at just the right time to be noticed, and listened to the voice telling me to help unload the ship quayside. To what but Providence could I ascribe my fortune? But what came of my father's faith? A warm tear, not unseen by Caddy, streamed down my cold face. I felt overcome with loss and gratitude and sadness and promise, all at once.

Leaving the chapel, Mr. Bracebridge came close to my ear and whispered, "Yes, chapel roof. Hm. On the list, it is, perhaps this year. No one nodding off during vespers, though!"

I joined them to bring in the log, which was decorated with holly, and it barely fit the great hearth. The Bracebridge family was exceedingly fond of carol singing, and, to my ear, it improved as the Wassail bowl emptied. With a final toast to The Child at midnight, everyone retired with promise of Christmas morning.

My sleep was sound, until a soft knocking at my chamber door awakened me. The fire was old, and lent scant light, but I arose to ascertain the source of the sound. I am reluctant to admit that, in the passion of youth, I briefly considered the possibility that Caddy had found her way to my door in the darkness, and knew not what my response would be.

I opened the door slowly, and saw nothing but the faint outline of the corridor outside. But, I cannot explain the feeling that came over me, one I had never experienced before, and only twice since, during times I will eventually reveal. I heard a small snap from the fire, glanced back into the room, and, when I returned my gaze to the door, saw a sight that made me try to scream, but the noise become stifled in my throat. The very hairs on my old arms and neck still stand erect each time I think of it!

Staring at me was the misty, semi-transparent figure of an ancient soldier, in full armor of the past. His helm had a small cross on the front, and rusted chain mail dripped from his wizened body like dew down a twig. He had a full beard, sunken cheeks, and hollow eyes. Despite this, his overall continence was complacent, and not threatening. His feet did not touch the stones, and he slowly bobbed mid-air, as if floating on gentle waves. Even in the dimness, I could see through him as if he were made of thin fog. In an instant, he was gone. I saw not where he went. He was there; then he was not.

My return to sleep came reluctantly, through sheer fatigue, and an effort to convince myself that what I had just experienced was simply a particularly queer dream.

The cost of the next day's feast could have, I thought, paid for repairing the chapel roof. The great boar's head, with an apple in its mouth, and a large goose, and a feathered pheasant-pie made up the centre of the table, while the servers were filled with mince-pies, frumenty, and all sorts of sweet-meats. The Wassail bowl seemingly refilled itself by magic, and the warmth and laughter was nutrition to the soul. After delivering our plates, the servants took their places at the table and joined the feast, with no difference being made between them and the rest of the family. I was seated beside Caddy, who increasingly found reason to pat my hand during our gay conversation.

"I am surprised our old friend has not visited anyone this Christmas, as is his habit!" she said, while battling a mince pie. Calls of "Not me!" "Once is enough!" and "I am still awaiting my turn!" answered her. Caddy laughed and explained, "There is a tomb of an ancient crusader nearby. He must have been a man of means, for his resting place is elaborate, with his full statue carved on top. It is said that, at Christmastime, he walks again, and there are many who will swear it is true. Perhaps he reminds us what has been sacrificed for our religion, or wants to ensure we remain faithful. I think," she repeated, loudly, as to gain everyone's attention, "I THINK he is in search of hot Wassail to warm his sleep! What soul, in this world or the next, would choose to miss Christmastime?" Her statement brought general agreement and laughter.

With great effort, I, too, laughed and held my composure over the mention of the apparition I had encountered just hours before, though I am certain the colour drained from my face. It was many, many years before I shared the story with another, and still do so only reluctantly.

To this day, that Christmastime is the one I relive each year in my mind.

On St. Stephen's, it was time to continue my journey. Never had I made a more pleasant stay, and I already knew the discomfort the next day's winter travel would bring. I was still lacking confidence that I would not disappoint Mr. Spills in my task. Before I entered the hall, Caddy caught me at the corner.

"I do so wish you could finish Christmastime with us. With me. I hope you will return, Will," she said softly, and hugged me. "We need no mistletoe." She looked up with her eyes closed, desiring to be kissed, and, though my experience was wanting, I did so, long and warm. She opened her eyes. "You will come back, won't you?"

"Will will," I promised.

Regis Bracebridge and his family fed me breakfast until I was about to burst, provisioned my saddlebag until it resembled a fat sausage, and bade me Godspeed until my return. A weak sleet fell from a grey sky, and I looked back at Bracebridge Manor with gratitude, but also a bit of wistfulness. What would it be like to be part of such a family?

The sleet continued as I turned the bay southward. The night was spent at a drover's inn of poor quality indeed when compared to the hospitality shown by the Bracebridges. I was reduced to sharing a bed with an uncouth, drunken man who bothered not to rise to use the bog. He also had a servant boy of about ten years of age, who slept on the floor without provision of a blanket. I allowed the youth the use of my greatcoat to cover himself from the chill." "Need naught fer tha'" slurred the master. "Digger's whelp, thrown off. Yoose t' th'cold, 'e is." I felt the boy's loss and sadness as if it were my own.

As I entered Herefordshire, sighting fellow travelers became more common. It was practice to be met with "Hi! Hi! Any news your way?" and exchange a word or two. Such was my encounter with two men on fine horses. One, curiously, with four white stockings, but the other was black as coal, all over. I had never seen such. After a moment of conversation, we parted, and I gave them not another thought.

About an hour from dusk (and, I hoped, an inn for the

evening), I came around a slight bend in the track, and a great blow found my face and knocked me to the snow. I was set upon by two men, struck several more blows, and pinned to the ground. Through the blood seeping onto my eyes from a bleeding forehead, I could see the coal black of my attacker's horse.

"Well, what news have we now, then?" I heard a familiar voice say. "Perhaps a fine young gentleman has a bit more time to give a poor traveler now, might he not? Away, Bess! All done here!"

My greatcoat, coat, waistcoat, shirt, and boots were stripped from me, and my hands and ankles lashed. I heard my mount resist for a moment, and then be led away. In an instant, I was laying bound, alone, and only partially clad in the snow. I struggled to rise despite my bindings, and managed to do so, but could only hop a foot or two before again hurtling to earth headlong, leaving behind a bloody impression of my face.

Over the throb of my head, I assessed my situation. Night was approaching, and the bitter cold was already robbing my limbs of feeling. I knew I would freeze to death in short order.

I remember, daughters, not the blackness of my thoughts as I lay there prepared for a frigid death, but the irony. I had overcome theft, kidnapping, a potential life of debauched servitude, loneliness, and poverty, only to freeze to death lying in the road like a squashed hedgehog. In my delirium, I found this funny, and began to laugh, until darkness came over me, inside and without.

My next sensation was that of being smacked on the cheeks, but gently, and "Sir! Sir!" being shouted in my ear. Life grudgingly returned to my body, and I saw, in the moonlight, rags being tied around my feet. I was helped into a standing position and covered with a coarse, foul-smelling blanket.

"Aye, he's still with us," exclaimed one of my benefactors, but such a great shiver overcame me and my teeth chattered so greatly that I was unable to respond. "You'll have to walk, sir. Sorry for the inconvenience, but we are on foot. We need to move, and get the blood back in yer." I was hoisted up by both shoulders, and half dragged along in the dark for what seemed like a frozen eternity. The males at each arm occasionally tried to make conversation, but I was too cold and shaken to give much response.

I do not know how long we traveled in this painful fashion, but we eventually came to a stop where I could see a pale light from a hearth through the crack between a set of shutters. A woman came up and said "Aye, we can come in and warm ourselves, then take shelter in the byre." We crowded into the small house, where I was placed closest to the hearth, and my senses began to return.

By the flickering light, I could see that my new traveling companions consisted of a man and woman around thirty years, a boy perhaps thirteen, and a girl of about twelve. The occupants of the house were an older man and woman. The man stood, warily, with a cudgel, at the door. "Now, to the byre as soon as yer thawed," he said, threateningly. "And remember, naught there shall be amiss. I'll keep watch on you, by God, I will!"

My new benefactor assured the holder that nothing would go missing, and thanked him for his hospitality. "This one," he said, pointing at me, "was set upon, and you most likely have saved his life, allowing us to share your hearth. He looks a gentleman. Who knows how he might be able to repay you for your kindness someday?"

At this, the holder became a bit more thoughtful, and

produced a cup, which his wife filled from a pot on the hearth, and allowed us all to drink warm broth from it. After that, and another admonishment to commit no theft, we removed to the byre, which was made relatively warm by the cattle. It was tight, cobbled, and mucked, and full of clean hay, providing adequate shelter.

Coherent again, I began to converse with the family that had saved me from certain demise, and thanked them profusely. Their name was Jones, and they, like me, were traveling to London.

"We were holders in Nottinghamshire." Mr. Jones explained. "Hard life, but we ate. But, what had been common for our use was taken. We had naught to graze, and nowhere to go. The city is our only chance. It's happening all over." He sighed. "The manor-born call it *containment*, but I call it thievery. But, maybe I speak out of turn, as you are a gentleman yourself, by the cut of what few clothes you were left."

"I am a child of the countryside, and know well the wickedness of *containment*," I said. "A man of commerce in Lincolnshire, who sent me on an errand to London, now employs me. I was robbed and left in the state you found me." I decided not to reveal too much of myself, for my trust in mankind was, understandably, at low ebb. They agreed to allow me to travel with them, at least as far as it took to again procure provisions and clothing, using their blanket as a coat, and their rags for boots.

"Perhaps I will be able to use the name of my employer as credit, or contact his associates, and I shall repay your kindness." I said, with hope.

"Naught to do there," said Jones (His name, it turned out, was Geoff, wandering with his wife Constantia, son Frankie, and daughter Annie). "We're not the kind to leave a man to freeze. But, I hope you can improve your lot, for your own good."

Despite my chill and throbbing head, I slept tolerably well on the hay that night. As we prepared to leave the byre to be on our way once more, I repaired to the manure heap to relieve my natural calling in private. Once there, I pulled my money pouch out of the crotch of my breeches, where it had been hiding since leaving Bracebridge Manor. Though it had been the source of some chaffing and irritation, there have been few objects I have ever been happier to see.

Yes, for fear of exactly the kind of evilness that came to pass, I had taken that precaution. Losing my horse and clothing was a setback, but my lifeline was still in my hand. I was greatly relieved when the highwaymen took only my outer garments, instead of stripping me naked and uncovering my wherewithal. On the other hand, I had been quite nervous when Caddy unexpectedly hugged and kissed me as I prepared to leave Bracebridge, fearing my assets could have been misinterpreted.

I knocked on the holder's door, and he opened it holding the cudgel. "You've had shelter; now, be off!" he exclaimed.

"Do you have boots or a coat to sell?" I asked

"As if you could buy!" he sneered. "But no, there are neither to spare. I have what I wear."

"Then bless you, sir, and thank you again for your help," I said, and handed him a shilling, which astonished him greatly.

The money pouch again safe in its warm hiding place, I set out to London with the Jones band. They produced a second set of rags to tie around my feet as substitute boots, and I wrapped the blanket tightly around me. I was able to return little of the favor, except to help carry some of the bundles that made up what little they possessed. The day had warmed, and the sun shone, but, as the melting snow soaked the rags on my feet, the tracks I left became increasing red.

Our progress was slow, but we came to a drover's inn late in the afternoon. We feared there would be no more shelter before nightfall, so Mr. Jones announced his intention to ask the proprietor if we could spend the night in the stable, in exchange for providing some service, such as mucking or chopping wood.

"Why, I believe this inn belongs to a friend of my employer," I lied. "I will speak to him privately, and perhaps we can have more in the way of hospitality."

I cannot blame the innkeeper for his look of skepticism when a half-frozen wraith, wrapped in a horse blanket and rag-wrapped feet leaving bloody prints on the floor, asked to hire food and lodging for an entire family for the night. A price of two shillings was agreed upon, and I left the room briefly to pull down my breeches and make a withdrawal of funds.

The Jones family greeted my news with joy and relief: the innkeeper insisted on providing his best for his old friend's downtrodden employee and the family that saved him. Or, so I told them. That evening, we ate and drank our fill, and seemingly could never get enough of the warmth emanating from the hearth. I nursed my oozing feet, and was able to buy a greatcoat and boots from the innkeeper, at what I considered to be an inflated price. To the Joneses, of course, these vital items were gifts of the house, just like the considerable amount of food packed for us to carry away the next morning.

The travel was somewhat easier with proper attire, and after decent food and lodging. I replayed the same scenario the following two nights, and I could see the positive effect on my traveling companions. The dullness left their eyes, and their steps quickened. The way became more populated, both with fellow travelers, and those living along the route.

On the fourth day after being left for dead, I entered the city of London, which is still my home. I have never desired another.

PART THE SECOND: *LONDON*

From the time of my kidnapping, each sight was new to me, and seemed to be of increasing wonder: the post-mill, the manor house, and the sea. None of these could have prepared me for the great city.

In my previous experience, winter snow made the world clean and white. That was not the case with London. In fact, one could smell the city before entering it, and see the darkness of the sky above even in mid-day. Smoke and soot turned snow to grey even before it fell. Openness with structures interspaced, as seen in the outskirts, was replaced by tightly packed buildings, most seemingly being held up only by their leaning on their neighbors. Melting snow in the streets mixed with all manner of filth, forming a wretched swill that sloshed past the ankles and ran in swift rivulets. People roamed these streets in swarms, some with purpose, and some with vacant looks and no spark behind their eyes. Many had no coats or shoes, and were wrapped in rags, as I myself had been only days before.

I had ascertained that Jones had neither specific plan, nor specific prospect. I imagined what it must be like to cast one's self and family into this bleak stream of humanity, through the necessity of nowhere else to go. Bereft of other ideas and as overwhelmed as me by the closeness of the city, he agreed to accompany me to find my employer's warehouse, with the hope that a position may present itself along the way.

Not knowing the extent of the city, it took many inquiries to be pointed in the direction of the Lea and its confluence with the Thames. Most of the poor souls I asked were evidently in the same state of being as my companions, and knew little but the squalor of their new home; more than once I was begged for food, of which I had none to give. Darkness found us before we made our way to our destination, and I conveniently discovered another lodging house owned by (I lied to Jones) a friend of my employer. I suspected this repeated coincidence was beginning to wear thin with him, but he was too grateful to ask questions.

The house was wretched, and I felt little safer there than I would have taking my chances in the filthy street. Our rest, such as it was, came on foul straw in a chamber with as many as twenty others; the stench made our night in the byre a fond memory. Jones and I agreed to sleep in turns, and, during each of our watches, chased away varlets intent on thuggery.

We reached the Lea the following day, finding fewer newcomers in that part of the city, and, after several inquiries, found our destination. The warehouse was of stone and seemed mostly solid, though a side dependency was tumbledown. A large and vacant expanse sprawled on one side. As predicted by Mr. Spills in his instructions to me, a small old man with an eye patch was found within. His name was Boyce.

"Spills's man, at last! I felt certain you had either absconded or met with your end!" he exclaimed. I was too fatigued at the moment to describe how close to true his second idea was. "Ho. Decided to take Christmastime with mutton-in-long-coats, I'll wager." I felt blood rise in my face.

"No matter. Why Spills sent such a wee'n to tend to his business here is no concern of mine. I'll show you the place, then my contract with you is at its end."

My initial assessment of the warehouse was confirmed. It was old and shabby and in need of repairs throughout, but of sound construction and structure. After seeing the bustling industry of the Great Grimsby warehouse, it seemed strange to occupy one so empty and quiet. There was a small lodging-room in the rear with a hearth and a supply of kindling and coal, a fuel with which I had little experience. Jones produced flint and steel, and soon a warming fire was crackling along, chasing part of the gloom and dampness from the air.

I was wondering how to explain my ability to suddenly produce coins from my nether regions in order to buy food, for hunger was overtaking us all, when Mr. Spills's solicitor, Mr. Whitlipped, came into the warehouse. I supposed, correctly, that Boyce had alerted him.

"Halloo! Here at last? Capital! Travel uneventful, I trust? No soft winter, this. Ah...who are your companions? he asked, spotting Jones and family.

"Traveling companions, indeed, Sir," I replied, "And good greetings from my employer, Mr. Spills. Might you and I look about the premises whilst they continue to warm themselves?"

"Oh, of course! Indeed! This way."

Mr. Whitlipped and I discussed lines of credit, operating expenses, duty payment, and labour. "I have to admit, Fezziwig, that I am not sure if this is a proper venture. The city is growing like a bloated tick, but the Lea-side is becoming less passable after the water-works and the new river have made their changes. The East India, though plagued by losses of late, is very effective in curbing intrusion into the Thames docks, and transport across the city is otherwise difficult, and expensive."

"Mr. Spills and I discussed much, and I have his instructions," I replied. "He is a cagey one. He looks not at today, but at tomorrow."

Whitlipped smiled. "You are young, but perceptive," he said. "I have been associated with your employer for many years, and I know he is at his best when others become comfortable with a certain path, whilst he chooses another."

I knew not at that time the long association I would have with Mr. Whitlipped. Indeed, there was little in our first meeting to endear him to me. His manner was brusque, and his appearance not inviting. He was perhaps twenty years my senior, and as thin as a prisoner long forgotten in the dungeons of times past. His nose was sharp, and his arms held close in. He had the slightest stoop and a high, rasping voice, giving him an altogether bird-like look. He gave the distinct impression that he did not want to be touched.

When Whitlipped left, I hid myself to retrieve my purse, and told Jones that I had been provided with initial operating funds by the solicitor. I sent him and Frankie out to find our dinner whilst mother and daughter continued their rest and warming. I assured him that his family would lodge at the warehouse until he found other provision.

"I don't know how to thank you," he said, looking at his feet. It was clear he had little experience in thanking people, for he had received little help from others in life. I pointed at some frozen offal in the road, being chewed upon by a dog.

"If not for your kindness, Mr. Jones, I would be no more than that cur's dinner at this moment." And I knew it to be true.

Over his protestations, I persuaded Jones and family to take the lodging-room while I slept in the garret. It was thick with dust, but reminded me of my first real lodging after my capture, and was wholly sufficient. By candlelight that night, I penned a long letter to Mr. Spills, detailing my adventures, and my assessment of the warehouse. The next day, I set about following the instructions he had sent with me, though they left considerable room for my judgment, or, given the situation, Lea-way, so to speak.

The first task was to ready the warehouse for commerce. I hired Geoff and Frankie, and another father and son named Hinton, also newly arrived in the city thanks to *containment*. The crumbling dependency was knocked down, and the stone stacked neatly on the barren lot. I asked Whitlipped why the space beside the warehouse had not previously been put to more useful purpose, and he laughed nervously.

"Oh, well, that. Yes. Pay it no mind, only prattle of biddies. But, the common tale hereabouts is that, during the great dying times of the past, several hundred years past, the plot is where the plague corpses of the city were buried. Dumped, more's the word. Even now, people fear unleashing it again if the ground is disturbed. That, and the spirits. Biddies' tales, nothing more." I shivered despite myself, remembering the chill of my recent encounter at Bracebridge.

"Have you ever seen or heard anything untoward?" I asked.

"Not once. I have lived my life within ten stones' throw, and all that have done me ill have been solid sort, indeed. But, the story persists, and the plot is considered unlucky. Perhaps so, in a way, for it is the very spot the Lea chose to silt up and impede commerce."

Within a week of my arrival, a gentleman called Dawks, a trader in shares and contracts, visited me. He solicited my involvement in a lottery to raise funds to build a new bridge at Westminster. I certainly had no money of my own to risk, so I tried to look upon the visit as a learning opportunity, as I knew Mr. Spills would see it. A new bridge could certainly improve our situation, allowing for easier movement of goods. But, in my view, a lottery was no more than throwing a die, so I rejected the offer quickly.

In those days, when masses were forced off their lands of self-sufficiency, men of commerce began to find new opportunities based on *capital* rather than *labour* and *goods*. Labour and goods I understood. If one works hard and is resourceful manufacturing or procuring commodities that are needed, his profit is earned.

I felt differently, and, indeed, still do, about those who become rich from selling one another shares, something without substance within itself, whilst dining and drinking and making sport of the lower classes. By what sweat (indeed, I should say, *whose* sweat) is their bread earned, but by that of the subjects of their ridicule?

At length, the warehouse was made ready, and goods began to arrive. All were fully taxed and duties; Mr. Spills's *other* business was handled elsewhere. Cotton from the American colonies, of which we had steady supply, was in high demand, since the India trade was still disrupted. The silted Lea added cost and time, for the river at the nearest wharf would only accommodate barges of shallow draft.

Labour, though, was cheap. Displaced country holders flowed in at a pace that seemed like it would soon empty the rest of the island, leaving no Englishman who was not a Londoner.

The filth and squalor increased with each day, and despite a new gin law requiring a fifty pound licence and twenty shillings a gallon tax (roundly ignored, if the words from men in the business were to be believed), gin houses continued to spring up like mushrooms after a rain.

I paid my workers one shilling per day, sun to sun, with no labour on the Lord's Day. In talking with Whitlipped and others, I ascertained that to be an average wage, and found no shortage of those eager to take it. The quality of their work, on the other hand, was a hindrance. Except for Jones and son, workers seemed to start off well when they were new to the city, grateful for a path away from starvation, but, as if there was no other solace for the lives they had lost in the countryside, they soon turned to gin.

It ravaged the city like a plague in those days. At any time day or night, one saw drunken men laying in the muck, sometimes never to arise. Women young and old, once respectable country daughters or wives, fell down and allowed carnal acts to be performed upon them in lanes and thresholds. (Upon first hearing the term 'three-penny upright,' I had to inquire as to its meaning, and was, at first, unbelieving, until assured by a reliable source). Babies cried for want of food. All for gin.

The salary I paid was, as stated, average. That meant workers might be attracted for just a bit less, and I could find a use for the small savings in providing myself with a more reliable workforce. My plan was to reduce wages by a farthing a day, but put that money into improving the lot of my workers, and reducing my overall costs. My announcement to my workers, now six in number, that their pay would be decreased was met with words I shall not repeat here. But, in the stead, I provided hot porridge each morning, and bread and a small sausage at noon. As labour ended each day, they were all required to spend a short time in a corner of the warehouse, where I taught them to read and cipher, oft by candlelight. I decided to try this method and keep close accounts, to discover its profitability.

Mr. Whitlipped thought me mad. "You can reduce wages by a farthing; I'm all for it!" he exclaimed. "But to what profit is it to spend the savings on bread and meat before it even enters your pocket?"

"If the practice adds to the negative column, I shall discontinue it forthright. I receive all the commodities to provide that small comfort at a low price for resale, so it will probably come close to a break-even," I replied. "But, you know the hold that gin has on the workers, and I am willing to try anything to ensure reliability. Already, on one occasion, a delivery of grain from up the Lea destined for the malter was delivered late because of the state of my workers. Mr. Spills has a good name, but it will take few events such as that to sully it. I believe in finding what works," I added with a smile, and Whitlipped seemed placated.

"You are a queer one, Fezziwig," he said. "Not long from the wolds, only as many years as a 'prentice, yet you make sense. The proof, of course, shall be in the pudding. But the part of it I don't understand is trying to make the strong backs into scholars!"

"Ah, that. I have observed that men often visit the gin-houses on the way back to their lodgings. Delaying that with contemplative work of the mind will, I hope, make the visits less likely. We shall see. It will also keep me from the streets in the evening as well!" The last was said with a smile.

As you know, because it is still my practice these many

years later, the policy was, indeed, a success. With less gin and a full belly, workers did naught to darken the reputation for reliability of Spills or Fezziwig. My added motive for teaching letters and numbers, which I withheld from Whitlipped for fear of sounding silly, has also returned me handsomely over the years. After I became part of the circles of business and had chance to converse with other commercial men, I found that my workers made fewer mistakes, being able to read brands and bills, and I was even able to have some of them make ledger entries before I was able to hire additional clerks.

During those days before our modern system of turnpikes and post roads, letters were greatly delayed and often lost. This caused me to have to make many decisions without consulting Mr. Spills, but he was pleased with initial returns and affirmed his confidence in my judgments. One of his letters, containing much business instruction, ended with: "Will, I have taken it upon myself to make inquiry among acquaintances in the interior of the County, as to the fate of Lemuel Fezziwig of Nene, but have discovered naught."

That same post also included the first letter I ever received from someone other than Mr. Spills. It was in a fine envelope, with a red wax seal, "C.B." I opened it and found the letter scented of lilac.

"Dear Will,

Oh, how I wish you had been able to stay with us throughout the twelve days! Your presence made Christmastime especially merry for me. Father thinks very highly of you as well. Please remember your promise to me for your return, and do not dance with another until our reunion. I hold you most affectionately, Caddy"

I know the words are exact, for I still have that letter today, along with many others.

In little time, the Joneses found lodging. Father and son continued in my employ, while the females found housemaid situations. I moved into the more comfortable rooms and was satisfied with my progress as spring came to the great city.

"Had I known the future." How many times is the line uttered? In this case, perhaps I would have ordered Jones, as my employee, to keep his family lodged at the warehouse, but who can blame a man for desiring independence? I knew he was distressed, and pressed him on it.

"I don't want to trouble you, Will. You have been so kind. It's a hard thing to say. The situation procured by my dear Constantia introduced her to drink. I don't know how it happened. She has always been a God-fearing woman. The Devil has her!" Jones cried like a child. "We never see her, and God only knows where she is. But today, I know where she is as well. She is in Newgate."

"Newgate!" I gasped. I had only seen the prison from the outside, but the name still brought chills.

"Yes. But of what she is accused can't be true! It can't!" With difficulty, I pulled from Jones that his wife had been accused of stealing a trifle in coins from a man whilst involved in lewdness. I couldn't believe it, either.

"Will…Mr. Fezziwig…you know I would never ask if there were another way. Please, please help us. We must pay her bail. I will work it off to you and live in the street, but we must have her back. It is the only way to save her."

"Of course we will," I assured, still stunned by the sad news. "I have not forgotten that I owe you my life."

I consulted Mr. Whitlipped on the matter the following day. "Nasty, nasty. Poor fellow," he shook his head. "I have seen it happen, and not just among the poor. You would be surprised, what I have seen. Gin is no respecter of class, apparently. My advice, Will, is to give Jones a prayer, but nothing more. It will only bring you grief. There will never be an end. Everyone denies the first run-in caused by the demon, but I have naught seen a case not soon followed by an encore. Leave them to their own devices, or they will pull you into their ruin."

Even as he gave me that advice, Whitlipped knew I could not take it. Careful not to comingle Spills and Company funds with my personal resources, I paid bail and returned Constantia Jones to her family. Her husband thanked me tearfully, and told how Constantia explained it was all a mistake. It remained a mistake, each of the following four times over that summer and autumn that I paid bail to return Constantia from Newgate, after her arrest for similar acts. And each time, Whitlipped sighed and raised his eyebrows, but said nothing.

In one of my letters from Mr. Spills, he suggested I should begin, work permitting, to spend a bit of time at the coffeehouses, in order to meet other men who may be in need of our services, and expand our own sources. Being ignorant of the workings of these institutions, I again turned to Mr. Whitlipped for advice.

"Ah, yes, Spills is right, you know," he agreed. "Much business is conducted in the coffeehouses. A part of my day is spent such. If you would like, you may visit the one I frequent to-morrow. It is the Root and Wallow, in Whitty Street. I will be there with my partner, and will help you make the acquaintance of others. Be sure to bring your own penny." He winked. I had come to consider him a friend.

The following day, I entered the Root and Wallow, and sighted, through a haze of bluish smoke from countless long pipes, Whitlipped seated at a small table with a sour-faced man with angular features who I assumed to be his partner. They were reading newspapers. I approached with "Hilli-ho!" but quickly regretted it.

"Bumpkin!" exclaimed the sour man, with a scowl. "Turnip, do you not know how to address gentlemen?"

"Oh. Oh. Meet my associate, Mr. Trembly," said my mentor. "I'm afraid I should have schooled you on the way of coffeehouses yesterday. Sit, and I will do my best." Events such as that reminded me of how unprepared for a different life one can be when moving between lines of a stratified society. I have oft considered how much time and industry is lost in attention to such lines, and for what real purpose they exist at all.

Trembly reinforced my first impression of him, and no affectionate feelings ever afterwards developed. On my employment practices, he said, "Porridge and meat for warehouse workers, at your own expense? And running a university for diggers at the end of the day? Enjoy your coffee now, Sir, for you won't be here long with such nonsense!" Then, to Whitlipped, "Has Spills lost his mind? Or does he know what his prodigy is doing in the city to bring him to ruin? Radish!"

"That, Sir, is the business of Spills and this young gentleman, and not ours to scold," remarked Whitlipped. "Sit, Mr. Fezziwig, and your first cup of coffee shall be my gift."

Upon leaving, I thanked my friend for the coffee and advice, and turned to his partner, with a slight bow. "It has been my great pleasure to make your acquaintance. Prune."

If asked, daughters, you would probably reply that your father has had only one love affair in his long life. It would not be entirely true. My other has been with the coffeehouse. Men there of all experiences and philosophies, vocations and views of God, educations and personalities, discussed the news and nature and the ancients and everything in between.

I attribute my success to many things, including my own hard work and ambition. But, the acquaintances made in the coffeehouses and the off-hand information offered like apples free for plucking (and learning which to eat and which were rotten at the core) have made up for my lack of privilege at birth. It takes both, it seems: industry, and connexion. Either, if not already in possession, can be had with determination. I am sad to see the fall of the coffeehouses and their replacement by clubs, to which it is harder for men of lesser means to gain entrance. The compote of ideas is less satisfying today, with fewer fruits in the pot. And, though tea now seems much preferred, coffee is still my choice.

Summer and fall progressed, and business at Spills and Company, London, continued to build, though the cost of land transport, owing to the silted nature of the Lea outside our warehouse door, remained detrimental. My correspondence with Caddy continued, and became ardent to the point that I shall not quote it further. One of her late autumn letters included an invitation to visit again at Christmastime, and Mr. Spills was kind enough to allow it.

Busy! Busy! Busy I was, but the thought of Christmastime at Bracebridge lightened my demeanor as much as the days began to darken. I was bone-tired each night, but thoughts of Caddy and her warm parting kiss and the intimate nature of our correspondence occupied my mind such that sleep became dear. I made plans to spend my first time away from the warehouse since my arrival there, cold, hungry, and with bloodied feet.

On the first of December, Jones came to me, and I knew by his look what I would be asked. I had determined that I was not going to pay bail for his wife another time, not just because it impeded my funds when Christmastime was approaching, but because it allowed the same act to be played again and again. This time, though, was different.

"No, no bail, Will. There's been a terrible mistake, and we must make it right, we must!" He was frantic. "She has been accused of stealing 36 shillings and a half a guinea from a...well, a liar...but one well known, and of an upper class. No bail. There is to be a trial. I need your help, more than at any time, Will. Please. If she is found guilty, she could..." His voice trailed. "We will get through this, and that will be the end of it, I promise! She has changed, Will. She is her old self again. Gin no longer has a hold on her. We just need her back! Please!"

The look in his eyes reminded me of the look in my Father's eyes, as he was being drug over the threshold of our hut. It seemed that a hundred years had already passed since then. Each time my anger at the Joneses rose within me, I imagined myself lying bound in the snow, laughing at my impending death.

After looking into the matter, Whitlipped came to me with a grim look. "Not the same this time, I'm afraid," he said. "She is no stranger to Newgate, the sum is more substantial, and testimony of the victim is likely to be believed. It is rare that such detailed testimony is given, under such vulgar circumstances, and it will be given great weight."

When I pled for his help, he said. "I will do what I can do. This sort of thing is usually more Trembly's area of practice, though he usually represents higher classes when they fall in such traps, but perhaps he will still advise me. I will do what I can do." I knew Whitlipped's concern was grave, since he referred to his partner by his actual name. In all our lighter conversations since my first visit to a coffeehouse, he had called Mr. Trembly "Prune."

Without sufficient funds of my own to both pay for his services (even at a much reduced rate) and make the trip to Bracebridge, I wrote to Caddy and tried to explain the situation as best I could, with a prayer that she would both believe me, and not take offence at my action.

Whitlipped did his best, I am convinced of it, but the outcome was assured. Constantia Jones was to hang, at Tyburn, on December 22. The word of a three-penny upright against that of a gentleman made no contest. Whitlipped implored me not to attend the execution, but offered to accompany me when I said I must.

When the day came, Whitlipped came for me at the warehouse, in his carriage. As we traveled the Oxford Road, we spoke little, though our conversations were usually animated. The day was clear and not at all cold, and we encountered many other carriages and men on horseback and afoot, all with the same destination. I was not prepared for what I saw upon arrival. It resembled, more than anything, a market fair. A great crowd pushed close, and vendors of hot chestnuts and other victuals did a brisk business.

A huzzah went up as a flat cart came into view, carrying two bound persons, robed in white, and with white hoods. I could tell from their shape that one was a female. Constantia.

The cart pulled up to the gibbet, which was lower than I expected. The white hoods came off, and Geoff Jones was allowed to climb up onto the cart and caress his wife. The condemned man, who appeared to be in a drunken stupor, had no such comfort. After a short while, a clergyman said a few words to all three, and the condemned were again hooded and stood upright. The executioner put the nooses around their necks, and led the horses away.

As the cart slipped out from under their feet, the bodies of the condemned writhed. I was aghast to see Geoff Jones make a great leap up and embrace his wife's body, hanging on as they all swayed gently.

"I'm sure he was counseled to do that, Will," Whitlipped whispered in my ear. "It helps them die quicker, so they should not suffer as long." I turned and ran to the edge of the crowd, and spewed the bile from my stomach.

Back in the carriage, Whitlipped said, "I have arranged to buy her body and her clothing from the executioner, and for her to buried with the fee you paid, Will. At least she shan't be going to the surgeons for dissection."

I never again saw Jones or his family, nor heard what became of them. It was long before I could rid my mind of the sight of Jones clutching the spasming body of his wife, swaying with a slow rhythm.

On Christmas Eve, I allowed the workers to leave early, with the next day as a paid break from their labour. They all left, leaving me alone in the cavernous warehouse. I wished each a merry Christmas, but it seemed anticlimactic, as they all wandered off.

A feeling of loneliness and melancholy overcame me. Christmas Day was spent alone in my chamber, after attending chapel. I was struck by the difference in my Christmases over the past two years. One was spent with my father, in a tiny but snug hut strung with greenery, drinking a small beer, and hoping for something, anything, different from our usual fare to be received as an annual pittance from the manor the following day.

The next had been a most glorious celebration, with warmth and food and drink and, dare I say it, the beginnings of love. I had opportunity for a gay reunion and reprise of that Christmas, but instead, out of a sense of duty and compassion, had a sight of unspeakable pathos burned into my mind. I stared into the fire and vowed that I would never spend Christmas in such a pedestrian fashion again, should it take everything I had to make it so.

When Whitlipped discovered that I had spent Christmas alone, he was incredulous. "Tut! That won't do, Fezziwig! Bad business! Connexions are made at Christmastime! You must know and be known! If only you had told me. Well, we can at least remedy it on Twelfth Night. I have been invited to take the evening at the home of Mr. _____ (I shall not name his name), a gentleman of means for whom Prune and I did considerable work over the past year, with satisfactory result. Since I have no other guest to bring (Whitlipped was long a widower), I shall bring you. Wear your best. Quite the Tory, he is. Old family. You will want to be seen in good stead."

As expected, most of the men had been late for their duties on St. Stephen's, but I was indulgent, and let them go early again that evening. The days leading up to Christmas had been quite busy for inventory, but the following week slowed, as if all humanity breathed a complacent, full-bellied Christmas sigh and drowsily prepared for the eve of Epiphany.

Twelfth Night arrived, and Whitlipped, having assured me it was convenient along the way, picked me up in his carriage, and we traveled west to the new May Fair. He gave me advice along the way.

"So much change, so many people, so much opportunity. London, yea, the world, can hardly be kept up with," he said, somewhat wistfully. "Hard work and products are making way for shares and connexions. Here's the lesson I've observed, Will. You must leave an impression. If it's the coffeehouse or Twelfth Night or chapel, perception has become more important than reality. To get ahead, you must leave an impression."

A crowd was gathered in the street outside our destination, and I saw my first pantomime. Not yet having become interested in political matters, I didn't fully understand the actors pretending to chop one another with a wooden "Walpole Ax" because they could not afford the Walpole Tax, but found it fully amusing, and have enjoyed theatre of all sorts since.

The house was fine, and the guests were many and richly dressed. Our host, Mr. _____, was a man with a red face, enormous belly, and wig slightly askew. There was music and food and Wassail, and Whitlipped introduced me to many of his acquaintances, making sure to provide me an opportunity to mention the type of goods in which Spills and Company dealt. The overall impression was festive, but lacking the warmth and sincere affection I experienced at Bracebridge. Watching the affectation of many of the revelers in their conversations with one another, I was much reminded of the bantam roosters Father and I kept penned at the close.

Perhaps due to my bleak mood, I ate and drank liberally, though my mind was still at Bracebridge. I chose not to join in the dancing.

As the evening wore on, everyone seemed to be anticipating something to happen, in much the same way as we look forward to the pudding on Christmas. "It's time!" exclaimed our host. "Biggs, bring in the cake." The tired and sad looking butler brought in a great cake, highly decorated, and sat it on the table with as much fanfare as he could muster. Whitlipped must have seen my confusion.

"Never seen a proper Twelfth Night? Hm. Well, that's the King Cake. There is a pea and a bean baked within, and whoever receives them are King and Queen of the celebration. He lowered his voice. "Silly old custom, if you ask me. That's why it's usually done only after the bowl has been practically drained."

Guests lined up to be served on fine blue-and-white china plates. I had noticed that the servants were excluded from all food and drink, and avoided the eyes when possible.

At the front of the line was the hosts' daughter, a buxom and loud woman about five years older than me. The butler began to cut the cake at a random spot, but she said "Oh, no, Biggs, that can't be right. Over here. That looks promising." The butler cut the cake at that site, and she seemed content to take her plate.

I was quite sated, but ate the cake out of politeness. It was of fine texture, though I profess I much prefer old pudding. In the last bite but one, there was a hard, green pea. "Well, now!" shouted our excited host. "We are about to be graced by royalty! Who are our king and queen?"

His daughter responded at once. "It's me, Papa! I have the bean!" A somewhat limp cheer went up.

"I knew it of you, especially when I received bills for your gowns!" joked Mr. _____, and everyone laughed. "Now, what about the pea?"

My intuition was to swallow the hard green offender and be done with it.

"Now surely, the pea has been discovered! No holding out!" Feeling equally obligated and tipsy, I raised my hand. "Capital! Capital! Young..um..Fuzzywig, Whitlipped's friend! There's a good fellow!" More cheers and pats on the back.

The host's daughter approached me. "Ah, my queen!" she exclaimed. When she saw my quizzical look, she said, incredulously, "Why, don't you know? My, in from the wilds, aren't we? On Twelfth Night, the natural order of things is reversed. I am the king, and thou art my queen! Come, I'll show you." She took me by the hand and led me into a corridor. I did not want to appear a bumpkin, nor offend the host, so I complied.

Once out of sight, she said, "Look up!" and I saw a sprig of green on the ceiling. "Remember, I am your king, and I shall have my queen!" she said wickedly, and pulled me to her by my cravat, kissing me deeply. I was so taken aback that I began to protest, but her hold became firmer, and one hand fell down along my body.

She eventually shoved me away, leaving my mouth aflame. "There, your highness. Let us return to court." She flounced back toward the hall. I lingered a moment to collect my wits, and unsteadily followed.

The crowd was thinning. Whitlipped found me and gave a quizzical look, but questioned nothing. "Hm. Yes, about a night, don't you think? I will tell the servant to fetch the carriage." I nodded and thrust my hands into my pockets.

My purse was missing.

"D---! Whitlipped! My purse has been stolen!" I exclaimed loudly, the Wassail having done it work on me over the evening. All eyes were upon me. I spotted the daughter, who was still sporting a wicked smile. I pointed. "You took it! When you kissed me in the corridor!" There was an audible, collective intake of breath. I saw her turn to her father.

"Papa! That dirty pig asked me to show him the portrait in the hallway, and tried to put his hands on me!" Mr. _____ immediately turned blood red and sputtered, and yelled, "Biggs!" Within seconds, the butler (who turned out to be much stronger than I anticipated) dragged me to the door and threw me over the threshold. I bumped down the steps and landed at the bottom. This being insufficient, Biggs dragged me out into the mud in the centre of the street and returned inside.

Wet and covered with fresh manure, I rose and shook myself off, my head still swimming. I sat on the kerb to collect my thoughts, and, in a moment, Whitlipped's carriage stopped before me and the door opened. He grimaced at my sight and smell as I sat down.

"Remember what I said about leaving an impression, William? Let's just forget that, shall we?" A faint smile crossed his lips. "Pea."

From my prior experiences, I knew that anything I carried was subject to be taken away, so, thankfully, only a small portion of my personal funds was in the purse. The overall store had already been greatly reduced by the unfortunate Joneses. It was some time before I could broach the subject with my friend. I described the actual events in the corridor, and it was very important to me that I be believed.

"They are upper class! Why in heaven would a rich woman steal the mean purse of a warehouseman?"

Whitlipped sighed his sigh, the sound that had become so familiar to me. "How do you think they become rich in the first place, Will? And maintain it? If something desirable is there, they believe it is their right to have it." He was thoughtful for a moment. "You will not likely ever get business from anyone who witnessed this affair. What was your mistake in this?"

I considered. "You will tell me I should have remained quiet and taken my loss. But, she stole from me! And in turn accused me of something I did not!"

"True. But, would it not be but your word against hers? And what is her station, compared to yours? A woman stealing from a man in a compromised position? We saw one possible result of that, all too clearly, at Tyburn. Change the class of the participants, and the results could just as easily be reversed. There is the thing to remember. Our *place* in life must determine our *action*. Forgetting that could cost you dearly, indeed."

Whitlipped was correct about business from the patrons of Mr. _____'s Twelfth Night celebration. Spills and Company never did a pennyworth of business with anyone in attendance that night. There was enough business to go around, though, in the burgeoning city, especially for those with sure supply, dependable delivery, and reasonable overhead expenses. I credit my labour practice in the last two.

A reply from Bracebridge came at last. Caddy wrote that she was heartbroken at my absence, but that, had it not been for Jones having saved me, her heart would be unmended for life, and the loyalty must be returned. Her letter helped remove some of the bitter taste left by the King Cake. I made plans to visit in early summer, praying that any rich, handsome fellows making their way toward the manor in the meantime would be waylaid by other matters.

That spring, the trial of a highwayman began to become a topic of conversation in the coffeehouse. The brigand's name was Dick Turpin, and evidence presented him as having murdered and stolen horses from York all the way to Essex. He was known by his coal-back mount, called Black Bess. His notoriety was such that the Duke of Newcastle desired the trial be moved to London, but it was convened in York. There was little doubt about the outcome; he would hang. The *Gentleman's Magazine* made note of the execution and its aftermath:

"Turpin behav'd himself with amazing assurance and bow'd to the spectators as he passed on the way to the gibbet. He mounted the ladder in an undaunted manner; but, feeling his right leg a-tremble, he spoke a few words to the topsman, then threw himself off, and expired in five minutes. For assurance, his body was left hanging until evening, at which time it was taken to a tavern in Castlegate, and buried in the yard at St. George's the day next. It was discovered upon the dawn that the body had been uncover'd, and taken, wherein a great mob formed to retrieve it and punish the body-thieves, which they accomplished. The body was re-buried, with a quantity of quick-lime, thus making it unvaluable to body-thieves."

With shame, I admit that I held no compassion for the deceased, and read the narrative of his hanging with great satisfaction. I remembered the dark feeling of being near death, the pain of my bloody feet (which persisted for some months) and the loss of an asset, the horse, which was to be sold for expenses upon reaching the city. May God forgive me for that lack of compassion, and my other transgressions. It did not occur to me until many years later to wonder why I was, though bound, left in the centre of the track rather than dragged into the wood, where surely I would never be found.

The return to Mr. Spills on his initial expenditures for the warehouse on the Lea began in May, and he was well pleased, though the silted channel kept us from the profit we would have liked. It was time to spend my first night away from the warehouse since I arrived over a year previous. I was on my way to Bracebridge, and Caddy, at last.

That spring was as pleasant as the winter had been severe. For a fee, I obtained temporary use of a middling horse from an associate, and no highwayman impeded my progress. Bracebridge Manor looked even shabbier than it had before, when snow hid many of its deficiencies (The current generation of Bracebridges, fortunately, has begun to bring the place back to a more wholly habitable state, though doing so in a manner that preserves its ancient nature). To my great relief, the atmosphere within was no less welcoming. My reception belied the fact that I had only encountered this family once before, and that was a year and one-half ago. They all seemed to know that the affection between Caddy and me had grown through our absence, and were encouraging of it.

During my brief stay, I helped with late spring agriculture duties at Bracebridge, and was much reminded of my previous life, and wondered where I would be and what I would be doing had not treachery overcome me. I remained (as, lo, I do even today, in my old age) sorrowful for my father, but resolved that my happiness should be his legacy. My budding success in business was a part of that, but the far greater part I took away with me as I mounted my hired horse and turned back toward London Town. Caddy and Mr. Bracebridge had agreed that, upon my next visit in the autumn, Caddy and I would be married.

With great difficulty, I tried to keep my mind on business that summer. The reputation of Spills and Company for reliability continued to grow, and I was able to hire more workers, still with only moderate salary, but added benefits of full bellies and education.

I rank our wedding day as the most transformative in my life, even more so than my salvation from the frozen road. Spills came down from Great Grimsby, leaving Barkers to mind the business, and Whitlipped provided himself and the groom transportation in his carriage. The local vicar read the prayers, and the gayest celebration followed, even compared to Christmastime. Having kept my promise to dance with none other, I danced and danced with Caddy until I could dance no longer. That night, we were given the same chamber I occupied during my first visit.

"You know there will be great joking at our expense," Caddy giggled as we retired that evening. "There always is after a wedding!"

"Aye, but let us join in the mirth, my love!' I replied. I told her the story of my money pouch that had been hiding during our first kiss, and the peals of her sweet laughter were such that I'm sure they were heard not only by others in the hall, but by the ancient crusader in his crypt (who, thankfully, decided to remain in place for the evening). No doubt the laughter added to the sly looks and grins from family and friends during the continued celebration the following day, and, for the duration of our lives together, her reference to my money pouch with the slightest raise of an eyebrow has always been enough to lighten my spirits, no matter how glum.

Before returning to London with my bride, I had a long business conversation with Mr. Spills, Mr. Whitlipped, and my new father-in-law. Mr. Bracebridge said he planned to cull many ancient but dying oaks from the manor forest, and the wood was strong, close-grained, and self-seasoned. He would like to see it go to more productive use than the hearth, and it would make particularly fine barrel staves. But, the cost of manufacturing and then shipping barrels empty to a place they would be needed was prohibitive.

Mr. Spills was quite pleased with our London endeavors and the reputation we had cultivated (Whitlipped neglected to tell him the story of Twelfth Night), but realised we were probably approaching our natural limit of what we could profitably do, given the silted state of the Lea. He asked if we should consider selling the warehouse and turning the profit into procuring a facility on the Thames instead.

"Forgive my presumption, but I have a proposal that may offer a unified solution to our needs," I said. "But, it is audacious." All were eager to hear it. "I have done my best to probe the obstruction in front of the warehouse. It seems to me made of two distinct layers, clean sand and rubble stone, both of which are much easier to move than muck. I believe we can open the channel sufficiently to allow flatboat access, plus build a sufficient wharf, by hiring no more than twenty-five men for the season." Mr. Spills seemed surprised by this statement, but considered it as he took snuff.

"From all I hear in the coffeehouses, sufficient funds will soon be raised to begin building a new bridge at Westminster." Whitlipped nodded agreement. "Hundreds of workers will be needed, making the cost of labour more dear, so we should act promptly. Now, as to the bridge, what are the tools that will be most needed in number?"

"Surely, shovels and buckets," said Mr. Spills.

"And barrows, I should think," added Mr. Bracebridge.

"Indeed, and indeed!" I exclaimed. "My observation is that

there is already a shortage, as I see men sharing them anyplace there are works. We can do nothing for shovels, unless we find a source. But, staves are much cheaper to transport than buckets and barrels. When our channeling project is at rest for the winter, we could set up a small manufactory on the vacant plot, with staves from Bracebridge turned into buckets and barrels by workers trained to be coopers after their labour in the channel is done each day. It shall be a condition of their employment."

The three men sat with furrowed brows, not speaking. It was almost as if their brains were ticking collectively, like a great clock. It was Mr. Spills who finally broke the silence.

"Bless me, Will! If it doesn't work, you know I will have to cut losses and be done with London. But, you're looking at tomorrow, not just today. I'm willing to take the risk. Gentlemen?" He turned to Misters Whitlipped and Bracebridge, who glanced at one another and nodded. "I think my kinsman has chosen well," said Mr. Bracebridge. "And so has my daughter."

You, daughters, have, by your own words, always known me to be a jolly man, a demanding taskmaster, perhaps, but thinking the best of humanity and rejecting the notion that there is any benefit to unfriendliness and a long face. You may be surprised, with all I had endured. I became the happy man I am on the day I married Caddy. The events of my youth could have caused me to remain calculating and suspicious, and few would have blamed me for it. Her brightness changed me for the better, and continues to do so today.

Caddy and I returned to London with Mr. Whitlipped. If she felt disappointment at the smallness of our lodging rooms in the warehouse, she did not show it, and the rooms (which, I will admit, had become a bit untidy from my own neglect) soon benefited greatly from her presence and attention. She had visited London many times before, as the daughter of a country squire, but took to the role of small merchant's wife with pleasure. Though I worked well past dusk each evening, the small rooms were alive with the passion of young love.

I set about to hire workers and procure equipment to channel the offending obstruction in the Lea. Small boats, dredges, ropes, buckets, and cant hooks competed for space in the warehouse, and two dozen more workers were hired from the constant stream of displaced country folk into the city. I paid a bit less, but, to some of them, the knowledge that every day spent working would be free from hunger, and that they would learn a trade that may continue to feed themselves and their families after the project was complete, was incentive enough to accept a small decrease. Like Mr. Spills, I was always taken by men who looked not at today, but at tomorrow.

Finding an overseer who could both direct the channeling and teach cooperage was a challenge, but I turned to my acquaintances in the coffeehouse, and was referred to a Mr. Laverty, late of Dublin, who had learned his trades at a brewery, but was a refugee from the latest famine in Ireland. His leathery hands and face would lead one to believe he had not once spent a day under roof. His language was foul and used loudly; I told him his voice opened oysters in the barrel at a distance of twenty paces. He was, though, an excellent judge of a man, and could tell within an hour if one was an innate worker. I liked him from the beginning, and learned to rely on him for the project while I continued with our primary business.

The warehouse environs soon resembled the encampment of a small army, with earthworks and great activity. The dredging revealed what I had suspected, that is, huge quantities of fine and peculiarly regular, basket-sized rubble. This was heaped in great piles on the adjacent plot, and I hoped it would not offend the souls resting there. The stone from the old dependency saw new use as pilings for the small wharf we hoped would emerge.

Some days I viewed it all with considerable pride, thinking that I had proposed a great work that I would soon see come to fruition, to substantial profit. Other days, I looked upon it with anxiety, wondering what would become of my lot should the scheme fail.

I found the dredging work most interesting, thinking back to my boyish fascination with water wheels. What came up and formed the huge piles struck me as odd. We all enjoyed plentiful eel pie that season, but the stones seemed almost of human manufacture, they were so regular, and many had parallel striations, as if they had been dragged along by some great force. Within the sand we often found bones, which was not a surprise, but some of them had turned completely to stone, and were not identifiable as fish or animals familiar to any of us. Since Mr. Whitlipped was an educated man, I asked his opinion of the matter.

"Not really my area of interest, you know, but I suppose the Flood of Noah would explain it, would it not?" he said.

"I can't see how," I replied. We know that water rounds rocks over, it's clear, but the marks were made by something solid. And, some of the bones and impressions are of fish unfamiliar to us. Would they not have survived the Flood, under water?" He had no answer.

Still in the grip of a series of harsh winters, work on the Lea came to a close with the year. Shipments of staves had arrived from Bracebridge, and the work of producing barrows and buckets began. For the barrows, Laverty found a wheelwright among the other Irish newcomers to the city. I procured the services of a smith through an acquaintance at the Root and Wallow, Mr. Binley, with the understanding that my need of him would only be part-time. It was several weeks before a shelter for the forge was constructed, but the warmth of it made its use tolerable throughout the season.

That Christmas Eve, I made it a point to make sure the workers had a merry evening, pretending confidence that our prospect for success and prosperity with our new endeavor was great, and hiding my own nervousness. We took Christmas dinner with Mr. Whitlipped, who had not hosted one at his home since his wife had died. He was quite smitten by Caddy's charms, and confessed that her presence moved him with a renewed spark of youth. Trembly and his equally dour wife attended as well, causing Whitlipped to joke, "So which pudding shall we bring in tonight? The plum or the *prune*?"

We used the occasion to announce that Caddy was with child. I desired to find larger lodgings for us, but, given the financial risk of the project, we agreed it not prudent at the time. She didn't mind; our rooms at the warehouse were comfortable enough, though I knew they would be barely sufficient once the child was born.

My visits to the coffeehouse became less frequent, out of necessity. During one in late winter, I encountered Mr. Binley.

"Fezziwig! I may need my man back for the full time come weather-break. Sufficient funds have been raised that work on the new bridge will begin in earnest, have you heard? Turns out the ferrymen had to be paid-off. A scandal, if you ask me. Must enterprise be held hostage by such rabble?"

"Hilli-ho, good news indeed!" I exclaimed. "Not just the construction, but it will ease commerce greatly! You had better start feeding your smith better, Binley, or he may decide to become solely a Spills and Company man!" I joked.

"Typical of radicals," he laughed. I had, because of my practices with workers, been called referred to as radical in the coffeehouse a number of times, though I barely knew what it meant. With all else that was going on in my life, politics were not an interest, despite their being on the lips of almost every other man of business.

"Such a threat, to one who recently did you a favor. Expect a visit soon from a Mr. LaVant. He is an associate of the bridge architect, Swiss, I believe, but speaks the King's. In our conversations, he mentioned a need for small work accoutrements, and I directed him to you. If you profit from his visit, Fezziwig, I expect to drink my fill on your penny," he smiled and raised his cup in my direction.

LaVant did, indeed, visit the warehouse. "So young," he said when I introduced myself. "You are sure you have authority to speak for this enterprise?" He seemed a bit suspicious, but I assured him I was the primary agent.

You might imagine my great relief when he examined the buckets and barrows, and said he would send a man to arrange payment for all that were ready to use, (at a close price to what I asked), provided I transport them to where they were needed. He also agreed to take all our future production until such time his needs were met, provided the quality remained unchanged.

To my surprise, he was exceedingly interested in the dredging work, which lay neglected awaiting better weather. On the plot, he rolled rubble stones around in his hands, and allowed sand to run through his fingers, brow furrowed.

"I will take two buckets with me today, Fessiwee," he said. (Though his English was good, he had difficulty with my name).

"Filled with sand. And a stone." You can imagine my perplexion, but I readily agreed.

Caddy's condition became more evident with late winter, and we expected our addition perhaps in early June. Her mother and sister planned to travel from Bracebridge in time to assist. One evening in late April, though, she began to have pain and issue, which disturbed us greatly.

In a panic, I sent Laverty to bring a surgeon. He returned, saying (to my horror) he could find none who would come to the warehouse without pre-arrangement and payment. He brought with him his wife (I knew not that he even had one) who was as hardened and grizzled as her husband. He told me she had experience in these matters, and I was in no position to refuse her help. Mrs. Laverty examined Caddy, beginning with a prayer in Latin and a crossing-sign.

Clearly, the baby was coming early. I had, of course, seen births among the livestock many times, but it prepared me not for that night. When the baby separated, I heard no cry and tried to comfort Caddy for our loss of the child, knowing I could not succeed. I looked up to see Mrs. Laverty with her mouth over the baby's tiny face, breathing life into his body. With a sputter, a tiny, faint cry came, but for a moment. Though tiny, Erasmus Fezziwig would live.

Mrs. Laverty moved into our rooms to help Caddy and Ras for a fortnight. Though I thought to sleep in the garret, I could not think of being that far away in case I was needed, so I slept on straw just outside the door, much relieved to be so close. Ras grew quickly, Caddy's sustenance allowing him to make up for his initial frailty. I know that these matters are in God's hands and but a mystery to us, but I later wondered if Ras's extraordinary need did not sap Caddy's reproductive strength, for she was never again with child, despite our ample and vigorous attempts.

It seemed that, though I was obviously not equipped to provide for Ras's needs during his frequent arousals through the night, I was awakened during them just the same. I found myself still pondering the origins of the regular stones and bones being pulled up with the dredgings. An unexplained question in the natural world has always kept me from rest, much as a husk stuck in the teeth. I just can't ignore it. So, by candlelight, I wrote down my observations, and drew illustrations as examples, hoping they would be of a quality that would make Barkers proud if he ever saw them. I had no definitive conclusion, but did note that it seems the world had changed over a great time, and forces other than the present course of rivers must have, at one time, been at work on the earth. I showed my work to Mr. Whitlipped when it was complete.

"I know there is great interest in such things, but I have little personally, I'm afraid," he said. "But, it is a novel little work. With your leave, I will show it around. Perhaps some good might come of it."

That summer brought another glad tiding, one that sealed the success of my gamble with the future of Spills and Company, London. When LaVant returned without warning, I feared some trouble with our products or deliveries, though I was continuously employed in making sure both were as agreed upon. His purpose in his visit surprised me.

"Fessiwee, I want your sand and stone. They are fit for our purpose with little preparation, and I have searched for a source closer to the bridge, but none are found. We must have it. But we cannot buy it." He saw I was confused.

"Here is our offer. You will keep the labour needed for

your warehouse and manufactory," he explained. "Any surplus, we will hire, plus send more of our own to finish dredging a channel sufficient to service your business. And, we will build your wharf."

My letter to Mr. Spills advising him of the arrangement could barely contain my excitement, and his reply was equally ecstatic, saying he had decided that Spills and Company, London, would now become the only *rest of the business* in which he cared to engage. His tone changed as his letter ended, though:

"Will, it is with sadness that I must tell you that Barkers died week last. He had reformed himself considerably, but the damage had been done, and he went to his Maker a very young man. Among other things, on his last day, he wished you well, and continued success. He was wistful that your path might have been his own, save his propensities, but he held no blame but to himself."

Poor Barkers! His short life was spent searching for something he lacked. Even with the support of a mentor like Mr. Spills, the same man who had propelled me into my up-and-coming life, he was unable to look over what he could not have, and failed to grasp what he *could* possess.

The scourge of gin still spilled out into the streets of London wherever one looked, and squalor and misery prevailed. Why are some enticed by gin's temptation even to death, while some, like myself, can make merry with friends and then go on about my business? It is due to the sins of fathers, or a defect of birth, or are there things, collectively, we could do to reduce gin's effect on humanity? In this, I have some little hope, because today, while still a source of considerable sorrow, the grip of gin is not quite as great as it was at that time.

Visiting the coffeehouse not long after receiving the sad news about Barkers, I spotted Mr. Whitlipped, and he hailed me.

"Good day, William. This," he said, pointing at the older gentleman seated beside him, "is Mr. Hadley, a fellow solicitor, who also has interest in the natural world. In fact, he is a member of the Royal Society." I made sure to look impressed, although I was not familiar with the said Society. "I showed him your work on the dredgings, and he wanted to meet its author. And this," he pointed to another gentleman seated at the table, "is an old friend of mine from school days, Mr. Bracken, engaged in the art of bookbindery, in Brickhole."

The gentlemen rose and offered their hands. "My pleasure, Mr. Fezziwig. Whitlipped advised me of your youth, but I must admit, I am still taken aback. But, I read your work with interest. It is clear you have no formal scientific training, but your observations are keen, and I had not seen the topic broached afore this." This came from the first gentleman, Mr. Hadley.

I thanked him for his compliment.

"The weather has always been the subject of my observations, particularly the winds. It's of great importance to navigation, of course. They certainly don't explain the winters we have been having. Wrecking havoc with agriculture, they are. The Irish are practically dying off; poor wretches just can't adjust. Anyway, your conclusion that weather changes over great periods of time, and your descriptions of novel things right around us, dredged from the Lea, may be of some small interest in the community of science. That is why I have a proposal for you. At my own expense, I will have a number of copies of your little work printed, and distribute them to those I know who may be interested in them. No profit in it, of course, but I can tell you from experience that there is some pride in seeing one's name on a page, especially if one did not first earn credibility through formal education."

I looked at Mr. Whitlipped, who gave a slight motion of approval with his head. "I would be honored," I said, and bowed slightly.

Mr. Bracken, who had a bit of a bored look on his face until this moment, entered the conversation. "Good, good. Of how many pages is this great work of science, Fezziwig?"

"Only about twenty pages, as written, sir," I relied.

"Probably about twenty-five, once set," added Mr. Hadley.

"I see, yes," said Mr. Bracken, a bit disappointed. "Probably best left with only the printer, then, without leather binding. Now, if you were to author, say, two more associated pieces of similar length, to be bound together?" He looked at me inquisitively.

"I am most sorry, sir, but I'm afraid I have written all I know on the topic, and consider that precious little," I apologized.

Mr. Hadley seemed a bit irritated at the conversation. "Good, quite good," he said. "Now, no offence to you, young fellow, but it does need a bit of revision, spelling, grammar, you know. Whitlipped here has an acquaintance who will work with it a bit for us, as a favor. The fellow writes for *The Gentleman's Magazine*, and wrote a poem a few years ago that became quite popular. Never read it myself, but I know many did. What was it called, Whitlipped?"

"London," replied Mr. Whitlipped. "The poem is called 'London' and the gentleman is Samuel Johnson. From Staffordshire, I think. Witty fellow, round, quite near-sighted, but he has no permanent situation. You will see him here, on occasion. I'm sure, though agreeing to do us a favor, he will not complain if few bob at least were involved for good measure. I will invite him to have coffee with us here tomorrow. But be prepared for his having forgotten his penny!"

"Yes, well, that will do it. The writing does need a bit of attention, but I do know some gentlemen who would be interested in it, when done. We shall make it worth Mr. Johnson's while, if it must come to that."

At this, Mr. Bracken laughed. "Ha!" he exclaimed. "Perhaps I had best stay involved. That Johnson is a wordy sort. By the time of his finishing, I may be commissioned to produce a three-volume set! Especially if his pay is in any way connected to his word-count!"

Both Hadley and Whitlipped also found this humorous, and I joined the laughter. The balance of our conversation was stimulating. Mr. Hadley talked of his interest in how the winds affected everything, from trade to agriculture, to our general disposition. Mr. Bracken talked of how the printing and bookbinding trade was, in his words, "shooting off like a volley of cannon."

"I think coffee is part of it," he said. "Just look around. All men of means now gather, and discuss the issues of the day; trade, religion, politics. It's like sport; no one wants to be off to the side. If one's opinion is not learned, he is quickly found out, in this crowd. So, they must read. And, after reading, think they can do just as well, and choose to write. Like *you*, young Fezziwig." He said this in a way that left me not sure if I should take offence.

He continued. "It all benefits my vocation, and I'm happy to be part of it. I am of the third generation in bindery, you know.

It is much more involved than many believe. In fact, one of my impediments is finding labour with talent enough to be taught the trade. Books and the lower classes just don't mix, no matter the amount of instruction, it seems."

I began to think less of Mr. Bracken at that statement, but he went on. "Now, I prefer the finer market, more quality. You are involved in commodities, Fezziwig? Find me something I lack, between writing your tomes on the natural world. For the finest books, the leather must be thick, but supple. I can find one, or the other, but finding leather that is both is increasingly eluding me." He pointed a crooked finger in my face. "Tough but supple, that's what I need, Fezziwig. Tough but supple." I apologized that I had no sources of fine, thick leather, but that I would be vigilant for what he desired, while Hadley rolled his eyes upward and commented, with a chuckle, that Mrs. Bracken probably made the same request, and she was left wanting.

That was how *A Description of Oddities Found in Stones Dredged from the River Lea, with Illustrations* came to be published, in a small number. I wrongly assumed that none of them would ever get further than London.

True to his word, LaVant saw to it that the mountains of sand and rubble were removed on the plot, the dredging completed, and the wharf built. My expenses were reduced, as a number of the workers transferred to his employ, yet still laboured on our improvements. The bucket and barrow manufactory continued to turn a profit, as did the warehouse business at our centre. Mr. Spills remained exceedingly pleased at our margin, and my salary increased.

That spring, I was finally confident enough to find separate lodgings for Caddy, Ras, and myself, close enough to walk easily to the warehouse, but separated a distance from the dampness of the river-side. The rooms were double plus half of the warehouse lodgings, with multiple fireplaces, and wholly comfortable. Instead of a raise in his salary, I offered Laverty and his wife use of the lodging rooms at the warehouse, thus avoiding the expense of a night watchman. I have always been exceedingly fond of such arrangements, calling them "You win, I win."

Ras continued to thrive, and Caddy and I found some opportunities to attend diversions with others of our station in the city. Spills and Company was developing a reliable reputation among London's men of commerce, and my popularity at the coffeehouse increased. We were especially happy to be invited to dances, as it gave us occasion to remember our first meeting, when I was a shy and half-frozen visitor to Bracebridge. I was pleased to see Caddy, always a social soul, nurture friendship among the wives and daughters of other businessmen of the city. Our lives were beginning to settle into a comfortable routine. Which, of course, is when fate decides to sneak up behind you.

PART THE THIRD: *AMERICA*

LaVant's hunger for sand and rubble stone and his hoard of workers, many of whom spoke languages foreign to my ear, made quick work of the dredging, and his skilled masons produced a small but tightly constructed wharf. Spills and Company now had shallow draft access to the Thames and thus, the sea, with facilities to transfer stores directly to and from its warehouse, the only enterprise to do so on that section of the Lea. Mr. Spills came to London to see it for himself, with great satisfaction.

"William Lucian *Fezziwig*!" he exclaimed. "What a thing we have accomplished! We may be smaller than many of our competitors on the Thames, but we now have great flexibility and lower costs. If we continue to look forward, we will be in whatever markets we choose. Who knows? Perhaps someday we will simply sell *shares* and have someone else do all the work for us, leaving more time for the coffeehouses!" At this we both laughed, knowing our mutual poor opinion of the practice.

Mr. Spills and I had several pleasant dinners with Mr. Whitlipped during the visit and, as always with Spills, the conversation turned to the future. "Now that we have the means, what will we be able to do to fill a need before someone else takes all the profit? What world events may open opportunity?"

Spills and Whitlipped were much better informed on such matters than me, though I had taken to reading the newspapers and *The Gentleman's Magazine* at the coffeehouse, and listening to the heated conversation they evoked. The latter couldn't be helped, for the volume.

"Trade with the Colonies will only expand," Spills continued. "We could try to involve ourselves in that already existing, with finished goods in exchange for molasses, and rice, and slaves." He saw Whitlipped and me frown. "No, no, you know I will never trade in man-flesh. It is the Devil's business, we all agree. You know the price of molasses has gone up considerably, owing to uncertainty in transportation because of the Spanish danger. The price of sugar cake has also increased, and the supply often suffers because there is more profit in distilling. In fact, prices were going up before war added the danger. My sources tell me that, since almost all the trees in the West Indies have been cut, casks and barrels have become dear."

"Now, there's no profit in sending empty barrels across the sea. But, looking at the success here on the Lea, I believe it could be of great profit to send a ship of staves, complete with the makings of a forge, and a few workers skilled in cooperage. Any excess capacity could be filled with implements for sale to the plantations."

Mr. Whitlipped frowned. "Hm. The troubles with Spain have settled some, of late, according to the papers. But it is still not without peril."

"And what, dear fellow, is without peril? Remember," he lowered his voice, "you speak to a man who profited greatly, and helped *you* do so as well, from the *rest of my business* for years." Whitlipped sighed his usual sigh, and Spills went on.

"Our agent would also use the opportunity to develop exclusive sources in the West Indies, then travel on to the North American colonies to do the same with our cotton sources. The main commodity we have to sell, gentlemen, is reliability, and we must keep it in good store through our relations on the yon side of the Atlantic."

"I do agree, Mr. Spills," I said, after thinking a bit. "It follows the path that has led us to success Lea-side. It will be most important that we find a trustworthy and knowledgeable agent, though. It will all hinge on that. Such men come dear today. Perhaps, Mr. Whitlipped, we could inquire of our acquaintances at the coffeehouse?"

Mr. Whitlipped rolled his eyes. "Pea, there are times you still surprise me. You see it not? You are going to America." Mr. Spills nodded agreement.

"What? Me!" The prospect had not occurred to me.

"It's the only thing that makes sense, Will," said Spills. "I know you are loathe to leave Caddy and Ras, and the business here, but I have decided that Mrs. Spills and I will move to London for the duration of your trip. I have a bright and honest 'prentice who can handle the commerce in Great Grimsby for a time. In fact, it will complete his education to do so. Mrs. Spills and I have long desired to take a season in the city, and, Will, the clock is certainly not turning back for us. She will be a great friend and help to Caddy and Ras in your absence."

Mr. Spills furrowed his brow, if more furrowed it could become. "I know this is asking much, but we should only have to do it once to ensure our continued success. At least for as long as it will matter to me."

Seeing my countenance still aghast, he winked at Mr.

Whitlipped and said, "I never knew dropping the *rest of the business* could be such sport!"

Caddy was not happy about the arrangement, but much assured by the fact that her distant relatives, Mr. and Mrs. Spills, would be moving nearby. "Remember," she breathed in my ear, "guard thy money pouch. You know the one I mean, Fezziwig!"

Preparations were made for a late winter crossing, on a ship of 120 tons, the *John V*. Mr. and Mrs. Spills were installed in lodgings not far from the warehouse, and Mr. Spills worked with Laverty and me for a week while the ship was being prepared and loaded. That winter had been a bit more moderate, and the day of our departure was clear, but cold. I clung to Caddy and Ras on the wharf, until I heard from Mr. Spills, "Chirrup! Will! Time to go! Godspeed to you, and to Spills and Company!"

Never having been onboard a ship whilst at sea before, my sadness at leaving my family was slightly offset by novelty. Our first several days were fine, though I can say there was naught a moment I wasn't cold. I had a tiny cabin to myself, chill and damp. The food was tolerable at first, but I suspected that wouldn't last, and I was proven correct.

Other than the cold and poor food, loneliness was a peril of the crossing. Many days went by without my having talked with a soul until evening, when I took dinner with Captain Browning and two of his mates. If I attempted conversation with any of the crew during the day, they would most often look right through me, as if I were a wraith, and go about their business. Appropriate for the venue, I had brought my parting gift from Caddy, a work called *Robinson Crusoe*.

Evening dinners did little to salve my lack of fellowship. Browning and his mates spoke little, and then, mainly about the ship and the sea conditions. He had a thick and angry red scar across his forehead, and great gaps in his teeth. His two mates were little older than me, but seemed to quiver in the presence of the captain, and ate nervously. When weather permitted, the food was cooked over charcoal in an iron box on deck; when not, we ate it cold. "It" consisted of hard tack that showed more tiny worms as time passed, salted meat that became more slimy by the day, and sour beer. I chose to pick the worms and maggots from my tack and meat before dining, but was alone in this practice.

As we proceeded south, the weather warmed, making the trip much more comfortable, but hastening the deterioration of the foodstuffs and beer. Winds and currents were favorable and the taciturn captain revealed that this could be one of his speediest crossings ever, but the isolation and sameness and loneliness for my little family eventually began to overtake me.

After I had read Mr. Defoe's work through twice, the fairer weather allowed me to spend time observing the sea, viewing dolphins and fish that fly, which I found exceedingly novel. I even fashioned fishing apparatus from a barrel stave, twine, and a bent nail baited with a meat rind, but the velocity of the ship stripped it clean with haste, so my thought of eating fresh fish was moot.

We passed two other ships in the warmer climate, both HMS. On both occasions, a small signal cannon was fired, with a reciprocated volley. I watched with interest, as I had never seen even so small a gun fired.

One night in warm climes, hails and commotions above awakened me. I tried to go above deck, but found the cabin door locked from without. After some time, the deck grew quiet, but the commotion moved to the hold. I debated whether I should make my own commotion, or stay quiet and unnoticed. The decision was eventually made for me, when the cabin door swung open without warning, and a large man with a sword drawn stepped inside. Beside him, a smaller, foul-looking lout held a lantern.

"Que tenemos aqui? No mucho, parece. Es usted ingles?" He saw I did not understand. "English?" he persisted.

"Yes, I am English," I answered.

"What is your place on this ship?" he demanded. His English was good, and I assumed he meant my position.

"I am an agent for the cargo, mostly barrel staves, bound for Barbados," I answered, truthfully. He spat, and left. I heard the door lock.

It was clear to me what had happened, and my fear was great. The ship had been captured by the Spanish. Was I now a hostage, who would be ransomed? A prisoner of war, to be exchanged? Or excess ballast, to be tossed overboard with no ceremony?

The man, whom I assumed to be in authority, returned the next morning. His wormy companion brought a small portion of equally wormy food and, more importantly, a jug of beer, for I had great thirst.

"Senor, this ship and its cargo are the property of King Philip, and you are a trespasser, and thus his prisoner," he pronounced. "Many of the other trespassers have been executed for their crime. You shall be removed from these quarters and, should I, as the King's agent, find it expedient, you shall be ransomed. If I do not find it so, you shall be cast off." I knew he did not mean onto a deserted island, to follow the path of Robinson.

I was allowed to eat and drink, and then I was roughly handled to the hold, and chained by the ankle to a timber. Daughters, can you imagine my despair? For the second time in my life, I was shackled and faced the bleakest prospect. This time, I had a young love and a fine son to lose, in addition to only myself. Providence, or chance, had not only saved me, but also brought me into grand opportunities and into the lives of good people who showed me kindness. Did all that happen just to have me drown like a bilge rat, or be run through by a Spanish sword? I thought of Caddy and Ras, awaiting word of me that was never to come. Would they return to Bracebridge, or remain in London? Would Mr. Spills make some provision for them?

Surely the Spanish devils could see the *John V.* was exactly what it seemed, filled with barrel staves and implements, I thought. And, as its agent, I was probably worth more to them alive than dead. D--n them, William Fezziwig *was somebody*, and had value! But then I rebuked myself for haughtiness. I was resourceful and hard working, but at how many places along the way had I been saved through the charity of others, instead of my own effort?

I wept, and prayed. Seldom have prayers been answered so swiftly, or in a more ignited fashion, other than perhaps Elijah's competition with Baal. After less than a day chained to the post, I heard great peals of noise, at first thinking them thunder. The third eruption was followed by crashing and splintering, as a ball passed through the hull, quite near me. More followed, and it first occurred to me that my salvation could also be my demise. If the ship sank, I would spend a watery eternity chained to the timber. What if the new combatants were privateers, who may have no hesitation of disposing of a wretch chained below decks?

Eventually, the sounds of full battle came from above, and,

to my joy, there were words in English hurled among the commotion. The action was hot by the sound of it, and my fervent prayers were for the Crown to have the day. When martial sounds silenced, I knew not which side would decide my fate, until a group of marine soldiers came into the hold, swords drawn. I did not recognize their colours.

"State your name and station!" a tall soldier demanded. He had a Colonial manner of speech and appeared to be in a position of authority, though only a few years older than me. I tried my best to contain my joy, but I am sure my reply was:
"MynameisWilliamLucianFezziwigandIamanagentforSpills andcompanyandIamaccompaningashipmentofbarrelstavesandimp lementstoBarbadosandIamaloyalsubectofHisMajestyfromLincoln shirelateofLeasideand.."

The tall soldier held up his hand. "I can see you are English, or hear, rather. I will attempt to find logs, and read them, and we will discuss your situation. In the mean time, Sir, you will be removed to the *Swansea* and kept under guard, just a precaution. You will not be abused."

One of the soldiers had a ring of keys and, after several tries, found one up to the task of freeing me. I was taken above decks, to a scene of great disarray. Several bodies were lying about, and large blood stains dyed the deck in places. Timber and sails were strewn, and had to be climbed over to reach the gunwale. The *John V.* was fastened to the *Swansea* with hooks, and sailors were busily binding her more securely. Compared to the huge warship, the *John V.* seemed no more than a boil troubling a great buttock.

I was taken to a small cabin in the *Swansea*, accommodated with a small portion of meat and beer, and a basin of seawater for washing. Even that was welcomed, after my captivity. I joked with the soldier set to guard me that the accommodations were superior to those I had just left.

"So you say today," replied the Colonial. "Are you new to the Indies? Have you had the fever as of yet?"

"No, until boarding the ship at our side, I had never left England," I said.

"May God choose to protect you from the scourge, then, Sir," he said grimly. "It is the enemy that makes the Spanish seem like a trifle when compared." Further conversation revealed the man was from Virginia, as were most of the marine soldiers onboard. His father, who still lived, was from Essex, but had come to the colony as a youth under indenture. Their ranks had been recruited under Governor Gooch, and his superior, the tall young man who had me freed, was Captain Washington, also of Virginia.

Within the hour, my liberator came for the promised interview. He extended his hand. "Captain Lawrence Washington, 43rd Foot, serving under Admiral Vernon," he announced, and bade me to sit. He had quite a stern face.

"You are a fortunate man, Mr. Fezziwig," he began, and I enthusiastically agreed. "We had been trailing the *El Churro* for some time, remaining dark. We were too distant to assist when you were taken. When we began to overtake you, the captain of the *Churro*, cowardly bastard, chose to save himself and leave crewmen with small guns, not even sufficiently installed as of yet, to fend for themselves on your ship. They are all dead. And, I'm afraid, your ship is badly damaged and not fit to continue under its own sail. Sufficient crew also survived, but not the captain. Filled with staves and implement, I see, and the makings of a forge? Your destination was Barbados?"

"Yes, to set up a small, temporary manufactory for barrels, and to discover other business prospects. I was then to continue to Charles Town, with the prospect of meeting with cotton merchants."

"I see. Not a bad plan, that. But I'm afraid you will be delayed. We are on our way to rendezvous near Cumberland Harbor. There are small facilities along the way, however, that will be able to make your repairs, but they are some days away. We will see you safely to one of them." His face turned even more serious.

"I'm told this is your first trip to the Indies," he said. "You probably know about the fever. It runs its course everywhere, even on this ship, I'm afraid. I wish I could tell you how to avoid it, but it seems the only avoidance is to have suffered it already." His face suddenly lightened "Do you, by chance, play whist? The fever has left me without a partner."

It is remarkable how many things happen because of something that may seem of little consequence. Due to my skill at whist, Captain Washington and I became almost inseparable, and found our personalities were quite complimentary. Being gregarious by nature and having been deprived of conversation for so long, I spoke to him of my life as I had seldom to another, over cards and the stale beer that served as our daily drink, and, on occasion rum with lemons, which I cared for but little.

Lawrence, as he eventually insisted I call him when not in the presence of his subordinates, turned out to be but three years my senior. He had been schooled in England, at Appleby. His mother died whilst he was away, and he returned to manage a portion of his father's plantation on the Potomack, until he had earned a commission by the Governor. Though it was clear our situations at birth had been very different, he was most interested in me and how I had made improvements at the warehouse, asking many questions about commerce. He was somewhat surprised to find I already had a wife and child.

"A good marriage, for you, Will!" he exclaimed when I told him about the Bracebridges. "A good marriage is most important. Oftimes, one plus one is equal to three or four, if families are chosen properly. I am associating myself with a fine family in Virginia, that of a cousin of a Lord, of Cameron. I feel his daughter will not be sad to see my return." He smiled wryly. "She is most young. Most. But, her father has seen to her education. We shall see."

"The thought must be quite comforting amidst this peril," I said, "though it is a bit odd to me to think of marriages as akin to commerce. And, if you saw the tumbled state of the ancient manor house, you may have counseled me to run! The staves in the hold of the *John V.* will go a way towards keeping the weather in its place next Christmastime! But the warmth and affection is beyond value. Chirrup! That is the reason to marry, Mr. Washington!"

He laughed. "Of course it is, Fezziwig! Don't misunderstand me. I view the Fairfax family in much the same manner as you do the Bracebridges. They are a jolly lot. My family is a bit more taciturn, I'm afraid. My father re-married to one also quite young, but well situated." His brow furrowed. "Not much mirth there, I'm afraid. Loss has been a companion to our family, as it has to so many. Tobacco is not as profitable as it once was, and it depletes the land remarkably. We have plans for our plantation on Little Hunting, with hopes to diversify our efforts and discover productive practices. Provided, of course," he said grimily, "I return at all!"

"Surely you will!" I assured. "You have already come

through great adversity."

"True" he admitted." "No thanks to the Spanish, and especially no thanks to the fever. You have seen how it has brought death to my Virginia boys. I feel my earlier arrival and exposure to the fever saved me from the fate so many of them have met. I fear only a fraction of them that came will have happy reunions with their loved ones. God grant that I am among them."

Fearing a black mood was overcoming my friend, I divulged to him the story of my money pouch, and Caddy's parting admonition, which brought great laughter and a lightened disposition. He continued. "I have greatly enjoyed your company, Will, but our time is coming to an end. Tomorrow, we shall deposit you, your ship, and its remaining crew in Nassau. We will stay two days for reprovisioning before continuing toward Cumberland. I have subordinates to see to the needs for my marine-soldiers; I will assist you in arrangements for your repair so you can be on your way. Your plan is still to travel on to Barbados, and then Charles Town?" I affirmed.

"I do wish your business were in tobacco, instead, Will. If so, I would persuade you to travel to the banks of the Potomack instead, and tarry with my family there during your stay. You would carry a letter of introduction from me, and be greeted with enthusiasm."

"My objective is more cotton than tobacco, I'm afraid," I replied, fully believing his offer to be sincere. "My employer believes advances in weaving will continue, making even more of it needed to feed the mills. He is a man who looks forward. But, when war is done and you are the most successful planter in the Colonies, I shall find reason to visit, hoping Fezziwig is a name you remember!"

"Do not worry. It shall not be forgotten," he said, gripping my hand.

Captain Washington was good as his word. In Nassau, he helped me locate an agent associated with the owners of the *John V.*, and an agent from the Lloyd's in Lombard Street, a coffeehouse I had visited on occasion with Mr. Whitlipped, in order to be introduced to the assurance trade. The Nassau agent, Mr. Phillips, had only been posted there for a year, and had met Whitlipped and some other men of commerce that I knew, and had even visited the Root and Wallow. It was a comforting thing, to speak to someone with mutual acquaintance, so far from home, and reminisce about places we both knew so well.

Nassau, my first landfall, was far from anything I had ever known. The lushness of the vegetation and the abundance of flowers cannot be described, nor could the oppressive heat and dampness. Most of the white occupants were English, but I also heard speech in languages I knew not.

The novel and disturbing thing, though, was the hoards of African slaves. They were everywhere; bodies glistening with sweat, and usually dressed only in filthy clothes about their middles. They swarmed the wharves and warehouses, some accomplishing hard labour tasks with the additional burden of shackles, often so tight they caused great wounds, with skin growing over the iron so that it became an immovable part of the leg. Many had backs so scarred from whippings so as to be unrecognizable as human skin.

I thought back to my youth, and knew no horse, ox, or swine in those days was ever treated so poorly by the holders as those African people were treated there, by their masters. I was not prepared for the effect my first exposure to human bondage would have on me. Having experienced shackles and captivity, I knew my own travails were nothing compared to the misery of these people, and I felt ashamed of my own times of self pity. While Spills and Company never traded in humans, I knew many men, both with whom I had business and at the coffeehouse, who made it part of their everyday commerce. I wondered if they knew what their contracts and agreements actually looked like, in practice?

While in Nassau, I lodged at a middling boarding house, in which I had a private bed. The proprietor, a Mr. Krupt, seemed of low character, but I had few other options given my resources. I was careful to carry everything of importance with me each day when going to watch the ship repair, as I had no trust that anything of value would not be stolen at the house. Meals often had indigenous fare which, I admit, was not to my liking. One evening, after I was served such a meal by a young African servant of around fifteen years, Krupt motioned me over to the doorway.

"Wot say, squire?" he asked. "Send 'er up to you tonight? Long way from 'ome, you know. Clean as a whistle, that, with spirit."

Instead of immediately rebuking him, I turned and looked at the girl. She was long-limbed and graceful. I was a young man who had been away from hearth and home for months. I hesitated. "No," I said, probably without enthusiasm, and pushed him. I am not proud of the closeness of my decision that evening.

The following day, I wrote a long and affectionate letter to Caddy, and, with some difficulty and expense, made arrangement for its passage to London. I was not confident it would ever reach her.

With the help of Mr. Phillips, the *John V.* was eventually

DANNY KUHN

made ready, and a new captain hired. Phillips gave me various packets, including letters of introduction, to deliver to his associates in Barbados. The new Captain, Joseph Matte, was a young man from Portsmouth in the place now known as New Hampshire; he was of French descent, but long in the past. He was quite a contrast from the unfortunate Captain Browning, being outgoing and gregarious. I was anxious to get on with my business, and be gone from the Krupt lodgings.

The passage to Barbados was uneventful, despite my nervousness upon seeing any approaching sail on the horizon. I took evening meals with Matte and the first mate, a survivor of the Spanish attack. With liberal portions of rum, Matte became even more talkative than at other times, though not disagreeable. As evenings wore on, he always turned to a certain topic, quite foreign to me.

"And why, good subject Fezziwig, do we have kings?" he asked one evening.

I thought for a moment. "I'm afraid that's a question without answer, Matte. It's in the vein of 'why is there a sea?' or 'why is the sky blue?' Because they simply are. It is the order of things. Without them, by what rules would we know to live, other than by God's alone?"

"Ah, so God's are insufficient, are they?"

"That's not what I meant!" I defended. "God's are supreme, and our leaders should follow them as well. But the passions of man sometimes run amok." At this, the mate gave a leering laugh. "That's when the King protects us from the greedy interests and intrigues of Parliament."

"Protects us!" exclaimed Matte. "Zounds, who protects us from the protector?" He slapped the rough table with an open

106

hand. "What was it that almost took your life but a squabble between protectors? War after war. Who might it be this year? Spain, France, Holland, take your pick. Are they not all but family squabbles amongst spoiled cousins?"

"Answer me this, Fezziwig," he said, as if the question would have great importance. "When your King George gasps and groans in the clutches of one of his mistresses or his cousin-wife, in what language does he sputter, do you think? English?"

When I had no answer to the question, having been quite taken aback by the crudeness of it, he slapped and table and exclaimed, "Not even his third choice! And I expect his girth prevents the need to ever beckon a third choice, indeed!"

"And you plead protection. What do they protect but their own interests, and those of the rich? Is not all they do to scratch one another's a---? But, in the end, who sweats and toils to support their incestuous salons?"

I had heard complaint about government, but never such outright treason. He continued.

"My first sailings, as a lad, were on a whaler. We followed the prey north in season, and encountered icebergs. You did not see them on your passage? No? They are mountains, mountains! Afloat, bluish-white and carved in wondrous shapes at the edge. But, the visible part, behemoth as it may be, is only a tithe of the whole. Nine parts lies underneath for each part seen. That's why they are so dangerous." He leaned back. "Remember that part, if nothing else, Fezziwig. It's the nine parts unseen that are dangerous."

His eyes narrowed, and his finger became a pointing stick. "The nine parts hold up the other. They toil in the freezing water, all to support the right of the tithe to sunlight and air. It's the way of nature, you say. But is it not the right of man to change the course of nature? Do we not build fires and ships and canals, and make clothes to cover our nakedness? Adam and Eve are out of the Garden, Fezziwig, and the nine parts desire air and sunshine!"

I had no ready response, so I said, "I wish you a good evening, Sir!" and rose to retire. "And a good evening to you, fine fellow!" Matte replied, sounding sincere.

That night, I struggled with Matte's argument and sleep was difficult. Had some radical in the warehouse presented such fiery claptrap, I would have dismissed him with haste. But, after having been so affected by the sight of the hundreds of bound humans in Nassau, my thinking had been shaken. When sleep finally came, it was fitful and filled with nightmares of our little ship, though in the hottest of climates, being inundated by a great, crumbling iceberg.

I avoided Matte the next day, until the evening meal. He seemed glad to see me. "Ah, Fezziwig! It is good you are here. I was afraid you might be writing letters to put afloat in bottles, pleading for His Majesty to send a ship to carry me to the gibbet. No public sport in simply tossing me overboard, you know!" He laughed, and spoke not of governing matters to me again. But, as you can see from reading this, it was a conversation that has stayed with me for all these years. And, Matte was not finished with me, for, on our last evening before reaching our destination, he said, "I shan't want my young friend to take his leave before his education is complete!" His brow furrowed and he leaned in close to me.

"So, tell me, Fezziwig," he said. "What proof have you of God?"

By mid-day, we were berthed in Barbados and slaves were

unloading our cargo into a warehouse. The heat was murderous, as the sea breezes were still, and the sky overcast, thus holding in the warmth and moisture. Matte bade me well, saying he regretted not being able to dine with me that evening, but that he had more pressing duties. The last was said with a sidewise grin that left little doubt as to his meaning.

The agent with whom Mr. Spills had made arrangements in Barbados was a Cornishman named Trees, a dark-haired man of philosophical nature, though I was still smarting from the dose of philosophy force-fed me by Captain Matte, like grain to a pate' goose. Trees said he had given up on the shipment, since it had been so delayed, and was interested in hearing each detail of the eventful trip. He referred me to suitable lodgings, of a slightly better ilk than those in Nassau, and helped arrange for a builder for the forge. I asked if it could be accomplished without the labour of slaves. He looked at me incredulously, and gave me a short "No."

Seeing the staves being unloaded made me think of Bracebridge and its forest and my family, bringing with it loneliness. I was a long, long way from the Lincolnshire hut where I was born, and from Mr. Whitlipped's subtle humour and wise counsel, and Caddy's warmth, and Ras's ready smile, all in London. Though Trees knew the name Spills and Company through correspondence, I was far away from anyone who had ever once laid eyes on any of my friends and family.

The Barbados port was busy, and the speech was predominately English. I delivered letters of introduction, both from Mr. Spills, and from Mr. Phillips. I had learned a great lesson, that a known name, or common experience, or some sort of intersection in one's path opens many doors, and are worth taking time to find when meeting someone new.

I am afraid, daughters, that, as an old man, I now give too much resource to this belief. I am guilty of pursuing such connexion as a good hound after a fox. If dining at a club, and a gentleman introduces himself as Mr. Thusandso, I make inquiry of him as if he were in the dock. "Ah, Thusandso! I once knew a John Thusandso, of Little Epping. But, I know there are Thusandsos also in the northwest, though I know not of any connexion between the two. Might you be of either family? Or shall I add another locale to my knowledge of Thusandsos?" By that time, I finally notice that my new acquaintance has made polite excuse to remove himself, and is eating oysters at a different table.

I was able to arrange the sale of the implements quite easily, and had good prospect for all buckets and barrels that would soon be produced by our craftsmen. My business took me into the interior, to the sugar plantation of Mr. John Downes. The production of sugar is as different from the type of agriculture I experienced as a child as a rock is from an apple.

By that time, the farming of cotton and tobacco had all but disappeared on the island, and smaller plantations had been merged into great ones. Cane grew higher than a man's head, and was cut and hauled by manpower, as the climate was conducive to neither horse nor ox. The mills were similarly man-powered, and I saw slaves struck with long leather whips when they slowed, the sharp *cracks* bringing bright red trickles on their backs. At the boiling pots, the smoke choked me and made me regurgitate.

I was anxious to finish my work and be off north, as I had gotten to know two most interesting men from the American Colonies, Captain Washington and Mr. Matte, and had heard that Charles Town was the city of greatest comfort and sophistication in the Colonies. My time in the heavy, wet heat of the Indies had also taken its toll on me, and I was ready to be quit of it.

My weariness of the heat increased, and I began to feel as if it pulled me down as heavily as the shackles I had recently experienced. I shared my distress with Trees, who looked deeply in my eyes and had me open my mouth, to peer into my throat. He asked me some questions about my daily constitution, and sighed.

"I'm afraid, Fezziwig, you have dodged the bane of the White man in the Indies as long as you can. By morning, you will be ill, as you have never experienced it. You have the fever."

Trees was correct. He made sure the landlord engaged a servant to care for me, a young female slave who, he was assured, was experienced in caring for sick Englishmen. A physician, Dr. Alexander Kincaid, a Scot from Edinburgh, also visited me daily.

I had heard many stories of the fever, and knew it could be a mild inconvenience for a few days, or it could quickly kill, or do anything in between. Lawrence Washington had confided to me that he fully expected for no more than a tithe of his Virginians to return to the colony, all taken by the fever. I had experienced fevers in the past, as most people have done, but it did not prepare me for the hell to come.

My body shook violently, as if it were in the hand of an angry giant. All my body, especially my back, was in such pain that I constantly whimpered. The contents of my stomach and intestines found the nearest points of exit unrestrained. A great roar took over my head, so loud I could hear nothing else. The servant kept me clean and dry, and tried to get me to drink, but the pain of retching kept me from doing so. Even in my state, I remember being embarrassed at my nakedness before her when she undressed and bathed me, though I was too weak to raise protest.

For the second time in my life, I seemed to know that death was imminent. It was so much bitterer than the first, lying bound in the snow after being robbed. When freezing, one becomes numb, and I even laughed with irony at the form of my demise. With the fever, there was no relief from numbness, rather, every inch of my surface became hypersensitive, a raging, boiling, molten, roil of pain. My eyes ached such that, had I the strength, I am sure I would have plucked the offending organs from my skull. There was no sleep, no relief, and no hope. I prayed to die.

The delirium set in, and I cannot separate what actually happened from my mind's projections, as my perception of both was equal. More than once, my father was in the room with me, shouting, "Do something, Will! Will!" over and over. The servant girl became Caddy, but instead of being gentle, she was angry and offered no comfort. Most heartbreaking was when the shade of my wife shouted in my face "Ras will die, Will!"

I remember it not, but I was later told Dr. Kincaid administered a tincture from the east, that was rare and of great cost, but brought sleep even to someone gripped by the delirium of fever. The difference between an amount sufficient for sleep, and one for death, was tiny, and varied with the person.

I awakened to being swabbed by the servant girl, and having great thirst. My tongue was stuck to my mouth, and my eyelids cemented with pus, so I could neither see nor speak. The girl must have understood my want, and put water to my lips. Since I could not lift my head, a quantity of it ran down my face, but enough entered to make me sputter. She said, "You will live, now."

It was several days before I would consider myself actually again alive, but I slowly gained strength and was able to drink without retching. Broth came next, then the same with bread soaked within it. Kincaid was pleased. "You have done a rare thing, Fezziwig," he said. "The luckiest among Christians here contract a very mild case of the fever, yet are protected from it in the future. Most who feel the full severity, as you have, die. But, you have survived, and I dare say you will not be bothered by it again."

I have always been stout by nature, but I had been reduced to skin and bone. Even after all the pain and fever dissipated, I remained so weak that I still required the help of the servant girl for my daily routines. My thirst continued for days, but Kincaid insisted I drink only beer, or fresh rainwater, or Madeira; I know not why.

During my illness, Trees had overseen the operation of the cooperage. We negotiated a commission for his services, which ended up being more generous than I had wished, but I was not in the strongest bargaining position. He could have chosen to wash his hands of the whole affair while I lay in delirium, so I was in his debt. The whole enterprise ended up being profitable enough for us both, fortunately, and I found a lucrative lease for the cooperage.

When my recovery was sufficient, I made arrangements for passage back to Nassau on the *Burcale*, where I would be able to find sail on to Charles Town. When it became known among the merchant class that I would be traveling there, I was given many packets and letters to deliver to various citizens, most with a promise of either some small remuneration, or a letter of referral that could be helpful to my business endeavors. I was surprised to find that Barbados and Charles Town were, in a manner, closely associated locations. Many of the old families with royal connexion in Barbados had members go on to Charles Town in the generation past, including the Gibbses and Moores, and several others.

Another who gave me a packet to deliver to Charles Town was Dr. Kincaid. "A colleague of mine is in that city, and he will be interested in this. I recorded the particulars of your course of fever. His name is Lionel Chalmers. He is from Argyllshire, but his father removed his family to Charles Town when Lionel was a bairn. He returned, though, to study medicine in Edinburgh, and that's where we became friends. You are a fortunate man in many ways, Fezziwig. Charles Town is surely no stranger to the fever itself, and now you are likely safe from it for life. Fever and its treatment are the particular interests of my friend Chalmers."

The *Burcale* was not a comfortable ship, but the passage was without event. My stay in Nassau was brief, and I purposely avoided the Krupt lodging house, though the one I found was no better.

From boyhood, I had dreamed of visiting the American colonies. My playmates as a lad made up stories of exotic India and Jamaica and Africa, but mine were of America, with its vast wilderness and plantations and Indians. News from America was plentiful in *The Guardian* and *The Gentleman's Magazine*, and the two Americans I had met, Captain Washington and Mr. Matte, had been interesting men. While their characters were quite different, there was something similar in them, which I couldn't quite identify.

I procured passage on the *King's Dog*, a small ship, but well fitted. I still found myself fearful when other sails were sighted, but I did not share my experiences with the Spanish with anyone else onboard, not wanting to bring bad luck. As we tracked northward, the temperature moderated, with autumn coming on, and the last few days of the journey were tolerable, save for the food and sourness of the beer. Knowing Charles Town to be the largest and richest city in that part of the world, I envisioned a smaller London, but cleaner, due to a much shorter human habitation.

We slipped past the island known as O'Sullivan's, into the finest natural harbor I had seen. Another passenger, a dealer in slaves, remarked that O'Sullivan's was his destination, as that was the location of the market dealing in humans. From a distance, I could see what appeared to be a fine church spire, and, indeed, it was of the church of St. Phillip, a landmark of that city.

What greeted me upon disembarking astonished me. Instead of a freshly washed small London, I viewed a flat, swampish land with putrid streams running through, stagnant pools, and plains of sticky grey ash with waste weeds growing up through it. A few years earlier, a great part of the city had burned, and rebuilding had not yet been fully accomplished. The sulphurous smell of decaying vegetation and stagnant filth-water was considerable, and burned the eyes.

By now, I had become accustomed to the sight of slaves doing all manner of labour, but I still found it repugnant. I found lodging in Mrs. Bedon's lodging house, which had been recommended to me by Trees. It was wholly sufficient. My bed was assured to remain private, and the food was much more familiar than that in the Indies. Oysters, crabs, and prawns were in great supply, and venison was common. A novelty to me was the abundant use of turtle-meat in meals, and another beer flavored with spruce-tips, the latter being almost my only drink, for the water was unpalatable unless mixed with rum.

I noticed that some of the finer private architecture in the area surviving the fire had a great similarity to that in Barbados, with tiled roofs, high ceilings, and large windows situated to catch the breeze.

The Spills and Company associate in Charles Town was a Mr. Thomas Gates. The fire had taken his place of accounting, but he was working out of rented rooms barely adequate for the task. His warehouses had been spared, though, so he was wholly engaged in commerce. Like Trees in Barbados, he had expected me much sooner, and listened with interest to the story of my delay.

"Bloody wars!" he spat. "The one thing a man of business needs is predictability. If we make a contract, it is based on a promise to fulfill it. Kings and armies are fed by our efficiency, then return the favor by holding us hostage to war, one after another, it seems! Well, that is our lot, I suppose. If Spaniards or the French or the Indians or whomever it happens to be this season do not bring us to an end, the fever is always there, willing to take up the task!" This last was said with wry laughter.

His mention of the fever reminded me. "Speaking of such," I asked, "Are you acquainted with a physician named Chalmers?"

"Chalmers? Lionel, a Scot?"

"The very one," I affirmed.

"Yes, I am indeed. Good fellow, in the opinion of most. Do you have need of him?" he asked, brow furrowing.

"Oh, no, thankfully not," I laughed. "I was treated for the fever by an associate of his in Barbados, and was given a packet for delivery. My illness and recovery is noteworthy among physicians, apparently."

"*Anyone's* recovery from fever is noteworthy, Fezziwig!" he said. "At least you are most likely protected from it, when it begins to rage again. But, don't feel slighted. There's always the small pox and cholera willing to make your acquaintance!" he laughed. "Oh, I had almost forgotten. I have had it for some time. A letter for you, from London."

After some searching, he produced an envelope, addressed WILLIAM LUCIAN FEZZIWIG, ESQ., in care of THOS. GATES, MERCHANT, CHARLES TOWN

"It could be further instruction from Mr. Spills!" I said, excitedly. The seal, though, was initialed "W."

The letter read:

Dear William,

I trust your travels have been safe and productive. Let me assure you that Caddy and Erasmus are well, the latter growing and exceedingly active. The business has continued unabated; though little grown, it remains as profitable as when you left.

The purpose of this letter is, I fear, a sad one. Two months past your departure, Mr. and Mrs. Spills had relocated to this city, in the vicinity of the warehouse. Spills quite fancied visiting the coffeehouses, enjoying comforts and entertainments not available to him in Great Grimsby, and Laverty's diligence with the business left the old man ample time to partake of them, as little supervision was needed.

One evening, on his way back to the Lea, Mr. Spills stopped at a public house for a libation and, upon leaving, was set upon. He had but little coinage on his person; his walking stick, watch, and cloak were also taken. He was found by someone who recognized him from the coffeehouse, and returned to Mrs. Spills, but his injuries were such that he ever again spoke. Within two days, he was no more.

We are greatly grieved by the loss of a good man, as we know you will also be. His estate will continue to operate Spills and Company in Great Grimsby; he had a competent apprentice there who will supervise the operations for the benefit of Mrs. Spills.

As to the Leaside warehouse and accounts, his will specifies his wish that it be sold to William Lucian Fezziwig for the price he initially paid for the property in its unimproved state; nothing more. He noted he had profited greatly already from your diligence, and any capital increase should be yours. I have taken the liberty to initiate the transfer, a small sum indeed, compared to its present value, from your personal account to the Spills estate. Mrs. Spills has decided to stay in London until your return, as she has become most attached to Caddy and Erasmus.

The will also specifies that you should have his watch, but, of course, it has not been recovered from the thief or thieves.

Finally, William, if it be your desire, I humbly offer you my services as solicitor for Fezziwig and Company.

Your Obliged and humbl Servant.,

M. Whitlipped, Prtnr., Whitlipped & Trembly

"Fezziwig...not bad news, I trust?" I do not know how long I had been staring at the letter before Mr. Gates's voice roused me from my thoughts.

"Yes, Mr. Gates, I'm afraid it is bad news. Bad news, indeed. Mr. Spills has died, in London."

"Oh. Oh. I see," said Gates, "I never met him, but our business dealings have always been on the level and square." I recognized the terms as Masonic, with which I knew Mr. Spills had involvement. "Ahh. Not to be indelicate, as I am sure you will spend a time mourning the loss of your employer, but where does that leave us in our contracts and negotiations for future intercourse?" he asked, seeming genuinely uncomfortable in asking the question.

"That leaves us, sir, proceeding along the present course, with Fezziwig and Company. It will be my pleasure to continue our association." It was the first time the name of the enterprise that still occupies me today, even in my old age, passed my lips.

That evening, I chose to take my meal alone in my room. I was briefly overcome by grief and, truth be known, fear. While Mr. Spills had granted me great independence in my operation of the Leaside enterprises, I knew his experience and advice were there to guide me, and, should I stray, he would have no hesitation in setting me back on course. He was the closest thing to a father that I had, since my own was taken from me so cruelly. Now, to whom could I turn? Whitlipped and my father-in-law, thank God, would still be my counsel.

I thought about the first day I viewed the tall old man on the Great Grimsby quay. I came to him having naught but clothes on my back, even those having been given me for perverted purpose. Where would I be if he had not called me out of the line of workers, and given me shelter that night?

Awaiting sleep, so very far from those I loved, I felt even more lonely than usual. Trying to conjecture what my station would be if not for the whim of the tall old smuggler from Great Grimsby, I vowed to be open to seeing small things in people that others did not see, little sparks of promise that I could help fan into flames that might do some good in the world.

The following day was spent better understanding my surroundings. While part of the city was still ashen and mucky, the part that had not burned had an overall elegance to it, very different from any section of London and but a village compared in size, but remarkable all the same. Delivering one of the packets I had received in Barbados, I found myself in Church Street, easily found by the spire of St. Phillips, which I had spied from the ship. Unable to find the person I sought, I asked a shabby passerby.

"Um, no, he will be found in Church Street; ask anyone. It shan't be hard."

"But," I stammered, "Sir, am I not in *Church Street* already?"

"Bloody Hell!" he swore. "He is in *Old* Church Street, d--- you! You are in *New* Church Street!" And so it went until I learned the city. It was not a simple task. Dock Street and Queen Street were, it seems, one and the same, as was the case with Cooper Street, and the more descriptive Broad. It was not difficult to remember that Bay Street, one of my common business destinations, was also the Front Street, due to its location.

I later learned the entire city had been moved at some time in the past, as it had originally been settled on the banks of the Ashley River, while it now faced the Cooper River. I am sure there was a reason, though I found the Ashley to be most pleasant and agreeable. The country was so low and sandy as to defy adequate description to an Englishman. No natural stone appeared in sight; that in the foundations and chimneys of buildings was brought from some other place. I was told that some of it came, like me, from England as ships' ballast.

Perhaps this lack of stone also led to one of the more curious aspects of the city, to someone arrived from London, that being the lack of cobbled streets. But, neither were they simply muck. They were made of sand and shells, carried in, and built up to a higher level than the base. During the frequent rains, and occasional higher than normal tide, the water seeped through, and they dried quickly. Slaves and drunkards from the gaol could be seen cleaning and renewing them. The overall effect was one of quiet passage, compared to the all-present clop-clop-clop of London's streets.

The church of St. Phillip was a fine brick structure, and so well attended as to be inadequate for all to be seated. There was also a church for dissenters, and a substantial powder magazine that had been built years earlier. Like all port cities, the front street had a smattering of bawdy taverns and ill-houses, and there was no shortage of low women to be seen there, and, even more notoriously, in an alley off the old Church Street belonging to Beresfords.

On my third day, I made acquaintance with one of my fellow lodgers, at the evening meal. When I heard him speak, he sounded much like my brief captor upon the *John V.* "Would your first language be Spanish, Sir?" I asked, making sure to sound friendly and curious, instead of threatening.

"No, Sir, Portuguese, but it is a common thing to think, as they are similar," he replied. Further conversation revealed him to be Mr. Joseph de Garza, who had begun his life in Portugal, but lived most of it in the colony of Georgia. He was also newly arrived in Charles Town, and attempting to begin business in small implements. I described my business, in case there be opportunity for cooperation. We continued our talk with a stroll. I remarked on the steeple of St. Philip as being a landmark to keep one's bearings, and asked if he had visited the church.

"Ah, Mr. Fezziwig, I am afraid I would not be welcomed."

That admission, along with his name and origin, made me lower my voice. "You are a Papist, then?" I asked.

He gave a short laugh. "No, Sir, I can assure you I am not a Papist. I am a Jew."

I felt quite embarrassed by my ignorance, and he noticed my discomfort.

"No alarm, Mr. Fezziwig. Our numbers are few here, and unexpected, perhaps. But, to the great credit of the town's people, Charles Town is a place we can live in peace, at least thus far, and I expect our numbers will greatly increase for just that reason."

"Much to their credit, indeed!" I said. I must admit that, in London, I had seen men identified as Jews only from a distance, and there was little contact between us, and that generally accomplished through third parties. In the years since, I have counted many of their number among my friends and business associates.

"So, many more of your brethren from Europe may arrive?"

"Oh, that is possible," he said. "But, sooner, many more from the colony to the south. My relatives have been there for years, many of them involved in the growing of grapes, and we have made good stead. But, of late, we are becoming less welcomed, and ordinances are being passed to restrict our involvement in trade and the civic life. Many of us have the feeling it is best to seek new opportunity, before things may get worse."

He sighed. "One of our strikes is that many of us are very much against an economy based on a foundation of slavery," he said, nodding toward a servant in the street, carrying a large basket on her head. "But we can't find a place to avoid that, it seems." Mr. de Garza became my usual dinner companion, and eventually did business with Fezziwig and Company.

Within a week of my arrival in Charles Town, a letter from Caddy arrived, addressed in care of Mr. Gates. It was a Godsend to my loneliness. Reading it showed she had not received the letter I posted from Nassau. She revealed her own grief at the death of her distant kinsman and our benefactor, Mr. Spills, and the affection she held for Mrs. Spills and Mr. Whitlipped, with their kind attention to her during my absence. She told of her tears, thinking of Mr. Spills lying in the street after being so cruelly treated. She had arranged with Mr. Whitlipped to engage a constable to find the brigands, but nothing had come of it. She closed with:

"Will, our son has become the brightest and most active child. He is in constant motion. He will not likely be a tall man, and is rather solidly built, and altogether in other ways resembling his father as well. Passersby remark on his handsomeness. We are very anxious for your return to us. Our loneliness will be especially acute at Christmastime, which will approach afore we are ready for it, as it always holds such special happiness and memories for us. Please return correspondence, and have faith that, until you are here, we hold you most affectionately in our hearts." I wrote her back and made arrangement for posting the letter the next day.

Mr. Gates turned out to be quite a jester, especially in his own opinion, but he was anxious to help me make trade connexions, mainly because he sold many of the implements of shipping, and acted as broker for several inland suppliers, thus ensuring profit for himself.

"You will find the arrangement of commerce a bit different here than in London," he told me. "You are used to men getting to the point. They will come to you and offer their proposal or list their needs within a moment of your first meeting. Not so here, no indeed. In Charles Town, you must first remark on how well someone looks, and then comment on the heat and dampness, as if either is ever likely to change. Next, you must inquire of the health and demeanor of family members, and wish to be favorably remembered to them."

"After all that," he went on, "you are to thank God you had the opportunity to see and talk with such a fine and respected gentleman, and bid peace and health until your next meeting."

"But, there was no business conducted!" I exclaimed.

"I am getting to that," he said. "As you are leaving, turn and say 'Oh! Oh! By your way! There is a thing I should like to ask, if you have one more moment! A trifle, really, a small matter of business, and it can wait if you are indisposed!' Then, Mr. Fezziwig, you may talk commerce in Charles Town!"

I felt Mr. Gates exaggerated, as people often do to newcomers for sport, but I found he was accurate. In fact, perhaps he underestimated the amount of small talk required before business could be discussed. Listening to him in his close, sweltering room with sweat streaming down my face, I concluded Charles Town was, indeed, at times a city of hot air.

When Gates introduced me to his associates, it was always as 'an accomplished young merchant from London.' Since he had brokered cotton for Spills and Company before and his terms were satisfactory, that part of my list of tasks was easily disposed. One day, he handed me a length of cotton cloth.

"What is this?" I asked.

"Feel it, Will," he replied.

I examined the swath carefully. It had the longest staple and finest nap of any cotton cloth I had ever felt. It was like silk, but more substantial. "This is remarkable!" I said. "It's the finest I've ever seen!"

"You did not encounter that in Barbados?" he asked, and when I shook my head, he said, "It is a specie of cotton that probably originated in Egypt. It is rare, and only thrives where the soil is sandy but rich; there is adequate rainfall, but enough sea breezes so that the leaves do not blacken from the dampness. It has been tried inland, but with poor result. There is hope, though, that the islands off our coast may be suitable for its cultivation. Together with some of my associates, we plan to import seed, buy plots on the sea islands, and attempt its cultivation. Just now, it's more or less a hobby. We want to see if it is suitable, in small plots with little investment, before risking much on it. Any endeavor on the islands is perilous. Storms, pirates, plagues…perilous indeed. But, should we someday be able to produce it, even in small amounts, do you think you would be able to find a market for so fine a cloth, in small quantities, at a cost that would make it profitable?"

I thought for a moment. "Mills in England are sprouting up like seed in the spring, and their output is gobbled up as fast as it's sewn," I said. "It appears that quantity may be more important than quality at present. But, when I return, I will make inquiries and let you know if there is promise. May I take this with me?" I could almost hear my mentor, Mr. Spills, saying "Think not only of today. It's already crowded with competitors. Dwell in tomorrow, where you will find much more room for your elbows!"

"That's why I gave it to you, Fezziwig. Frightful heat and

dampness we are having, wouldn't you say?" He grinned, for the day was quite moderate. Gates considered himself a man of humour; I'm not sure the thought was widely held, but he had become a friend and was very considerate of me, though I was fully aware his aim was to profit from our relationship.

"I have made arrangements for you to visit inland, and see the Indians, as you requested. There should be no danger now; it has been more than twenty years since they were subdued. But you will travel with Mr. Summers, my agent who deals with the tribe. We broker their venison and skins. The market for the latter was quite smart in the past, but is dissipating, for the demand for buckskin pantaloons is no more. Funny thing, style. It changes on a whim, and the consequences can be felt around the world. Venison is still much enjoyed here in Charles Town, though."

He went on. "Along the way, you will stop at a plantation on Wappoo Creek, part of the holdings of Colonel Lucas. His Majesty has seen fit to return the Colonel to Antigua, so his spinster daughter, Eliza, oversees the plantation. She does quite well, really. She was educated in London, and studied botany and agriculture, with a good result. Quite a head for that sort of thing, for the fairer sex, of course. She has sent word that she would like to meet any new merchants visiting, and Wappoo is along the way to the Indian settlement."

"Just so you will not be surprised, though, Fezziwig, be aware that your overnight at Wappoo will not be a lark. Miss Lucas is known as a hard old woman when it comes to commerce, and even harder to gaze upon. We all have talents; being fair to the eyes and personable are just not the ones she possesses."

I assured Mr. Gates that I was up to the task of dealing with a hard woman, and looks were of no interest to me if there were productive arrangements to be made. The next morning found me on a borrowed horse, leaving Charles Town over a path that could barely be called a road, with Mr. Simpson Summers. He was a native Colonial, dressed in buckskin, and had a perpetual brown stain of tobacco at the corner of his mouth. He answered all my questions fully, but said little else.

By then, the season made the moderate temperature and dampness perfect for our task. Along any edge in that country grew odd palm trees, much different than those in the West Indies, shorter and stouter, with pointed remnants of previous leaf-fronds along the trunks. The further from the city we found ourselves, the denser the pine forest. Anywhere not shaded out by their thickness (the pines in that country having exceedingly long needles) was covered with undergrowth so luxuriant, even after many plants had lost their leaves, that passage would be impossible. I pointed to one such place without tall pines and asked Summers why it had not been cultivated.

"If you were to walk into it, you would find out quickly," he said. "You would be sucked up and never again seen. What appears to be dry land is really swamp. It can be cultivated, but only with great ditches being dug to drain it. That's how our rice plantations are built, on just such swamp, and along the rivers, which are slow and still affected by tides."

"I can't imagine ditching and cultivating such land!" I exclaimed. "What work that must be!"

"Aye," said Summers. "It was first done by Indians, but, even though this was their land, they died when put to the labour. One day, work would be at full force; the next, they were all dead of small pox or some other plague. It became more profitable to sell them off to foreign markets, and import

Africans instead. I suppose there are great numbers of Indian slaves on the Continent. I hear they were novelties and well liked by the Dutch. There was some attempt to use indentured men from England for the tasks, giving them promise of land at the end of their terms, but their terms always ended early." I got his meaning. Even at home, I had heard that an indenture to the plantations in Carolina was a death sentence for Englishmen, owing to the fever.

Summers went on. "The Africans do much better. They are not decimated by fever, I suppose because it is present in their own land. Many die, still, but not in numbers that keep the work from being accomplished." Being satisfied that my question was answered, he again went silent.

I, too, fell silent. Though enjoying a pleasant ride, with clear sunlight but free from heat and mosquitoes, the images from Summers' matter-of-fact explanations disturbed me greatly. I suspected there would have been more remorse and pathos in his voice had he been describing a plague of foot-and-mouth that had denuded the land of livestock. Did not the Romans once descend upon England and enslave our own ancestors? And was it not done again by the Vikings? Yet, we have no hesitation in enslaving anyone we encounter, and bartering them like so many bushels, and viewing their decimation as only a setback to commerce. Spills chose to never deal in human flesh, and I would certainly never do so, but was not almost everything I traded still dependent on slave labour at its root?

By evening, we came to the Wappo plantation. The house was substantial, the centre-part being made of brick, with chimneys on either end, and timber additions. We were met by a liveried slave, who took our horses and directed us to enter the hall, where a similarly dressed young slave met us.

"The Madame wishes me to direct you to rooms, where you may refresh yourselves. She is disposed, but will join you for dinner." I was amazed at his short speech. No finer diction could be had at any coffeehouse in London, but it had a musical lilt that I never again heard after leaving Carolina.

The fixtures in the house were English, and sparse. The plaster was not finely done in places, and a pane-hole was covered with parchment in my chamber window, awaiting replacement, but the surroundings were comfortable. I found that I needed refreshment and a basin more than I thought, but I was quite ready when the young servant summoned me to dinner. Darkness had fallen, but candles were abundant. I was ready to meet my hard, unattractive old spinster hostess.

I descended into the dining room, and was met by radiant beauty. That Gates! I'm sure he later had great sport in telling how he had misled me.

Eliza Lucas was about my age, if not just a bit younger, tall and slender, with clear complexion, and large brown eyes. She wore a pale green gown, tight about an ample bosom. She curtsied.

"I am pleased to make your acquaintance, Mr. Fezziwig. Thank you for your visit. I am always interested in speaking of commerce with merchants such as yourself." She gave a delightful smile when I found myself unable to immediately reply. Her attention was diverted when Mr. Summers entered the room, and she greeted him and offered that we all sit for the meal. There was venison, rice, long potatoes, and baked pumpkin custard. Summers said little during the meal, after Miss Lucas asked about Mr. Gates and his family.

"Mr. Fezziwig, do please tell me of London!" she said. "I was schooled there, but have not found the time to return. Since my father was called back to Antigua, duties here have kept me from all else, I'm afraid."

As Madeira was served, I found my tongue and began to recreate the great city for my eager listener, telling her of the construction of the new bridge that had benefited our business, and of the masses streaming into the city from *containment*, and the scourge that gin had become.

"And what of *you*, Mr. Fezziwig," she eventually asked. "What is your story?" I was taken aback by the question, but it was offered with such sweetness that I could not refuse. I told her of my origins, but not, of course, of the uncouth circumstances that brought me away from my first home and to London. I described my travels before arriving in Charles Town, and I mentioned my association with the Bracebridges, and Caddy and Erasmus. At the latter, I must admit I looked away, as to not see her face in the candlelight.

"Mr. Gates was right. You are quite accomplished indeed, Mr. Fezziwig! It seems fate has thrown us both into great responsibility at young ages." She laughed, and the sound was like music.

"I have something to show you!" she said, and went to a sideboard. She retrieved a small box, which she handed me. I opened it and found it full of dried vegetation. "Do you know what it is?" she asked. I admitted that I did not.

"It is indigo. You did not encounter it in the Indies? With the mills producing more cloth, the demand for dye is great. In the Indies, it must compete for space with sugar, and usually loses the battle. I think it can become greatly profitable here, if only we learn its proper culture."

I could hear genuine excitement in her voice. "My father

sent seed from the Indies. I have been cultivating it, and only planting the most productive the next year. It failed to thrive, until I purchased a slave familiar with its culture in Africa. There was a great increase in the year past, and I hope next year there will be sufficient quantity to export!" She tilted her head such that the candles reflected in her eyes.

"Do you think there may be a profitable need for this, in England, among your business associates, Will? Ah, Mr. Fezziwig?"

"I am quite certain of it!" I said, with perhaps more enthusiasm than was warranted. She smiled. "Good. We shall, then, stay in communication on the matter. Now, tell me, do you dance?"

"Hilli-ho, indeed, Madame, dancing and whist are my favorite pastimes." I said.

"Oh, good! Then you must know the latest steps. We are so separated from England here that they are quite out-of-date before we even know of them. Have you much opportunity?"

"Some little, thanks to Mr. Gates, among his business acquaintances. There have been a few dinners after which the chairs were cleared and the fiddle sang."

"Well," she said, with breath. "It is unfortunate we have none this evening, but promise me you will show me at the next opportunity."

I promised, and the evening came to an end. After breakfast the next morning, our hostess saw Summers and me on our way. We both thanked her for her kindness.

"It was only commerce, Mr. Fezziwig. Do not forget your contract to repay me, with a dance!"

Summers was even quieter than the day before, and I wondered if he had observations about the evening that he chose not to share.

The smell of smoke told us we were approaching the Indian settlement. Two of the natives, mostly naked despite the cooling weather, stood in the path and nodded to Summers as we came into their view. Without words, we followed them. They were the first of their kind I had seen.

The habitations were of timber and hides, and there were many small cooking fires. Naked children ran about, and many of the women were exposed at the top, causing me to avert my eyes. Summers was apparently well known by the men of the settlement. A young man took us into one of the dwellings and we sat upon a deerskin, on the ground. We were each given an earthen bowl of cooked, pounded maize, of which, following Summers's lead, I ate with my fingers. An older Indian entered, and began to speak with Summers in the native language, which I understood not.

Eventually, Summers turned to me. "The maize crop was good this year, as was the mast, and they should be able to continue to be abundant with venison for the Charles Town tables. The signs tell them of a cold winter, though, as the hornets have built high, and the autumn skins are thick. They are disappointed that the price for skins has fallen, with fewer being needed for pantaloons."

"They predict the weather by the hornets, and the skins?" I asked, never having heard of such a thing.

"Yes, both, and there are other ways as well." The Indian must have understood some of our conversation, because he rose and left, but returned in a moment with a deer hide, which he handed to me. The native rubbed it between his fingers as he did so. "See. Thick," he said.

I also rubbed the skin between my fingers. The skin was, indeed, thick, but fine-grained and flexible. Like being struck with a cudgel, in my mind I was transported back to the coffeehouse in London, with a crooked finger pointed in my face, and sneering words of Mr. Bracken. "Tough but supple, Fezziwig. Tough but supple!"

"Mr. Summers," I said, softly. "Let us negotiate the meanest price for this season's deerskins, on behalf of Fezziwig and Company. I have something in mind other than pantaloons."

Upon my return to Charles Town, Mr. Gates could hardly wait to hear of my experiences. 'So, how did you find the old spinster of Wappoo?" he asked, unable to hide his mirth. I chose not to acknowledge his prank, fearing it would only spawn more like it.

"She was an adequate hostess. Quite keen on the idea of growing indigo, it seems." I replied.

"Miss Lucas is *quite keen,* indeed!" Gates roared with laughter, very satisfied with himself. "As far as her experiments with indigo, I will wait for the proof in the pudding," he said. "You know I am not adverse to experimentation, such as with cotton, but indigo has been tried before, and proved too difficult to cultivate in sufficient quantities to develop a reliable market. But, I wish her good with it. The whole endeavor is quite remarkable. She has run her father's plantations very successfully; not only the one you saw, but also a larger one north, rice, on the Waccamaw. "

"The woman is rather looked down upon by some, you know," he went on. "The Meddlers Club is scathing of her, saying she debases her sex by barging into the business of men.

There are rumors that, instead of using the refinement from having been schooled in London to her advantage as a lady, she prefers the manners and, uh, *proclivities* of the Indies, where she grew up."

"But, who knows, Fezziwig? If her indigo scheme is successful, it may help the *poor old spinster* to finally attract a mate!" He roared with laughter once again, but saw I failed to join his humour.

It was my plan to finish my business in America in the spring, after contracts had been made for the future planting. I cultivated my agents and contracts as carefully as Miss Lucas did her indigo, because I desired to make them all so durable that another crossing would never be needed.

Correspondence from Whitlipped revealed that the cooperage in Barbados, now on its third cargo of Bracebridge staves, was turning a small profit, and the warehouse continued to operate at a busy and efficient pace, but not one that required any capital expansion. My letters to and from Caddy became more reliably delivered and received, and they were salve to my loneliness.

As winter approached and there were fewer agricultural interests to keep people industrious, the city became more social. Some of the finer homes were not occupied by their owners at all through the hot, damp summer, but only during the winter, when owners could afford to be absent from their inland plantations and live a life less isolated. I found myself being known about the town, though I missed the fellowship offered by coffeehouses of London. They had no direct counterpart in Charles Town. I found some pleasure in making drawings of the stranger plants I had encountered, and playing whist with Mr. de Garza when we could find others so inclined.

I showed my drawings to Mr. Gates one day, only because I was quite pleased with them. He admitted they were good, though he had little interest in anything that grew without sowing a profit potential.

"If this is a pursuit of yours, it is a pity you have not visited the coast a little to the north." he said. "I have seen specimens from near the mouth of Cape Fear, brought and shown as a curiosity, that I am sure would be included in your drawings. A small plant, but with a stem that looks for all the world like an open mouth, crimson inside, with projections like eye-lashes around the rim that interlock. This mouth lies normally open, but, if a fly lands upon it, snaps shut like the maul of a lion, and the fly is thus eaten."

I told Mr. Gates that I had read the fables of Aesop long ago, and his cry of "Wolf!" no longer moved me to action. He appeared to begin to protest, but then let the matter of the fly-eating plant drop, seeing that convincing me of the existence of such a thing was unlikely.

In mid December, I was invited to dinner at the home of Dr. Lionel Chalmers, the Scottish physician to whom I had delivered the packet from Dr. Kincaid of Barbados soon after my arrival. Dr. Chalmers had taken to calling me Lazarus, a name suggested by Dr. Kincaid's report, because I had practically been raised from the dead. His home was modest, as he was one of those physicians who seemed more interested in healing than in profit. There was a small group assembled before dinner, most of whom I knew, and the conversation was merry.

I was talking with my host when I heard from behind me, "Mister Fezziwig! It is a pleasure to see you still in Charles Town!" I knew the music of the voice immediately, and turned to see Eliza Lucas in a pale blue gown. I bowed.

"The pleasure is mine, Miss Lucas. Please pardon my neglect in not having written you a note thanking you for your past hospitality."

"Oh, none needed, William," she laughed. "You thanked me quite sufficiently. And, I hope, the English dyeing industry will some day thank us both, with considerable profit!"

Fate seated Miss Lucas and me beside one another, and the company and oysters and Madeira provided for a pleasant evening. Other guests knew of the indigo scheme, and two were going to plant a quantity of Miss Lucas's seeds that spring. She offered to send her African 'indigo master' to advise during the planting, when he could be spared from Wappoo.

After dinner, the furniture was cleared away, and one of the guests produced a fiddle. "Finally, William, an opportunity to repay my kindness with a dance!" She smiled.

We danced, wine and warmth and politeness leaving no choice. It is said my love of dancing cannot be missed; it takes hold of me and turns me into a Dervish, and I'll not deny it. We danced until it was time to thank Dr. Chalmers and leave.

"Where will you spend Christmas, Will?" Miss Lucas asked as the servant brought her wrap. I had assumed I would be invited to take Christmas with Mr. Gates and his family, but no invitation had come. Otherwise, it would be spent alone at the lodging house.

"I am not yet sure," I said, hoping to hide the uncertainty from my voice. "Mr. Gates will, I'm certain, have something arranged for me."

"But you have not yet accepted an invitation? Oh, good! You must take the dinner with us at our town home. I'll take no excuse! You must never turn down a lady after a dance!" The last was said with an impish smile.

When I went back outside into the cool night air, with the damp sand of the street scuffling under my shoes, I felt both exhilarated and guilty. It had been the most peasant evening I had spent since leaving London, by far. I had done nothing more than have dinner and dancing with casual acquaintances. Then what was the source of my guilt?

I tried to put the matter out of my mind over the next fortnight, until Christmas. I attended services at St. Phillip's with regularity, and even enjoyed a play staged in a warehouse. The city had its own separate playhouse, but it had not survived the fire a few years earlier, so plays were put on at intervals with a mix of traveling actors and citizens in smaller parts. I remember the play to be a farce, called *All Without Money*, and I laughed at it greatly.

Eventually, a halfhearted Christmas dinner invitation did come from Mr. Gates. "Ah, yes, Will, if you have nowhere else. It may be a bit crowded, family visiting, you know, but we will make room. Not Christian to be alone on Christmas, they say! Though you are so often seen strolling with de Garza that the Meddlers may think you have no need of Christmas pudding. Ha!"

I had almost hoped for such a vigorous invitation that it could not be turned down, allowing me to give honest excuse to Eliza. Mr. Gates's limp offering did not provide it. I struggled for just a moment, and thanked Gates for his kindness, but said I had already accepted another. He seemed relieved.

During the crowded Christmas Eve service, an intense conversation, back and forth, issued in my own head. It was just a kind invitation to Christmas dinner from a business acquaintance, nothing more! But, then, why did I feel contriteness about it all? Surely, Caddy would not want me to take Christmas dinner alone in my lodging-room, and I hoped she was preparing for a happy feast with Mrs. Spills and Mr. Whitlipped and others.

But, thinking of Christmas dinner with my friends and family was probably a mistake. Loneliness overcame me, and, in the dim candlelight of the church, tears streamed down my face, and I stifled a sob, to save others around me from thinking I might be a dissenter overcome with the spiritual emotion for which they are notorious.

Christmas Day was bright and cold. Breakfast was more festive than usual at the lodging house, with tankards of warm cider. I wrote a letter to Caddy, wishing her and Ras and all a Merry Christmas, and determined to find the fastest and most reliable posting for it the following day, no matter the price. That evening, I donned my best suit and made my way to the townhouse of Miss Eliza Lucas.

The Lucas town house was fine, though not one of the most imposing in the city. Like most of the homes, each door and window was hung with a green wreath for the season. I hesitated for a moment before entering, and struggled with a debate in my own mind.

On the one hand, I was a young man of business in a foreign city, with the mission to make contact with the merchants and commodity sources of that land. I had worked very hard to bring success to my employer, and now had only myself on which to rely if I intended to prosper further. Caddy and Ras depended on me, as well as Laverty and all the other workers at Fezziwig and Company. It was Christmas! It would be bad business to sit alone in my room, and I had risked my life more than once for the sake of this enterprise. And, surely, no one could begrudge me a bit of fellowship and a pudding, so far from home.

For each hand, there is another. I was attracted to Eliza Lucas. I had thoughts of her as I lay in my bed the previous night, and the thoughts inflamed passions that had not been so engaged by thoughts of anyone but Caddy since my first Christmas at Bracebridge.

Did the Gospels really mean that a thought was just as sinful as a deed? But, is a young man even as able to control one, as the other? Nature, itself, dictates certain responses even when the mind resists.

I went in, was greeted by the same liveried servant I had met at Wappoo, and was led into the hall. The hostess wore a festive red gown, of a type similar to what had been in fashion in London a couple of years prior.

"William! Merry Christmas!" she exclaimed, and laid her hand upon my arm. "It is so good to see you! Come, and I will introduce you to the others. I'm sure you will know most of them, if only by their good names!"

I did, indeed, know many of the other guests. Dr. Chalmers was there, as was Mr. Eddings, who dealt in tar and pitch and other such stores, and Mr. Teasdale, an associate of the wealthy Mr. Manigualt, who was not present. All the men were escorted by ladies, wives or others, except one, Mr. Charles Pinckney, an eminent planter, who had, in recent past, been the Speaker of the Assembly. When Eliza introduced me to him, she said, "Will, I am afraid this Christmastime is touched with great sadness for my dear friend and neighbor, Mr. Pinckney. It will be his first since the passing of his wife, of the fever, in the late spring."

I bowed deeply to the sad faced gentleman, who was about

twenty years older than me. "I extend to you my very deepest sympathy, my dear Sir," I said, sincerely.

"Thank you, Mr. Fezziwig." He returned a short bow. "It is but for God to made large decisions, whilst we men quibble over laws and the price of rice, isn't it so? But, to help us through seasons of loss, he gives us faith, and friends. Like," he turned to Eliza, "Mr. Lucas, spending Christmas far from us in Antigua, and his very able daughter, to whom I am most appreciative."

Eliza took him by the arm. "Charles, you know you will always be with family as long as there is a Lucas in the colony!" she said. "Father would never have been confident in leaving me to tend the plantation had he not known I would depend on your kind guidance."

While the dinner and atmosphere were less regal than the one at Bracebridge, so firm in my memory, it was splendid by the standard of the colony. There was ham, which I saw less often there than venison, and turkey, which I had not seen in America until that night, though they were supposedly wild in abundance in some areas. The Wassail was made with rum and tea and lemons. After the pudding (not quite the same in America, though I am at a loss to explain how it differed), Dr. Chalmers and I were partners at whist, and ruled the evening, defeating the hostess and Mr. Pinckney. The Scot was elated, but I was repentant for the outcome.

"So, now he wants to show mercy!" laughed Eliza to Mr. Pinckney. "I am afraid, Charles, that we will find Mr. Fezziwig just as aggressive a dancer as he is a card player!"

Soon, the furniture was pushed back, and a fiddler appeared. Another, older servant joined him, with an instrument with which I was not familiar. It had strings, and a long neck,

"Ah, you have not heard the banjie? It is common in Antigua, among the Africans, and I have always loved it. It is a happy sound, you will see!"

It was happy indeed, and the spirit of Christmas and the warmth and Wassail and the exertion of the dance all beckoned, and I was a willing recruit. Far too quickly, guests began to bow to the hostess in thanks, giving their final wishes for Christmas Day, and take their leave.

Mr. Pinckney offered passage in his coach to my lodgings, "As soon as I can have the thing summoned! My driver is likely to be found with a full season of Christmas cheer, I'll wager!" I declined his kind offer, and bid him goodnight whilst he waited. I took Eliza's hand, kissed it, and thanked her for the kindness shown a vagabond so far from home.

After the servant brought my coat and I was about to exit, I heard Eliza's voice behind me.

"Will," she said, with a glance back to see that we were unobserved. "Did it seem strange to you that the house is decorated, but there is an absence of mistletoe?" she asked.

"Ho!" I replied. "I had noticed not, but, now that you bring it to my attention, it does seem odd. Surely there is no shortage; I have never seen a place more infested with it!" I said softly, staring into her eyes.

"It is because it would be wrong for a young, unattached lady to invite temptation," she breathed, and closed her eyes.

I intended a gentle kiss, a friendly kiss, but it was not to be. We clutched each other, our hands moved. Her lithe figure pressed against me was so different from Caddy's rounder, more solid form.

"But, I *am* attached," I mumbled.

"That I know. You have not hidden it," she said, with her lips brushing my ear. "But the ocean is wide, and you are here." Her voice became more resolute. "In the Indies, life is more honest. Here in Charles Town, people are no more faithful, but only pretend to be, and are self-righteous about it until they are behind closed doors. Whose transgressions are greater, then? I am what I am in this place and at this time, Will, and so are you!"

I looked again into her eyes. "I wish you the very best, Eliza. Thank you again for a lovely Christmas dinner." I smiled and walked out into the chill evening.

The season leading to Epiphany and the Twelfth Night did not seem to be as much ado in the colony as in England. I spent it dining and drinking Madeira with de Garza, and, I must admit, relished telling the story of a previous Twelfth Night, which was much funnier recounting than it had been living it.

Over the next two months, I continued to become a part of the circle of commerce in the city, and found that most deals were made at this time, while the planters were in their town houses for the winter. Many would make only tentative contracts until spring, though, until they returned to their plantations and saw what the variable spring weather would be like, and made decisions affecting the distribution of plantings. Had it not been for this necessity, I would have returned to England earlier.

A curious thing happened that February. I called a house servant one day, and he entered my chamber to ask how he could be of service. I pointed to a letter on my desk, addressed to Mr. Whitlipped, and told him to take it to Mr. Gates for posting. He looked at the letter and remarked "Strange name, Whitlipped."

When he realised he had been overheard and saw my surprise, he entreated me, "I am so sorry, Sir! Please, please, I beg forgiveness! It just looked strange to me, little figures, but they mean nothing!"

I was perplexed by his agitation. "What does it matter?" I asked. "Whitlipped is, indeed, a strange name. I was just a bit surprised that you could read it."

"Please, Sir, tell no one!" he pled. "It could be a hard thing for me, and for someone who only wanted to show me kindness so I could read the Scriptures." He sounded desperate. With my silence, he added, "Don't you know, Sir? There are laws against us reading, and teaching us to do so." I assured him that his secret was safe, and he went on his way, still shaken.

I was true to my word, but inquired of Gates a few days later. "There are restrictions on the education of servants?" I asked.

"Of course," he replied. "The Negro Act has been in effect for a couple of years now, and it's very clear. The penalties are strong. There's only rudimentary education necessary for their physical duties, limited number of Negros that can be assembled at once, even for good purpose, and they can only move from place to place with permission and scrutiny."

When he saw my surprise, he winked, and said, "I hope I have not ruined all your future prospects, Will. I would not have guessed it. You came to Charles Town to set up a Negro university to rival that at Oxford, did you not? You should have told me this before today!" With this, he laughed loudly.

"I fail to see the humour," I said. "All those restrictions can even lessen the utility of the servants to their owners, can they not?"

Mr. Gates changed abruptly, and an uncharacteristic glare came to his eyes. "You were not here to experience what we endured," he snapped. "You see things as they are today, but just four years ago our very existence was threatened. It only took one Negro to flame an insurrection that left more than five score of our friends and family dead, butchered most heinously. No one slept for weeks. Grown men were afraid to go out of their homes, even to tend their plantations in late summer. Why, children are still having terrors in their sleep, and I'm not immune from them myself, I'll admit."

He went on, becoming ever more agitated. "That *Cato* was educated, and thus able to rally his brethren to him. He had all the Devil's work in him, all right, because he was a *Catholic* as well. Some say the Spanish had put him up to it, somehow. The whole affair tore the fabric of our colony. Without the most basic safety, how can we provide a reliable source for you and other London merchants? How many victims would it take before the King and Parliament think that we are unable to administer our own affairs to the extent that we do? "

By now, Mr. Gates finally seemed weary of his tirade. "We are a tolerant people. We welcome dissenters. We even welcome Jews...your friend is beginning to do well for himself, I hear. It might be treasonous to utter it, but I dare say we would even welcome Papists, if it weren't for their being thought infiltrators for the Spanish, or French. But, there has to be some order to things, and cowering in our bed chambers afraid of what the slaves will do to us and our children, by God, to our *women*, if you think of it, by a few merry-makers being too familiar and lax with their property, well, William, I should think you see the folly in it, Sir!"

I had seen Mr. Gates's temper flair on several occasions, and I knew he could be sometimes cruel with his pranks. I had never seen him as animated as on this topic, and I did not raise it with him again.

Spring time and planting comes early in Carolina, and with great beauty in blooms and temperate days. My interactions had brought me into contact with Miss Lucas a number of times since Christmas, but never alone. Each time, she put her hand on my arm and chatted pleasantly, as if I had entered the street on Christmas night without having seen her in the hallway at all.

Our last meeting in America came at the dinner Dr. Chalmers hosted in the spring, as a farewell for me before I began my passage back to England. Mr. Gates and Mr. de Garza were there, as well as the taciturn Mr. Summers, and several others I had met during my stay. The dinner was at The Lion, a tavern in the Bay Street. Eliza was as cheerful and beautiful as ever, and full of anticipation of that spring's planting of indigo.

"Indigo will someday fill the warehouses of Fezziwig and Company, Will, I assure it!" she said, with a lovely smile.

"My lady, I am afraid Fezziwig and Company is only in possession of a single warehouse," I laughed.

"At present," she said. "You may soon have a need of builders!"

That last evening in Charles Town, I was proud of my accomplishments, and was confident they would do well for my future, and that of Caddy and Ras. My thanks to all assembled were sincere, and I collected many packages and envelopes for delivery to London. The following morning, I boarded the *Anemone*, which held, among other things, a large quantity of deer hides for the bookbinderies along the Thames.

Having spent more than a year as a trade agent in the
Colony of South Carolina amongst the natives and cotton
merchants, I had my fill of adventure and hoped for strong winds
and no enemy sails on the horizon as I returned home to London.
Boredom, wormy food, and sour beer were the worst of it,
though there were two events that remain in my memory. One
left a more pleasant implant than the other. The one, filled with
pathos, involved a prisoner being carried in the hold of the
Anemone, to face justice in London. I cannot say with certainty
his crime, for I heard several different versions of it. He was
consumptive, and, being chained to a timber in the hold (Not
conducive to health, I could say from experience), it
overwhelmed his body, and he died.

I had heard of burial at sea, and envisioned a body, wrapped
in black wool and chains for weight, being placed on a board
and, after a few words to Providence were spoken, tipped to slip
into the sea for eternal rest. What I saw, while taking air on the
deck, was a filthy, emaciated body being dragged by two sailors,
one on each arm, hauled up through the hatch like a hogshead.
When they reached the gunwale, they grabbed the body by
shoulders and knees, and heaved it over on a count of three. It
made a splash in the wake, and was no more. I was keenly
aware that the scene could have been my fate a year earlier, had
it not been for the intervention of Providence, and perhaps
Virginian marine-soldiers on one of the King's ships.

The other, fonder, memory is of a fellow traveler, a seaman
of middle age who had been in the Colonies exploring
commerce. His name was Mr. Greenshaw, and he had been
involved in sailing out of Kingston-upon-Hull in the past, but
was now retired from that vocation due to his age. We took our
meals together, and, with rum at the ready, he told of his travels
to almost every sea in God's creation. One evening, after our
relationship became more familiar, he told a remarkable story,

which, though the years have rounded over the edges of my memory as a stream does a pebble, I attempt to recount here:

"In the eastern sea, I found myself the only Christian on a small island. I will not go into the circumstances that brought me to that isolation, other than that I was wrongly accused and left without resources. I greatly feared that the natives of the land, being Hindoos, would have no use for me and I would quickly meet my end, but I knew a bit of their language and was able to strike a deal to work like a common servant for my sustenance.

After two seasons, I knew I had no chance of rescue if I stayed, the location having nothing to bring civilized visitors to it. I worked and ate, and was not cruelly treated, but my life held nothing more, and I was willing to die in an endeavor to escape, rather than to grow old and do so as a servant to others.

My master, if called such under the circumstances, had a type of boat called a 'dhow' in that part of the world. It was small and low, but had a short below decks, sufficient for rising while stooped over. He was about to send three of his other servants on a voyage to a nearby place, and it was provisioned for departure the next morning. My duties to him never took me from the settlement, for fear I would be gone.

My stealth aided by a new moon, I left my mean hut in the midst of the night, and untied the dhow, quietly pushing it out and pulling myself onboard. I was pleased that, since Providence had allowed me to slip out unseen, I reasoned, He may also lead me to Christendom, despite having no map or other means of navigation.

When just away from the wharf, I heard a noise from below.

It was only then that I realised that another servant had been put into place to guard the boat, was asleep, but was now being aroused by the change in motion. I listened for conversation, fearing that there may be more than one man in place, but there was none. I looked about for a weapon in the dark, but in the little time I had, found none suitable, so I had but a second to use my wits instead. I positioned myself at the opening of the below deck and, when a form emerged, jumped and gave a great push, forcing him over the gunwale and into the sea.

He thrashed about with loud oaths, many of which I understood, and tried to climb back into the boat. Having nothing but my fists as weapons, I struck his hands as they grabbed the edge, and struck downward into his face as he reached. At one point, he was able to grab my arm, and I feared he would pull me into the sea as well, and all would be lost. His grip was wet, thought, and I was able to twist away while pummeling him in the face with my other fist.

He eventually went quiet, and I anticipated his strategy, for it was the same as what I would have done in the circumstances. He held a tenuous grip onto the slippery hull, while working his way around to a spot I would not be watching to defend, and pull himself aboard. The night, as I stated, was very dark, and I could not see to defend all the areas of the boat at once. My hearing was, then, quite keen, and more than once I heard him attempting to grip the side, and responded with my fists.

Then, a remarkable thing happened. In that strange part of the world, jellyfish travel in great hoards, thousands upon thousands, and a faint, bluish glow emanates from their numbers, even in the darkest night. I know that seems like either jest or delusion to those who have seen it not, but it is true. At some time in that night, dark as ink, we drifted into the midst of such a swarm, and it accomplished two things that helped secure my existence. It allowed me just enough light, ghostly as it was, to see my enemy, and it weakened him though many stings, each of which caused him to utter a little cry.

As dawn approached, I could see that he was still clinging onto the hull, though his condition was dire. He summoned the strength to make one last attempt to gain the boat, but, in the light, I had found a pike and a hook with which to defend myself. I tried to force him away from the hull with the pike, but he grabbed onto it with more force than I thought him capable. With my other hand, though, I had opportunity to swing the hook, caught him in the eye, and he slipped under the surface with little sound.

I lay on the deck, exhausted from my effort, but relieved. I was adrift in the southern sea with nothing but the stars and sun to guide me, but was equipped with food and water sufficient for some time.

Some days went by, in which I was able to catch a few fish to preserve my stores. I ate them raw, but I had become accustomed to that on the island. The light breeze eventually died away, and the air became completely still and heavy. I knew such doldrums would only be broken by a storm.

It started with low thunder. Then, the first raindrops fell, sparse but so large as to half fill a bucket. I secured whatever I was able, and went below deck for shelter.

The swells were large, but slow and gentle at first. They became quicker and sharper, and the sound of the wind became like standing at the base of a waterfall. Looking out through the cracks in the opening, I could see nothing, though the time was mid-day. The storm progressed, and all I could do was hold on as tightly as I could to the fragile timber. Seawater rushed in through the opening. I feared being drowned below deck, but knew going above would mean certain death. I had no choice but to try to avoid being washed out into the sea, and to go to the bottom with the craft should it capsize. My hope of survival was small, indeed.

I thought I was only projecting my hopes when I felt the swells start to slow, and the howl of the wind begin to ease. The storm had lasted all day, and by then it was pitch dark. Knowing I could do nothing to improve my lot until light, I spent a hellish night partially submerged below deck.

When the wind allowed hearing, there was a curious sound from the port side of the hull. It was a thud, thud, thud that had the same rhythm as the swells, as if something large was traveling alongside the craft, and gently bumping into it with each crest. It seemed to be at least the same length as the boat, but not solid, as a log or other craft's hull would be.

At dawn, I pulled onto the deck. It had been swept clean. I immediately looked to the side to find the source of the sound. What I saw shocked me, though I had been a sailor for some years even at that time. Floating next to the hull was the bloodied carcass of a calf whale. It was about the same size as the boat, and stained the water around it red.

The great creature must have been killed by the storm, but I knew not what force kept it attached to the small boat. My first order was to bail out the below deck with a bucket that I had successfully secured below. Almost all my stores had been either washed away or ruined by the seawater, but I tried to salvage all that might still be used.

In my rattled state, I did not immediately realise that the whale could be my salvation. Having only a small knife that had survived on my person, I leaned out and began to cut chunks of whale-flesh from the carcass, and heaving them onboard. It provided my first meal after the storm, and I was most grateful for it. I continued my task, hoping to dry whatever I could, and to eventually reach some of the innards to use in fishing.

It wasn't long before I was not alone in exploiting the carcass. Sharks began to swarm, tearing off great chunks of it, and sometimes even biting one another through their lack of discrimination. The water around the boat became a red, roiling, hell. I had to cease my own harvest, or risk losing my arm. After a time, the carcass was so depleted by the sharks that it finally sank, and I eventually drifted away from its red stain. At least, it had given me a supply of flesh sufficient to keep me alive for a time.

One cask of water had survived the storm, but some seawater had seeped into it, so it was scarce better than drinking bilge. The moisture gained from eating the whale flesh helped sustain me. I knew, though, my survival would not be assured for many days without rescue or landfall.

That night, sleeping on deck was more comfortable than the soggy below deck. Increasing swells aroused me, and I feared another storm approached. When I looked up, though, I saw stars with the intensity only seen whilst at sea. Then I heard the strangest sound I had ever heard, and even the thought of it causes my blood to chill today. It was a series of long, low, tones, most mournful and sorrowful, as if grieving, seeking, calling. At first, I was sure I was mad, or that the ghost of the heathen who I sent to the bottom with a hook through his eye had found me, and was singing an invitation to join him.

It was a whale, not a calf the size of the boat, but a great leviathan, as large as a mountain afloat, with its upper surface barely exposed. Its motion matched that of the boat, which was no more than a sixth-part of its size. My fear was extreme, but I dared not utter a sound, and huddled below the gunwale.

The monster held back, and came to the hull with its maw, bumping it with a force that almost sent me into the sea. It did that several times, then swam ahead and did a half-turn, exposing to the hull what could be nothing but mammoth, engorged teats. I knew it must be the mother of the dead calf.

She continued to try to nurture the little boat at intervals through the night. The dawn brought a change in her. She came to and brought her eyes to the boat and remained in that position for a time, then, with a great splash of her tail, as big as a carriage with team of four, disappeared.

My relief lasted only for a moment. The great monster surfaced again right beside me, straight up out of the water, almost capsizing the boat. Only at the last second did I catch hold of a timber and avoid the sea. I barely regained my grip before it happened again, and again. At the last, the tail came round and whipped at the boat, sending it skipping across the waves. The entire boat went under and I felt myself beginning to drown, still afraid to let go. The boat was barely buoyant enough to reemerge.

I lay gasping on the deck, and looked over to see a huge eye, blue as ice and the size of a waggon, staring at me. There is no other description for it, and no question. The leviathan was staring me in the eye.

Sure I was about to die, reason left me, and my reaction was uncontrolled. I rose and waved my arms.

'I didn't kill your calf!' I screamed. 'It died in the storm! I didn't kill it!'

How long our direct gaze lasted, I cannot say, But I know,

as God listens, that I was not staring into the dumb eye of a soulless beast. I know that, somehow, it made a decision, slapped the little boat with its tail once more, and was gone, not to be seen again."

I was so enthralled by the sailor's story that I could not speak for quite a time. I poured more rum with lemon and sugar for him, and, although it was not to my liking, for myself as well. He was silent for a time, drinking from his cup, with a sad and plaintive stare into the air.

He was the first to break the silence. "I floated for another few days; I'm not sure how many. I was mad with thirst and had resolved myself to death, when I began to see gulls, in the air, and branches afloat. It was land. I was too weak to try to guide the craft, but was met by a long boat with three natives and a white man. He spoke to me in Dutch, of which I knew little, but my plight needed no explanation. In short, I was, through the mercy of God, brought back to life and eventually earned my passage back to England."

The last cup had already been drained, and I refilled it. Another silence followed, until I finally broke from my trance to ask, "What to make of it? Surely you have some idea, what to make of it?"

"What to make of it, young Fezziwig? The question is still with me. I believe, to my bones, that the great beast thought the boat was its lost calf, from the smell left by the carcass and the meat onboard. It tried to suckle the boat through the night, to reanimate the lost babe. With light, the monster saw its mistake, and lashed out with sadness and anger at the only possible culprit at hand. Then, when it saw the fear in my eyes, it made a choice, and let me live."

"You see, Fezziwig," he said softly, "there are many junctures in life when a tiny change, yea or nay, makes not only a difference in the course of our paths, but the length. Is it by chance? By Providence, solely? Or can a beast grieve and decide to show mercy? I know not the answer. But, the junctures are there nonetheless, my friend. Every day."

I grasped his hand, like old, weathered harness leather. "I already know this to be true," I said.

My dinners with Mr. Greenshaw for the rest of the voyage were interesting, but mostly light and in good humour. None had the import or grave nature of the evening with the tale of the whale, and I have never heard another story to compare. I have observed, with age, that men have a curious habit of feeling a bit guilty after sharing an intimate conversation, and, upon their next meeting, will act as if it did not happen.

The list of countries whose ships would have pursued us had we been spotted was long, since we were at war with half of Europe, it seemed, but none materialised, and my excitement grew as we slipped into the estuary and past Gravesend on our way up the Thames. It was mid-morning when we reached the wharves. I made arrangements for the transportation of the hides and other implements onboard, and then for myself.

It was a fine day, warm but not yet damp. I exited the carriage and saw a woman and boy at the door, speaking with an older woman. It was Caddy, Ras, and Mrs. Spills.

PART THE FOURTH: *RETURN*

I must admit that, had I been sworn to identify my son, I could not have done so with certainty, for he had grown so much. He was solid and strong and clear-eyed, and smiling, with exceptional energy. He did not know me, of course, but, being not shy at all, we soon became inseparable.

I am confident this will only be read by our descendants, so I will also admit that Caddy had grown as well, in girth, as she would continue to do over the years, and I along with her. The length of our separation, my fatigue from the trip, and the need to regain familiarity limited the extent of our congress the first evening, but that was soon remedied.

There was a fine sign over the warehouse, proclaiming "Fezziwig and Company," that, Caddy revealed, had been a gift from Mr. Whitlipped. She said he had been as good as gold to them in my absence, and she would remain ever grateful both to him, and to Mrs. Spills.

"And, I do believe being here with Ras and me has been good for her, as well," Caddy said. "She is like a grandmother, indeed, becoming even more affectionate after her poor

155

husband's death. It was so sad, Will. He was brought to us covered in street filth and blood. He spoke not a word until he died, no moans, no moving lips, though his eyes were opened wide, as if still in fear." Her voice softened even more. "I know he was very dear to you, Will, and you owed him a great debt."

"Indeed, it is true, Cad. Where would I be today, if not for his decision to offer a poor boy compassion?"

"It was through him that you first came to Bracebridge, and to me" she said. "For that, I owe him a great debt as well."

The next day, I visited Mr. Whitlipped, who had not yet heard of my return. He stood up and offered his hand. I was momentarily overcome with joy to be safely home, and that, with the loss of Mr. Spills, my other mentor and source of counsel stood in front of me. I hugged him tightly, which surprised him greatly.

"Ho! Well, indeed, so now. Back from the colonies in one piece, I see!" he sputtered.

I thanked him for his diligence in looking after my family while I was gone. He produced a decanter of Madeira, and we drank a toast to the memory of Mr. Spills before having a long business discussion. "I have engaged the service of a thief-taker, but, I'm afraid, the cruel murder of our friend is still unresolved," he said. "As much as I have no desire to repeat our trip to Newgate, I would welcome the chance to see such a good man revenged."

Mr. Whitlipped continued. "You have done well, Will, and I am certain Mr. Spills is looking down upon us favorably. The contracts you made in the colonies are solid, and the cooperage in Barbados is profitable. Not a big source of income, mind you, but I hear your father-in-law may soon be able to again convince the weather to stay outside the chapel, instead of inviting it in to prayer, by next Christmas."

"By the way," he said, almost an afterthought. "That little work you wrote on the rocks and sand from the dredging? There must be learned men much more interested in it than me, for it has become quite popular among those types. Mr. Hadley has had it reprinted twice more, to meet demand, and I hear he is about to order a third. No profit in it for you, of course, since you gave him the right. But, should you ever write another such work on the natural world, perhaps your name could help it find a market." I could tell Mr. Whitlipped was surprised the little work would be of that much interest. He had, at my request, delivered my Carolina drawings to Hadley as well, but there were many similar works already, and they were returned.

"I have handled your business correspondence, and any personal letters that have found their way to me, very few, have been sent to your home. Has Caddy shared them with you?"

"No, not as yet," I answered, "but I will ask for them today." I was surprised that any personal letters at all would await me, and I could not think who might have sent them. One, I found out that evening, was from Captain Lawrence Washington, of Virginia. It had been addressed to me in care of Spills and Company, London. It said:

William,

I heard through friends there that you contracted the fever during your stay in Barbados, but survived and reached Charles Town without further peril. I thank Providence for your delivery from the fever. My nightmares from that time are not from the horrors of battle, but of my men disappearing from the sickness like wine poured from a bottle.

The time of a soldier is described as boredom interspersed with short periods of fear and misery, and my service in the West Indies was no exception. Looking back upon it, I must say your good company made at least part of the boredom more than agreeable. Your prowess at whist even helped make it profitable!

Much transpired, almost all to the good, upon my return to Virginia. I am now most happily married to Anne Fairfax, a kinswoman of the Lord of Cameron. I have been made a Major by Governor Gooch, and am engaged in bringing my farms back to full productivity.

My new interest, though, is in opening trade to the interior. This is a matter I would, some day, like to discuss with you. My endeavors may bring me to London in the future, and I trust you would be agreeable to seeing me, as nothing would be more pleasurable than a reunion under more civil circumstances than our last meeting.

If your travels should ever bring you to Virginia, know that you have a friend and a glass at my little home, which I continue to build, and have named in honor of Admiral Vernon. We shall find room.   Your Ob't Svt,

Lawrence Washington

The deerskins turned out to fit the need of Mr. Bracken and other bookbinders quite well, and my reliable supply of them from Carolina remained profitable for several years. Over time, I also found a market for hartshorn from Carolina, bought for almost nothing and rasped into powder in our warehouse. While the commerce afforded Fezziwig and Company did not grow at a pace that necessitated expansion, it was sufficient to hold our employees and slightly improve their lot, while developing a reputation for reliability.

I have heard few fathers complain that their offspring are dull, until the youths reach a certain age, but Ras was exceeding bright, of amiable personality, and in constant motion. Mrs. Spills encouraged Caddy and me to, on occasion, allow her to keep the boy whilst we enjoyed an evening of dancing.

That Christmas, the longstanding custom of Fezziwig and Company to hold Christmas Eve festivities with our workers and friends at our place of business began, and, as you know, it will be so until my last breath is drawn. Even then, I pray that my descendants will continue the practice, for I believe it returns many times over the little cost.

The great hub-bub of the spring is of little consequence, but I mention it because I found it instructive of human nature. It began with small talk in the coffeehouse between Hadley and other acquaintances with scientific interests, that a comet had been spotted by some French observer, and it seemed to be growing at a rate that it might be seen without devices. Indeed, it eventually came to brighten a substantial portion of the sky, with multiple trails behind it giving the impression of a celestial octopus. It was quite a sight.

Then, as now, there were reasonable ideas about the origin of comets, but anything out of the ordinary becomes fodder for the hysterical. And hysteria, it seems, spreads fastest among the religious, readily filling the gaps left by the mysteries of faith. I wish our warehouse had profited an extra pound for each time I heard that the *World Was Ending*.

The night sky, just then, gave a well-timed boost to the writings of Mather, from America, and of Doddridge, and their followers gave everyone else little rest from their zeal. Though Cromwell was long in his grave, out of his grave, and mostly in it again, his personage lived on in those Puritans and their like, who not only believed that almost everyone other than themselves was to suffer the fires of Hell, but giddy with happiness over it.

One such was a young man, though not many years separated us, that I had taken as my first apprentice, David Brown. He was of a middling family, bright and hard working (at first), and, for the most part, personable. A change came over him when the comet became visible, and his ideas of its meaning kept him from his work. The fog of Puritanism enveloped him like the fog of gin, and to similar effect. He harangued the other workers and our associates to such an extent that I had to separate him from my business.

Some men suffer for the Gospel. Some men suffer because they are asses, and choose to blame it on their love of the Gospel.

"Mr. Fezziwig, I hold you no grudge," he said. "We who truly believe are set apart, and it is to be expected that the rest despise us. But, it is not too late. You may still join the elect. Even the heavens call out to you to repent, Sir, and follow. In the twinkling of an eye, we will be caught up, and you left with the damned. Give up your tobacco, your wine, your dancing, and follow the Star of Bethlehem, for it has reappeared as a sign to the righteous!"

I have found that irrational opinions, when faced with fact, do not dissipate; they become more entrenched. If the great comet was a sign that the True Believers were about to be caught up, their numbers must have been small indeed, for I missed no one. Even young Brown remained. Though no longer in my employ, he sent word to me that, through the fervent prayers of his kind, sinners like me had been given a short reprieve, but surely it was my last chance. He also suggested that, should I wish to take advantage of the opportunity, I could show my gratefulness by allowing him a stipend, to give him the wherewithal to spread the good news to others. I declined, respectfully, saying that my plans to be 'caught up' involved my work at the warehouse.

The whole affair did, though, push me to examine my own feelings toward matters Providential. I had always been a believer, as was my father, just as a matter of fact, such as "The sky is blue." I had experienced hours of despair, like Jeremiah in his pit, and, in each case, I called out to God for His help, and He always saw fit to aid me. The circumstances were such that pure chance was not sufficient explanation. And, when I received blessings, I hid not my thankfulness under a bushel.

I could not help to think, though, that anyone who claimed to know the mind of God was seeing what he desired to see, instead of what might actually be present. I have been in the countryside with friends, when one would say "Hark! See the hedgehog! Just there! Look closely!" Then, if not seen by the companions, "Are you going blind? Just there!" With more cajoling and in little time, everyone present eventually agreed. "Ah, yes! Well hidden, he is! Just there!" Of course, there was no hedgehog at all.

I compared it to reading Scripture with eyes closed, in order to ensure that all the words read were only those already inscribed on the inside of one's own lids by choice. Surely, the meaning of words was debated in the coffeehouse every day (especially if Mr. Johnson happened to be present), and was one opinion not as valid as another? It was only when prefaced by "this is the one and only truth; any deviation from the letter is folly, indeed," did I dismiss a statement out-of-hand.

How many lives, within a grandfather's memory in our own country, had been taken by one or another claiming to know God's will? Best to leave judgment to Him, I have always thought, and accept what He gives, whilst working to improve the lot of not just yourself and your family, but to those around you, no matter their beliefs, as well. I trust that sentiment will allow me to be caught up, even without the help of a comet.

While the comet caught-ups received little but derision at the coffeehouse, there was much more serious discussion of Whitefield's sermons, and of Wesley, and of the outdoor preaching of the day. Whether they were trying to transform the Church of England, or destroy it, was hotly debated. The question has not been exhausted today, nor may it ever be. I'm sure similar questions were asked just as much by the followers of Baal and of Moses and of Luther. Who knows of what beliefs, unknown to us today, the same question may be asked in the future? As my days shorten, I am confident that how I treated my fellow man will account for something. As to the specifics of what that something might be, I suppose anyone's opinion is of equal worth as my own.

As the comet and the failure to be caught-up passed, a new threat, this one of much more solid material than the many-tailed star, came down from the north, with grave consequence. The Young Pretender arrived from France.

At first, rumors of another such attempt were scoffed at. When he arrived with all of seven men armed with broadswords, many crude jokes, usually told in pretend Scottish speech, made their rounds. The joking ended when the Young Pretender entered Holyrood, and it began to dawn on the people of London that the King's troops were busy on the Continent, leaving the city largely exposed.

The effect a threat has on commerce cannot always be anticipated. If it stills transportation, goods already on hand become very profitable, but, when current inventory is gone, failure looms. If goods continue to move, the populace is split. About half desires to buy and hoard goods against possible shortages in the future, while another half choose to hoard their gold instead, as it is more easily hidden or taken whilst fleeing. Early in the affair, our goods continued to move, both in and out, and the overall result was positive for our enterprise. The Bank did not fail, as some feared, though *shares* decreased precipitously, renewing my view of them on principle. Our cost was greatest when counted in anxiety, rather than pounds sterling.

After the weather turned cold, the Young Pretender reached Derby, though, and the city panicked. Food became short; little came in from the north, and the wealthy hoarded much of what was left. There were rumors that a ship stayed at the ready, to remove the King at a moment's notice should the Highlanders swoop down and pillage the city. Two of my men left their work and marched north with Cumberland, and only one would return. Low whispers spoke of this or that politician or member of the aristocracy or rich man of business who was ready to declare for the House of Stuart.

Such was my anxious state of mind when, one night, I heard knocking at the door of our lodging, in the darkest hours. I told Caddy to remain quiet, and Ras was not aroused. Our rooms had a trap beside the hearth, and I crawled out of it, clutching my knife, and came around to the front to accost the offender, unshod and trembling with cold in my nightshirt.

I saw a man in a black traveling cloak rapping at the door. "Fezziwig! Fezziwig! I must speak with you!" I heard him say, and the voice was familiar, though I could not place from where.

It was definitely Scottish.

I was in a quandary as to what action to take. I assumed the man was armed, though I could see no weapon in the darkness. Should I use my surprise, and set upon him with my knife? Was I justified to do so, for the offence of knocking on my door at night? I had never killed, and, though I had desired it during the trauma of my youth, had no such want of the experience. If I called at him, he could turn and attack me. If I were overcome, what would he do to Caddy and Ras?

My decision was made for me in a moment. Without turning, the man said, "Do not attack me from behind, William. Or, should I call you Lazarus? I once saved your life. At least you can now spare mine." He held up his arms and turned, and I faced Dr. Alexander Kincaid. "You do remember me, from your fever in Barbados, William? Now, it is I who is in need. May we enter, and talk?"

I was dumbstruck. I had never anticipated seeing the Scottish doctor who had treated my fever, so far away, again. I lowered the knife.

"Yes, Dr. Kincaid, of course. You can surely forgive me for my surprise. We will talk by the hearth." We entered and he found a seat near the embers. I went up to reassure Caddy that there was no danger. When I returned, I found the doctor looking haggard in the sparse glow.

"Again, Doctor, you have given me a great surprise," I said. "I never thought I would see you again, unless commerce took me back to Barbados. But I have often spoken of my gratefulness to you. What is your business in London?"

"I am glad you view me with favor, Fezziwig. In years past, I would have had many friends in London, but times have changed. At the first, I must ask you. What are your sentiments on the restoration of the rightful house?" He had no threat in his voice; it was only an inquiry. The way it was phrased, of course, left no doubt about his stand.

"Well, I know the City is as distressed as any time I have known," I replied. "It has yet to affect my business, but the future is uncertain. The Highlanders are in Derby, if reports are correct. As close as that! And there are daily rumors of a French fleet being sighted here and there. If the French really had as many ships as are reportedly sighted, they would already rule the world. With the King's armies on the Continent, though, the fear is real."

"But, Fezziwig, what are your sentiments on the legitimacy of that *King*?" He was insistent.

I sighed. "Doctor, I am a man of cotton bales and deerskins and barrel staves. Kings, I look upon like, well, like birds. Sometimes they are pleasant to look at. Sometimes they can be useful, as when they pick insects off our crops. But, sometimes they eat our seed. They just *are*, and we have to live with them." I thought of that comparison again, quite proud of it. "As for which of all these cousins sit in which palace, it matters little to me. As long as I can sit at my hearth and move my inventory, I care not. I just wish to be left alone."

Kincaid considered this for a moment. "Your King is not native. His family blood is not in this soil. He came through incestuous plotting and deception and murder. Does that not change your opinion?"

"I am clearly not as well versed on history and politics as you, Doctor," I said. "But, unless I'm wrong, those things can be said about most kings, in most places, if one examines ancestry long enough. Again, I just want to be left alone."

My visitor stared into the embers. "So, then, Fezziwig, I come to you as a man of business with a proposition. I need an agent to procure stores and send them north, quickly and quietly. You will be well paid for your service. Your reputation for being honest and reliable is solid; I have made inquiry. Speed is most important, and I have associates who are waiting to meet with you to discuss details."

Perhaps it was because of the sudden awakening, or my surprise at being reunited with a man whom I thought I would never again see, but that was the first moment Dr. Kincaid's mission became clear to me, and my jaw dropped.

"What?" I exclaimed, so loudly I was immediately afraid I would awaken Ras. "Sir, you are asking of me nothing less than treason! Did you help save me only so I could dangle at the end of a rope? I will have nothing of it!"

His voice became fierce. "You said, yourself, Fezziwig, that the true King is in Derby. How long until he crosses into London? Do you not know the support he has in this city? His opposition is minority, under watch, and will be quickly dispatched. A ship awaits to take your German away to the Continent, and what thought will he give to Fezziwig and Company? But, Will, if you help us now, think of the benefits that can come to you in just weeks, when the Stuart is restored. We will know who his friends are, and there will be many opportunities open left by the demise of those who follow their German king, to their folly. It is only because I know you to be honest and reliable, and I want you to prosper, that I make you this offer, instead of to some other."

From the look of desperation on Kincaid's face, I doubted his last statement to be true.

"As I said, Doctor, I will have nothing of it."

Kincaid considered a moment more, and said, "Then, at least, a passive transaction. Who could have objection to simple commerce? We will obtain our own goods through our other sources, which know opportunity when it arises. But, we lack storage. We will pay you for that, so what we need will be here and available to us when the Highlanders arrive. Which will be soon. Surely that, at least?"

"No, Doctor. I have no space at present, and you know as well as I that there is no 'passive transaction' in the games of kings!" The first part of my statement was a lie, for the panic had caused our stores to be much depleted, and the warehouse stood nearly empty.

Dr. Kincaid reached over and gripped my arm. "Will, please. Our cause is at a critical point, and some little assistance now will tip the outcome. And," he said with finality, "you owe me."

I paused, and looked directly into the Doctor's eyes, seeing more reflection from fire within than from the faint embers. "Doctor, I am grateful to you, and wish you well. In the matters of kings, though, I wish to be left alone. How many times must I say it? The best I can do for you is to promise that, while it may matter, I will not tell anyone of your plans, or of your presence. That is all."

My visitor let go of my arm and leaned back in his chair. "You are making a mistake, Will. In weeks, the country will change, and you could be part of the new era. It is the same with many of my countrymen," he sighed. "They think only of their own kettles and sheep and whisky and lasses. They do not hinder us, but nor do they help us. Chalmers, in Charles Town, whom I hear you befriended, is such, comfortable in his new life, and no longer interested in the cause in his native land, one way or the other. Remember what our Lord said about spewing out the lukewarm. But, we will prevail, Fezziwig. It is God's will."

"I have heard that invocation for many things, Doctor, some of them directly contradictory. I feel inadequate to determine the mind of God for myself and my little warehouse, much the less for kings."

"I see. If you change your mind, you will still have opportunity. There will be a time, though, when it will be too late. Thank you for your hearth. It is good to see you well and with your family, instead of rotting in the damp ground of Barbados. Guid eenin." He rose and left, into the cold and dark night.

I returned to bed, and clutched Caddy to warm myself. She was not one to be easily put off, or accepting of minimal explanations, and she demanded a full recounting of the conversation, despite the hour. She was distressed.

"Scoundrel!" she said in a harsh whisper. "He should be hunted down and hung!" Then, more worried, "What if the Young Pretender does enter the city, Will? Surely it can't happen, but would your refusal to participate in treason cause the varlets to retaliate against you? Against us?" she said, nodding toward the sleeping child. "Should we leave?" She now sounded truly scared.

"No, Caddy, I have done nothing wrong, and we will not leave," I said. "If the city is overcome, and we exchange one King for another, I fear our inventory might be taken, but I do not fear for our lives, and we would build back our business."

"How can you be so sure we would not be harmed?" she asked, voice trembling.

"It is God's will." I replied with a smile to myself, and turned to sleep.

The following day, near the early dusk of December, Laverty came to speak to me in the warehouse.

"Beggon the pardon, Sar, I have a matter most delicate to take up with you," he said. "Might you stay a bit later here tonight, so we may speak, after the others have gone?"

"Why, Laverty, you know you are welcome to come to my lodging to talk," I said. He was a most loyal and skilled employee, and I knew I owed much of the success of Fezziwig and Company to his hard work. I also, probably, owed him and his wife for the lives of my wife and son. He had gone about his work and caused me no trouble since our first meeting. I paid him well, and he never asked for more. This made his request to talk in private seem odd.

"'Twould be best, Sar, iffen we talk here, as to not raise an eye." I agreed to stay.

After everyone else had left for the night, Laverty and I sat at a table in the warehouse, which seemed bigger and colder than usual because it was nearly empty. He seemed most agitated.

"Sar, you know I am grateful for the living you give us."

I laughed. "Laverty, you know that my family and I could say the same thing to you, and be more justified," I said, and it seemed to calm him a bit.

"Tanks to you, Sar. You know, with the panic and all, the laws are being enforced again." His voice quavered, and I knew what laws he referenced, the tax on Catholics and the prohibition of their worship.

'Now, I obey the laws, I do. But, I haven't been paying the extra tax. I really don't think it applies to me, Sar, because I'm just a believer, no more or less. Not a participant, and any strict sense of the word. But I thank God for blessings, and ask Him for guidance."

"We are similar in that, Laverty," I said.

"Well, Sar, I'm not sure that protects me in any way, during these times. I have no fault with any King, this one or that, as long as they leave me alone."

"Laverty, would you believe I said almost those same words, not a day ago?" I asked.

"Then I have even more confidence in them, Sar, that being the case," he said. "But I have another thing pressing. It involves family."

Fearing some serious illness, and knowing my indebtedness to him, I asked, "What is it, Laverty? Who is in distress? Not your wife, I hope?"

"Shar, no. It's the laws. They have said that all priests must leave the city by tomorrow. There is even a hundred-pound reward for finding one in the city, or within miles of it.

"I heard. But, Laverty, you're obviously not a priest, or, if so, your missus is in for a bit of a shock!" I laughed again, in hopes of calming him.

"Ah, Sar. Over here." He picked up a candle and walked to a dark corner of the warehouse, obscured by bundles of staves. I followed, and he held the candle aloft to reveal a small man in a black cloak, seated upon the floor. "My brother, John Laverty, Sar. Brother, and Father...Father John Laverty."

That is how I came to commit treason by sheltering a Papist priest in violation of the Penal Laws during the '45 uprising.

Father John Laverty turned out to be an amiable fellow, more talkative than his brother. They had all come to London at the same time to flee one of the regular famines, and, though their family had once owned land, they had lost everything to the Protestant nobles. He had been ministering to his flock in secret for these years, and later told me there were hidden Papists in the city who were well known men of politics and commerce, though he would not reveal any of their names. He was willing to leave a city where he was persecuted and not wanted, but for two things: his flock was there in London and would not be moved, and he had not the wherewithal to go anywhere else.

As for politics, he shared considerably in the views of his brother and me. "Of Popes and Kings and their alliances, they are all well and good, but mean little to me," he confided. "My employment is birth and marriage and death, and repentance. Some say the Stuart will return the entire realm to the Church, but we know that cannot be. And, as fact, looking back at the Stuarts, did the bulk of the people fare more justly under them? Or under any Kings or Queens? Except for those terrible times, (I knew he referred to the Protector), things change but little. We, Mr. Fezziwig, just want to be *left alone*."

The full import of those words, in regards to politics and religion, were beginning to become clear to me.

It being too risky to hide Father Laverty in the warehouse, I decided to bring him into my home, until the crisis passed. Caddy failed to see it as a practical course of action, at first.

"You are going to harbor a fugitive, here in our home!" She was able to make a whisper sound like the loudest of admonishments. "Do you wish to have me jump up and embrace your wiggling body on the gibbet? You so willingly risk your life and our future? For what? You are not a Papist! You turn away treason when it offers you profit, but embrace it when it comes with empty pockets?"

"You know our debt to the Lavertys, better than anyone, Caddy," I attempted to sooth. "It will only be until the crisis passes. And, look at this: it is like a contract at Lloyd's. If the Pretender does prevail, which we know he will not, but if he did, having Laverty here to vouch could save us. Even the word of Kincaid would not negate the blessing of a priest, I'm sure."

She thought about that for a moment, and I could tell she was unconvinced, but she said no more on the matter. Father Laverty was with us for more than a month, until after Falkirk, when he decided it was safe enough to go back to his secret life with his followers.

That Christmas was sparser and less festive than many after, owing to shortages and anxiety. There was ample room for dancing in the warehouse in Christmas Eve, and that, along with Wassail from stores tucked away for that purpose, made up most of our evening celebration. Father Laverty had asked that he be able to hold his prayers for a small group of followers in the warehouse after all my employees had left, but, feeling this too dangerous, I had to disappoint him. The priest and I became friends, though, and when the threat from the Young Pretender was over and he returned to his home, he left with a blessing for us.

"You know you would be welcome in the One True Church, William," he said, with a twinkle in his eye.

"Thank you, Father," I replied. "But, I feel I am already a member of it. And, I am not referring to the one in Canterbury. I have much confidence in the one that could find you and me seated beside Jews and Hindoos and Muhammedans." As is often the case, explaining my views to someone else clarified them for me as well.

"I view it much like my first trip to London. I believed London existed, yea, I *knew* it existed, despite the fact that I had never seen it. My journey here included pleasure and pain, love and treachery, greed and charity. But, I worked hard and was mindful of others along the way, and eventually arrived. Now, the city has taken good care of me as I try to take care of my workers. I believe all should be welcomed here, and can thrive, should they be diligent and treat one another fairly."

Father John could see how pleased I was with my own explanation. "Shar," he said with a wink, and was gone.

Commerce with the north was renewed after Culloden, and the escape of the Young Pretender, dressed as a lady's maid, caused many a jest that I would not repeat, even to other men. The King's troops were still engaged in so many places that I could not recite them all, causing various panics and transportation scares, but not long-lasting. Ras grew like the lush plants in the Indies, and, when time allowed, I found great pleasure in showing him the natural world, along the river, and teaching him to scribble little drawings of what we saw.

Mrs. Spills had returned to Great Grimsby, after receiving my heartfelt thanks for her help with Caddy and Ras whilst I was gone, and my eternal regards for her late husband. His body had been returned there to be buried, and we grieved at the sad news, in the spring of 1747, that she had joined him in eternal rest.

Mr. Whitlipped received a letter from her estate manager, that some small matters would require his attention there. He asked if Caddy, Ras, and I would like to accompany him, stopping at Bracebridge along the way. Caddy, not having returned to her childhood home since our marriage, was anxious to do so, and I felt obligated to pay my belated last respects to a man who had shown me so much favor. My new apprentice, young Mr. Chess, was fully up to the task of running the business for a while, with Laverty's help.

Ras became the King of Bracebridge during our visit, cavorting with the small spaniels and running amok in the forest. Upon our arrival in Great Grimsby, we were in a jovial mood, despite the sad event that brought us. When I visited the Spills and Company warehouse, I surprised myself by being overcome with emotion, thinking of the poor prospect I had when I first entered it, and how my life had changed. Caddy had heard the story many times, and was anxious to see my first little garret room, and other scenes of my deliverance. When we visited the Spills's resting place in the churchyard, I was not surprised to see a carved stone for Barkers next to it.

Something most curious delayed our leaving from Great Grimsby. At dinner, Mr. Whitlipped said he had met the physician who had tended Mrs. Spills, and, to the former's surprise, the doctor knew the name William Fezziwig and desired to speak with me the following morning.

Doctor George Stovin was a serious man of middle years, greatly interested in the natural world. He had a copy of my little work on dredgings, and had something he wanted me to see. The next day found me accompanying him to Amcotts Moor. "Wear not your best suit," he warned.

It was common practice in that area for rural folk to dig peat from the bogs, to be used for fuel after a year of drying. A local youth had been so engaged, when he dug up something gruesome, almost six feet in depth, that caused him to run away and not return. It was only later, when he had told the tale in a drinking house, that anyone investigated. The young man had uncovered two small, strange shoes, with skeletal feet still in them. Dr. Stovin, having some skill as a coroner, was called upon to look at the body.

"What I saw was most remarkable," he said. "Indeed, feet were still in the shoes, which were rudimentary and strange indeed, blackened by the stains of the peat. There was enough of the pelvis to reveal the skeleton to be female, and, though the skull was smashed, even some hair and nails remained. There was an inquiry as to when the woman was killed and buried in the bog, but I believe the evidence is that he body is old, Fezziwig. Unbelievably old. Hundreds and hundreds of years."

"How could it be so?" I asked. "Would not the dampness rot all matter away in that time?"

"It's an odd thing," he replied. "The muck is so tight, and full of tannin, than it keeps out the air. Small frogs and bones that defy identification are often found, but I have never before heard of a person. When you see the shoes, you will marvel. They are of a type I have never seen, nor anyone else who has viewed them."

The remains were stored in a dim stone hut near the moor, laid out on a table. We carried them, table and all, out into the bright sun, and I was amazed at what I saw. The entire remains were charcoal black. The shoes, still with skeletal feet within, were styled in a manner I had never seen. Stovin had removed one of them, and skin and nails were still attached to the bone within.

"Most curious, don't you think, Mr. Fezziwig? I know, from your writing, that you are of the opinion that some things in the natural world are older than commonly thought. In my opinion, this skeleton perhaps even goes back to near the time of

Our Lord. Others will think me mad, I'm sure, and be searching for a murderer still afoot on the moor. That's why I need your help."

"My help? What can I do?" I asked.

"You already have a small reputation in the community of science, and your drawings are quite easy to decipher. I have no such talent. I would like you to produce a description of the skeleton and its discovery, with illustrations, in hopes of printing it. The thing is too notable to not record its finding."

That was how my second work, *A Description of the Curious and Ancient Skeleton Found in the Amcotts Moor, with Illustrations*, came to be printed, with the assistance of Mr. Hadley. He found the subject to be quite interesting, but was little more satisfied with my writing than before. Mr. (Not yet called Doctor at that point) Johnson was no longer available to help revise it, because he had, according to Hadley, "Finally found the perfect position for himself. He's writing a dictionary. Instead of having to decide which words to use, he will simply use them all!"

Hadley procured the service of the sister of a magistrate, who had written books and had some scientific and historical interest herself. Her name was Sarah Fielding, and Hadley said she would do the revisions very cheaply. "Still, it's just for those interested, you know, Fezziwig. There will be no profit in it. Not a penny."

Upon our return to London, I was surprised to hear from Chess that a Scot identifying himself as a physician and an old friend of mine had come to the warehouse, and wished to speak with me. I knew it could be none other than Kincaid, but wondered what further business he thought we might have, since the Pretender had fled, silk stockings and all.

"It is again good to see you, William," he said, sincerely, when he found me at the warehouse a few days later. "I trust our last meeting didn't leave you with ill blood. Some days are won; some are lost. I do not feel the game is over, but that's not why I'm here."

"I must admit, Doctor, I am glad to see that *your* game isn't over, with its last dance dangling from the gibbet. You walk abroad, so I trust you are not a wanted man? I shan't be caught harboring one," I said, feeling no remorse for the statement. After all, I hadn't *been caught* harboring Father Laverty, had I?

"No, I am of no interest, and I will soon return to Barbados. The favor I ask today is small, and will cost you nothing. I simply need an introduction. You are associated with the partnership of solicitors Whitlipped and Trembly, are you not?"

"Indeed, I am. In fact, Mr. Whitlipped is a close friend, and I am well acquainted with his partner as well."

"I see. It is Mr. Trembly in whom I am most interested. He has a reputation of skill in criminal matters, having won cases that were deemed lost. It is to him I need a reference."

"For yourself? You just said you are not pursued."

"For a distant kinsman, who is a supporter of the *true king,* and being brought here for trial. He is aged, and guilty of no more than self-preservation, and his story must be brought out, very skillfully. Our family has raised a fund to retain Mr. Trembly for representation."

"I see. Who is your kinsman facing the dock?"

Dr. Kincaid leaned back, seemingly proud to say "He is Simon Fraser, Laird Lovat, of the Fraser Clan, to which I am kin."

"Ah. Notorious, yes, I have read of him. Do you know the Root and Wallow? It is in Whitty Street."

"I can find it, I trust."

"Come tomorrow at two o'clock," I said. "Trembly and Whitlipped are often both there at that time, if not otherwise disposed. I make no promises, though. Trembly is not a charitable sort, and does little he wants not to do. But, I will make you an introduction."

Kincaid rose and grasped my hand. "Thank you, Will. That is all I ask. Know that I have no ill feelings toward you, and this kindness, in my account, put us even. I will see you tomorrow."

I thought back to my illness in Barbados, and of the five pounds Dr. Kincaid had required for treating me. That didn't make it into his ledger, apparently.

Trembly was an unpredictable man, except for being reliably disagreeable. His denunciation of the Pretender and his cause was loud and laden with oaths. Kincaid attempted to persuade him to take the case as a point of law, regardless of sentiment for the cause, but to no avail. The doctor left the coffeehouse despondent.

"I shall have to look elsewhere, but I thank you for your help, Will. When this is concluded and I am returned to Barbados, I will write to you. If your business ever brings you again to the island, you will still have a friend." I never returned to Barbados, and fate dictated that Dr. Kincaid would never do so, either.

My companions at the coffeehouse followed the Lord Lovat trial closely, and pronounced sentence before the trial had even begun. The old treasonist called upon the personal mercy of the his captor, the Duke, reminding him that he had held the Duke up as a baby, to the face of the Duke's grandfather the King, so that he may be caressed. Such pitiful pandering only served to make the old prisoner more despised in the eyes of the public. The coffeehouse prediction of the trial's outcome was only wrong in one respect. The Highlander was not sentenced to hang. Instead, he was sentenced to beheading.

There was some surprise at that, for the method so favored by Henry VIII had fallen out of fashion, and, to my memory, there have been no other beheadings at the Tower since. The verdict and anticipated execution brought an air of festivity to the city I had not seen since before the Pretender's arrival from France two years prior. Great throngs assembled at the Tower to view it. Almost all of my coffeehouse acquaintances attended, with the exception of Whitlipped, who had views similar to my own. While I had no sympathy for sedition, I had better ways to spend a day than seeing the head chopped off of an eighty-year-old man, and drunken crowds cheering the scene.

Some years later, a full recounting of the beheading was printed in the *Newgate Calendar*. I still have it today, and cannot improve on its description, so I copy it here, *ver batim*.

"On the morning fixed for his execution Lord Lovat, who was now in his eightieth year, and very large and unwieldy in his person, awoke at about three o'clock, and was heard to pray with great devotion. At five o'clock he arose, and asked for a glass of wine-and-water, and at eight o'clock he desired that his wig might be sent, that the barber might have time to comb it out genteelly, and he then provided himself with a purse to hold the money which he intended for the executioner. At about half-past nine o'clock he ate heartily of minced veal, and ordered that his friends might be provided with coffee and chocolate, and at eleven o'clock the sheriffs came to demand his body. He then requested his friends to retire while he said a short prayer; but he soon called them back, and said that he was ready.

At the bottom of the first pair of stairs, General Williamson invited him into his room to rest himself, which he did, and on his entrance, paid his respects to the company politely, and talked freely. He desired of the general, in French, that he might take leave of his lady, and thank her for her civilities: but the general told his lordship, in the same language, that she was too much affected with his lordship's misfortunes to bear the shock of seeing him, and therefore hoped his lordship would excuse her. He then took his leave, and proceeded. At the door he bowed to the spectators, and was conveyed from thence to the outer gate in the governor's coach, where he was delivered to the sheriffs, who conducted him in another coach to the house near the scaffold, in which was a room lined with black cloth, and hung with sconces, for his reception. His friends were at first denied entrance but, upon application made by his lordship to the sheriffs for their admittance, it was granted.

Soon after, his lordship, addressing himself to the sheriffs, thanked them for the favour, and taking a paper out of his pocket, delivered it to one of them, saying he should make no speech and that they might give the word of command when they pleased. A gentleman present beginning to react a prayer to his lordship while he was sitting, he called one of the warders to help him up, that he might kneel. He then prayed silently a short time, and afterwards sat again in his chair. Being asked by one of the sheriffs if he would refresh himself with a glass of wine, he declined it, because no warm water could be had to mix with it, and took a little burnt brandy and bitters in its stead. He requested that his clothes might be delivered to his friends with his corpse, and said for that reason he should give the executioner ten guineas. He also desired of the sheriffs that his head might be received in a cloth, and put into the coffin, which the sheriffs, after conferring with some gentlemen present, promised should be done; as also that the holding up the head at the corners of the scaffold should be dispensed with, as it had been of late years at the execution of lords.

When his lordship was going up the steps to the scaffold, assisted by two warders, he looked round, and, seeing so great a concourse of people, "God save us," says he, "why should there be such a bustle about taking off an old grey head, that cannot get up three steps without three bodies to support it?"

Turning about, and observing one of his friends much dejected, he clapped him on the shoulder, saying: "Cheer up thy heart, man! I am not afraid; why should you be so?" As soon as he came upon the scaffold he asked for the executioner, and presented him with ten guineas in a purse, and then, desiring to see the axe, he felt the edge and said he "believed it would do." Soon after, he rose from the chair which was placed for him and looked at the inscription on his coffin, and on sitting down again he repeated from Horace: *"Dulce et decorum est pro patria mori"* [it is sweet and fitting to die for one's country] and afterwards from Ovid: *"Nam genus et proavos, et quae non fecimus ipsi, Vix ea nostra voco."* [As for things done by our ancestors and other people than ourselves, I say we can have no credit for them]

He then desired all the people to stand off, except his two warders, who supported his lordship while he said a prayer; after which he called his solicitor and agent in Scotland, Mr. W. Fraser, and, presenting his gold-headed cane, said, "I deliver you this cane in token of my sense of your faithful services, and of my committing to you all the power I have upon earth," and then embraced him. He also called for Mr. James Fraser, and said: "My dear James, I am going to heaven; but you must continue to crawl a little longer in this evil world." And, taking leave of both, he delivered his hat, wig and clothes to Mr. William Fraser, desiring him to see that the executioner did not touch them. He ordered his cap to be put on, and, unloosing his neckcloth and the collar of his shirt, knelt down at the block, and pulled the cloth which was to receive his head close to him. But, being placed too near the block, the executioner desired him to remove a little farther back, which with the warders' assistance was immediately done; and, his neck being properly placed, he told the executioner he would say a short prayer and then give the signal by dropping his handkerchief. In this posture he remained about half-a-minute, and then, on throwing his handkerchief on the floor, the executioner at one blow cut off his head, which was received in the cloth, and, with his body was put into the coffin and carried in a hearse back to the Tower, where it was interred near the bodies of the other lords.

His lordship professed himself a papist, and, at his request, was attended by Mr. Baker, attached to the chapel of the Sardinian ambassador; and though he insisted much on the services he had done the royal family in 1715, yet he declared, but a few days before his death, that he had been concerned in all the schemes formed for restoring the house of Stuart since he was fifteen years old.

This nobleman's intellectual powers seem to have been considerable and his learning extensive. He spoke Latin, French, and English, fluently, and other modern languages intelligibly. He studied at Aberdeen, and disputed his philosophy in Greek; and, though he was educated a protestant, yet, after three years' study of divinity and controversy, he turned papist. He maintained an appearance of that facetious disposition for which he was remarkable, to the last; and seems to have taken great pains to quit the stage, not only with decency, but with that dignity which is thought to distinguish the good conscience and the noble mind."

What the Calendar failed to mention, being of little consequence to history, I suppose, was what happened the moment the old conspirator's head hit the kerchief. A scaffold had been hastily built, so more of the crowd would be able to see the proceedings. As the ax fell, many of those on it stood and raised a cheer, some of joy, and some in opposition. The sudden shift of weight caused the structure, made of heavy logs that were not well connected, and it collapsed. Under the weight of the logs and people, more than twenty were crushed to death.

I first heard of the tragedy the day after it happened, at the coffeehouse. Mr. Trembly had attended, and all present listened to his recounting. He told of seeing the body of a young child uncovered at the bottom of the pile of logs and people. At the end, he said to me, away from the hearing of others, "Fezziwig, that damned fool Scot doctor you brought here was in the pile as well, serving him what he deserved!"

The next spring, my great alarm was of a more personal type. Ras had been born before his full time, but swiftly made up for it and grew heartily, generally avoiding the many diseases that spread through the city. He first complained of a discomfort in the throat, and became hot. Small pustules began to erupt, and we feared the small pox. His mouth and tongue began to glow bright red, and the spots covered his entire body, revealing his illness to be the scarlet pox, instead. It spread through the city that year, and I do remember seeing bodies, mostly of children, on the kerb awaiting removal. Parents who knew not what else to do placed some there, perhaps suffering the effects themselves or preoccupied caring for other children with the disease. Others were unclaimed from quarantine houses.

I was no stranger to fear and helplessness, but I had never felt it more keenly. I hired a physician, who bled the boy until his colour lightened, and told us we must burn everything he had used of late, and only touch him while covered with a sheet. This grieved Caddy mightily as she wanted to hold and comfort the boy, and I had never seen her is such a state. His condition became more dire with each day, and we feared he was slipping away from us. The physician offered little hope, but continued his visits with his bleeding-knife.

"Do something, Will! *Something*!" I had only once seen such desperation in her eyes, when Ras became his entrance. Knowing not what else to do, I turned to the same one who helped us during that time. I went to Laverty, and he saw the fear in my face. "I wish I knew more, Sar, truly," he said, pity in his eyes. "For us, if a physician gives no hope, there is only one thing more, but it woulna' fit your believing."

"What would you do, Laverty? If this were your son, what would you do? Please. The physician has given us no hope."

"The only thing left, Sar, the anointing."

"Then we must do it, Help me, Laverty."

He sighed. "We must wait for darkness. I will have John come tonight. But, you must know, Sar, that for us, it us more preparing for," he paused, "for the end, than to give any hope for the present."

Father John Laverty appeared as promised that night, accompanied by his brother. He carried a pouch, and produced candles and a vessel. Showing no fear of the disease, he said Latin prayers and anointed Ras with water (or oil, I know not which). The boy was near death.

"The physician's bleeding knife is no longer needed," the priest said, grimly. "Bleed no more, so it will not add to his discomfort. Pile him with blankets so that he stays hot, and give him salted water to spit, if he be able. I pray for his recovery, Mr. Fezziwig." At this, he turned, raised his hands over Caddy and me, said another Papist prayer, and hugged us.

We were resigned that the night would be our last with our boy, and, at dawn, he was more dead than not. Toward mid-day, he uttered "Ma," and we feared it was his last word, but, within the hour, his eyes became more animated, and continence more calm. He asked for water, and the pain in drinking seemed slightly lessened. He took broth that evening, and, over the next days, grew stronger. Within two weeks, he was left thinner and with a number of scars on his face and body, but revived.

What saved my son? The physician with his bleeding knife? The Papist prayers and anointing, or the King's prayers said by his mother and me? Or was it chance, or a change in the vapors in the air, or Ras's own strong constitution? In questions such as these, it's only the opinions of those who knew they are right, beyond question, that I dispel. I gave God the thanks, and whether He heard the English or the Latin or the waves of the Lea at high tide matters not to me. The boy lived to become a man.

One evening in early December, I was quite surprised when Laverty told me I had visitors from America. I had not heard of a pending visit from any of my sources, and could not think of another reason for anyone from the colonies to call. You may imagine my shock when Eliza Lucas and Charles Pinckney entered the room.

"Oh, William!" Eliza exclaimed, and ran to hug me. Charles's face was wry during the display, and he appeared to be trying to see right through us, as if we did not exist. Still, when Eliza released me, Charles offered a warm and sincere handshake.

"I wrote to you that we were coming to London, and had business to discuss. Did you receive my post, dear?" Blushing at the term of affection, I replied that I had not, and that their arrival was a great and pleasant surprise.

"Ah, the unreliability of the post! Don't we all wish we had but a tithe of the commerce lost to such poor communication? Well, Will, in addition to business, the letter held happy news!" At this, she twined her arm with Mr. Pinckney's. "Charles and I have been married!"

I was stunned, and quite angry with myself for the feelings the news made well up in me. I offered congratulations, which initiated yet another tight squeeze and handshake.

"Oh, we are so happy – so happy indeed!" she said, her face aglow. She looked at Charles and said, "I am resolved to make a good wife to my dear husband in all my actions, and sincerely hope I have thus far followed that path."

Pinckney looked wry again. "Indeed, my dear, you have. But, all that should not keep Mr. Fezziwig from his hearth this evening."

"No, of course not! But it is so good to see you again, Will! And you look so hale. I do wish to meet your family! But, since my letter did not arrive, you do not know what matter of business, besides old friendship, brings us to see you."

"Alas, I have never been good at guessing-games," I said, "But, might it involve indigo?"

It did, of course.

The Pinckneys took Christmas with us that year. When we were together, Eliza was as familiar with me as she had been in Charles Town, her arm frequently through mine. Charles was evidently accustomed to such behaviour, because the wry look was his only reaction. Even that caused me to wonder, since a wry look seemed to be the only type his face ever had available for use.

Caddy, on the other hand, had a much greater store of looks available to her, and used many of them when we were in the presence of the vivacious Mrs. Pinckney.

"William, how did you ever meet such a woman at the first?" she asked, with an edge in her voice. "Your letters from Charles Town certainly didn't mention *her*."

"Ho, my letters failed to mention many people met in my search for commerce, Caddy," I replied. "She was just another, who happened to have offered me a most remarkable product, with enthusiasm, one in short supply!"

It has happened to most people, probably, and to me more often than my measure. I have said something I thought to be of little importance, but a tiny fraction of a second after the words left my mouth, yea, while their echo still rang in my ears, I knew they would bring something ill. That was one of those times.

"Humph! Short supply indeed, William Fezziwig. You shall find out about *short supply!*"

As you well know, daughters, I later became friends with a great man of science and inventor of that age. I distinctly remember, one evening, proposing to him a device, perhaps like a great bellows, to be held at the ready in conversation, so that it could either blow words right past the ears of the listener, or suck them back in before they were able to do harm. While my friend agreed on such a device's usefulness, he was never able to perfect a working model.

The indigo trade did turn profitable, and the largest part of it, almost 100,000 pounds that year alone, went through the humble warehouse of Fezziwig and Company. I was wary of mentioning indigo to Caddy for any reason, but it remained a significant part of our business for many years. When it came time for the Pinckneys to return to Carolina, Mr. Whitlipped and I saw them away at the wharf, and the lady was as affectionate as ever. She said they were quite pleased with our business arrangements, and that they planned to return to London before not many years.

That spring, I received a summons to appear before the magistrate in Bow Street. It worried me greatly, for I could not think of why I should receive such an order. All my accounts were current, and I had no altercations or pending suits. Mr. Whitlipped was also without an idea on it, but was unable to accompany me on the appointed day, having to appear in other proceedings.

London had, of course, more than one magistrate, but I was ushered in to the chambers of the better known, Magistrate Henry Fielding. He wore an extensive wig and had a rather hooked nose.

"Yes, yes, Fezziwig," he greeted, without offering his hand. "Thank you for coming."

"I was not aware the choice was mine, your, um, grace?" I stammered, not quite sure how to address him. "I am confident I have done nothing wrong."

"Oh, none of that, Fezziwig! 'Your grace' makes me sound like a Papist wanting his ring to be kissed! Though there is plenty of kissing of extremities in the office of a magistrate, I'll assure you!" He laughed loudly at his jest.

"I know you to be an honest man of several interests, Fezziwig, and up-and-coming in commerce. The little work on the mummy found in the bog in Lincolnshire? It was my sister who did some rewriting on that for you, at Hadley's request. That kind of writing is very safe, I think. The worst that can happen is that your suppositions be proven wrong. My little works, on the other hand, can cause people to pucker and weep and come to the window with pitchforks. Little matter." He also laughed at this, but it was more subdued.

"Anyway, it's my job to know all that is afoot in the city. I know how long you have been here, and I know what sort of goods you import and store. I also know you suffered a loss of a friend when your employer, Mr. Spills, was set upon, and killed." His eyes narrowed, and his stare was intense. "A loss of a friend and benefactor, no doubt. But not a loss at all financially to you, Mr. Fezziwig? In fact, quite profitable." He paused, and I'm sure the look of horror on my face was evident. What could he be suggesting?

He leaned back and broke his stare. "Ah, but you were in the Colonies, and had no knowledge of the provisions of his will. And, your associate, Whitlipped, hired a thief-taker in the matter, though to no resolution, unfortunately."

"Sir!" I exclaimed. "Mr. Spills was my friend and great benefactor! I was greatly saddened by his death, and would like to lay my hands on his murderer! Through his kindness, I have profited, but not without hard work of my own. Surely you do not...." He raised his hand.

"No more, Fezziwig! Take no offence. I find it useful, upon meeting a man, to view something of his character under a situation of surprise. Pay it no mind. No, what happened to your friend is far too common. Our city has become filth-filled, and in need of a flushing, such as happens during high tide. The gin-houses and the whores and the thieves have their run. The gin and the Jacobites are at the root of much of it, no doubt, but all the lost souls pouring in from the countryside with no better prospect, well, they arrive with good intent but are dragged down. It's easy enough to just blame them all for it, and wish for plagues that would selectively contain themselves among the lower classes, but we all bear some responsibility."

Hearing the man's mention of gin seemed a bit ironic to me, because he, himself, exhibited all the signs I had learned to associate with its enthusiastic consumption, including on that day.

"I do agree with that, Sir," I said. "I have found it a profitable practice to provide a meal and some level of education to my workers, even if it means a slightly lower wage. At the end, we both benefit, I've found."

"I know that about you, Fezziwig. Remember, it's my job to *know*. But, to our purpose. You deal in oak staves, well seasoned, from old forests to our north?"

"Yes, I do. At first, we supplied buckets and barrows for the bridge that nears completion, but now many go to Barbados."

"Good. I will be in need of smooth, stout oaken cudgels, made to my specifications, about twenty-five in number. I have assembled a group of men to serve writs and make investigations, mostly from the best of those already employed as thief-takers. But these are employed by the public, and subject to the Court. I want them to be uniform in their manners and equipment."

The magistrate fumbled about in his desk, and produced a paper, with a detailed rendering of a cudgel. "This is what I need, and you have the means to supply them. You will, I'm sure, choose to do so at your own expense, since it is to your advantage as a man of business to assist in this endeavor, hmm?" He glanced up from the paper.

"Of course, your, um, Sirness." I said, knowing no other option.

"Good. One month, then. Capital. I'm sure you have the means to deliver them here, so no need for me to send someone 'round, right? Good day, to you, Fezziwig."

"Good day, Sir."

I walked back out into a grey day in Bow Street, and wondered at the conversation that had just ended. I wasn't sure if I should feel honored, or robbed. I decided on the former, since the latter would neither change the outcome nor make me feel any better. In similar situations since, I have taken the same path, and usually found it to be best.

The cudgels were delivered as promised, as a public duty. Over the next years, the magistrate found other little ways for me to assist his efforts, as a public duty. But, I also found profit in it; more than a few offers of business came to me with the preface "The magistrate mentioned you to me," or "You come recommended by Fielding, you know." The name was soon to become even more known, by his books, which were scandalous to some, and praised by others. I found them to be overly eager to lay blame for every evil on the old Church, but you know my personal views on those matters. His books are too indelicate to be read by the fairer sex, but I know that presents no barrier to you, daughters of mine!

Shortly after my interview with the magistrate, I received a visit from Major Lawrence Washington. Unlike the previous visitor from my journey to the New World, the Major brought with him nothing but gladness to see an old friend. He was traveling without his young wife, and I insisted that he abide with us for a few days. We brought Ras, though now a large boy, into our own bed for the time, in order to give Lawrence sufficient space.

He insisted that the real reason for his crossing was to again become my partner at whist. We recruited Mr. Whitlipped, who wasn't very good at the game, to make our four, and, despite Caddy's proficiency, the pair of Washington and Fezziwig reigned victorious in almost every match.

Caddy liked Lawrence a great deal, but young Erasmus came to idolize him during his stay. He was enthralled by Lawrence's stories of battles, and the sea, and the West Indies, and tales of red Indians and pirates, and of rescuing the boy's father from his Spanish captors.

Lawrence was excited about prospects in the American interior, called the Ohio country, and about his latest project. He had invested and been made an officer in a company formed to exploit the wilderness. One of the initial needs was for a new deep-water port, sufficient for moving goods directly to England. He had secured the votes and permission from the Governor in order to have the new port built upon land already largely owned by his family and that of his in-laws, insuring him a dominate place in the new town.

While fellowship and whist were greatly appreciated, Lawrence eventually admitted his crossing was to secure prospects for the Ohio Company, and I was able to offer some assistance with my connexions in business.

It was plain to me, though, that he had another purpose that went unmentioned. He was clearly a sick man, and he was there to consult physicians. Lawrence was half-a-head taller than me, and of sturdy build, but now his features were sharp and gaunt. He tried to hide a rasping cough and a slight tremble to his hands. I was not the only one to notice. Though Mr. Whitlipped had never seen Lawrence before, he commented on the man's appearance to me privately, and feared for his future.

When it came time for Lawrence to leave, we exchanged warm affections, and I promised to redeem his standing invitation to visit the Potomack one day. Caddy was most impressed with the Major, commenting that he most favorably compared to my other American acquaintances she had met. Washington's biggest impression, though, was on Ras. I thought it would be passing, as is wont for the young, but from that time on, I heard but one desire from the lad.

"When I am a man, I will be a soldier, like Major Washington."

By that time, Fezziwig and Company was thriving and providing my family with a good living. We were able to move into larger lodgings, and I began to have a small amount of leisure time. I instilled in Ras my love for the natural world, whether it was through day trips into the countryside, or just walks by the river. He continued to grow strong and handsome and bright.

One advantage London has over the rural areas is the availability of day schools, which we used, instead of sending Ras away. He desired a military education, but I wanted him to become a man of business, like me. I seldom see men who are not adamant about their sons' paths either following their own, if they be successful, or not doing so, if they feel inadequate.

The business was not such, though, that I found it necessary to expand to the Thames, or build another warehouse. I did add a new dependency on the adjacent lot, and hire a few more employees. I developed a reputation for treating my workers well, and was both praised and condemned for the practice. I remain, today, most demanding of my workers, and will not tolerate idleness or dishonesty. I had known want and meanness and greed, and felt their hellish effects, and owed too much to Providence to contribute to either of those vices. I did what was right.

On the other side, though, I did what was profitable. I knew I could not be too generous with wages, or else my services would become expensive, and business would not come. Finding the finest line between the two, and being willing to keep my own compensation at a comfortable but reasonable level, was a profitable calculation.

I seldom had the problems with theft and other treachery so loudly proclaimed by other men of business at the coffeehouse, and that helped me build a reputation for reliability. My employees were, for the most part, loyal, and knew I had some concern for their welfare, and met them as other men, not beasts. That commodity, a smile and pleasant word instead of a scowl and curse, cost me nothing, yet returned a healthy profit. If a man were to be fired by Fezziwig, though, he had a hard time indeed finding another position.

Those were days when men, and their characters, were of more importance than massive machines, which consume on one end and produce on another, serviced by poor wretches who live only to perform a certain task until falling, just to be replaced by the next.

My penchant for keeping old letters has been a bane for Caddy and our house servants over the years, but it has been so useful to me in this endeavor. I recently uncovered two letters and a small package from that era that brought mist to an old man's eyes. The first, I remember receiving in my usual packet from Barbados, in a hand familiar to me:

William,

I hope this finds you and your family well, as I hold you in my deepest affection. I had a faint hope that you might be here in Barbados looking after your West Indian interest, but at least I have remembered you to you associates here.

I have traveled here with my brother George, in hopes of regaining vigor. You may not have noticed when last we met, but I have become a bit consumptive, and I am sure experiencing the tropical climate for a time will be restorative. I seemed to thrive in it during my service here, though so many good men met their demise.

George is here for his first time, and I feared the fever for him, but he contracted the small pox instead. By the kindness of Providence, his affliction was mild, and only left a few barely-noticed scars.

I sought, both to consult myself and for George, the physician who so successfully treated your fever here, but my inquiries after Dr. Kincaid indicated he had left for a visit to his homeland, and not returned.

If not here in Barbados, we shall next overcome all challengers at the card table on the banks of the Potomack, and I shall find time to teach drill to Erasmus.   Your Ob't Svt.

Lawrence Washington

Stored, carefully, with that letter is another, along with a small package. They were, if I recall, received around Christmastime of that year, though it was the time of the calendar change, and my recollection of dates may be confused. It reads:

My Esteem'd Mr. Fezziwig,

It is with great sadness that I inform you of the death, of consumption, of my dear brother, Lawrence Washington. He had been in ill health for some time, and had of late visited Bath (the one here in the Colony) and Barbados to seek relief, but, unfortunately, Providence found not the reason to spare him.

He spoke of you most affectionately, and always hoped that you would be able to visit us here in Virginia, and we would find mutual interests in commerce. Rest assured that his offer stands, and your name will always be remembered in good stead here at Mt. Vernon.

I have attached a small article from his desk, upon which he had written "Fezziwig." The meaning is clear to me that he would wish you to have it. His passing leaves a great void for me. I shall always remain, Sir, Your Ob's Svt.

Geo. Washington

The package contained a box of playing cards, the very ones with which the Virginian and I had such success upon the sea.

Another set of events during that era of my life was a result of my strange (still in my mind today) involvement with the magistrate, Fielding. It began with something that became a public spectacle, and ended with something secretive and personal, that haunts me still.

The case of Elizabeth Canning is, of course, still

remembered and debated today. It had more turns and twists and reversals than the streets of London and the Thames during the tide, both combined. A young girl of about eighteen, employed as a maid, disappeared on the late night of the New Year, and was thought to be either dead or absconded.

A month passed, and hope waned, when she showed up at the house of her mother, in Aldermanbury. She was in a poor condition, half-naked and bleeding at the head. Near delirium, she told of how she had been abducted and taken to a house, where an old gipsie woman demanded she go the way of a paid trollop. When the girl refused, she was partially stripped and thrown into an attic, with naught but bread and water. Near death, she finally escaped by prising off a loose board and falling into the soft muck of the street.

It so happened that an employee of mine, Bob Scarrat, who rasped the hartshorn that came from Carolina with the hides into powder, lived nearby and was present when Canning reappeared. With my man's help, the girl identified the house that was her prison, and her captors were arrested. Their names were Mary Squires, the principle renter of the house, and Virtue Hall, a boarder, and other assorted members of the Squires family.

Suing for justice, the young Miss Canning was interrogated by Magistrate Fielding, and found to be truthful. He also questioned Virtue Hall, who confessed that the maid had been abducted, her stays stolen, and kept captive because she refused a life of debauchery. At the Bailey, great mobs gathered outside to hang on each turn of events, and provide the useful service of preventing many witnesses for Squires and company from entering. The captors were convicted, and sentenced to Newgate.

I was surprised at the amount of sympathy Miss Canning

aroused at the coffeehouse. Most of the men there would think little of seeing a young maid starving or dying in the street for lack of shelter or a physician. Still others supported many desperate young women living through debauchery by being their customers, or felt justified in taking advantage of their own servant girls, and were unrepentant of it.

I took a lesson from that, about how the opinion of even the more learned and influential can be so easily shaped, like a soft wood by a skilled turner. Some of the men did contribute to the fund set up for Miss Canning's legal fees, but it seems the most vocal of her supporters had, that day, forgotten their purses. I, on the other hand, had no such excuse, for, early in the case, one of Fielding's Bow Street Runners (as his men had become to be called) had visited me after dusk at the warehouse to inform me that the magistrate was certain I would feel obliged to contribute a pound, as a public duty.

When all in the city thought the matter done, a strange thing happened, one that I could not know would have consequence for me. The judge, Sir Gascoyne, had decided the witnesses for Miss Canning were all from the lower classes, and heard differences in opinion from men of higher station. He interrogated Virtue Hall again, and she recanted the facts as had she told them to Magistrate Fielding. He had a pamphlet printed (I still have a copy, of course), and her statement caused the currents of coffeehouse opinion to shift. When asked why she had not told the truth, she said, "When I was at Mr. Fielding's, I at first spoke the truth, but was told it was not the truth. I was threatened to be sent to Newgate and prosecuted as a felon, unless I spoke the truth."

You can imagine the uproar. I had not seen the city so animated since the Young Pretender was on the horizon. It even became common to hear someone ask, when incredulous about something, "So, which time were you lying, Virtue?" or, to add emphasis to a story, "And that's the truth, Mr. Fielding!" Gascoyne had Squires freed, and prosecuted Elizabeth Canning for perjury. She was convicted, and, it seemed, so was the reputation of Magistrate Fielding. Canning was sentenced to a month at Newgate, and then seven years of transportation.

The new verdict brought another nighttime visit from the Runners, all grasping Fezziwig and Company cudgels. I was beginning to wonder if these men even existed in the daylight. I was informed that the magistrate wished me to use my business sources to find a suitable, respectable position in Carolina for Miss Canning, as he was attempting to negotiate, on her behalf, a lawful emigration instead of transportation. I agreed to try.

The magistrate's negotiations must not have been successful, for Miss Canning was transported to the colony of Connecticut, and supported there by Methodists, if reports are to be believed.

A few nights later, I was awakened at our lodging by the Runners, and told to dress and come with them to the warehouse. The magistrate, it seemed, had a small task he was sure I would feel obliged to accomplish, out of public duty. Once there, I was instructed to build a box, about five and a half feet long, a foot and a half wide, and a foot deep, with no need of particular sturdiness nor fineness of joinery. I had everything at hand to do so, and my carpentry skills are adequate, but you can imagine my wonderment at such a request.

When the box was finished, the Head Runner (for I know not what else to call him) held a candle close and examined it. He nodded at the others, and two stout fellows carried it out. I was about to follow, but was motioned to stay. At length, one of the carriers returned.

"Now, Mr. Fezziwig, the magistrate has one more small favor to ask, of a citizen interested in the public good. Small, really, just a hand. With the box." We walked out into the night, and along the wharf. A small boat was tied to it, and the box and two other burly runners were aboard. "After you, Sir," the Head Runner said, politely, but with a tone that said it was not up to me.

The two began to row us out into the Lea, and I assumed that night would be my last, but I had no idea what my transgression had been. The Head Runner seemed to be enjoying the evening, and commented on the serenity of the river at night.

When out of sight from the wharf, the Head Runner told the others to stop rowing, and said to me, "Now, Mr. Fezziwig, if you would be so kind, the box has served its purpose. Surely such a small item will not hinder navigation in this part of the river, so, if you please, let it go overboard. I would do so myself, but I do have an old injury of the back, gained in the King's service, you know."

I did as I was told. The box was heavier than it had been before it had left the warehouse. It slipped under the surface with little splash, given its shape, and was instantly gone in the darkness.

"Thank you, Sir," was all the Head Runner said, and we were rowed back to the wharf. Out of the boat, he said, "The magistrate would like to give you his personal thanks, in Bow Street, tomorrow, if you please." The runners all quickly disappeared, and I was left standing on the wharf in the darkness, totally confused by the events. That is, until my interview with the magistrate the following day.

When I entered his chamber in Bow Street, it appeared

Magistrate Fielding had aged considerably since our last meeting, and he made no attempt to shield the bottle and cup before him from view. The Canning affair had taken a toll on the man.

"Fezziwig. Capital. You are a good subject, the kind we need."

"Thank you, Sir," I replied. "I am sorry for your setbacks." I didn't know what else to say, but knew he would come to the purpose of my summons in time.

"Yes. Well. You know something of my duty to the city, Fezziwig. I have given it my all. I have allowed myself to be scorned and libeled and parodied. I know who is loyal to reform, and who isn't. It's my job to know." He paused and stared at his desk for a time.

"I still have faith in law, Fezziwig, but it's plain that it wins not all its battles. I have come to believe that, at times, tempering it with practicality becomes necessary. Justice and procedure are amiable traveling companions, but sometimes their paths diverge. Last night was one of those times. Thank you again for your help. You have not failed me in the little favors I have asked."

He reached into his desk and pulled something out. It was wrapped in paper, and he handed it to me.

"I think this is yours," he said.

I knew not what to expect. I unwrapped the item. It was a large, gleaming watch. The inscription said: Time SPILLS, to be Caught.

"You have avenged your friend and mentor," he sighed. "It would not have happened another way. He was of an upper class, and his word would have won him the day. In this case, when law sailed the Thames, justice rowed a boat on the Lea."

Neither of us spoke. Not another word ever passed between us. My thoughts were like so many colours of dye, blended together into something dark, so they were no longer recognizable in their original forms. I rose, bowed slightly to the magistrate, and walked out. I received no more visits from his runners, and he asked no further favors.

PART THE FIFTH: *CROSSINGS*

As Caddy and I grew in comfort and wisdom, we also grew in girth. My gains around the middle were offset by losses on my head. I had always worn my own hair, tied back with a ribbon, but over time took to wearing wigs of the Welsh kind, and I do even now, though they are fading from style.

Ras grew to be a man, though barely one, when he went to be a soldier. There was no convincing him otherwise, though I tried. I went as far as suggesting apprenticeship under Mr. Gates in Charles Town, or a position with Eliza Pinckney, who had recently become widowed. I felt either of these situations would satisfy his need for adventure, and the desire to see the America that had figured so prominently in his father's life. The vision of soldiering left in his head by my late friend Washington, though, could not be erased, nor its desire quenched with anything else.

While there was much soldiering to be done around the world in those days (which has not changed, though I wish it had), I told myself that it was much preferable for him to go to America instead of India. I felt his chances of falling to disease were not as great and, after the reversals of the idiot Braddock, things had been improving on that front.

Caddy would not be reconciled to Ras's decision. She refused to speak for days, even up until the time he was to board the ship for his crossing. I took her aside and told her that the future was in God's hands, and her obstinacies in bidding him farewell could be a regretful thing. In the end, she embraced him, and the image of that embrace is one burned into my mind.

He was attached to troops under Brigadier General John Forbes, who had been with Cumberland during the rout of the Young Pretender. Forbes had, according to the papers, been at Louisburg, but it was not reported where he had gone from there.

The plight of those whose sons are at war has changed little over the years. I suppose parents of Spartan soldiers set off to fight the Athenians were no different. They went about their work and lives, drank wine, made love, and sang songs, but, all the while, the burden of separation and worry was upon them. I ran the business (though, by then, had more time for leisure), visited the coffeehouse, and found excuses to attend functions that allowed Caddy and me to dance, still our favorite pastime together. We wrote letters often, knowing that one in ten would likely be delivered, and quickly looked through each packet in hopes of seeing familiar writing. I still have, of course, every letter he wrote. One said (only in part):

"You are right, Father. This is a wondrous country! The city of Philadelphia is quaint, with but few buildings of any height. It is not small, though, and would likely take a full day to walk around. The streets, except at the river, are regular, and cross at right angles. It has nary a steeple containing a bell or clock, and there is no tolling of the hours.

In some places, it does not seem that I am in British America at all, but rather in German lands, as that is the language most heard, and a strange speech it is, sounding much like someone being choked on a mutton rind, trying to rid himself of it. Even the English Americans have speech different from our own. In London, I can readily tell from what part of the city one is from by his speech, or if, in fact, he is newly arrived from the north or coast. To my ear, all Americans sound alike, but their dialect is a bit more primitive, and not like any I have heard in England.

You will be glad to know that I have attended prayers while here, but also, out of curiosity, attended them once at a German church, of Luther, and understood little of what was said. I still felt that I had worshipped, though. I think I have chosen to follow your belief, Father, that the differences among the faiths are smaller than the similarities, and should be less of a focus. When I take a gross of French soldiers prisoner, as I am sure to do, I will even question them about their Popishness in good humour, as I will the Red Indians about their faith, whatever that may be (I regret that I have not read about it, nor heard it explained, though our mission here will likely cause many of them to experience their version of the afterlife firsthand, sadly).

Much of my time is spent in drills, and I am becoming quite proficient. We are quartered with residents of the city. The family with whom I lodge, the Kunders, is of German descent, but generations back. They are amiable enough, but some of my fellow soldiers tell of resentment of the lodging practice among some of the residents. I cannot fathom how Provincials want the benefit of protection from the Crown, without feeling the need to pay for it, or be inconvenienced in any way.

The biggest threat here is small pox. I have lost two acquaintances to it, and more are ill. There is an open pit to receive all such victims, and it is filled in little by little, covered with dirt only as needed. There seems to be a good chance, though, of developing a mild case, and surviving with not much more than a few scars to show grandchildren someday. It is said among soldiers that these mild cases are protective against more severe ones later, no matter how badly it spreads.

I am most anxious to see the interior of the country, and believe I will do so soon. There have been successes, and I am confident we shall soon prevail. I know the thought may be premature, but, when my enlistment is finished, I may, indeed, travel south to Charles Town, if there are still opportunities there. There may be room to enlarge Fezziwig and Company on this side of the great sea. Or, if I continue to find this part of America agreeable, there could be a chance to begin commercial intercourse for us here in Philadelphia."

Around the same time, I received another letter, this one only from Craven Street, near Charing Cross. It was from a gentleman recently arrived from America on business, who had scientific interests. He had read my little work on the dredgings, and on the corpse in the bog. He desired to meet me, if it should be convenient, and discuss what common thoughts we may have on the natural world. Knowing my vocation, he also said he had many business contacts in America, and would like to hear more about any possible commercial connexion.

I was always interested in such opportunities, so I readily agreed. The visitor, Dr. Benjamin Franklin (as I always find myself referring to him, even in writing about earlier times, though he was not generally called Doctor until later, when he became so at Oxford), was quite famous for his scientific experiments, though, and I felt I could offer him little in that area.

The house was in a neat area and, I learned, owned by a widow, a Mrs. Stevenson, willing to let to a reliable boarder of quality. I was met at the door by the mistress's daughter, Polly, a handsome girl of around 18 years or so, who took me to a windowed room upstairs. Dr. Franklin was seated at a desk, which was piled with books and papers. He arose when I entered, and extended his hand. "Mr. Fezziwig! I am so glad to make your acquaintance, Sir! Please have a seat. Madeira, I'm sure? Yes!" He was about my size and build, though, of course, older, and afflicted with the same balding as myself, only more advanced and not covered by a wig. He was dressed plainly, and had a friendly face with sparkling eyes.

"I have desired to meet you since seeing your pamphlet on the Lea dredgings," he said, after the glasses were in hand. "I would like to see the site, if you would please. I once was sent a skeleton to examine, from the western lands of Virginia, the Kentuck territory, that was clearly of an elephant. So, it is thought, there must be elephants to our west, though none have ever been seen, or even spoken of by red Indians brought into our conversation. And, this elephant had differences from illustrations I found. It seemed even bigger. It gets quite cold there, you know, and sometimes snows heavily." He had leaned back, fingertips pressed together, and seemed to be lost in his own comments, almost forgetting I was there. After a pause, he broke from his thought and remembered me.

"Oh! Yes. So, what you observed about things possibly being very old, and the weather changing over time. Interesting. If the deluge covered so many things at the same time, they were uncovered over the years by what? Where there is no stream washing the rock away? The process does seem quite slow." He was at risk of drifting into a conversation with himself again, and recognized it.

"Please forgive me! I have gone on! But the subject is of interest. Please tell me, Mr. Fezziwig, about your business, and your travels, and such!"

Once he turned his attention to me, it was complete. I have never known anyone who could wheedle more information from a person he had just met. I was probed as if by a physician, but felt an immediate affection for the gentleman, and felt at ease being forthcoming and familiar. I lost all track of the time, and, to my surprise, the mistress of the house knocked gently and announced the evening meal. I rose to leave.

"No, no, I won't have it, William!" my host proclaimed. "You must dine with me. I seldom do it alone, and do not like doing so, but this evening you will save me from it!" The meal was simple, but the conversation not. He was there as an agent for not only Pennsylvania, still at that time a Penn family concern of sorts, but for other colonies as well. He made it clear, though, that his work on their behalf would not stand in the way of scientific pursuits, as he had retired from a lucrative printing concern in order to do so. When I left Craven Street, it was agreed that our next meeting would be Leaside. He also asked me to inform him if he could be of any service to Erasmus in Philadelphia, in the way of letters of introduction or other referrals.

I distinctly remember the words with which I met Caddy that night: "I have met the most remarkable man today." So little I knew.

At the coffeehouse, I often heard men bemoaning correspondence from their sons away at school. It seemed their only letters began "Dearest Father, I find myself in need of..." Their complaints only served to swell my pride in Erasmus, who wrote frequently, but never asked for anything, despite my probable ability to provide it. I saw in him a budding skill at looking forward, instead of just at the present, and thought of how Mr. Spills would have been proud of it. One letter said:

"With the influx of Germans and Scots as well as Englishmen, land here near Philadelphia is quite dear. In the west, it can still be had, but the threat from Indians causes many to be leery of it. I know the threat will eventually end, and speculation here may yet be worthwhile.

My larger interest, though, is southward, and westward, in Virginia. There is a waggon road that originates in this city, and goes westward to turn south into the great valley of Virginia, and on, even, to Carolina. Near the end of the Valley, turning westward, the Indian lands of the Green Briar river leading to what is called the New River are said to be rich, in hunting, timber, and fine for agriculture. Though I have not been able to confirm the fact, it is believed the New widens to become navigatable and is called by the Indians the Canawagh, which flows into the great Ohio. When we control that western border, as we one day will, the area could become most valuable indeed.

Many Virginia soldiers are also present here, to be engaged in our efforts, and my conversations with them convince me my future may lie in that colony. The names of our late friend, and his family, are well known to them. I have no need to tell you of the usual preoccupations of soldiers, since you spent time among them, but I can say a dominate one here in America is talk of land, and its profitability."

My old friend Lawrence had left my son as fascinated with Virginia as with soldiering, it seemed.

My visit from Dr. Franklin came much earlier than I expected, both in interval and time of day. The dawn had not yet fully come when a rap came on our door, something that had not brought particularly good tidings so many times in the past. But, to my surprise, he was cheerful and wanted to go to the river straightway. When we came to the warehouse and wharf, he went to the water's edge and looked up and down. Seeing no one, he surprised me greatly by stripping off his clothing, all of it, and wading into the still-cold water.

"I find it stimulating to the constitution, William! Will you join me?" I thought not. "Really, early and brisk, setting the tone for the day! It invigorates the mind!" After a short while, he climbed back onto the wharf and dressed, as unconcerned by his nakedness as a baby.

He spent half of the day examining my warehouse and its workings, and the sand and stone left from the dredging. I had kept many specimens from becoming part of the new bridge, and he considered them carefully. He asked many questions about the goods in the warehouse, and the extent of my trade.

The appearance of another comet that year brought more religious fervor and hand wringing. Franklin joined me at the Root and Wallow a few times to meet Mr. Hadley, joined by Mr. Bracken and, of course, Mr. Whitlipped and Prune. He listened intently to Hadley's ideas on winds and currents, and, having spent much of his life as a printer, had common interest with Bracken as well. He fell easily into our circle, as if he had long been a part of it.

"This comet, of course, is significant in its regularity," he explained. "It is, as Mr. Halley predicted, right on time. Those who try to put God on such a schedule amuse me, but they persist. Signs are seen in the smallest of things, and I think He probably looks down upon us likewise amused. It is hard not to find what you are seeking, if you look hard enough, regardless of its existence." We all agreed.

Franklin enjoyed visits to the coffeehouses, but seemed more inclined to the clubs instead. The clubs seek, and are sought by, men of like opinions and interests, while the coffeehouses were a much richer mixture, and open to anyone with the penny needed to fill a cup. He once invited me to join him, as a guest of a guest, at a club meeting held by Sir Francis Dashwood, which went by the ridiculous name of the Brotherhood of St. Francis of Wycombe. I respectfully declined, and he later revealed that I had made the correct decision, as he found the goings-on distasteful.

My next letter from Erasmus indicated he was finally on the move from Philadelphia, and the letters could hardly contain his excitement:

"Instead of being a soldier, Father, I have come to America to be an engineer. Our objective is Fort Duquesne, at the confluence of the Allegheny and Monongahela Rivers (Those are the spellings, though I hear the latter called differently each time I hear it), which become the Ohio. That is where Braddock failed, but we shall succeed. We are building a road, a fine one, westward from Philadelphia, so that we may be supplied and reinforced at will.

We entered the domain of the Indians not far from the city, surprisingly close, I would say, but most of the ones here have become reconciled to the Englishman and we have seen no action. We stay long enough to build small fortifications and commodity depots at sufficient intervals, and that should help ensure our success. General Forbes is a keen thinker, and is not likely to repeat the mistakes of his haughty predecessor.

I have just learned that we will soon rendezvous, at the head of the great valley, with a native force from Virginia, which is commanded by Colonel George Washington, brother of your departed friend. I am most anxious to meet him, and give him the regards of our family, and tell him of the fondest memories we all held for his late brother. I do not know the protocols of the native force, however, or how to approach its Colonel, when I am but a private soldier in His Majesty's service. I will assess the prospect when we rendezvous, and promise I will follow the strictest rules of demeanor; it would be a shame, though, to meet him and not mention our family connexion, do you agree?

The land here is fair and lays well, though becomes hillier as we move westward, which slows our progress. The small pox continues to be a problem, and already more than one of our rank has found final rest in the soil of Pennsylvania. I, being a Fezziwig throughout, remain hearty and strong, except for the occasional bout of the camp runs, which, as indelicate as it sounds, is the only name used for it that I might repeat in a letter sure to be read by mother.

The longer I am here, the more I listen and learn, and plan for what may come next. Soldiering has brought me to America, but I feel I will soon have had all it can offer me, and I will be ready to follow your trade, on this side of the sea."

I was swollen with pride in my son, and shared the letter with Whitlipped, and my new friend, Franklin, who said his own son, named William like me, was soon to arrive from America to work as his assistant. He also had a proposition.

"William, it is part of my purpose to improve and increase my acquaintance among persons of influence. I have had an invitation that will serve me well in that, I think, and I would like you to accompany me, because my hosts will have interest in you, and vice-versa. One of them, Mr. John Michell, has done work on layers of soil, and has ideas about their ages and how they were deposited. I'm sure your presence will add to the conversation. You must come with me to Lichfield!"

Since my return from America years before, I had been concentrated in London, and traveled no further than

Lincolnshire. Our trips for leisure were mainly to Bracebridge Manor, with shorter jaunts into the countryside with Ras. Business was stable, so much so that I had taken on a second apprentice, and I knew it could easily stand my absence for a period. Franklin was such an interesting personage that the idea of an adventure into the west midlands appealed to me. Whether or not it would appeal to Caddy was a question. I took a chance greater than any trader in shares, and agreed to go.

"When, Sir, do we leave?"

His broad face brightened. "Ah! In two days. I have hired, or really had loaned, a coach and driver. We will also meet with two of Mr. Michell's associates, young fellows, I think, and very accomplished. Mr. Matthew Boulton is a manufacturer. You may very well have common business interests. And there is a physician, who shares a name with your son, Dr. Erasmus Darwin. There could be more as well. They have begun meeting for scientific and philosophical conversation during the full moon, they say for safety, but mainly so they can call themselves 'Lunarticks' I think, and wear the label proudly! They also have great interest in electricity, and I am invited to speak on the subject. We will lodge with Dr. Darwin, in Lichfield.

Caddy was not enthusiastic about my plans, but was assuaged by my suggestion that it would be an opportunity for her to visit her parents, who were, by then, quite aged. I talked with Mr. Whitlipped and Laverty and my two apprentices (Misters Timpkins and Lews) to assure smoothness in my absence, and met Dr. Franklin in Craven Street at the appointed time. Mrs. Stevenson met me at the door and took me up to my friend's chambers. I walked in and was surprised, indeed, shocked, to see her daughter seated on the stout man's lap, with her arms around his neck, and they were kissing.

"Oh! Fezziwig!" he said, when I was noticed. The girl blushed slightly and left the room. "What a fine girl she is, Polly," said my host, without the slightest embarrassment. 'She has come to regard me as a beloved uncle, and the thought of my leaving distresses her. I will call for the coach!"

The borrowed vehicle was old, and so was the driver, but we were soon off to Lichfield, a city I had never before visited. After leaving London, the way was smooth and pleasant for a time, but became wilder, and my bones and joints began to feel the strain. My companion, though twenty years my senior, seemed not to feel the jolts, and was attentive to everything viewed through the window, making comments on trees and waterways and sheep and rocks and everything else we passed.

Where is it written that we must lose our wonder of nature when we cease to be children?

We had cheese and bread and beer in the coach, but the weather was exceedingly hot and damp, making it uncomfortable. The villages and farms had fallen away, and forest surrounded us. We requested a necessary stop, and walked a little way into the wood. Before us was an astoundingly beautiful, clear pool, formed at the foot of a small waterfall on a fine stream. My companion could not resist.

"Will, what luck! What could be more refreshing? You must join me!" I said I would gladly wait for him, but he said "Bosh! Tell the driver we will be a moment. This is just what is needed! Here, lay out the clothes upon that rock on your way, if you please."

I knew it was wise indeed to hire Benjamin Franklin to be one's agent, for telling him 'no' and staying with it was almost impossible. Two men, one approaching forty and the other approaching sixty, were soon splashing like stark naked schoolboys in a clear forest pool. He stopped to observe minnows and salamanders and plants along the edge, and recounted how he had hoped to make a living at swimming when he was young, but was unable to find just the right structure for the business.

Dr. Franklin was right. Acting a boy again for a while rejuvenated us greatly, and the coolness of the water made it hard to bring our little diversion to an end. When we did, the initial embarrassment I felt at being naked had, to my surprise, disappeared. (I later learned that the feeling is common when visiting Bath. Men enter the pools most aware of their state, but leave without a care of it).

Yes, my embarrassment had disappeared. So had our coach.

And our clothing.

We had heard nothing from the direction of the road, but our preoccupation with recreation may have prevented us from doing so. We looked up the road, and down. There was not a soul to be seen, and dark was falling. We looked at one another, in the eye of course, and the full weight of our situation fell upon us.

"Eventually, someone will come upon the road," he said.

"Yes, but how do we hail them? I asked. "Who would stop to give aid to us, in our state?"

"True. We must try to cover ourselves as best we can, and warn any traveler upon the road with a hail first, to explain our plight."

Lacking any better idea, I followed Dr. Franklin back toward the pool, and we went in separate directions to find natural materials, vines and leaves, to weave some sort of protection for our mid-parts. When we met back at the pool in the gathering dark, I could not restrain myself, and fell to my knees with convulsive laughter.

"Is my appearance that comical, Mr. Fezziwig?" Franklin asked, with a bit of an edge. "Let me assure you, that yours is little different!"

"No, no, my dear friend!" I gasped. "I know we are quite a sight. But, I cannot resist the irony of the world's greatest man of science, in a forest full of plants, choosing to cover his extremities with stinging nettle!"

Dr. Franklin's mouth dropped open, his eyes became as wide as eggs, and he threw off the offending girdle with vengeance, adding to my laughter.

By the time I was again able to breathe, and my companion had found more suitable attire, it had grown quite dark. We decided to walk on the edge of the road and hope for deliverance. There was no moon, and we each fell and sprawled upon the ground more than once. No travelers came, but, at length, I spotted a pale light off the road, and I suggested our best course was to go toward it.

Even in the darkness, we could see the moldering state of the house we reached. The trace leading to it was disused, though small bent bushes indicated some recent activity. It was altogether of a good size, but most of the structure was falling down and uninhabitable, leaving only a small portion of stone, about four rooms and very ancient, upright. It was not inviting, but we had few options.

Franklin gave a halloo, while we stood to the side of the door. It creaked open, to reveal a large man, powerfully built, around Franklin's age. He had a fringe of greasy hair, wore no wig, and had no discernable teeth. I could see a cudgel at his side.

"Who disturbs me?" he barked. We stayed out of sight, but Franklin answered.

"Two travelers, who have been abandoned along the road through no fault of our own, Sir!" he answered. "We stopped for the necessary, and our coach went on without us, on our way to Lichfield. And, Sir, circumstances have left us without clothing, I'm afraid, and that prevents us from seeking help from fellow travelers."

"Wot? Without clothes? You are in a state, then, I suppose. Show yourselves to me."

We exchanged a glance, and came around in front of the door. The man opened the door wider, so that more light escaped, and stared for a moment, as if making a decision.

"Yes, a state indeed. We can't allow this. Our Lord praised the Samaritan, you know. Come in. I think I can find something to assist you." He opened the door fully.

We entered to a strange sight. It was clear that the rooms and furnishings had once been fine, but were very old and neglected. A heavy candelabrum sat on the table, with two candles flickering but spaces for several more. Dust covered everything, and piles of rubbish sat in the corners, looking long undisturbed. A plate with a greasy bone was set upon the table, along with a clay jug and cup.

Our host pointed us to a bench by the hearth. He picked up a knife from beside the plate and took one of the candles from its socket. "I can find something for you, I think. Move not!"

He left the room, and I glanced at Franklin. He shrugged. "Little choice," he said.

The man returned with a pile of clothing under his arm, and shoes dandling from his fingers. "I don't know how suitable, but better than leaves, I'll reckon. He dumped the pile on the floor in front of us. We had no choice but to defoliate and don them whilst he watched.

The clothes were ill fitting, but I was glad to be in them. Franklin thanked the man, and told him that, once we had reached our destination, he would be well compensated for his kindness. "One more thing, Sir, if it isn't stretching your charity, we have been without food and drink for some time, and need it greatly. If there is something you could spare, we will sleep in your barn and be off with the light, if you please."

I gave Dr. Franklin an incredulous look. We were not particularly hungry or thirsty, and I certainly didn't want to eat anything from those surroundings. He didn't return my look, but smiled serenely at the big man.

"Should have known that. Shan't be much." He rose and turned to a cupboard.

What next transpired astounded me. With unexpected quickness, Franklin leapt up from the bench, grabbed the candelabrum, and pummeled the big man on the back of the head with it. It took the man off guard, and he stumbled, but arose with a roar and started to strike at Franklin with the knife. 'Will!" Franklin yelled. Dumbstruck, I jumped to my friend's aid, lifting a chunk of wood from beside the hearth, and swung it at the man's head. He struck back toward me, but, fortunately, his knife stuck in the wood and he lost his footing in the rubbish as he pulled back on it. Franklin was waiting with the candelabrum, and struck him solidly. This time, the man lay still.

"What in the devil have you done?" I yelled at Franklin. "We seek help, and we have set upon the man who offers it! Do you want to hang?"

"Help me tie him, Will, quickly. If he awakens, we may not fare as well. Quickly!" Finding cord near the hearth, I bound the man hand and foot, still stunned at our actions. As soon as I finished, Franklin hurried me out to door. "Quick, now, behind the house, I'll wager. Step, step!"

When my eyes became reaccustomed to the darkness, I gasped at what I saw. In the back of the house sat our coach, with the horses tied to a tree, still in harness.

We hitched the team and were off toward the road in the dark, having no means of lighting the lanterns. We made very slow progress, but, just before dawn, reached a settlement with a tavern. Our chests were still on the coach, but the purses that had been with our clothing were gone (this being one time that even my favorite hiding place for it was insufficient). I had some extra coins hidden in my chest, just enough to continue us along our way. Dr. Franklin wrote out a detailed account of what had happened, leaving it to be delivered to the sheriff. We later heard that the body of our unfortunate coach driver was found in the forest.

After we were happily out of danger, supped, and washed, I told my friend how surprised I had been at his quickness. "Hilli ho! You were altogether like a cat, Sir!"

This caused him to smile. "Yes, I suppose so. A very old, well-fed, gouty cat. I will consider that a compliment, William."

Then I asked, "But how did you know? If we had acted such and you were wrong, if that man had not been the one who stole the coach, we could have hung for what we did!"

Dr. Franklin looked pained. "Sometimes, Will, compulsive observation is a distraction, when needing to focus on something else. But, in this instance, I think it saved our lives."

"But what *was* it? What did you observe? " I wanted to know.

He still looked pained, but gave a tiny smile. "Your shoes, Will. The man gave me shoes that had, only hours before, been on your feet, and I recognized them. Now, please do not be offended, but I must scratch myself."

We agreed to leave out the part about losing our clothing when recounting the story, but, as the reputation of my late friend is forever enshrined around the world for his discoveries and diplomacy, and no one but my own descendants are ever likely to read this accounting of my life, I think that, wherever he may be today, he is smiling at the memory.

The home of Dr. Darwin in Lichfield was a work in progress. He had recently acquired it, an ancient half-timbered affair, but large, and he was busily turning it into a fine, modern lodging. Our host was, himself, large, with a bulbous nose and a couple of chins, though quite young. He had a perpetual skeptical half-smile, and I found him most agreeable. His young wife, Polly, was great with their first child. He was openly excited to meet the esteemed Dr. Franklin, and, to my surprise, had read both my little scientific works. He was also quite pleased to hear my own son was also named Erasmus, as it was an old name in his family.

The following evening, we met Dr. Darwin's fellow "Lunarticks." They included the scientist Mr. John Michell, Mr. Matthew Boulton, a metal manufacturer, and Mr. John Whitehurst, a clockmaker. Dr. Franklin relished the attention, and they hung on his words, with many questions, and clear admiration. We met for the next three evenings, and conversation turned, for a time, toward my works on the sand and stones and petrified bones of the Lea, and the remains in the moor. I was greatly surprised that all but Mr. Boulton had read them.

Our host, Dr. Darwin, was particularly interested in the dredgings, and Mr. Michell recounted many instances of similar observations he had made. We all agreed that many things in the natural world seemed very, very old, and that the world all being covered with water at once, and then receded, did not seem to fully explain what was present. Dr. Franklin told of the elephant bones, and Mr. Michell talked of other examples of bones of creatures that seemed no longer to be present today. Mr. Boulton expressed little confidence that such matters could ever be resolved, until we ask the Great Manufacturer such questions directly, and the mysteries did not interest him enough to rush into that interview.

"In the mean time, Gentlemen, He has given us great wealth to exploit, if we are only industrious enough to discover it. We have the materials, but we are limited to the toil of our hands and our animals to use them. When we overcome that barrier, of harnessing sufficient power, as surely we shall, every man shall live as a King!

Dr. Franklin scoffed a bit. "Then, all our manufacturing shall be of the implements of war? Open the way for the individual to be industrious, and all shall be better by it. I fully believe that each has a talent, but it can never be called upon if hunger and ignorance covers it with a bushel."

"Ah, that brings me to ask a question, perhaps delicate, that I would like to ask you, Doctor," said our host. "I have come to think, as have a few others here in England, that the Colonies will, one day, be ready to become wholly separate and independent." I heard Mr. Boulton harrumph politely. "Is that a common sentiment in America? What are your thoughts?"

Dr. Franklin smiled and leaned back. "You are speaking, Sir, to a loyal subject, who fully intends to meet Providence as such, later rather than sooner, I hope. I know there are some who advocate such a drastic move, but they are few. I am employed to advocate our rights as Englishmen before Parliament and to make connexions for business. We are more important to the realm than most will admit." He paused and reflected for a moment, then continued.

"I was in London as a very young man, in hope of furthering my career as a printer. I was ambitious, willing to work hard, and, though I never had the opportunity for formal education, fairly read for my age. London was filled with a thousand other such young fellows, I'm sure. But, I found that this Loyal Subject was, from the beginning, considered lower than the others simply due to my origin across the sea. Even today, our requests are often met with an expression like that of a father hearing requests from his son, who is away at University. But, we ask little more than protection, and offer much." He nodded toward me. "Just ask Mr. Fezziwig, whose single crossing years ago established trade that is still supporting many employees today. In turn, his own son is, even now, engaged in protecting my home from the French, and their native allies. It is a road wide enough for travel in both directions, I think."

Dr. Darwin nodded. "I see, Doctor. Your comparison to a university student is apt, and one I have used. That student will, one day, complete his education, and become fully separate, though available for support and counsel to his father. It is nature's way. And, a world with strong, independent allies in it will greatly benefit England as well, I think."

We passed a most pleasant week with Dr. Darwin and his Lunarticks. Most of the discussion on subsequent evenings focused on Dr. Franklin's electrical experiments. I had the opportunity to see all the gentlemen several times over the years, and became quite good friends with Dr. Darwin, who still makes a point to call when he is in London; in fact, I have seen him lately. I eventually had some small commerce with Mr. Boulton, meeting him several times, along with his associate, Mr. Watt.

Caddy had not yet returned from Bracebridge when Dr. Franklin and I arrived back in London, after an uneventful trip that left us with all our clothing. I had much to do at the warehouse that had accumulated during my absence, but, overall, things had been well handled. When Caddy returned, she was grateful for the visit, but distressed at the decline in her parents' health, for they were, by then, quite infirm.

Whilst alone, still awaiting Caddy's return, the second of three of the strangest moments in my life occurred to me. Late one night, I thought I heard something, or someone, downstairs, at the hearth. Since most of my midnight disturbances in the past had not ended well, I came to investigate, hoping I did not have a visitor.

There was the faintest glow from the fire, which had not been large, it being only mid-October. I did not light a candle, but stood still and quiet, listening, but heard nothing. I was about to return to my bed, when the room fell cold, and each hair on my body stood on end. It was exactly the feeling I had experienced years before, when visited by the old Crusader on my first visit to Bracebridge. Fear overcame me, but then it ebbed, and I felt I was no longer alone. The presence was as familiar to me as my very own, and I felt it surround me, and embrace me, and whisper to me.

It said, "Father."

And then it was gone, as quickly as it had come. I stood for a time, and then returned to my bed, though I could not sleep. What to make of it? Had my anxiety and loneliness for my son created a visit from him in my mind? By dawn, I was not sure if I had really even descended the stairs that night, or simply dreamed the whole affair.

As our means by that time allowed it, I was searching for us a new lodging, and knew Chelsey (some spell it differently, but I'm not sure why) to be of the most pleasant and agreeable nature, as it remains today. When I first saw the timber, stone, and brick structure in which I now sit, I knew it was to be our home. It was but a few years since its construction, and of modern style. I could not help but to compare it to the ancient hut that was my home for the first years of my life, and wish my father could somehow see it. Who am I to say what the capabilities of those passed on might be, and that he did not?

We were moved in before Christmastime, and proud to entertain our friends in our new home. We made merry for the workers in the warehouse on Christmas Eve, and Mr. Whitlipped, Dr. Franklin, his son William (who had joined his father in London in order to study law), Mrs. Stevenson and her daughter Polly joined us for Christmas dinner.

William's guest was a young lady he was courting, named Elizabeth Downes, whose father I had met many years before on my trip to Barbados. The couple eventually married, and Caddy and I attended the ceremony. Some elements of conversation at the table caused Caddy's eyes to widen, and Mr. Whitlipped's to narrow, a time or two over the evening.

It was two days after Epiphany, I know, that I received a letter from Pennsylvania, dated October 15, 1758.

My dear Mr. Fezziwig,

You may recall that I had sad cause to correspond with you some few years ago, to inform you of the death of my dear brother and your friend, Lawrence, and to send you a token in remembrance of your association. Though I am reluctant to do so, I fear I must write to you again, under circumstances that will bring you and your wife the greatest grief and shedding of tears.

Having followed my late brother's vocation as a soldier, I am attached to the forces of General Forbes in our mission to unseat the French from the headwaters of the Ohio. Only a fortnight ago, I first saw the name Erasmus Fezziwig on a roster of the General's troops, and called for him. The name is uncommon, so I assumed a connexion with you. We spent a pleasant evening meal with remembrances of my brother. I pleased me to hear of his admiration for Lawrence, and of your hospitality when he was your guest in London.

Three days ago, our forward post, called Fort Ligonier, still being constructed, was attacked by the French and their native scouts. The attack was repulsed. However, at night, the enemy made another attempt, but was again repulsed by cannon fire. Erasmus was one of the brave soldiers who fought valiantly, and helped win the day. Colonel James Burd, a Pennsylvanian, was in command, and he has informed me that, as the enemy retreated, a stray bullet found your dear son's heart, and he gave his life in service to his God and King. He suffered not; he was jubilant in victory in one moment, and delivered to Providence the next.

Please know that writing this letter to you is a most difficult task, and my deepest sympathy is with you.

I have arranged, at my own expense, to procure a leaden coffin for your son, and plan to have him interred with dignity and clergy, with said coffin filled with brandy for preservation, in case that you someday have the desire to retrieve it and have it transported to England for final rest. Should that be, please so inform me, and I will offer every assistance within my means to see that your wishes are fulfilled.

My prayers for you and your good wife are constant during this time. Should God spare me during this campaign, I would hope we should, someday, be able to pay each other regards in person, either in England, or here in America. My little home in Virginia would be honored to receive such a visitor, should you ever be inclined to grace it. I am forever, Sir,

Your most Affectionate and Ob't Servant,

Geo. Washington

I was at the warehouse when I read the letter, and fell to the cobbles, overcome by my grief. Laverty came, and quickly deduced what had happened. The man, who had been present at Ras's birth, held me, and we both cried. He sent for his wife, who had helped deliver my boy to life, and she joined our misery. When our tears were spent, Mrs. Laverty said, "You must tell your wife, Mr. Fezziwig, may God help you both."

"I cannot do it. I cannot. I am not able. You must do it for me," I sobbed.

"We will be with you, may God help us, Mr. Fezziwig, but she must hear it from you. It has to be from you."

I knew she was right. They took me to our new home, which had been so novel and bright and pride-filled when I left it that morning. When we arrived, I'm sure the look of it had not changed, but to me is had become dark and fearful, and I wished not to enter. But, I now understood my strange experience in front of the hearth the previous October. Erasmus had stopped to say goodbye on his way to heaven.

I was not prepared for the sincere sympathy offered by so many people when the news became generally known. Whitlipped, not a man given to emotion, hugged me whilst tears streamed down his face. Even Mr. Trembly's eyes glistened; I had not before known that he had lost a brother to a different war many years ago. Dr. Franklin offered his assistance in bringing Erasmus back to England, using his many contacts in Pennsylvania to do so. Caddy and I discussed it, but decided that Ras's enchantment with America was such that we would let him rest in peace in its soil, knowing he had given his life for its protection.

Caddy. Truly, a man cannot fully understand the loss of a child to a mother. We lose love and hope and happiness. Their sex loses all that, plus an actual part of themselves. I feel certain our loss quickened the decline of Ras's grandparents. Indeed, within less than a year, they had both left this world, and Bracebridge passed to Caddy's oldest brother, who continued restoring the manor to more livable condition throughout. Caddy retreated from me, and from everyone, into the blackest depths. For the rest of the year, she hardly left our house. There was no joy in her, and I knew not what to do to change it.

Caddy's misery continued into the following autumn and early winter. I dreaded the coming of Christmastime, fearing the anniversary of our sad news might affect her even more. I shared my concerns with Dr. Franklin. He had a suggestion.

"Will, sometimes doing nothing is the best treatment, I have found. But, if a glass is falling, it does no good to stand by and hope something happens to prevent it from reaching the floor. What I am going to propose will sound strange, dangerous and perhaps even cruel, perhaps, but you know my affection for you and Caddy is such that I am most concerned for your welfare. Is it not?"

"Of course it is. I know that to be true."

"Indeed. I have strong reason to believe that an electric shock, applied to the cranium, can be most therapeutic in treating melancholia. I have received such shocks, by accident, on more than one occasion myself. They induced unconsciousness, but, when I aroused, I had no memory of the event. I did, though, feel refreshed and clear of thought. I have been corresponding with a Dutch doctor, Dr. Igenhousz, who has reported the same thing, and we have contemplated using shock in cases just like Caddy's. Are you willing to try it?"

I was without speech. I trusted my friend, but only knew electricity as something dangerous (since he had found lightening to be nothing but the same) or an oddity. I had seen his demonstrations of making animals twitch with current, and had a horrible vision of Caddy as the subject of a parlour game. But, I was losing my wife, day by day.

"I will give it thought, Doctor. We shall at least wait until after Christmastime, but I will give it thought. I thank you for your concern."

That Christmas Eve, Caddy did not join us for our dancing at the warehouse. Whilst my workers made merry, I made a show of it myself, but my heart was not in it. My losses had been great; I could not bear another. I decided there and then to arrange with Dr. Franklin to administer his treatment for Caddy.

It was dark and cold when I returned home that night, and found Caddy sitting in our chamber, which was only lit by the fire. She raised her head to me as I entered, and smiled. I had not seen her smile in almost a year.

"He found me, Will. We moved, so it took some time, but he found me. He is happy, and now, so am I."

She said no more, and it was not necessary. I had not told her of my experience the night Ras had died so far away. Neither of us ever discussed it again. But, that night before our hearth, she began to hum, and then to sing, and she took my hand, and said, "Let us dance."

I had my Caddy, my happy Caddy, back. Dr. Franklin's treatment was not needed. From that day until now, we celebrated Christmastime with abandon. But, at dinner the next night, when a toast was called to the King, I saw Caddy discreetly lower her glass and her eyes, and drink not. The next year brought a new King, but her refusal to drink his health persists.

Dr. Franklin's time as an agent for Pennsylvania internal affairs and trade came to an end, and he announced that he would return to America. His main objective had been to alter the relationship between the remainders of the Penn family and the populace, seeking a charter similar to that of Virginia, but he had not seen that accomplished.

He had a large and adoring circle in London, and Caddy and I attended many farewell parties for the old gentleman. Our adventures together had been many, and we agreed to keep up regular correspondence. He promised to make sure Ras's resting place, far from Philadelphia but still in Pennsylvania, was marked and tended. Though saddened by the prospect, I assumed I would never see my old and esteemed friend again. His promise to correspond was well kept. Within a few months, I received detailed letters from him concerning the currents he encountered in the crossing, and he asked me to distribute them for comment, to various mutual acquaintances with scientific interests.

Around that time, Mr. Whitlipped allowed a young Scottish solicitor to work with him for a few months, an aristocratic but brash dandy of a man. He brought him to the Root and Wallow one day, and I could tell by Whitlipped's expression that he was not particularly compatible with the young man. Prune was there, and Mr. Goldsmith (a writer and occasional visitor to our table, after the death of Mr. Hadley), and Bracken, and Johnson (who we saw but rarely after the success of his dictionary. He was in the company of the bookbinder, who usually ended up paying for the writer's coffee).

"Please accept my apology for being late today," Whitlipped sighed. In the years I had known him, this was the first time he had ever been late for anything, for he was a man of exceptionally regular habit. "My companion was…detained. This is Mr. James Boswell, recently having passed his examinations in the law at Edinburgh University. You are already acquainted with Mr. Trembly. I present to you Mr. Fezziwig, Mr. Goldsmith, Mr. Bracken, and Dr. Johnson."

"So, Sir," harrumphed Johnson. "Did you visit *Scotland* to become a scholar, or is your association with that country longer term?"

Boswell raised an eyebrow. "Dr. Johnson, I do indeed come from Scotland, but I cannot help it."

Johnson leaned his large frame and its substantial attached belly back in his chair. "That, Sir, I find, is what a great many of your countrymen cannot help."

Prune and Bracken could both be acerbic at times, but they were rank schoolboys when compared to Johnson and the newcomer. At their first exchanges, I thought they would surely end up in fisticuffs, but they both seemed to relish the barbed comments aimed at one another so much that they became sport. The others at the table barely got in a word, on edge. Boswell eventually suggested a libation stronger than coffee, and Johnson pulled his girth out of the chair to leave with him.

"There," I said, as they left, "is a match made in heaven."

"Or, perhaps," sighed Whitlipped, "somewhere much warmer."

"Ha! Indeed!" laughed Bracken. "Our friend now has so much fame, that it is good for business to be his associate. But two coins barely scratch in his pocket. Each day, I hear 'Dr. Johnson said,' or 'According to Dr. Johnson,' or 'Now, what would Dr. Johnson think about' such or another. I would not be surprised if some thought he wrote the ten commandments, and, to prove it, pointed to his dictionary and said, 'See! All the words are in here!' I have never seen anything like it!" I commented that my friend from America expressed that similar things happened to him there, in regard to his almanack sayings.

Mr. Goldsmith gave a grunt. "It is, indeed, out of hand. I heard the best just the other day, from an uncouth driver. He had just narrowly avoided being kicked in the crotch by the horse, and he referred to his escape as having 'saved Dr. Johnson.' He saw my confusion, and said he calls it Dr. Johnson, because Dr. Johnson will stand up to anything! Bosh!"

The fond remembrances of the farewell parties thrown for my friend, Dr. Franklin, had hardly faded, when he returned. I came to know it through a letter delivered by a messenger. I recognized the handwriting at once, but was surprised to see it was not from a mail packet. It was brief: "My dear William, events and, if He is at all interested, perhaps Providence, have brought me back to Craven Street, and I am anxious to renew our association and friendship at your convenience. B. F."

My friend looked a bit older than he had at our last meeting, but the radiant faces of Mrs. Stevenson and her daughter showed how excited they were at his return. Midst chests and packing boxes, we renewed our acquaintance.

I first inquired to the health of his family. Though I had seen his son William a few times in the elder man's absence, I had not met Dr. Franklin's wife, or daughter, as they had never made the crossing. "William's prospects, I think, are good," he said. "His marriage has been satisfactory and, since he is about to complete his education in the law, he will soon be returning to America. He has a head for government, I think, perhaps more so than myself." He paused and looked toward the window. "I do wonder about some of his views at times, but that's certainly to be expected. My own father wished that I enter the clergy." He smiled. "That would have been a turn of events, would it not?"

Our conversation turned darker. "My time on native soil was distressing. There is turmoil in the west, as well as in the city. The wilderness is safer, thanks to the sacrifice of men like your lost son, and settlement continues, but I'm not so sure civilisation follows. Some seek to assert our rights as Englishmen when dealing with the Penns, whilst others seem intent on answering to no authority at all, man, King, or God. I am not sure what will come of it. Reason seems to flying like the years, and I fear I am beginning to feel the weight of it. Nonetheless, I always kept you in my mind whilst there, and I do have some correspondence concerning commerce for you, which may turn out to be profitable. Shall we go over it?"

Fezziwig and Company dealt mainly with products from the West Indies and Carolina, of course, but, thanks to Dr. Franklin, I was able to begin conducting some small business with merchants in Philadelphia, for which I was grateful. When I thanked my friend, he replied, "William, you are a rarity for men, or even women, because you ask nothing of me. For that, I am happy to provide any service. After all," he winked, "it is with few of my associates that I have been naked in the forest."

The demand for goods and space to store them continued to grow with the population of this great city. Yet another new bridge was being built, and canal work made passage into the Lea easier, but the increased competition did not seem to negatively affect our business. I had carefully followed the practice of looking forward, promising no more than I could deliver, and fulfilling contracts exactly as they were made.

My practice of cultivating the character and loyalty of my workers never gave me reason to reconsider it. None were more loyal than Laverty, and I suffered a great loss when he took ill suddenly. I engaged a physician, but to no avail. Even though he had spent so many years in London, his wife wished to have him sent to Ireland for his eternal rest, where he could be laid in ground that had been consecrated according to their beliefs. She would also return, and live with kinfolk.

Their youngest son, Finn (the workers called him 'Fishback'), already worked for me in a labour capacity, but I decided to make him a business apprentice instead, and tend to his education concurrent with his apprenticeship. Caddy and I owed the Lavertys much, and I was not disappointed with Finn's work. When his apprenticeship was over, I wanted him to stay, but, though he had been just a baby when the Lavertys arrived in London, and the most frequent news from Ireland involved famine, he eventually decided to join his family there as well.

When the controversy over taxing the colonies to finance their own protection erupted, I had not seen such heat in conversation since the Young Pretender was knocking at the gate. I was surprised that so many desired to simply cut the colonies off, to their own devices, and be done with them. For some, it was a matter of expenditures and bloodshed; for others, it was a matter of natural rights. Dr. Darwin shared the latter opinion. Accompanied by his young son Charles, he made a point to visit Dr. Franklin and me when in London. On one of his visits, he gave me a small book, with the writings of John Locke, which I have read many times, and may do so again. Each time I take it up, as new events occur, it becomes more enlightening.

Most of my coffeehouse associates, excepting Mr. Whitlipped, were of a different mind, and preferred heavier taxes and, if necessary, confiscation of American goods to punish the ingrates. When news that the King's tax agents were being cruelly abused reached the newspapers, some called for hanging all Americans, and starting over on the continent with a clean slate. Dr. Franklin, of course, was in the centre of the fray, and was formally engaged in debates in Parliament on the matter.

I could not ignore the crisis in America, since trade with the colonies provided my bread and meat, and my association with Dr. Franklin would not allow me to be indifferent. He negotiated a trade of another sort, which repealed the taxes and ended the tar and feathering of tax agents, while reasserting the right of Parliament to oversee, to some degree, internal governing matters across the Atlantic. I could tell he was battered, but relieved, comparing certain elements in the colonies to a collective powder keg.

I was quite surprised when he visited me at the warehouse one day with a small lad in tow. He was an active boy, with a large forehead. While the child explored the warehouse, Dr.

Franklin said, "Will, we have yet another William to keep track of in our conversations. This is William Temple. He is William's son, and thus, my grandson." I knew William was in America, and I had attended his wedding. The boy was of an age that he probably predated that event, so I looked confused, and Dr. Franklin noticed.

"Yes, it is a surprise to me as well. I did not know about him until a fortnight ago myself, but he is indeed my grandson. He was born shortly before William's marriage, and being cared for at his expense by a neutral family. Since it cannot be denied, I have decided to become involved in the boy's education and raising myself, as his presence in William's home at present would be problematic." He sighed. "There are so many advantages to older women, Will, don't you agree?"

I was not in a position to argue.

As the lad grew, he was referred to as William Temple Franklin, and became a companion to his grandfather. It was only later that my friend revealed to me that he had a young son himself, years before, who died of smallpox at four years of age, and that his son William had not been born to Mrs. Franklin. "We all arrive similarly in this world, and it is not as if we do not know the cause," he said, with a small smile.

Looking back on those times, it seemed we lurched from one political crisis to another. The American question had divided the government and those following it, and seemed to spread discontent that could be read in every face. It was as if London was an old blue china server, with a thousand tiny, irregular cracks in the surface that could only be seen by looking closely, but, when placed in the hot oven of dissention, began to open under the stress. One who stoked the fire in the oven was an exceedingly ugly and vulgar man named John Wilkes.

Wilkes, whom I know to have died a few years ago, was one who had a talent in stirring people up against authority. He was a Member of Parliament, but had respect for neither man nor God and wrote blasphemous and wicked things, such that I hope you will never read for fear of you not being able to rid it from your memory. He fled to France to avoid answering to that, and of writing sedition toward the King. He was imprisoned when he returned, but his hold on the minds of some was so great that they rioted, and several were killed at St. George's Field.

Such is the reason I have never understood politics: close upon being released from prison, the man became a sheriff in London. It was then that I was summoned to his chambers. As with my summons to the magistrate years before, I had no idea of its purpose, and a very ill feeling about the whole affair.

It bears saying a second time that Mr. Wilkes was an exceedingly ugly man. I know that is no fault of one's own, and not a reflection of character, but my statement is true. He gazed in two directions at once, the shape of his head gave the appearance of having been manipulated, and his chin protruded whilst his lips puckered. His voice was high and thin and lispy.

"Good of you to come, Mr. Fezziwig." he said. "I know many things about you, but you only know of me what is reported in the newspapers, I assume." I didn't know how to answer, so I did not at all. He continued.

"I know you are an honest man of business, having come to it through your own work, and comfortable, though rather middling. You are well acquainted with at least two men of my acquaintance also, Mr. Bracken and Dr. Franklin. Though they won't say it, neither holds me in much regard, I sense. But, no matter. It is men like you who will make the difference."

"Difference, Sir?" I asked. "Difference in what?"

"Our future, Fezziwig! Our government is corrupt! It should be serving men such as you, who toil and employ and provide! Instead, it works mostly for those who inherit and live off the work of others!"

I was careful with my words. "I, through the grace of Providence, have been able to eat and stay warm through the years, Sir, thank you. As to all the rest, like most, I just wish to be left alone to go about my way."

He sat back in his chair. Given the trajectory of his eyes, I was not sure if he stared at me, or at some apparition over my left shoulder.

"Indeed, Mr. Fezziwig, that is what we all wish. To go our own ways. But do not the layers of aristocracy impede us? Were you not born with the same rights as those who sit in judgment?"

"I have never felt ill-used, Sir. I have given my son, my only child, to our defence against the French, in America. My goodwife and I still feel the loss each day. But, I know thousands, millions, have done so over history, and I have no thought that it will ever end, I'm afraid."

"Right you are in that, Fezziwig. Especially if men such as yourself just want to be *left alone*." He spat the last two words out like something rotted. "But, if your men find a hole in your boat on the Lea, do they grant its wish to be *left alone*? That is what we face, Sir. The boat is sinking. The time comes when we must decide to seal the hole, get off the boat, or sink with it." I saw small blots of spittle forming on his puckered lips.

"I respect your views, Sir, as I do of many others. But, what are you asking of me?" I did not want to be there, and risked sounding impolite to a sheriff.

"I want you to join me, Mr. Fezziwig. To join loyalty and liberty. You are a man of means. Help me support our cause, and even, perhaps, to be seated in Parliament yourself someday, as one of my allies."

I could not help but to utter a tiny chuckle. "Sir, if you please, I stand as if gazing at the sky on a clear night. The stars swirl above me, yet I can name but a few of them. They leave me alone, and I them. I wish you the very best, but now I must go."

I feared a knock on my door that night. It did not come. I debated with myself on whether to mention my interview to Dr. Franklin, but knew I ultimately could not withhold it.

"You surely did rightly, Will," he said, seemingly with genuine relief. "I have met him several times, and under some circumstances I would rather forget. I know there are those who say we should be allies. Some of what he writes is true. We will reform or die. Some in the colonies see him as a great thinker on rights and liberty, but he is a dangerous man, and you are well served to avoid his association. Tell me, through all the time you have known me, with as many losses as wins in my endeavors with His Majesty's government, have you even known me to advocate separating ourselves from it?"

"Never," I said.

"No, because I am an Englishman. And an American. They are not incompatible." He paused, and then said, almost at a whisper, "At least, not yet."

A few days later, news arrived from Boston (not the one I trudged through from Great Grimsby) that British regulars had fired upon a rabble of colonists, killing several in the streets. From that day, I saw the weight of events begin to weigh heavily upon my friend. There were diversions, of course. He made several trips to visit the Lunarticks again, and traveled in Ireland. The latter brought him back rather despondent, though, saying that, once a colony has used up much of its resources, there is not much left to rebuild for its own people, if wealth continued to flow to the empire.

We attended the wedding of Polly Stevenson to a young physician, William Hewson, and Dr. Franklin played the role of a father in the ceremony. "Our list of Williams continue to grow, and, as my faculties give way, I fear I will not be able to keep them straight," he laughed. Upon telling me that his daughter (I do forget her name, I'm afraid) in Philadelphia had given him a grandson, he said "And he is not another William, but a Benjamin, thank God!"

His scientific demonstrations continued, even throughout those turbulent times. He once asked me if I had ever witnessed a human dissection. When I answered negatively, he said, "Oh, you must! It is most interesting. Dr. Hewson performs them regularly, on Craven Street. I shall let you know when next he has a body!" I politely rejected that offer, and never again felt quite comfortable with any refreshments served to me there.

He was much more insistent with another invitation, though. Lord Huskings had invited Dr. Franklin to view antiquities he had acquired, some from the east midlands. Since I was familiar with that area, I was to accompany him. "Huskings is interested in science and history, but known to be not a whit inclined to the causes of any Colonials, no matter from what corner of the realm, I'm afraid," he said. "I will, I promise, keep conversation to scientific matters only."

We arrived at the Huskings town home in Dr. Franklin's borrowed carriage. The host was nondescript, except for the

angle of his nose, which gave the impression he was looking
down it. Perhaps he was doing so. We had a fine meal, attended
by servants with very good wine, and sprinkled with our host's
tirades on what should be done to the American, as well as the
French, Catholics, Irish, Scots, Methodists, and so-ons.

Not soon enough for me, we were shown to another
chamber with glass-topped oaken cabinets. There was some
equipment that I recognized as having to do with electricity from
seeing Dr. Franklin's demonstrations, some stuffed animals not
hailing from Britain, and several other oddities. We were seated
at a table, and Lord Huskings brought out a small chest.

"This I have recently purchased, from Lincolnshire,' he
said, opening the chest. "I know it is very old, and I want your
opinion on it." He brought out a small object, wrapped in cloth.

I gasped when I saw it. Dr. Franklin said, "Ah, it is good
that I have my Lincolnshire friend here, your Lordship, for I
think he can, indeed, enlighten you as to the object's origin."

Before me was the shoe from the bog mummy.

"Where did you get this?" I asked, perhaps too bluntly for
the circumstances, and Huskings scowled. "As I said, in
Lincolnshire. A gentleman there, whom I shall not name, has
been collecting items for some time, but has need of a bit of
liquidity, and contacted me. Do you know something of this, or
not?"

"Indeed I do, Sir, and it is a great pity that it has been
separated from its whole. A great pity, for a curiosity, instead of
kept for learning. But, I can provide you with a pamphlet that
tells it story, at least as far as is possible, that I wrote shortly
after it was first excavated. Do you know where the rest of the
mummy is now?"

"I do not," he said. "I suppose other parts were similarly sold, though none would be, I think, as interesting and as presentable as a shoe." He looked on the object with pride. "So, I will expect your pamphlet to be sent 'round tomorrow, perhaps?" I knew it was an order rather than a request. "And, oh, yes, this. Old jewelry, I suppose, but who can really tell? Gold, when cleaned, could have been wrought yesterday, or a thousand yesterdays."

I glanced down. The blood seeped from my face, and my throat gurgled. Huskings looked surprised. "William, are you alright?" asked Dr. Franklin.

The lion's one bright blue eye stared up at me with inner fire. It was the jewel I had plucked from the turnip patch, more than thirty years before.

"William?" Dr. Franklin said again, shaking me lightly on the shoulder.

"Yes, sorry. The wine, I suppose. You are right, of course. It could have been fashioned yesterday, or long, long ago. There is no way to say for certain."

"That's what I thought. It is a pretty thing, but not complete. It has some value, in the gold and the stone. I could not know the purity until it is melted, of course, but it does remain a curiosity."

"Indeed, it does," said Dr. Franklin, giving me a glance from the side. "My friend Fezziwig is gifted at drawing such articles. If you could provide him pen and paper, he will make a drawing of it for me, and I will consider it further."

A servant brought the items, and I took the jewel in my hand, the very hand that had freed it from its resting place, the hand that was unable to keep its father from being dragged away. I made a careful drawing of it, and we took our leave of Lord Huskings.

When settled in the coach, Franklin said, "William Lucian Fezziwig. Indeed, my friend, you hold a secret, as sure as I am an old man troubled by gout. And I shall have it."

Until that night, only two people had heard the story of the jewel, and one of them rested under the sod in Pennsylvania. Caddy was the other, and, though I knew she believed me, she was used to my occasional enhancements for the sake of a story, and probably felt the tale of the jewel held some of those. I held nothing back, and that evening Dr. Franklin knew the entire story. He was silent for a time. "Remarkable. What shall we do?" he asked.

"Surely, it is what *can* we do!" I exclaimed. "It was stolen from us, and my father most likely did not see the dawn because of it. What we thought a blessing turned out to be a curse!"

He paused again. "Has it, Will? Did not your loss set you upon the path that brought you to this carriage on this night, on the way home to the arms of a loving wife, and with a prosperous business? In this, I have questions only, not answers. Those you will have to provide."

There was more silence, and then, "I am saddened, like you, of the ancient shoe being separated from its owner. The girl had worn if for a thousand years, most likely, and now they are separated. Not as much can be learned by looking at parts instead of the whole. It is good that the world has your drawings, for that will be the only way the maid will be remembered. It seems an affront, somehow."

More silence, for a long while, but I could almost hear the cogitation and feel the heat emanating from my friend's bulging forehead. Finally, he said, "We have detailed drawings. We could have an exact copy made. Huskings is keen to know more about it. I could tell him that an electric current could be employed to tell the age of wrought metal. The jewels could be switched."

I thought for a moment. "Do you really think it could be done?" I asked.

"It's not without risk. He would probably not allow it to happen except under his watch, but it is easy enough to arrange a substitution, perhaps in a black box with a false floor. Of course, we could simply offer to buy the jewel, but I know he would expect a great price. We must not be hasty. Let us both think tonight and tomorrow, and talk again in two days." I agreed.

When Caddy asked me about the evening, I told her about the shoe only. In case we implemented Dr. Franklin's plan, and it turned out badly for us, I wanted her to know nothing of it. In two days, I visited Craven Street.

"Have you considered our options, Will?" asked Dr. Franklin.

"Indeed, I have. I lay in the arms of my wife and thought it through. I have known loss and tragedy, but, as you said, have a goodwife and am prosperous. I also have a friend, perhaps the most famous scientist in the world, willing to risk his mission and reputation, and perhaps even the gibbet, to return to me what was lost. I have, kind Sir, all the treasure I need. Let Huskings have the rest."

After that night, the pace of American events quickened to their inevitable conclusion. The only talk was of what had happened in Boston and other ports in the colonies, when the India Company's tea was viciously destroyed.

I could tell Dr. Franklin felt helpless, though he tried his best to broker some type of accommodation, as he had on the earlier occasion concerning tax stamps. "The cry at home is 'Taxation without representation,' but it's show only," he confided. "The last thing that would benefit us would be representation. Just think of it. A few members in Parliament? To be ridiculed and voted down upon every turn? Our plight would be worsened, not bettered. But, I still have hope that reason will prevail. We have our friends in Parliament, and they are not without influence."

We tried to make that Christmastime enjoyable, but both a loss in Dr. Franklin's London family and politics made it difficult. Dr. William Hewson, Polly's husband, had cut himself during a dissection, and could not be saved from the sepsis, leaving her a widow after only four years of marriage. As to politics, there was the feeling as if a great storm approached. The storm broke in January, when Dr. Franklin was called before the Privy Council in Whitehall. The solicitor, Mr. Wedderburne, abused him most foully. Even the newspapers did not print the full extent of the invective hurled at my friend by the solicitor, and by many of the Lords themselves.

I went to see him early the next morning. He was breakfasting with his friend Dr. Priestley, who was visiting, and appeared a broken man.

"My friends, up until yesterday, we were countrymen," he told us both, "But I regret to say, we are so no more. It is clear the colonies are but beasts of burden, though treated more poorly. It is time for the harness to be unattached." His eyes glistened. "My reputation in my homeland has suffered, because

I held faith that reasonable men could, indeed, reason together, in order to avoid bloodshed. I now know that I was wrong. It is only a matter of time that I will be called back to America, and, my friends, you and I will technically be enemies."

Dr. Priestley and I both protested. Surely, there would be a reaction to the cruelness of the Lords' action, and violence would be averted. Surely, the King would intervene, after seeing such action.

"I no longer look to the King, Will. From today, I look to liberty."

The next year was like a slow, lingering, and painful death. We knew each day could bring the end of our association, and there could be no news but bad. There was no longer hope of a cure. Some days, we could forget and have pleasant conversation and even have short jaunts, but he was aging before my eyes, and everyone knew not to make plans ahead, for the end was near, and would come suddenly. Such was the anxiety the following Christmastime, that of 1774, a dark year in which John Wilkes became Lord Mayor of London, and the Fezziwigs had Christmas dinner with Benjamin Franklin for the last time.

In late winter, he prepared to leave. We had become so attached to him that it equaled any heartache I had experienced, but one. As if the gods of old were plotted against him, he received word from Philadelphia, not long before leaving, that his wife had died. He had not spoken of her very often, except to say that she was a homebody, but sent her pretty things and, I know, wrote letters. He had sacrificed a life of leisure with her for a cause that was flying apart.

There were no cheerful farewell parties upon his second leaving. He knew that, shortly, he would occupy a cold cell if he did not soon make the crossing. When we bade farewell, Caddy and Mrs. Stevenson and Polly were sobbing, and our own eyes glistened. It would be reasonable to think, because of his age, we would never see one him again.

Providence, though, had a different plan. If, indeed, Providence makes plans.

PART THE SIXTH: *FULL CIRCLE*

Trade was not immediately affected. Customers started to hoard everything coming from America, and the warehouse inventory moved briskly. Products continued to make the crossing from Carolina for almost a year. Correspondence from Mr. Gates (the Junior now, who had taken over from his deceased father long before) and other sources indicated they wanted to continue trade as regularly as possible, and I agreed.

The port of Charles Town was in the hands of the rebels early during the conflict, but was then reopened by our Navy after a time. Prices rose, merchants found new sources in the east, and still needed warehouse space. While the overall effect of the war years was a negative one, Fezziwig and Company survived.

Among some of my friends and acquaintances, my reputation suffered by my association with Dr. Franklin, and my good relations with Americans in general. Dr. Darwin, who continued to visit me whenever he was in London even in Dr Franklin's absence, was an exception, since he was adamantly in favor of independence as soon as a people evolved and matured to a point it could be successfully accomplished.

I had no strong thought on the matter. My son had shed his blood to protect the Americans, and his thoroughly English body rested there. Did that mean he was now in hostile ground, with no gratitude for his sacrifice, and that, should the rebels prevail, he would lie forever in a foreign land? It was some comfort to me that his grave was in Pennsylvania, because, while Erasmus was far from Philadelphia, Doctor Franklin was from Pennsylvania. I also thought of my affection for Lawrence, the great friend from my youth, and the kindness shown by his brother, whom I had never met. To hear how the name George Washington was misused in London, one would think the postmark on the letters from him I kept must read 'Hell.'

It was during that time that I first began to feel the years, more than fifty of them. Caddy and I had both become quite stout, and my only hair was that I purchased. In a strange way, losing my considerably older friend had taken away my feeling of youthfulness and adventure. He could convince me to do things and to meet people I would not otherwise consider, and see mysteries to be solved in the most mundane. The conversations at the coffeehouse, while still lively and especially heated during the war, slowly began to dwindle as my old associates began their decline, and younger men of influence chose to join clubs instead.

When one is old and details the story of his life, it necessarily contains many tales of losing friends to old age. It was during the war that I lost one of the dearest and best. I was still a lad when I first met Mr. Whitlipped, and I came to him dirty, cold, and hungry. He seemed old to me then, and never appeared to age an additional day in the more than thirty years that followed. Even now, I cannot say how old Mr. Whitlipped actually *was*. His steady manner helped me through every crisis that life brought during those times. He took a boy from the fields and helped make him a successful man of business.

Except for suicide, I suppose, we do not choose the manner or time of our own demise. I think Mr. Whitlipped was an exception. Mr. Trembly (though I'm sure his ghost would not be angered if I called him Prune, as he had gotten used to it) had died a year before, and Mr. Whitlipped had taken on a new, young partner, Mr. File. The young man was quite amiable as well as able, and, while he seemed always anxious when compared to the reserved Whitlipped, the two became friends, as well as colleagues. That meant, of course, that Mr. File became my friend as well.

On that particular day, I was seated at the Root and Wallow with Dr. Darwin, who was visiting the city, and was a bit surprised that Whitlipped had not already arrived. The Doctor had some involvement in designing the mechanics of improved navigation on the Lea, with the workings of the locks. His reputation as a physician was growing, but, at the same time, he was becoming known as a bit of a radical. His support of American independence was well known.

Even more than the colonies, though, his views on education for young women, of all classes, drew derision when mentioned in the newspapers. He believed that schools should be established for their formal instruction, which caused hot discussion in the coffeehouse. My only comment on the matter was that I had, fortunately, met some success in life, after having been taught to read and write by a young girl, sitting under a tree in the fields.

Dr. Darwin had just stated that he would wait no longer for Whitlipped before having his chop, when a boy came with a message. It said: "Mr. Fezziwig, if at all possible, please come to the home of Mr. Whitlipped at your earliest convenience. He has urgent business with you. Your Ob'd Svt., B. File"

I had never heard the words Whitlipped and Urgent in the same breath, so I went immediately. I had only been to his personal chambers a few times over the years, and they were exactly as I remembered them. Nothing, it seems, had changed from the first time I had entered them more than thirty years prior. Not a chair, nor a tablecloth, nor a carpet, nor a candlestick.

Mr. File met me at the door, and I asked the nature of the urgent business.

"Ah, yes, Mr. Fezziwig. I am so glad you came. Mr. Whitlipped is, well, apparently, you see, Mr. Whitlipped has scheduled to, ah, die today, and he wishes to see you."

"What?" I was shocked, for I had seen him but three days prior, with no change in him whatsoever. 'What do you mean, scheduled to die?"

"Oh. Poor words, sorry. He is, indeed, dying, and it does seem it will be today. He has known it for some time, for I looked on his calendar to see what appointments need to be canceled due to the sickness that came upon him yesterday, and his entry for today says die."

I felt for young File, for there was great pain in his face. "Come this way, please," he said, and I followed, not knowing more to say.

The room was dark, and Whitlipped was laying, propped up and tucked in with blankets, on a tall, ancient bed with the curtains pulled back. His face and hands were all that were visible, and those were the colour of unbleached wool. I saw no movement, and thought I might have been too late, but his eyelids flew open as I bent over him, giving me a start.

"William! Thank you for coming. I knew this time would be convenient for you." His voice was otherworldly, rasping like an ancient, rusty hinge. "I want you to know that I have thoroughly schooled Mr. File in your accounts, and you will receive a complete ledger within a fortnight. All is in order. You are free to choose another solicitor, of course, but I advise against it, for Mr. File will serve you well, for a fair price."

I looked into his pale grey eyes, almost lifeless. "Tut, Mr. Whitlipped! We will fetch a physician! Think not of business now. We will have you better, and back at the table at the Root and Wallow!"

"No, my seat at the table is now vacant, I'm afraid. I have taken the liberty to suggest that Mr. File begin to occupy it, if it is your pleasure. Our association has been most profitable, Will, and I am grateful for it." He closed his eyes and laid back, though the rasping breath continued.

I heard Mr. File's voice behind me. He said, softly, "Mr. Fezziwig, Sir, I'm afraid Mr. Whitlipped's next appointment has arrived. He scheduled them every quarter-hour, you see."

I was stunned. "He scheduled in all his clients? Whilst he lies dying?"

"Yes. As you know, Mr. Whitlipped is a man of regular habit, and much detailed in his life." He paused, as if considering whether or not to tell me something further. "I feel that he knew his end was near, and has such self-control that he willed it to be today, because, you see, today is the end of the quarter, and it coincides with the termination of several contracts, and it is, from a business and accounting view, very neat." It seemed every word was difficult for Mr. File.

"I know, Mr. Fezziwig, that he has great pride in you, and

considers you his closest friend. But, another client awaits, Sir, I'm sorry. But, if you would be able to see me in our offices tomorrow, I do have a small matter to discuss."

"Certainly, Mr. File. And please let me know if there is anything I can do for Mr. Whitlipped."

"Yes, of course."

Caddy was distressed to hear of my old friend's demise, for she also loved him dearly, and we had suffered so many losses. She knew that we owe much of our success to Mr. Whitlipped, and that he was the last remaining mentor from my youth. He had been a father, in a way, to a young man who had lost his own.

I saw Mr. File the following morning, and he answered my question before I asked it. "Yes, Mr. Fezziwig, our friend's journey is done. It was without pain or agitation. He simply sighed and closed his eyes, and was done. It came on the stroke of seven o'clock."

We stared at one another for a moment. "Close-of-business time," I said.

"Precisely."

"I am very sorry to have to ask this, after my years of affection for the man, but does he have family? He was widowed many years ago, before our meeting, and he had no children. Beyond that, I know not."

"No, he did not. None whatsoever. I am his administrator, and none are listed in his will."

At that very moment, the thought struck me for the very first time: the same could be my fate. Caddy had siblings and many nephews and nieces, but I had no one, not a single living blood relative. It hit me like having a bale dropped upon me from the top of the warehouse, and I began to sob, as I had not since Ras's death. I could tell Mr. File was taken aback and knew not what to say, but was sympathetic. When I regained myself, I apologized.

"No need, Sir, none indeed. I know you were a good friend to him, and he had the greatest affection for you, so your loss is felt."

"I will pay for the funeral and mourning," I said. "It is the least I can do for him."

"That is what I need to talk with you about, Sir," File said, gently. "It will be no surprise to you that he had everything well planned. He is leaving his estate to the company, of course, with a few charitable contributions. He not only specified funds for his funeral, but also left very specific arrangements for it. There will be no expense to you, Sir, and all will be fitting and following his wishes. But, what I needed to tell you, is that he had already procured exquisite gloves for the mourners, a better quality than usual for such occasions, and, well, here is a pair, so you can see."

The handed me a pair of kid gloves from his desk, and they were fine indeed, supple and strongly stitched. Embroidered on the cuff was "In memory of Mister Whitlipped, by Wm. Fezziwig, Reliable Imports and Warehouse, Leaside."

I smiled. "He has done you one last favor, Mr. Fezziwig," Mr. File said. "They have even already been tied up, with silk."

I managed a small laugh. "A man of business, with my interest in mind, to the end!" I said. Mr. File produced a bottle and we drank a toast to the departed, and I rose to leave.

"One last thing, Mr. File," I said, turning back toward him. "In all our years, I have never seen or heard our friend's first name. Under the circumstances, I am most ashamed to admit it. I never asked, and never knew, but I wondered about it over the years. I considered him like family, but he never shared with me his Christian name. I have seen him sign his first initial as 'M.' Was it Michael, as I assumed?"

Mr. File looked puzzled. "Why no, Sir. I thought you knew. His first name was Mister. Mister Whitlipped."

It seemed most fitting.

The following day, again whilst seated with Dr. Darwin at the Root and Wallow, the same messenger boy found me. This time, his message was only verbal.

"If it pleases, Sir, Mr. File requests that you come to the home of the late Mr. Whitlipped, immediately if possible, Sir. Something dire has happened, and he is in need of assistance!"

I gave the boy a coin and left at once. Dr. Darwin, who had become well acquainted with Mr. Whitlipped during his visits to London and coffee with Dr. Franklin and me, offered to come as well, and I welcomed it.

Dr. Darwin was amazed at how much the Whitlipped digs looked like a box that had been sealed decades ago, in perfect order. We found Mr. File seated just inside the door.

"Oh, Mr. Fezziwig! Thank goodness you are here. I am so sorry to disturb you, Sir, but I didn't really know upon whom else to call. Something terrible has happened!"

"What is it?" I asked. "Has Mr. Whitlipped's house been robbed?" I knew it was not an uncommon event just after someone's death.

"Yes! Um, well, no. In a way, I suppose, though nothing is gone. No *thing*, that is, is gone."

I'm sure the look on my face said all I needed to say. "File, please, get a hold of yourself and tell us, what happened?"

"Mr. Whitlipped, I'm afraid, Sir, is gone."

I sighed. "Yes, Mr. File, I know he is gone, and we all feel the pain of it. But, you have the responsibility to carry out…"

"Sir!" Mr. File shouted, which quite surprised me. "Sir, what I mean to say is that Mr. Whitlipped is *gone*. Someone has stolen his body!"

Dr. Darwin and I looked at each other, flabbergasted.

"Yes, I know," said Mr. File, almost in tears. "It is ghoulish, but I have heard of it happening. I brought in the undertaker, within an hour of Mr. Whitlipped's last breath. He worked for some hours, doing what he does, with an assistant. They left before midnight. I met them here yesterday afternoon, when they brought the coffin, and all was in order. I came back in this morning to prepare for this evening's wake, and, as you can see, no Whitlipped. What are we going to do?" The young man was clearly horrified.

"Collect yourself, File," Dr. Darwin commanded. "And find me quill and paper, if you please." Mr. File did so, and Dr. Darwin settled his girth into a chair opposite the young man. "Now, tell me every minute of your actions regarding Mr. Whitlipped over the past two days. Omit nothing!"

Mr. File seemed to calm after having been given a task, and he gave a detailed narrative of events. The doctor asked questions, and occasionally scribbled notes.

When Mr. File had exhausted his memory, Dr. Darwin leaned back, closed his eyes, and pressed fingertips together for a moment, then hopped out of the chair and produced a small glass from his pocket. He dropped to hands and knees, which was not easy for him, and examined the floor carefully. He made his way from the empty coffin to the front door, and then to the back, and all around the perimeter of the ground floor of the house, before coming back to the desk and making more notes and some sketches.

"Whatever happens in this world leaves marks," he said, with some authority. "Most never see them, because they know not where to look. I have much information about the thief, and that will help bring him to justice. He acted alone; only one man entered and removed our friend. He came in through the unlocked back window, and removed the body the same way. There is a hole in his left boot, and the brigand even felt comfortable enough to pause to take snuff during his treachery. He is moderately strong, for he worked alone, even though our friend was not all that heavy a burden, I suppose."

He leaned back, quite pleased with himself. "We shall right this wrong, gentlemen!"

Mr. File looked dubious. "The funeral is scheduled only," he looked at the clock. "Six hours from now, Doctor. Shall I send messengers to cancel it? How on earth shall I word such a message?" He winced.

"Nay, Mr. File. Fezziwig and I will be off to deal with this matter. I knew our friend well enough to think any last minute change of schedule would not be to his liking!"

I could not disagree with that statement, but I also did not want the memory of my friend, who had never missed an appointment in his life, to be sullied by missing his final one.

"Let's be off, William! We have work!" Dr. Darwin seemed so energized by the challenge that he moved like a man of smaller girth. We went to the back of the house, and he bent down. "Ah! See! Drag marks. They go to the back street!" We walked along, bent over, with Dr. Darwin seeing signs that were invisible to me. The trail ended at the kerb. "He loaded our friend into a waggon here. Now what? What from here?" Dr. Darwin muttered to himself.

"We must tell the sheriff, and the magistrate, and the Runners!" I exclaimed. "We will never be able to find him on our own!"

"Tut, Fezziwig, modern methods are much superior. The Runners are nothing but a band of part-time brigands themselves! But, I suppose it is necessary, and your powers of observation, no offence, my friend, are of no help in this stage. You and File initiate those channels, but be sure to leave something in the right palms to prevent word from being spread that the body is missing. Meet me back here in two hours' time."

I collected File, and made a decision to go directly to Lord Mayor Wilkes, not knowing if I would be able to find him, or if he would see me. I was surprised to find both happen, and Mr. File and I were standing in his presence within a half-hour. I had not seen him since our interview some years before, and I cannot say the time had improved his look.

"Ah, Mr. Fezziwig! It is good to see you again. I trust you are well? I know losing our mutual American friend has been a blow." I was surprised as the extent to which my association with Dr. Franklin was known. "As you might know, I believe making war against our American cousins is immoral. Your reputation as an honest man of commerce has been maintained, from what I hear, and I am proud to say it. Are you wishing to discuss how we might cooperate in our endeavors?"

I was in a great hurry, so I simply bowed, thanked him for his interest in me, and spilled our crisis, and our need for help. He listened attentively, and seemed genuinely distressed.

"It is a devilish problem," he said. "The effect of gin is beginning to dissipate, I think, but the masses come to the city for work, and they expend themselves, with others ready to take their places when they fall dead. It is no wonder some are driven to even desecrate corpses. These resurrectionists run rampant, and their methods grow more sophisticated. Of course, there is actually a good cause behind it all. I know churchmen are against it, but how else should doctors be trained, but through dissection? And why should we make them criminals by doing so? The supply of executed is declining, thankfully, so we need to find another way."

"I do hope your friend, Dr. Darwin, has not fallen into a world that will bring him harm. I have not met him, but would like to do so. I have read his writings, and know we agree on many things. Of course, I will help in any way I can. We will first notify the Runners. Go back to the deceased's lodgings, and I will send them with haste. They will fetch you if you are needed."

I saw real concern and compassion in his eye, the one that pointed my way, at least, and my attitude toward the man changed. A still-nervous Mr. File and I returned to wait at Mr. Whitlipped's house, and nothing I could do would divert File's stare at the clock face. At last, a Runner knocked upon the door. "Compliments of the Lord Mayor, Sir, your friend's corpse has been located, as has your friend, the Doctor. If you would follow me in your carriage, you can collect them both."

Mr. File was so relieved that I thought he would collapse, for we had very little time before mourners would begin to arrive. My carriage and driver were ready, and I followed the Runner, who drove his own small waggon into a wretched part of the city, nearby, but very different. It reminded me that, since my situation had changed over the years, it was easy for me to forget about my initial arrival in London, and the plight of the poor classes who continued to swell it.

We came to a stop before a wretched, filthy warren of paths too narrow for the carriage, and followed the Runner through to a dark hovel that stank of waste and death. Inside, we found, crowded around the tightly shroud-wrapped corpse, four Runners, a dirty, vile-looking man with no teeth who was tied hand and foot, and Dr. Darwin. The latter was nursing a bloody nose, and one eye was dark purple.

"Ah, Fezziwig!" Dr. Darwin announced, pointing at the bound man. "Behold the villain! I have found and subdued him, and he shall pay for his sins! He attempted to flee and fought me, but you can see the result," he said proudly. I noticed the Runners glance at one another and roll their eyes. "But, we must hurry. The funeral hour approaches. Help me, here, men."

Two of the Runners picked up the corpse, for and aft, and carried it out to my carriage. Being too long to lay cross-wise on a seat, we arranged it into a seated position. I sat beside it, and held it into place. The carriage tipped in his direction as Dr. Darwin entered and seated himself opposite, still holding a handkerchief to his nose. "Observation, Fezziwig, triumphs in the end, but sometimes force, most primal, is also needed. We must hurry!"

The driver had his instructions to make haste, but, after a time, I heard his voice urging the horse, and the flip of his whip, and we began to rock and lurch dangerously.

The corpse fell forward onto Dr. Darwin's ample lap. "What the devil?" he said. "I know we must hurry, but it will do no good for us to overturn, except to produce more corpses!" I looked out the window to see the cause of the driver's actions, and found another carriage, with a team of two, was close behind us, and the driver used the whip liberally. We were being pursued!

"D---, Fezziwig! The villain must have associates! If they catch us, they shall try to put us on the dissection table, I'll wager! Driver! For your life! We must not be caught!"

The carriage that chased us was light and pulled by two, and we could not outrun it. To my great relief, even though I could almost feel the breath of the huge horses that pulled it, the carriage broke off onto a side road, and was gone.

"Ha! Thought better of it I suppose!" cried Dr. Darwin. "I would have dealt with them as I did their cohort, the brigands. They would rue the day!" I noticed his nose had again begun to bleed.

Suddenly, the horse protested loudly, and the corpse and I both were thrown forward onto Dr. Darwin. When I recovered, I looked out the window to see the pursuing carriage had cut us off from a side road. A man got out of it, and approached my carriage door. I was as stiff as my seatmate, with fear.

The man came to the window and said, "Halloo, Mr. Fezziwig!" I was surprised, and relieved, to see a face I knew. It was Dr. Magnus Falconar, who was married to the late Dr. William Hewson's sister, Dorothy. I had met Dr. Falconar in the company of Polly and Dr. Franklin several times, and I knew he had taken over his late brother-in-law's practice.

"Mr. Fezziwig!" he repeated. "I have a most urgent matter with you. I am sorry for the brusque manner, but I must speak to you!"

"Dr. Falconar, if you please, we are in quite a rush! Can it wait until tomorrow? You see, my friend Mr. Whitlipped, I know you have met him several times, has expired and, it's a long story, but this is his corpse, and we must deliver it to his home for his funeral!"

The young Doctor looked at the shrouded corpse with great surprise. "Yes, Mr. Fezziwig, that is exactly the nature of my business. You see, I have Mr. Whitlipped, or his corpse, of course, in my carriage, and I must give it to you, with all respect."

"What?" Dr. Darwin and I exclaimed, at once.

"It's true, I am afraid," said Falconar, with some degree of shame. "You know that dissection is important to instruction in my field, and we do have to obtain, ah, *candidates* where we can. I obtained a specimen this morning, after having been assured that it was from a criminal executed at Newgate. But, upon examination, I saw it was your late friend, Mister Whitlipped." When he saw the look on my face, he added, "There is no mistake. It is him. I recognized him immediately."

"Then who, pray tell, is this?" I cried, pointing at the corpse sitting beside me.

"I'm sure I have no idea, Sir. Shall I take a look?" He produced a penknife and made a small cut in the cloth, turning the face of the corpse away so that I would not be forced to see it. "Hm. Young man, teens, I would say, blonde hair, tall but malnourished. Cholera, most likely."

Dr. Darwin and I were both speechless, which is a rarity. Finally, Dr. Falconar broke the silence.

"Ahem. Shall we trade?"

"Indeed, Sir." In the street, we carried the corpses to and fro, until I was assured the correct one was seated beside me. Whilst accomplishing the task, I introduced the two physicians to one another and gave Falconar a brief account of what had transpired.

"It is fortunate, indeed, I was able to find you, Mr. Fezziwig. I have great respect for you, and your deceased friend, and am thankful to be able to help him receive the disposition he deserves. And," he turned to Dr. Darwin, "it is a great pleasure to meet such a famous fellow physician, Dr. Darwin. I hope we shall again, under less exceptional circumstances."

We were soon again on our way, but, as we approached Mr. Whitlipped's lodgings, we saw a number of people assembled at the door, awaiting the funeral.

"Doctor!" I exclaimed to my companion. "What are we to do? We can't be seen carrying my friend in through the front door to his own funeral!"

"With luck, the back window will still be unlocked," said Dr. Darwin. "Let us drive 'round, and carry him from the lane out of sight."

Climbing through a window was not going to be an easy task for either of us. Though I was a decade older than Dr. Darwin, and quite stout myself, I had a slightly better chance of fitting through, and thus it fell to me. Halfway in, I could not move further forward. To my dismay, neither could I back out. My wig fell upon the floor and I could not reach it to put it back on, my arms being immobilized. I yelled for Mr. File, hoping no one else was yet in the house, and that he would come to my rescue.

When he came into the back room, the young man was apoplectic. In his panic, the first thing he did upon seeing me was to pick up my wig and place it back upon my head.

"Mr. Fezziwig! Thank God! Mourners are pounding at the door, and demand to be let in! Where is Mr. Whitlipped?"

"Open the back door, Mr. File, and we shall bring him in."

Mr. File and Dr. Darwin carried my old friend into the front room and laid him in the coffin, whilst the commotion at the front door became louder. As soon as the corpse was suitably arranged, Mr. File ran to the door and opened it, and the mourners entered. He gave a nervous apology for the delay, and the ceremony began. It was not until it was over that Mr. File and Dr. Darwin returned to the back room and, with great difficulty, dislodged me from the window, in time to run to join the end of the procession.

With the whole affair finally over, Mr. File, Dr. Darwin, and I returned to Mr. Whitlipped's lodging, and had a last drink to his memory. It was only then that Mr. File noticed he had placed my wig on backwards, and apologized profusely. "You know that Mr. Whitlipped would have been greatly amused by this whole thing," I said, "if only it had happened to someone else."

Mr. Whitlipped's departure left a great void for me. There had been few days since my arrival in London almost forty years prior that I had not seen him, except for the time I spent in America. I had other friends and business associates, and did not lack for company, but his passing also made me miss my old friend from Philadelphia even more. Reading that Dr. Franklin had moved from Pennsylvania to Paris in order to procure assistance for the American cause from the King, I attempted to write to him, but, during wartime, the mails with an enemy were almost always destined for failure.

The next great disruption came from within. I have said before that I believe I have benefited from Providential intervention, but am wary of those, of any belief, who are certain theirs is the only path to knowing God. The character of a man or woman, be they Church of England, Methodist, Jew, or Hindoo, is of more importance to me; the rest is none of my affair. I have some reason to believe that my own mother had come from a Papist family, and you know of my involvement with the Lavertys. The bile some harbored for Catholics, which had flared when the Young Pretender approached London, flared again in 1780, and I understand it not even today.

The laws that caused the Lavertys to fear for their lives had, a couple of years earlier, been lessened in penalty, and some had been stricken altogether. It made sense to me, but rumour at the time held that it was done mainly in order to recruit more soldiers destined for America. As oft happens, a loud man with hatred and hidden motives can turn the tide of opinion among the weaker minds, finding the tiny sparks of fear and prejudice present in the hearts of all men, and fanning them into a raging fire. Such was the case in those days with Lord Gordon.

It is ironic that, from what I read, his Lordship now resides on occasion at the rebuilt Newgate Prison, for it was his hateful actions that led to the old structure's destruction, and that the founder of the Protestant Association is no longer Protestant. I wonder if he has time to reflect upon the deaths his hatred caused, and if it was worth the brief self-glory he experienced.

By then, the coffeehouse was no longer as lively place as it had once been, and the more influential discussions were held in clubs instead. Nonetheless, voices were raised, with some adamant that the Papists were trying to "take over" and destroy our way of life. If not dealt with severely, they would soon overrun us, taking our livelihood. The answer, said they, was to return to the values of our fathers.

When asked my opinion, I said, "With many things, I suspect we would all be better off to be simply left alone."

Perhaps, if words are needed for my crypt, those would be as good as any.

"You have always been such, Fezziwig," said Mr. Olin, a brash man who made a comfortable living selling liquor. A pompous, self-important naysayer, he always proclaimed himself to newcomers as the only voice of reason to be had in the vicinity. "Yes, you have. You are successful, yet do not support those institutions that brought you that success, God and Country. You would allow radicals to upend our values, just because you wish to be left alone! Not two doors from mine, a Papist grows rich from a warehouse, taking away business from true Englishmen. You, of all people should be aware of that, Fezziwig! How much business are they stealing from you? They perform their rituals in the dark, and the pox abounds. They are ruining us, and we must take our country back!"

"Sir," I replied, wishing one of my more articulate friends, such as Dr. Franklin or Dr. Darwin, were present, "Being left alone is, to my believing, counted among our *values,* and, if it is not, very well should be. My way of life is of my own making, and others should be allowed to make their own as well. I would say, Sir, that, in some other time or place, your ancestors have needed that sentiment, but, now that you have become comfortable, you would deny it to others. That, Sir, is the difference between you and me."

I could tell he was surprised at the heat of my retort, as I am generally seen, and see myself, as an amiable old man. He sputtered, "Well, Fezziwig, it is clear where you stand, having put in your tuppence!"

He then flopped down in his chair with his back to me, muttering to his supporters. Such is the way of a bully. But, their bluster can have serious consequences. In early summer, Gordon became vapid in Parliament, and whipped up his hateful followers, with their blue cockades, into frenzy. They rioted, pulling many Catholics out of their homes to be murdered. Their churches were destroyed, and businesses burnt. The Moorfields, where some of my Irish workers lived, were ravished. The embassies of Papist countries were attacked, and Newgate prison all but pulled down, allowing prisoners to flee.

The Catholic-owned warehouse near Mr. Olin's business did not escape the violence, and it was burned to the ground. The fire could not be contained, though, and spread to consume Mr. Olin's distillery in its entirety. I later learned that the Catholic warehouseman had insurance, with Lloyd's in Lombard Street. Mr. Olin had none. A hat was passed for his assistance at the coffeehouse sometime thereafter. I contributed tuppence.

The city was recovering its sanity when, a few months later, it was rocked by news from America. Lord Cornwallis had been cut off by a French fleet in Yorktown, and taken prisoner. While some hoped it only a setback, I saw that we could no longer continue our war with America with hope of success. Under the leadership of my old friend Lawrence Washington's younger brother, the Colonies had won. I would have liked to have been present to see Dr. Franklin's face when he received the news.

My trade from Charles Town (which now calls itself Charleston) had been interrupted for about a year and a part, but soon resumed. An unexpected export from there also began: that of loyalists.

This story is so well known to you that I hesitate to record it, but I will do so for your descendants. I was at the warehouse, when my lone apprentice at the time, Mr. Sheaves, announced visitors, and I was surprised to see a pretty young woman with three of the most beautiful little girls, with light hair and grey eyes all. One was still in arms. She introduced herself as Martha Byrnes. I had refreshments brought, and she settled to tell her story.

"Mr. Fezziwig, I am not accustomed to seeking assistance, but I know not where else to turn. I am newly arrived from Charleston, with my three daughters. My husband, Robert, took ill and died during the crossing."

"I am most sorry for your loss, Mrs. Byrnes. Most sorry, indeed. In what way can I assist you?" I knew it was a common ploy to send young women with children to men of business, always with a sad story, to ask for charity, though their stories were false.

"I seek a position. I have funds to carry us for awhile only, and you see that I have three daughters I must support." She took the opportunity to introduce them: "Iris is five, Lily is three, and this is Violet, but a year. I have worked with my father in mercantile since I could walk, and have been well educated in the ways of business. You were well acquainted with my late grandfather, and did business with my father, his son, before the war. I am the granddaughter of Thomas Gates the Senior, daughter of Thomas the Junior, if you recall the names."

I was astounded. "Of course I recall them. Our association

goes back more than forty years, and your grandfather was quite a friend of mine whilst I was in Carolina as a very young man. I am, indeed, sorry for your situation, Mrs. Byrnes! What brought you and your family to make the crossing?"

She glanced at the floor. "I have no interest in politics, Mr. Fezziwig. The war was hard for everyone. Most of us simply wanted to be *left alone*, but we were occupied by one side, then the other, and many people took harsh advantage of the situation. My husband, late husband, was loyal to the King, but not hostile to the rebels. He was accused of it, though, and, after Yorktown, we were treated criminally. We feared for our lives. Our property was burned, and no one would do business with us." Tears began to run down her face.

"We had no choice. Some of our friends were murdered, and we saw others covered with tar and feathers. We had to leave. We intended to begin anew here, but now Robert is lost. Oh, Mr. Fezziwig, I have heard your name all my life as an honorable man. I will do any work, chambermaid, or spinning, or anything, but my daughters must eat. Please, please help us!" She began to sob, which had a disquieting effect on the children.

I called for Sheaves to fetch the carriage and take Mrs. Byrnes and her daughters to our home. Many single days changed my life. That day is among them.

Our house was wholly sufficient for the added lodgers, and Caddy was much rejuvenated by having children again under foot. We sometimes hosted visits from the grandchildren of her brothers and sisters, and we always felt young again during them. Her heart melted at the sight of the three girls.

I knew I could find domestic or factory work for Martha, but I had another idea, influenced, looking back on it, by conversations with Dr. Darwin. I assessed Martha's abilities, and found her education had been good indeed, and her knowledge of business substantial.

"I have just lost an apprentice, so I have only one instead of two." I told her after watching her cipher. "You shall fill that role. Welcome to Fezziwig and Company!"

She could hardly believe my offer, in a good way. Almost none of my workers or business associates could believe it, either, but in a bad way. Even in the intervening years, I have not heard of a woman apprentice in a warehouse business. Sheaves, a tall and handsome young man, thought it sport, but I heard grumbling among many of the others, and oft times they refused to take orders from Martha unless the same order was repeated by Sheaves or me. I had stern conversations with more than one of my men over the practice.

Dr. Darwin, who visited not long thereafter, was delighted at my action, and was anxious to meet Martha. He quizzed her about the extent of her education in America, and was much enchanted.

But, what a head for business she had! She could add figures upon sight, keep ledgers neater than any I have seen, and was always thinking for *tomorrow* instead of today. In many ways she caused me to think of Mrs. Eliza Pinckney, though I did not feel compelled to mention that fact to Caddy.

And when she died in the great sickness the next winter, when her dear, sweet light was extinguished, Caddy and I hesitated not a moment. We adopted the three of you, and, with Mr. File's help, made you our legal heirs. Most decisions in life are either mostly right, or mostly wrong, with a small element of the other. That decision, daughters, was completely right. Our lives were again filled with laughter and purpose. And you are as well educated as any man I know, and doubly able, in the opinion of your proud father.

Some months later, I received another surprise visitor, this one at our home. It was prefaced a few days by a note, which, of course, I still possess:

My Dear Mr. Fezziwig,

After many years absence, I am returned to London, and would like to visit you and your fine wife, if it be convenient. I trust you are well, and let me assure you that I hold you in the highest regards. I seek your assistance in a personal matter that I think you shall find agreeable.   Your Ob't Sert,

William Franklin

It was good to see my old friend's son again. He had aged, and began to resemble his father to some degree, though he was taller and his face not so open. The most notable difference was that his mouth was set in a perpetual frown, instead of his father's smile.

"I am not sure this is all over, Mr. Fezziwig. There may still be room for reconciliation with the Colonies. A separation does not make sense, for either of us," he said, looking sad. "But, politicians will do what they do. The new government here may be beneficial to us. Who can know? But, a personal reconciliation is why I am here. I am sure you know my father has been in France for all these years, and has become quite attached to his friends there. My son, Temple, has been with him the entire time, but now visits me regularly. We are both greatly desirous of my reconciliation with my father. Temple believes it possible, but feels my father needs a small added incentive, a gentle push, if you will. I know the high regard he holds you in, Mr. Fezziwig, and feel a letter from you encouraging a visit to London on his way back to Philadelphia may be all that is needed."

I could tell the proud man was trying his best to cling to a small bit of dignity, given his situation. Using his father's influence, he had risen to a substantial position in America, but had lost it all. His father was, by then, a very old man, and time was short.

"Nothing would make me more happy than to see my old friend again, Sir. I will be most glad to correspond with him, should you feel it would be of help, and offer my home as a place for your meeting."

William looked relieved. "Bless you, Mr. Fezziwig. I know he loves you, and counts you amongst his most precious friends. Had this unpleasantness not intervened, I know he would not have stopped until he convinced you to visit him in Philadelphia, which he may still do!"

I saw Caddy's eyes narrow. "Oh, no, William, these old bones shall not make the crossing again. I have not the adventurous spirit or constitution of Dr. Franklin! But I shall begin my letter at once."

William smiled and grasped my hand. "Thank you, Mr. Fezziwig! Your letter will be attached to mine, that I shall send to Temple, and he will deliver it." I saw a twinkle come to his eye, and in that moment he did, indeed, remind me of his father. "And just wait," he said, "until you see how it shall be delivered!"

The day was cold and clear when I traveled with William Franklin to Dover Castle, having left the evening before and spent the night at an acceptable inn. Upon our arrival the next morning, there was a large group was assembled, and William was expected. A great balloon, tethered and wholly contained within a giant net, which supported a wicker boat underneath, was being inflated.

We approached two men who appeared to be in charge of the whole affair. William said, "Mr. Fezziwig, please meet Monsieur Jean-Pierre Blanchard, and Dr. John Jeffries. They are the bravest men I have ever known."

"*Non*, Monsieur Franklin, we will be safer than you in your coach!" one of the men exclaimed. "Are you sure you will not accompany us?"

William laughed. "No, Monsignor Blanchard, I'm afraid the adventurer of the family is already in France. I feel certain, even at his age, he would be honored by the offer! My son will meet you in Guines."

"Yes, we expect it!" said Dr. Jeffries, who, by his speech, I could tell was American. "You have the letter, as we discussed, Mr. Franklin?"

"Indeed, I do," said William, as he pulled a package from his pocket and handed it to Dr. Jeffries."

"Thank you, Sir. Post by air. I am sure there will be a future in it! Thank God you are not a smith, sending your son a new anvil!" he laughed. "We shall give your regards, and your letter, to your son before midday."

William thanked the two men, and we retreated to watch the balloon continue to rise. Once it was full and round, the two men climbed in, the tether was loosed, and two great flags, the Fleur-de-lis and the Union Jack, were unfurled from the boat. The balloon floated upward and east, out of sight.

"Godspeed," I heard William say, softly, and I agreed.

The reply to my letter came through much more conventional means, and was shorter than I imagined:

Dear William,

I received your letter, and am most appreciative for the airiness of it. I shall be traveling back to Philadelphia in August, via London, and it would be a pleasure to see you whilst I am there. Thank you for recommending that I also meet my son William, for we have some property matters to resolve.

B. F.

William arrived at our home early, and was clearly nervous. He gladly took each glass of Madeira as it was offered in turn, and paced until I feared a depression in the floor. The day was rainy, so, when the knock at the door finally came, it was a soggy Dr. Franklin and Temple (who had grown into a handsome young man) who entered. Temple wore a cloak that dripped as he removed it; his grandfather wore none, and rain droplets streamed from his bald head.

My friend had aged greatly since last I saw him. His remaining hair, present only around the edges, was thin and stringy, and wrinkles around his eyes and mouth resembled maps I had seen of the Nile delta. His neck flesh resembled a goose freshly plucked. Always stout, he had now grown even plumper, and he hobbled with gout. But his eyes were bright, and twinkled as he grasped my hand, telling me how he thanked Providence that we could meet again, for he was sure his days grew short. He hugged Caddy, and made a small joke that he was available, should her husband ever meet his demise under a falling cotton bale. He also delighted in you, charming girls.

Temple shook his father's hand warmly; Dr. Franklin's greeting for his son seemed cordial, but formal. We all sat, with a glass, and the old man took on the air of one holding court. His first questions were for me, about business and how it had been affected by the war, and about our mutual friends. He was most interested in the sample of exceptionally fine cotton I showed him, from the islands off Charleston, which I had just begun to broker.

Dr. Franklin was quite sorry to hear of Mr. Whitlipped's death, but had no hesitation to roar with laughter and slap his leg at the story of Dr. Darwin's investigation and Dr. Falconar's saving us with his last minute chase through the streets of London. He had followed the news about the anti-Papist riots, and had been dismayed by them. "I have now lived among the Papists for several years," he said, "and have never been treated more humanely," he said. And then, with a glance toward William, he added. "Anywhere."

"I am afraid the world is to be challenged," he said. "For all of history, we have been subject to clashes amongst kings, and used like pieces on the chess board. But, I am beginning to see a new tyranny, which may be as dangerous. Men with speaking and writing skill and selfish motives can inflame the populace by finding the dark corners of the heart and exploiting them. It is most often done in the name of God, or patriotism, or fear. I have seen it, already, in our country, and I fear the beginnings of it in France. England, clearly, is not immune."

There was a bit of uncomfortable silence, until William said, "Father, you were always proud to be an Englishman. You worked for years to bring about reconciliation. It is still possible, and there is much support for it. I carry on correspondence with men of influence in New Jersey, and New York, and Pennsylvania, and so many of us here who have been chased from our homes for remaining loyal. I know it is true. All that is needed is a man respected by both sides to bring cool heads together. The hotheads, the mob that you speak of, must be put back in the box, Father, or their work will spread, and no one in the world will be safe again. Who to protect us from what you just described, but our King? You and I want the same thing, Father."

The next moments, with no words spoken, were among the longest I had ever spent.

Finally, Dr. Franklin said, "William, we have an issue of property, in New Scotland, that is titled jointly. I know it will be to your advantage for us to agree on disposal. Temple has the documents necessary for us to take care of the matter." The last time I saw the look that appeared at that moment on my old friend's face was when I met him the morning after his interview before the Privy Council.

Caddy and I found an excuse to leave the room, and Temple soon followed, I assume at the request of his father or grandfather. He looked embarrassed, and more so as we heard the conversation in the next room become increasingly heated. Caddy had mercy on him, and he gratefully accepted the hot rum and lemon she offered.

"I am sorry," he said, with a tear forming in the corner of his eye. "They are both strong willed, and I love them. They will come together; I know it." He looked at me. "He would not have come, except for your letter, Mr. Fezziwig, and I shall be forever thankful to you."

For almost two hours, into the darkness, the three of us sat together, and the heated conversation continued, sometimes dying in volume, and then flaring up again. We would occasionally attempt small conversation ourselves. Temple had, himself, recommenced a regular relationship with his father only a year before, and it was plain a reconciliation between the two men in the next room was his fondest wish. He was very enamored with life in Paris, and insisted that Caddy and I must find a reason to visit it, as well as Philadelphia.

Temple accepted every glass Caddy offered, and had caught quite a fox by the time he heard his grandfather call for him. He went into the next room briefly, and then returned for the pouch he carried. All was quiet for a short while, and then Dr. Franklin called for me.

Both men were red in the face, even as seen by the light of the lamps. Their expressions were identically sour, but Dr. Franklin's softened as he gripped my hand.

"Ah, my old friend William, who has such affection for me, and I for him," he said, and grasped my hand again. "Some of my most pleasant moments whilst residing here in *England* have been shared with you, my friend, and they shall never be forgotten. You must make the crossing again, and be my guest in Philadelphia, to allow me to return some small degree of the hospitality you have shown me. Perhaps Providence will allow me just enough time for you to do so. But now, I must take your leave." He hugged Caddy once more, and, uncharacteristically, me as well. He then said, "Come, Temple." The young man retrieved his cloak, gathered the document pouch, and they were gone.

William Franklin was left standing beside his chair, and he did not speak for some time. After he heard the carriage leaving outside, he bowed slightly and said, "Mr. Fezziwig, I am most grateful to you and your lovely wife. Thank your for your efforts, and your hospitality, and your great friendship with my father. You shall always be held in high regard by the Franklin family, across the generations." He left without speaking more, but the pain on his face made words unnecessary.

I have seen both William and Temple Franklin on a few occasions since that night, but I have not traveled to America, and never again saw Dr. Franklin. It was not hard to keep track of his activities, as the newspapers reported them. He helped set the course for the new country with a constitution, one that brought Mr. George Washington again to lead.

Around Christmastime in 1789, I received a letter from Philadelphia, from Polly Stevenson Hewson. She had gone to live with Dr. Franklin, and she revealed that he probably had not much longer to live, and that a last visit from me would do him good. Despite my age, I considered making the trip the following summer, but death came for my old friend that spring. The newspapers reported twenty thousand mourners at his funeral, and, since my experience with America was quite antiquated, I could not imagine that many people assembled anywhere there.

Temple Franklin had also been with his grandfather when he died, but returned to Paris to live, with visits to his father in London. During one of these, he brought me papers his grandfather had entrusted to him, and that visit gave me the thought that I should write down an accounting of my life, this very document.

The papers were Dr. Franklin's memoirs, and they had been left to Temple for editing and printing. The old man had worked on them sporadically for years, and they were complete only up until his work in London as an agent for Pennsylvania. I read through them, and found that my old friend was even more remarkable than I had known.

"I do have a question, for you, Mr. Fezziwig," said Temple. "Whilst Grandfather only finished the writing to the point you saw completed, he did leave an outline for the rest of the work." He shuffled through papers in his satchel. "There is something here I wish to ask you about." He pointed at a fragment of Dr. Franklin's writing on a page. It said "Naked in the forest with Fezziwig."

"You must tell me, Sir," asked Temple. "Do you know what he means?"

"I am afraid not, Temple," I said. "What an odd thing, indeed, but it is to me a mystery. I'm sorry. Now, I think Caddy has tea."

The success of the Americans did seem to unleash a lust for both freedom and power. Things were written and said about the King that would have been unthinkable when I first began my visits to the coffeehouse so many years before. Some called for a similar revolution in Britain. Others insisted that even uttering that sentiment was treason, and that every pike in London should have a head on it, as in days past. Parliament was a battlefield. It all seemed barely contained, and could have spilt at the least jostle.

Across the channel, of course, what spilt was actual blood. The royal family had been on the throne much longer than our own, and the thought that a King and his lady could be dragged through the street to lose their heads to an efficient machine invented for that purpose was unsettling, no matter what one's politics. I had no strong opinions in either direction, as is my usual stand in matters political, and suspected most Frenchmen just wanted to be *left alone*.

Shortly after the arrest of the French King, but before the most explosive violence broke out, I received a letter from Dr. Priestley, sent from his home in Birmingham. It contained a piece from a newspaper, and a note. The note said:

My Dear Mr. Fezziwig,

Several of the mutual friends of our departed mentor Dr. Franklin, including fellow 'Lunarticks' with whom you are familiar, will gather at a dinner here in Birmingham to celebrate the breaking of the Bastille, on the fourteenth. Dr. Franklin was the greatest supporter of freedom of our time, and his influence will continue to help us reform our present system. Many glasses will be raised to his honor, and I thought you, as one of his close friends, might be interested in joining us. You will, of course, be welcome to reside at my home during your visit to Birmingham. With Reg'rds,

Joseph Priestley.

The newspaper clipping read thus:

"A number of gentlemen intend dining together on the 14th instant, to commemorate the auspicious day which witnessed the emancipation of twenty-six millions of people from the yoke of despotism, and restored the blessings of equal government to a truly great and enlightened nation; with whom it is our interest, as a commercial people, and our duty, as friend to the general rights of mankind, to promote a free intercourse, as subservient to a permanent friendship. Any Friend to Freedom, disposed to join the intended temperate festivity, is desired to leave his name at the bar of the Hotel, where tickets may be had at Five Shillings each, including a bottle of wine; but no person will be admitted without one. Dinner will be on table at three o'clock precisely."

The thought of seeing old acquaintances and toasting the memory of Dr. Franklin was attractive to me, and I had not traveled from London for awhile. But I was, at the time, shy of two apprentices, one having served his term, and the other taken ill, so the expediency of business did not allow me to attend.

Yet again, either luck or coincidence or Providence smiled upon me. I have had many a memorable dinner in my years, but the one I missed on that date would have been memorable indeed. Many of the same type of people who had set London alight more than ten years earlier, who believed they had the mysteries of God in hand directly from the Source, had great hatred for Dr. Priestley and many of his associates. In their own eyes, only the small few who believed exactly as they did would avoid eternal damnation, and, being the elect, felt they could treat everyone else as they pleased.

Dr. Priestley drew their ire because he believed there should be no religious test to hold public office, and that books with open views should not be banned from the town's lending library. I know Dr. Priestley as a physician and a man of science; I did not know he was such a wild radical as to have seditious beliefs such as those!

The dinner I did not attend was stormed by a mob of religious purists, who drank up all the liquor, and rampaged the city, burning down Dr. Priestley's home. If they sang a hymn whilst it burned, I cannot say.

Caddy and I did an adequate job of educating you, daughters, in reading and writing and ciphering, and I was glad to see you take an interest in the natural world as well. But, when you came to the age that more formal education was required, I was surprised and disappointed to discover how difficult the task. There were schools for young women in London, and I visited one after another, but found them inadequate, concentrating only on domestic concerns and offering no further classical education than what we had already given at home.

Remembering Mr. Spills's philosophy of looking forward, which has served me so well, I decided to embark upon my first business venture outside of goods commerce, opening a school for the equal education of young women. I had no idea of the resistance that would meet me for providing what seems an obvious need.

I have seen the attitudes concerning so many things change over my lifetime. The sin of slavery had, thank God, been outlawed in England several years before, and there was a strong movement afoot to abolish the trade throughout the empire. I had hoped to see the great sin addressed by the Americans after the war, but they have not yet done so. Having been influenced over the years by the great intellect and ability of women, I knew that their equal education, and the realisation of their equal ability, must soon come, and each day of delay was wasted opportunity. I believed there would be enough sensible people in the great city who agreed, and that I could accomplish a substantial good, while making a modest profit for the service.

I discussed the idea with Dr. Darwin, who approved, and referred me to a friend of his, Miss Mary Parker, who established such schools in his environs. She was able to provide two excellent young teachers, Miss H. Pence and Miss G. Coalgrove, who were anxious to move to London. Through inquiries among my business associates, I also hired Mr. J. Patton as an instructor in scientific studies.

To house the school, I found a most suitable lodging for rent not far, coincidentally, from the Stephenson home in Craven Street. I met the owner of the building, Mr. Hollingsworth, at the coffeehouse to make a contract.

"You will not be sorry, Mr. Fezziwig, and it is through my great charity that I offer you the location at this price," he puffed.

"It is worth much, much more, but I know you to be a reputable man, and I am a great supporter of education, so I am willing to take a loss for the good of humanity."

The price we had agreed upon was quite fair to him, though I knew there was no use to pursue the matter, but he persisted. "In fact," he said, "if your standards turn out to be high enough, we may consider a caveat to provide education to my own son when he comes of age, at a substantial discount, of course?"

"I am afraid you would not likely to find that suitable," I replied. "The school is for the classical education of girls and young women."

Hollingsworth reacted as though he had been struck. "Classical education? Beyond domestic concerns, or what is needed for factory work? Bloody hell, Fezziwig, are you daft? I thought you a man of business, not one of those radicals!"

"I do not consider myself a radical in any respect, Mr. Hollingsworth. I simply want to provide the best education for my daughters, and I know many others have the same desire. Seeing a need and moving to fill it is radical, in your view? Then," I swept my hand to include all the men in the room, "Welcome to a den of radicals!"

His face reddened, and I could almost feel the heat from it. "You shall not use my lodgings for such foolishness, Fezziwig! The world seems to be unraveling, and you and your type are bent on helping it do so!" He jumped up and stood over me, so I felt compelled to rise as well, which caused him to increase his volume even more, and drew the attention of everyone in the house.

"I often wonder about men such as you!" he yelled. "In what other areas of your life do you defy the natural order of things? Are you the result, yourself, of a father who knew not how to be a man, or a mother who desired to be one?"

Mr. Hollingsworth was taller, and considerably younger, than me, and his nose was quite large. It made my fist pain considerably when I struck it, and the spurting blood stained my shirt. He plopped back down into his chair, and a general cheer went up from the other patrons. After a stunned moment, Hollingsworth, holding a handkerchief on his injury, stormed out, shouting "Vew wilf pay fo thith, Feffiwith!"

And pay I did. As you remember, I had been summoned to the magistrate on occasions in the past, but never as a defendant. Magistrate Combs heard my explanation, and ordered I pay Mr. Hollingsworth one pound, and that I pay a fine of five pounds. I thought we were finished, and I prepared to leave, when he said, "Wait, Mr. Fezziwig, I am not finished. I believe the contract between you and Mr. Hollingsworth had already, in effect, been verbally consummated, so I order him to supply the lodging to you as originally agreed upon. And, if you please, meet me at The Plow at noon tomorrow. I wish to discuss with you the enrollment of my daughter, if you please."

That was the origin of the Philadelphia-London Academy for the Education of Women, named in honor of my old American friend, which you, daughters, so successfully run today. I allowed Miss Pence to continue at the school after marrying, since she is a gifted teacher, but Miss Coalgrove left of her own accord. Mr. Patton has turned out to be extraordinary, sparking interest in the natural world in even the most recalcitrant minds, and acting as the steadiest mentor to not only students, but you as well. You have done well to make him your role model in your profession.

The first of my two new apprentices, hired soon after establishing the school, came from an unexpected source. Mr. John Wilkes, the former Lord Mayor and Member of Parliament, had fallen from favor, as his harsh reaction to the riots and support of revolution revealed conflicts in his nature. He had retreated to the Isle of Wight, but was still a frequent visitor, and visit me at the warehouse is precisely what he did one day, without notice. He had accompanying him a slight, pale, shy youth, altogether homely, though not as much as the older man.

"It is good to see you still about, Fezziwig. For a man of your advanced years, you are still spry, indeed (I note that Mr. Wilkes, only recently deceased, was but a couple of years younger than me). I trust that both your successful commercial trade and your belief in an obligation for compassion are still as robust as your physic?"

I hoped he was not about to ask my help in a plan to regain political power, for the times were already too volatile for my taste. "Thank you for your kind compliments, Sir. My business is above water rather than underneath, and my practices have not changed."

"Good. I am glad I was able to be of service to you in retrieving the body of your friend. Your concern showed you to be a good man. Now, Sir, I have need of a return from you, but one that you will find of great benefit to yourself in the end. This," he said, pointing to the frail young man, "is Dick. He is my son, though, given the unofficial nature of the circumstances of his birth, we have decided on the surname Wilkins. I knew about him from the beginning, and contributed monetarily to his upbringing, but we have only recently become acquainted. He has a frail nature, not suited to much physical work, but his mind for figures is sharp, more so than mine, as a matter of fact."

I could see what was coming, and was relieved that it would involve neither money nor politics.

"He is at the age to become independent, and lacks a position. I have already made inquiries, and know that you are in need of an apprentice. If it pleases you to do so, you will not regret giving Dick such an opportunity. And, if not, perhaps you could assist us in finding a similar opening among your peers?"

I looked the young man in the eye. I saw intelligence, a bit of shame in his circumstances, but also hope. His looked moved me. I agreed to take him on.

"Capital! Fezziwig, I knew you were to be counted upon. He may start immediately, then? His bag is in the carriage."

I didn't expect such immediacy, but found no reason to deny it. He settled into one of the apprentice cubbys, behind the counter. Mr. Wilkes shook my hand, thanked me, gave his son a handshake and admonishment to work hard, and was on his way. That was our last meeting.

The circumstances that led me to employ Dick Wilkins could have brought me disaster, but did not. He proved to be quite bright and able. His greatest obstacle was a lack of confidence. He was shy by nature, and sought approval from others by being too eager to please them, at his own expense. He would agree to do someone else's work, when his own could not be completed. I am proud to say that, with time, I helped him with those things, and he became quite successful because of his early involvement with the power of steam.

Sadly, his success held the seeds of his end, when a boiler exploded, because of the shoddy work of a manufacturer. Dick was quite attached to me in his youth, and I felt it was compensation for not having the guidance of a father as he grew.

Not long thereafter, a second apprentice came to me through more conventional means, from the southeast. Ebenezer Scrooge was a handsome young man with a moderate boarding education, and great ambition. His skill with figures was not initially as good as Dick's, but he applied himself and they soon equaled. The two also became inseparable. It was as if Dick had never had a close friend, and Ebenezer was a captive. Ebenezer was clearly the leader of the two, and was not above using Dick to his own advantage. I kept an eye on the equity of their dealings, but only intervened if necessary.

My involvement with young people is what invigorates me most. At the time, having my three darling daughters just beginning the flirtatious age, and the eagerness of Dick and Ebenezer, made Caddy and me feel again like the two youngsters who had first danced at Bracebridge so many years before. I think the comfort of knowing that we were to go into our old age with such security also gave me the freedom to enjoy each day, knowing they numbered fewer and fewer. Commerce was changing, but I knew my way of doing things and our savings would be sufficient to keep us until our natural end.

That may not be said for the future, though. Great mills are swallowing the small manufacturers and tradesmen, and workers seem to be employed by machines, instead of the opposite. Instead of water and animals supplying power, it is fire, and it never sleeps. The men in fine suits and clubs they establish for themselves only buy and sell capital and futures and paper, with no regard to the human fodder fed to their great boilers. I am glad my life spanned the last world, instead of the next.

These thoughts caused me to rejoice in the great health and vigor I still possessed, and made me determined to use both to their fullest whilst I had them. Dr. Franklin's memoirs, describing his own origins and his visit to his family's ancestral home, inspired me to do the same. Though I had returned to Lincolnshire several times during my adult life, I had never sought the place of my birth.

Thinking it would be of use to Dick's development to have him in charge for a short time, I decided to leave him behind to mind the warehouse (knowing that my Irish foreman, Kelly, would let nothing go awry), and take Ebenezer to assist me. We would visit Bracebridge along the way, and Caddy would stay there to visit her brother and his family.

Bracebridge, though ancient and still with much be done, was in much improved condition, even from my last visit. Caddy's brother had proved to be an astute man of agriculture. Timber products were no longer a large source of income, since he did not want to deplete the forest, but grain and wool were profitable, and he applied modern methods in order to not ruin the soil.

The best part of his restoration, though, to my mind, is what he chose not to do. The hall, as far as my old eyes could see, remained unchanged, to the smallest detail. The ancient Bracebridges still stared down upon us through a layer of dust. Brown and white spaniel dogs still ruled with mayhem. The china was still cracked, the silver still bent, and the cushions still threadbare. My mind went back to my first visit, as a young man with no formal education, and hardly tuppence, but who had been shown kindness.

The purpose of the trip had me in a nostalgic mood, and I thought of the importance, especially in old age, of having a place unchanged from youth, to again visit. Most do not have such a luxury. I think it could even be a pastoral place, such as a river, or bridge, or view from a hill, as long as it remains as it is remembered. It reconnects the two ends of one's life.

After the evening meal, a servant took up a fiddle, and the younger amongst the family were astounded at the agility with which Caddy and I, stout and aged, danced, as they put it, 'rings about' them. Ebenezer had been wide-eyed and enthusiastic during the trip, and enjoyed himself thoroughly, especially since he was the recipient more than one shy glance from assorted younger Bracebridge great-nieces and cousins of the fair sex.

Ebenezer and I continued on to the vicinity of Nene, and settled into an acceptable inn. The area was beautiful, and resembled most of the east midlands, but seemed no more familiar to me than any other.

The next day, I sought directions to the manor house, and we set off down a series of bumpy country lanes. The house itself had been modernized somewhat, but was still recognizable to me, though it appeared considerably smaller than I remembered. Without a definite plan, I knocked on the door, was greeted by a servant, and presented my card.

In a short time, Ebenezer and I were escorted to the Lord of Nene, a nondescript fellow about twenty years my junior. He seemed eager to know our business, and then for us to be off.

With some small talk (infinitely less than would have been required in Charleston), we discovered that we had a couple of mutual acquaintances amongst commercial men in London, which led to his saying, "So, what brings a successful warehouseman from London to the countryside, Mr. Fezziwig?" somewhat impatiently.

"This is not a trip for business, though I am never adverse to new opportunity, Sir," I replied. "It so happens that I was born on these very lands, some seventy-five years ago, and happy to see them once more before I meet my ancestors face to face."

At that, he smirked. "Ha! Meeting them, depending upon where they may be residing these days. Well, Sir, you are welcome to ride around the manor, if you desire. You will see it well run and profitable. I am sure you won't be interfering with any of our activities. Early summer is a busy season, you know."

"Indeed, Sir, I shall not, and I thank you for your hospitality. You are a direct descendant of the House of Nene, and were raised here, I assume?"

"Of course. I was schooled at Oxford, and came into my inheritance several years ago."

"Do you remember ever hearing the name Fezziwig, at all, Sir?"

"No, never, I'm afraid."

"Or Meade, as a vicar?"

He leaned back. "Meade. It does sound familiar, from childhood perhaps, but I cannot place it. I know of no Meades living here now. I'm sorry, Sir, but business does press upon me."

I rose, as did Ebenezer. "I thank you again, for your time, Sir. One more thing. Does the manor still have freeholders?"

"Oh, no. I am sure we did in the past, but not today. It is inefficient, and is no longer the way of things. Our workers are employed, and pay rent for their lodgings."

"And there are no longer commons, for their use?"

"Of course not. Where would be the profit in that? Why do you ask?"

"Curiosity, nothing more. Good day to you, Sir. "

Using the manor house as a landmark, I was able to find (though with difficulty) the hut in which I was born. It was still occupied by a manor tenet, though hardly fit to be called lodging. There were great gaps in the thatch, and the door only leaned into its opening, with broken hinges. A young woman with a filthy baby huddled inside, and she cowered with fear when I arrived. Her husband was in the fields. I assured her that I meant her no harm, and just wanted a look at her home.

The floor of the hut was now unpaved. I'm sure all the cobbles had been taken up in hope of finding more treasure after that frightful night. There was no longer a close for growing family vegetables; every inch of land was used for the manor's benefit. I gave the woman ten pounds before we left, and I was not sure who was more astounded by the act; the woman, or Ebenezer.

"I do beg your pardon, Mr. Fezziwig, Sir," he exclaimed as we left, "But, what, other than by chance living in the right hovel, did that woman do to earn such an amount from you?"

"Nothing, Ebenezer. Nothing at all."

Our next visit was to the church. It looked unchanged, as did the vicarage. The young vicar was present, and outside when our carriage pulled up. I explained to him that I had been born in the vicinity, and would like to see the churchyard.

"Have you ever heard of a Reverend Meade or his family, here, Sir?" I asked.

"Meade? Yes, though, of course, he has been gone many years. In fact, you will find him buried yonder." He pointed toward the yard.

"And any of his family? Do they remain, perhaps? A daughter, Pricilla?"

He shook his head. "No, I only know the name from records, and, of course, the gravestone. I am sorry, Sir, but I am sure you honor Reverend Meade's memory by asking."

"Reverend Meade's memory? Oh yes, it is quite clear to me, indeed, Vicar, and always shall be. Thank you for your help."

Ebenezer and I entered the walled churchyard, and walked slowly along the rows, as I looked at each stone. I had some small hope of finding one with the name Fezziwig, but there was none. In a neglected corner, though, was a weathered rock in which had been carved the initials 'S.F.'

In a place of honor in the yard was a slate stone, which must have been quite expensive in its day. It proclaimed, "Rev. Thos. Meade 1700 – 1762 Man of God."

"Was he influential in your childhood, Sir?" asked Ebenezer.

"Indeed, he was, Ebenezer. Quite influential," I replied, and what I did next surprised him, and even myself. I looked around, and finding no one else within sight, pulled down the front of my breeches. "I have need for relief, and I have found the perfect spot."

Before leaving, I made arrangement with the vicar to buy a stone and provision for the grave set with the rock. I will never know, in this life, if the grave holds the body of my mother, but the weathering of the rock seemed of the right age, and the chisel carving would have been a thing my father could have done.

Ebenezer was silent in the carriage as we traveled back to the inn. I know he was curious to know the source of my animosity toward a long-dead vicar. Over Madeira after the evening meal, I told him the story of the lost treasure, and my kidnapping, and he was astounded by it.

"Treachery! Treachery most evil!" he cried, "How could a man of God betray another so? It was theft and murder!"

"Ebenezer, when I contemplate how another person can commit a most sinful deed, and fail to be able to understand it, I rejoice." I said. "That means it is not in my heart to follow suit. Most foul acts stem from the same source, and that source is greed. If it be money or a share of business or a carriage or the affections of a woman, men want what is possessed by another, and are willing to kill or steal or otherwise violate their souls for it. Be it a country vicar, or a king, or a nation, it's all the same. It's greed."

He was silent for a while. "I am sorry for the loss of your father, Mr. Fezziwig. My own saw to my education, but with little affection, and we are no longer associated, I'm afraid."

"Is there yet hope for change in that, perhaps, Ebenezer, if you initiate it? A great friend of mine, now gone, failed to reconcile with his son awhile back, though I tried to facilitate it. I regret it did not happen. Time eventually runs out for such matters. It is a great comfort to me that my own son and I were on the most amicable terms when he was taken. I could not bear it if it were different."

The young man was silent. I continued. "Ebenezer, I delayed this trip until I grew old enough to profit from it. It is clear to me that the things we leave behind do not matter. The jewel I dug from the close was once possessed and treasured by someone long gone. It was in my father's hands but a short time, and now belongs to another. Someday, it will be lost again. The only thing that outlasts us, as our legacy, is the good we do for others. I'm more convinced of it now than ever. An abused, captive youth once decided his lot could be made no worse by showing kindness to a boy brought to share his misery. Mr. Spills gave a vagrant a chance to work. Poor migrants shared their meager rags with a stranger left to die in the snow. Those things retain their value today more than all the gold earned from the warehouse."

"They do, Sir," he said. "You now have wealth, and you make people happy with it. I hear of other employers, and the way their workers are treated, and know you choose to make better the lives of those around you."

I considered this for a moment. "No, Ebenezer, I think I have never made another happy, and I am incapable of it. Happiness is self-made. All another can do is be fair, and have some small compassion. I have wealth because I have worked hard, and not squandered, and was treated fairly by many others who could have chosen to do otherwise. In turn, most made a fair profit from my efforts, and it was deserved. I profit from my workers as well, and charge a fair price for my services. But I do not succumb to greed. I have seen it be the downfall of many, and, when they fall, their flailing and grasping take many innocents down with them, like a drowning man may sink his would-be savior."

I paused to let the thought develop, more for myself than for Ebenezer, then continued. "I suffered many injustices when I was young, and some brought me near death. I could have been scared of the world because of them, and dedicated myself to gaining the false security of wealth. Wealth came, but I chose to be a part of the world, and not fear it. The small investments I make in others come back to me tenfold. I have said many times that all I wish is to be *left alone*. But, what would have become of me if, at those times in my youth, I had been so? And how can I know what may live after me because I chose to do more than to leave someone alone? Do not be afraid to go into the world, Ebenezer, and you will be successful, indeed."

"I will be successful, Sir," he said, solemnly. "I promise."

The trip exhilarated both Caddy and me, and the next Christmas was as joyful as any we remembered. But, there was a strange thing that happened, one that I can hardly describe, and, upon writing about it, confuses me greatly. On Christmas Eve, as we had done for more than a half century of Christmases, we made merry with the workers in the warehouse.

As customary, at seven o'clock, I was anxious to be done with work. "Yo ho, there! Ebenezer! Dick! Yo ho, my boys! No more work tonight. Christmas Eve, Dick, Christmas, Ebenezer! Chirrup! Clear away!" The bowl and table were set, the fiddler arrived, and it was a most joyful time indeed. What is the reason, today, that the young cannot dance like their forebears? Do they spend too much time in sedentary pursuits? For, that night, Caddy and I danced as though our feet had wings, whilst the youth in the room, including you, daughters, and your bevy of suitors, could barely follow!

The strange thing occurred as the merriment ended, and I wished each a Merry Christmas as they left into the dark night. After the last had gone, I glanced up the road and saw something in front of the window. Perhaps a better word would be felt it, or sensed it, for I am not sure I saw more than a reflection. It appeared to be a strange, small person, with thin strands of light escaping from under a hat instead of hair, standing with an old man in a nightshirt. The man seemed familiar to me, but I cannot say who it was. In a blink, they were gone.

What I can say for certain is that the vision, if called that, was accompanied by a sensation I had only experienced twice before. The hair of my body stood on end, and, despite the chill, I broke out in a cold sweat, and my heart pounded.

When I went back inside, Caddy said, with concern, "Why, William Fezziwig! What on earth is the matter? You are as white as the snow. You look as if you have seen a ghost! Did you catch a chill?"

"Yes, a chill. That must be it. Warm me." And then I wrapped my arms around her, and kissed her, which took her by surprise. "My Will! Still no need for mistletoe, I see," she breathed, and we laughed at a joke regarding a money pouch so familiar to us both that it did not have to be spoken.

Wars and rumors of wars continue. The Irish starve, then rebel, and are further persecuted for their rebellion, so they starve some more, in a circle. I suspect they would prosper if only they were *left alone*. When Dr. Franklin visited Hibernia, he invited me to accompany him, but I declined because of work at the warehouse. I now wish I had gone; it is said to not be an arduous trip, and I believe I could still manage it. We are supposedly now a united nation, but I see little unity, except, perhaps in our fear of the small man in France.

The thought of having missed an Irish adventure with Dr. Franklin by my own doing reminds me that the final stories of very few old men include the line 'I wish I had spent more time at the warehouse.' Like most, I regret more things undone than things done.

I was quite surprised, two years ago, to find myself, and Caddy, still here to see the turn of a new century, and even more surprised that we were able to dance the year in that night. To everyone's delight, it was not our last night of dancing, though, as the complaints of the joints have finally become louder than the music, how many more we have left in us is unknowable. I considered an offer from Ebenezer to buy Fezziwig and Company, but rejected it. He is now associated with a man called Marley, and they are doing quite well indeed. I may yet reconsider his offer, but we could not at the time come to an agreement on continuing my labour practices.

I found that, with less time spent on business, my mind turned back to scientific topics. I had always read scientific papers as I had time, and associated myself with their writers at every opportunity. An idea came to me whilst walking along the Lea, remembering the water wheels I made in my youth, and, I decid

(The text ends here, with a scrawl of ink)

AFTERWORD

What brings a certain person and a certain object together, at a particular place and time? Is it ordained, or does it happen like the card shuffling done in preparation for a cosmic board game? In this case, I did it, with an eighteenth century manuscript purporting to be the autobiography of a person I thought to be a fictional character, in London.

In 2010, I was fifty years old and had just retired from my job as a conscientious bureaucrat in a federal government agency. My wife and I were packing and moving to a warmer climate. The biggest challenge we had while downsizing was dealing with the mountain of old stuff (poor man's antiques, I'll call it) I had accumulated over the years. None of it was of much value, but just the fact that something is *old* is usually enough for me to find a place for it. It could be piece of broken pottery, a nail, or a tattered book from a flea market, no matter. The contents of the latter, a tattered book, is what you just read.

My daughters were grown, but when they were young, we had spent a week on a budget bus tour of Great Britain, and those memories are still some of our best. My retirement present to myself was a return to London, in a tourist-class hotel. A week in

London is barely enough to have your picture taken in front of all the obligatory tourist sites, much less actually have fun and get to know anything about the city. While my wife's checklist included Harrods and seeing *The Mousetrap* in the West End, mine included something I had secretly wanted to experience since I was twelve years old: The Portobello Road Market.

In 1971, the Disney movie *Bedknobs and Broomsticks* contained a scene (actually shot in Burbank, I'm sure) in which Angela Lansbury and company traveled to the Market in search of the other half of a book of spells, because, of course, Portobello Road is "the street where the riches of ages are stowed."

While my verging-on-adolescence buddies bragged that year about sneaking into the theater to see what happened in Jennifer O'Neill's beach house in the *Summer of '42* (whether they actually got in to see it or not), I was fascinated by the idea of Portobello Road, where the detritus of a city inhabited for four thousand years is dredged up and put out in stalls once a week. I made sure our trip included a free Saturday morning.

We stayed out later than usual on Friday night, insuring my wife wouldn't mind sleeping in while I went out the following morning. I took the tube to Notting Hill station, and quite a crowd had already formed at 8:15, despite a grey and threatening sky.

The Market was everything I envisioned, mixed in with much I didn't. There were tables and carts bowed down with everything imaginable, some specialized and some so eclectic they defy description. Victorian penny licks could be found beside bundles of old Escort magazines beside stacks of scratched Gramophone Concert records beside Staffordshire dogs beside hypoallergenic tongue studs. Amazing.

Given the late evening before, finding coffee and crumpet and sausage was important and mercifully easy (though overpriced) from a stall. After juggling my breakfast, I wormed my way into the now-large stream of people going down each side of the street. I was frustrated at first, having made the typical American mistake of walking on the right hand side of the street, progressing with the difficulty of a spawning salmon. I eventually fell into step and got swept along with the throng, stepping over to let people pass when something caught my eye.

By 10:00, I had bought a Coronation magazine and a bent spoon purported to be Regency for myself, and a brooch in the shape of a bird (probably 1950s) for my wife. I didn't have to feel the first raindrops falling on my neck to notice the change in the weather; I could see it in the scowls of the other market patrons. The drizzle caused a flurry of activity, with vendors pulling out sheets of plastic and tarps to cover their wares.

As the crowd began to thin and I pondered what my own rain abandonment point might be, I came to a makeshift stall loosely billowed with clear plastic and saw a small trunk of dark wood, bound in blackened brass. It was scarred and tattered and, to my eye, beautiful. I knew it would be difficult to get home. I knew there would be no place for it in my new, smaller house. I knew I could not afford it. I also knew I wanted it.

The woman minding the stall appeared to be around my age, and quite soured because of the rain. I asked if I could look at the trunk; she admonished me to keep it under the polythene and not let it get wet. The trunk was heavy and oily and tight. It spoke to me and seemed to respond to my touch.

"What's its history?" I asked.

"Don't know much." she said. "We just came by it this week. It's out of an old building in Stratford that is being

299

knocked down to make room for the Olympics." She struggled to light a soggy cigarette. "There were several things in the garret, and we took the lot. Old, it is. At least Georgian. And in good nick, that."

"How much you asking?"

"Well, people love chests. Especially this small size. It's worth at least six hundred pounds, but I would rather not tote it back again. For a fine southern American gentleman, I will take five-hundred fifty, y'all. Are you from Texas, love?"

I am from West Virginia, but was in no mood to discuss her knowledge of regional American accents.

"I would like to have it, but I can't go that."

"Five–hundred, dear, and I know I shouldn't do it."

"I can go three-hundred." This wasn't a ploy. I really couldn't afford more than that, knowing I had just become a retiree, and my new gig as a self-employed management consultant hadn't exactly caught fire in the Worldwide Recession.

'Oh, no, dear, I can't do that. I have to have five-hundred."

I was disappointed, but knew it was for the best. I thanked her and turned to go.

"I do have a couple of other things from the same place, sir. I didn't have everything out, for the rain." From under the table, she pulled out a covered plastic bin. "Have a look, but keep the cover over it, please."

The bin contained some ornate brass gas fittings, a tarnished candlestick, an inkwell missing its glass insert, an incomplete set of balance scale weights, and four small leather-bound books. I leafed through the top book and saw lines of faded figures in spidery handwriting.

'I just looked through those a bit. Definitely Georgian. The dates are clear. People love those old leather books, you know."

"How much for the books?" I asked, though I really wanted the trunk.

"They always sell best as a set. I will let you have them for one-twenty."

I had recently given away literally hundreds of old books, but none this old. I could see them between the two bronze elephant bookends on my desk. Very stylish. There was nothing much to actually *read*, but they were more than two-hundred years old and came from the Portobello Road Market. It had to happen.

"I have ninety pounds."

She frowned over her cigarette. "Ah, you had three-hundred just a minute ago. I have to have ninety-five, dear."

"I'll take 'em."

I was thoroughly damp by the time I reached the tube station, but my treasures were safe in their plastic bag. I rationalized that I had refrained from buying a thousand other little things that caught my eye during the trip, so these small items weren't too offensive. Of course, for the difference of two-hundred pounds, I would have been lugging an oak trunk into the hotel room and warning that we could eat nothing but airline peanuts on the way home in order for me to pay the excess baggage fee.

We had been home about a week when I had time to examine my finds more closely. I read the magazine first, and found a place for it on the second tier of an end table in the hallway, knowing it would probably soon live in the attic. I triaged the condition of the spoon, and decided refurbishing it would make a good winter project. That brought me to the books.

They were pretty typical of utilitarian books from the late 1700s. Each and every cover had separated from the binding, and been stitched back on with four ringlets of twine. The bottom and top books still had their front pages, proclaiming J. Shaw and Son had printed them. There was no other mechanical printing in three of the books, but line after line of faded copperplate entries, beginning in 1790. The latest date I found was 1799. The entries were very general, such as:

Jn 17   W. Duncan 3 c. bot. D

  "   J. Smyth   1 h. pitch D

On and on, hundreds of lines in the first, second, and fourth volumes.

Then there was the third book in the stack. Something was different; I wondered why I hadn't noticed it before. In leafing through a stack of four seemingly identical books, I suppose Number Three gets the least attention.. This volume had hundreds of lines of ledger entries like the others, but with something added. Beginning a few pages in, the backs of the pages were also written upon.

The handwriting appeared to be the same as the ledger entries and was totally readable, but just made no sense. The first line I read at random, near the end of the book, was "city the in commerce of something know someday would I that resolved I that moment that at was it." Almost no punctuation. No capital letters, though there were a few italics (or what I assumed to be meant as italics) scattered throughout. What could all this mean? More than two-hundred years ago, someone had obviously spent a great amount of time writing gibberish.

Staring at it for a while, I tried sorting it out several different ways, and finally read the lines backward. I audibly gasped when it yielded, "It was at that moment I resolved that I would, someday, know something of commerce in the city."

Written backwards. On each page. Through the whole book. With this key, it wasn't too hard to figure out. The last line of the work was at the top of a page near the front, and the first line was at the bottom of a page near the end of the book, on and on, for hundreds of pages. But, with a strong light, it became completely readable. It is, apparently, an autobiographical work by an old man who wanted to leave the story of his life to his children as a legacy

When I first encountered the name of the supposed writer, I went straight to the computer to enter a name in my favorite search engine. All I found were the expected references to a minor literary character, along with images of an ale bottle and a cartoon toad playing a fiddle. Surely, there must have been a different person with that name! But, when I came to the last few pages...how else to explain it?

I spent the next year carefully transcribing the work, not altering the eighteenth century terms and spellings (and misspellings). Make of it what you will. The books do look really cool on my desk, between those bronze elephant bookends.

NOTES

The Autobiography of Fezziwig is a work of fiction written against a historical background. Any resemblance of the fictional characters to a real person, living or dead, is purely coincidental. The actions and conversations of actual historical characters, other than their participation in documented events, are fiction as well, and dates and chronology of actual events may have been modified for continuity of the story. Actual historical events include, among others: the policy of Containment, the rise of London gin houses, the hanging of Constantia Jones and Dick Turpin, the assault on Cumberland (Guantanamo) Bay, the Catholic Tax and Negro Laws, the promotion of indigo by Eliza Lucas, the discovery of the Amscott mummy, the beheading of Lord Lovat and the scaffold collapse, the battle of Fort Ligonier, the Canning trial, the Gordon Riots, the formation of the Lunarticks, Dr. Franklin's breakfast with Joseph Priestley after the appearance before the Council, the burning of Dr. Priestley's home, and the first letter delivered by air mail. The descriptions of the Turpin and Lovat executions, Canning trial testimony, and the newspaper advertisement for the Bastille anniversary dinner, are reprinted exactly as they originally appeared in the original sources noted in the text. A later generation of fictional Bracebridges (whose home was relocated a hundred miles or so south for the purpose of this novel) welcomed a visitor from America, Mr. Washington Irving, for Christmas dinner.

Cover art: Front: *Mr. Fezziwig's Ball*, from a hand-colored etching by John Leech (1809 – 1870) for the 1843 publication of Charles Dickens' *A Christmas Carol*. The work is in the public domain. Back: *La experience Aerostatique de Monsieur Blancard accompagne du Chevalier Lepinard 1785*, by Louis Joseph Watteau (1731-1798). This work is also in the public domain.

The Autobiography of Fezziwig is on Facebook! Join us at:

www.facebook.com/TheAutobiographyOfFezziwig

ABOUT THE AUTHOR

Danny Kuhn grew up in the coalfields of southern West Virginia, and holds degrees from Marshall and West Virginia Universities. His career has included stints as a social worker, high school science teacher, and Federal probation officer. He now lives in Myrtle Beach, South Carolina, and is an organizational trainer/speaker for Favoritetrainers.com. He has decided to relive, rather than just reread, the classic literature he has always loved.

23354524R00169

Made in the USA
Charleston, SC
18 October 2013